Finally, he lay down in the end zone and put his arms over his head, exactly as he had done when the whistle had blown the play dead on that fateful October morning. I walked into the end zone and gently said, "C'mon, Daryl. We better go." He just shook his head slowly from right to left. "Really, Daryl, c'mon," I urged him. "It's late, and we're not supposed to be here."

I waited and waited, but it looked like he needed to lay there in the dark night. I wasn't sure if he was just thinking or if he was crying because his arms still covered his face. Finally, I surrendered and just sat down right next to him and crossed my legs, as if I was about to meditate or something like that. I guess I was meditating because, since I didn't know what to say, there was nothing else to do. Together we rested, the only sound was Daryl's labored breathing.

After what felt like forever, he broke the silence. "Ya ever feel sad, Duchess?"

EXIT 14

GARY SCARPA

This book is a work of fiction. Names, characters, and incidents are either the product of the author's imagination or, if real, used fictitiously.

ISBN: 978-1-7365146-0-3

Book design by David Provolo
Photograph of Gary Scarpa by Julia Gerace

Printed in the United States of America.

For more information about books by Gary Scarpa, visit www.garyscarpa.com

for Edmund

1

Michael and I hadn't missed a Derby game all season, which may sound a little screwy since neither of us had ever attended Derby High School. As brothers, we have many things in common, but none was more unifying on this crisp, late October Saturday than our hatred for Derby football and our hope that Derby would finally lose a game. For me, hating Derby is completely natural because I go to nearby Shelton High School, probably Derby's greatest rival. But Michael is in college now. He hadn't gone to Shelton High, actually, but instead to a private high school, so what was his excuse? Maybe it was because Derby hadn't lost a game in two years. Maybe it was because of the way the arrogant Derby players strutted into the vestibule of Duchess, the fast food joint where Michael and I work, placing their orders and brashly predicting their next victory. Maybe it was the way they exploded onto the field in a pregame ritual, running two by two into what would soon evolve into a whirling tornado, the players melding into a human funnel of red and white power and energy. You almost knew that this storm of energy meant doom for their opponents. Or maybe it was just that we were sick and tired of Derby being so damned good.

As we walked from the parking lot to the field, I said, "I think Seymour has a good shot today, don't you? Novak and Andrews are a great combination."

"Dig it," Michael shot back. He's always saying *Dig it* to indicate he *gets* what I'm saying. Not that he made it up or anything, because there's no way he did. I'm almost sure the beatniks made it up. Michael wouldn't know that because he doesn't read weird stuff like me. I always have a book jammed into my back pocket. Even as we approached the field I was carrying *On the Road* by Jack Kerouac, who, along with his pals, are considered some of the earliest beatniks. From what I can tell, the beatniks eventually became the hippies of today. "Anti-establishment" and all that. I heard somewhere that Jack Kerouac may have even made up the word *beatnik*. I think he might have even made up expressions like *Dig it* and others that we use all the time. But like I said, Michael wouldn't know that, even though *Dig it* is something he says about a thousand times a day. It's weird, but most people don't even think about why they say the things they do. Michael probably falls into that category. I myself am more analytical.

"Hey, why don't we try to sit in the visitors' stands today? What do you think?" I offered.

"Give me a break," Michael said and continued to walk toward the Derby bleachers.

Like *Dig it*, Michael is always saying *Give me a break*, but I have no idea whatsoever who made that one up. Anyway, attending the Derby games was tricky. Michael and I had to kind of pretend we were Derby fans because we always sat on the Derby bleachers. The bleachers on the visitors' side were always filled up before we arrived, and we didn't want to stand at the chain link fence where players, coaches, and officials blocked sight lines to the action on the field. Sitting on the Derby bleachers gave us the best view of the action of the game. But Derby fans wouldn't have appreciated hearing us root for the opposition, so we couldn't exactly do that. We blended inconspicuously with the raucous crowd as we reservedly clapped when Derby made a good play or scored, like we were happy about it or something, and we suppressed our excitement when the opposition did the same. I liked the way Michael would kind of side-glance me, giving me a subtle nod.

Of course, Seymour being undefeated so far this season was no joke either. Ben Andrews and Daryl Novak, the best passing tandem in the state, were deadly with Andrews' accurate passing and Novak's speed, height, agility, and "sure bet" hands. Not only did Seymour have Novak and Andrews, but they had a big line and a couple of hard-nosed running backs.

The first half was such a thriller that I didn't even notice that it had been probably the chilliest October morning in the history of Connecticut meteorology. As Michael and I and probably everyone in the stadium expected, when the gun sounded ending the first half, the Seymour squad had given Derby everything they could handle and more. Andrews had connected with Novak for two touchdowns, and the score was tied at 14 apiece.

Michael and I were happy to peel ourselves out of the crowded Derby bleachers and escape all of that sickening Red Raider school spirit. We headed for the refreshment stand in the far south corner of the stadium.

"How about Novak?" I said practically skipping alongside of Michael.

"Dig it," he replied. "He's the real deal. The genuine article."

"What hands," I continued. "Did you see that down and out he caught early in the second quarter? I mean, the velocity on that ball... whoosh...and Andrews threw it just a little too high for any normal player to catch. How did Novak reel that one in?"

"He reeled it in because he's Daryl Fucking Novak...that's how." Michael squeezed his long body between fans at the food stand and ordered us a couple of hotdogs, which was nice of him because I didn't even ask for one. I was starved.

"Yeah," I said, blabbering away in my excitement. "And then he sidesteps that Derby player — who was it? — Foxy Belchak, I think — and Novak goes, like, what? Maybe 50 yards for the score. Nobody could catch him. All those white jerseys chasing after him. As if they had any hope of catching him. And Foxy is, like, standing there around mid-field saying to himself, 'What just happened to me?' "

"What happened to him is he got out-finessed." Michael handed me a dog and Coke and took a bite of his.

"Exactly! Out-finessed. And how about Novak's second touchdown? What was he? At least 30 yards out, right?" I noticed that I was asking questions and then answering them myself, but I didn't care. "And then he sidesteps one guy, right? And then another, and then he even fakes out Adamo...*even* Adamo...before galloping into the end zone."

With a mouthful of chewed up hotdog and bun, Michael mumbled, "Adamo can go fuck himself." Luckily nobody could understand what he said but me because, maybe Michael didn't care, but I personally wasn't in any mood to get into a fight with any Derby fans, especially since the last time I got in a fight I was in seventh grade.

"Yeah, I know. Right? I mean, Adamo scored both of Derby's touchdowns...but yeah...you know what he can do, right? He can...he can go...go do what you said he can do!"

"Derby's far from out of it, though, so don't go getting your hopes up too much," he said, now chewing with his mouth open. "They're dangerous, and they can really grind out the yards."

"Don't I know it," I replied. "Geez, if Derby wins it, we'll never hear the end of it."

"Dig it. Now let me ask you a question, Einstein. You ever see Novak come into Duchess and start bragging about how great he is or how great Seymour is?"

Thinking about it for a second, I replied, "Now that you mention it, no, I never did."

"You know why that is?"

"No," I said, maybe a little too eagerly. The fact of the matter was that I hadn't ever really thought about it, and now that Michael brought it up, I was really interested in knowing why.

"That's because — now pay close fucking attention to this, Gabe — it's because Novak's not an asshole."

Wow, I thought, *Michael really gets right to the heart of the matter.*

That's for sure.

As we headed back to our seats, I found myself thinking about how Daryl Novak wasn't an asshole. It made a lot of sense. Or at least a lot of sense to me. Of course, I had been processing Michael's logic for all of my fifteen years, so I was pretty good at it.

As the frosty morning melted into early afternoon, Derby came on strong, doing just what Michael said they would do. They ground it out, which could easily be seen by how their nice white pants were smudged black and brown with dirt and mud. Seymour's yellow pants were similarly besmirched. I like that word, *besmirched,* which I learned from reading *The Prince and the Pauper* by Mark Twain last year...something about the pauper's rags being besmirched with mud or something like that.

Anyway, getting back to the game. In the third quarter, Derby ground their way down the field twice, besmirching everybody and everything in their path in short, filthy five or six yard plays, with Adamo exploding into the end zone from just a few yards from the goal line each time for two more Derby scores.

Just when I was beginning to lose all hope, though, Novak did it again. Early in the fourth quarter, way back on their own ten yard line, Andrews threw a short pass to Novak right over the middle of the fierce Derby line. There seemed to be too many white and red jerseys around him for Novak to make anything out of such a short pass play...or so I would have thought...but he went and turned this little, nothing play into the Daryl Novak Show, brilliantly side-stepping around and dancing by player after player, not the least of whom was, once again, Frankie Adamo, the last obstacle between Novak and a touchdown. After he left Adamo talking to himself in the middle of the boggy field, Novak, the number 88 emblazoned in bold yellow on his royal blue jersey, pranced untouched into the end zone. The first thought I had was, *Novak's uniform is the only clean one on the field because I don't think anyone laid a hand on him all day.* My second thought was,

Number 88's career at Seymour High is the stuff that schoolboy dreams are made of. I didn't make that statement up; I heard it somewhere. But it was true. Tall and handsome and blond, with honest gray eyes, Novak was a three-sport athlete who excelled on the baseball diamond and the basketball court as well. I thought about what Michael had said at halftime. Daryl Novak was the strong, silent type — not some kind of asshole but, instead, just a kid who carried himself with a lot of humility. He didn't need to talk about how good he was. His actions on the field proved it. I not only admired Novak, I wanted to be him.

Unfortunately, even with Novak's incredible heroics, Derby was still ahead. In a last ditch effort, thankfully, Seymour got themselves in scoring position. With only nineteen seconds left on the clock, Seymour had a fourth and goal at the Derby nine yard line. The score flashed brightly on Derby's new electric scoreboard — Derby 28, Seymour 21. Seymour needed to score a touchdown and then decide if they would go for the tie or the win. Both teams had a lot at stake. I don't think there was anyone, player or fan, at Ryan Field who didn't know that Seymour's only real hope hinged on a pass play to Novak. When you have a Daryl Novak on your team, you go to him in a do or die situation no matter what. Derby only had to stop Novak from catching the ball, which would be very difficult to do if Andrews delivered anything remotely catchable.

For me, that play will be forever stamped in my memory. The huddle broke and Andrews approached the line of scrimmage. As he placed his hands under the center, he yelled, "Hut one...hut two... hut..." continuing into a long count. The entire offensive formation remained still except for Novak who went into motion from left to right, crossing behind Andrews and the offensive line in a long, loping trot. When Andrews called the fifth "hut" and the ball was snapped, Novak turned and foiled an attempt to slow him up by rolling off of a would-be blocker like the player wasn't even there. Accelerating, Novak sped straight down the sideline and then, as he crossed into the end zone, he made a sharp 90 degree cut toward the towering white goal posts.

The overworked Seymour line gave Andrews the best protection they could, and just before Derby's All State lineman Nickie Grasso broke through, arms flailing, Andrews let the ball sail into the air. Michael grabbed my forearm tightly with that "Oh my God" squeeze, and the action seemed to go into slow motion. A perfectly thrown ball appeared to be due on arrival into the reliable, outstretched hands of Novak who had beaten his defender by a yard. Just as Novak's nimble fingers got ready to wrap themselves around the leather pigskin, the camera in my mind snapped out of slow motion as Frankie Adamo, the star Derby linebacker, materialized completely out of nowhere and administered a crushing shoulder into Novak's ribs. Novak was launched upward before crashing to the ground as the ball seemed to just about be in his grasp, and then he fell into the muddy grass beneath him. The referee vigorously waved his arms, signaling the pass was incomplete.

It was bedlam in the stands and on the field. The Derby crowd erupted in jubilation, the puny band in their red blazers and Derby hats bleated the school fight song, and the Derby players began slapping, hugging, and pushing each other in a wild and exuberant victory dance.

I guess the only two people in the Derby stands who weren't happy were me and Michael. His face looked about as green as mine felt. I thought to myself, *Wow, Adamo just got some sweet revenge for the two times that Novak made him look stupid!*

The Seymour players stood motionless, most holding their helmets now, grimly watching the Derby celebration unfold before them. Only one player wasn't watching. As I looked down on the field, I saw that Daryl Novak was still lying on his back in the end zone, with his long arms crossed over his face mask.

Soon enough, the refs and the coaches were on the field restoring order because there were still thirteen seconds on the clock, so the game wasn't really over. The Seymour coach was hovering over Novak, probably making sure he hadn't damaged anything more than his pride. Derby's coach, Big Sal Costanzo, was yelling at his players. I couldn't hear what he was saying, but he was probably telling them to get their heads out of their asses and back in the game. Big Sal had come to high school coaching only a few years before. He had been a pro player with the New York Giants and then, eventually, an assistant defensive coach for the Giants. I guess coaching at Derby was his retirement job. Lucky Derby! We had heard a rumor that Big Sal had applied to coach in Shelton a few years before, but Shelton felt he was too old. Dumb Shelton! No other high school that we had ever heard of had a coach who was a former pro player and coach. No wonder Derby was so good.

Of course, with order restored on the field, all Derby had to do was run out the clock which would only take one play since Seymour had expended all of their timeouts. And that's exactly what they did. Grasso snapped the ball to Derby's quarterback Foxy Belchak, who took a knee, and the game was in the books. Another Derby win.

As we walked to the car, Michael was quiet. *Sullen* might be a better word to describe him. Tough losses like that made him moody. I don't think anybody hated Derby more than Michael. Of course, I hated them too, but not like Michael.

When it comes to sports, Michael really knows how to hate. That's just how he is. The thing is, he takes his sports seriously. I mean, I guess I do too, kind of, but nothing like Michael. I'm almost sure he came out of the womb a sports fan. We share a bedroom in our small apartment on Maltby Street, and I remember being confused by nightmares he had had as a younger kid, flailing between our twin beds in a spasmodic dance, crying out that Mickey Mantle had struck out. Dad would burst through the darkness and deftly lock Michael into a safe embrace until Michael calmed down. Then Dad would put him back to bed and tuck him in. With Michael now back in a deep sleep, I was left alone to contemplate what it's like to be the brother of a kid who has nightmares about famous baseball players. No wonder I'm an insomniac today.

I'm not saying that Michael's obsession with sports is the world's biggest hang-up exactly, but I have to admit that it is a little nuts. I guess that's what makes Michael uniquely Michael. I'm more a "Johnny Come Lately" when it comes to sports...and when I say "lately," I mean, like, two or three years ago. I had quit Little League at only eight years old because, lamenting my lack of playing time, I told my mother, "If I want to see a good game, I can watch one on television!" I was kind of a witty little kid. So besides playing on the playground and in the neighborhood, my interest in organized sports or pro games was nil up until the last few years. I guess I'm pretty decent at most sports. You kind of have to be to get any respect in the neighborhood or at the Boys Club. The way I see it, being able to compete in sports is part of survival in the game of life. I think my interest started to peak when I discovered the summer before ninth grade that I had a pretty accurate outside shot in basketball and an inexplicable competitive nature when in the midst of an athletic contest of any kind. It's simple — when you're shorter, you try harder. I guess if I want to be totally honest with myself, part of my growing interest in sports has to do with fitting in, but what's the point of being honest with yourself?

The truth is, even today, I would always rather be reading a good book. I guess Michael only reads when he has to. Growing up, he would rather have been playing football or Wiffle ball in the street in front of our house than be reading. Me, myself — I've loved reading ever since I got my first library card from the Plumb Memorial Library here in town when I was just a little kid. I've been devouring books ever since, which my mother will vouch for. I remember loving *Ben and Me*, a biography of Benjamin Franklin narrated by a mouse. What can I say? Like I said, I was a little kid. From there I gobbled up biography after biography like they were potato chips, from *Set All Afire: A Novel of St. Francis Xavier* (Did I mention I went to Catholic school?) to *PT 109* about the World War II exploits of former President John F. Kennedy. In seventh grade I found myself completely addicted to the *Brass Knuckles* series by Monsignor Raymond J. O'Brien about juvenile delinquents who eventually go straight.

I was hooked on *On the Road* the same as the *Brass Knuckles* series although I don't know if Monsignor O'Brien would approve of Jack Kerouac's main character, Sal Paradise, and his beatnik friends, their drinking and drugging, or their generally loose morals, unless maybe they were to go straight in the end, which I assure you they don't. And it isn't that I want to drink or do drugs or have loose morals like those guys because that's not my deal. I just want to be free and adventurous, just like Sal and the beatniks.

It was a long walk to the upper level parking lot behind the high school, so we took a shortcut through the woods. Michael, being a lot taller than me, was taking Paul Bunyan-like strides along the path, stepping on the dead leaves like he was mad at them. As I tagged behind him, I realized he was actually kind of built like Daryl Novak, except for the fact that Novak was way quicker and considerably more agile. Michael had never played a varsity sport when he was in high school, maybe because he had gone to a private boys' prep school out of town. As a younger kid, though, he was always on the Little League and Biddy League All Stars, but that might have been because he was a lot taller than most of the other kids, having reached his full height of 6'1" by the time he was in seventh grade. Towering over most kids his age, Michael easily snagged rebounds in Biddy League almost without jumping, and when he connected with a baseball, it often sailed for extra bases or home runs. One of my favorite Little League stories about Michael from the era is drawn from a game when the toughest kid and the best pitcher in town, Buzzy Wasielewski, had a no-hitter going with two outs in the last inning. Michael was to be the final out, except on the first pitch, he lined the ball into the left field gap for a double. Before facing the next batter, Buzzy turned to my brother, the spoiler, pointed his finger at him and said, "I'm gonna kick your ass after the game!" I'm not sure if Buzzy followed through on his threat, but I think it's pretty cool that my big brother ruined a no-hitter, especially a Buzzy Wasielewski no-hitter.

When we eventually reached Michael's '63 Corvair, he stuck the key in the ignition, slammed his fist on the steering column, and finally spoke up: "Fucking Adamo! Fucking Derby!"

"Yeah," I replied — because what do you say to a comment like that?

Like I said before, Michael takes his sports really seriously. Even now, while watching a Giants game on television, when things are looking bleak for the Giants and the game suddenly seems out of reach, it is commonplace for Michael to abruptly pull himself off of the carpeted floor, switch off the TV, pound his fist on the top of the television cabinet, and storm out of the room with absolutely no regard for the fact that I am watching the game too. A loss for the Giants makes him so furious, he seems to forget I even exist. I usually don't even turn the game back on after one of his tirades because our apartment is so small, and there's no use in exacerbating things further.

I guess that was the end of our conversation because he slammed an 8-track tape into the tape player, and for the rest of the ride, we listened to the unparalleled falsetto of Frankie Valli sing a collection of the Four Seasons' greatest hits, which at least distracted me from Michael's dark mood.

Here's where I'm at, though. When you have a brother who is four years older than you, you almost can't help but look up to him. Even if he's quirky, like Michael. First of all, let me say this. My mother told us she named us after angels. For some reason, that's how Catholics do it. I don't know exactly why, but they name their kids after saints and angels and people like that. The only reason I can think of is so you'll act like a saint or an angel instead of getting into a lot of trouble. Mom told us that Michael was the leader of all the angels and that he was a warrior. She told me that Gabriel was a messenger of God. So there we were — Michael the great warrior and me, Gabriel, the measly messenger. Anyway, the way I figured it was if St. Michael the Archangel was this big warrior who was the leader of all the angels, it was only natural that I looked up to my brother. I don't remember when we were very little kids, but by the time I was around eight, I wanted to do everything he did and be everything he was. The problem was what I wanted and what Michael wanted were not usually the same thing because when I was eight, Michael was twelve, and he wanted to pretend that I didn't exist. Oh, once in a while he would play with me, but these were often one-time experiences. For example, I remember Dad buying us a duet book for sax and clarinet. That night Michael grabbed his tenor and told me to get my clarinet. I was excited beyond explanation by the experience of playing these harmonious arrangements with Michael; he seemed to enjoy it too, but a day later he was less enthusiastic. In the ensuing weeks and months, no matter how much I pleaded with him to play from the duet book again, he refused. And not to belabor the point, but here's one other simple example. When we walked to grade school in the morning, Michael and his pal Paulie walked side by side, and I was left to follow ten yards behind while wishing I could walk with them. It's rough being a younger brother.

But when I entered high school, everything changed. Michael suddenly became my advocate. In fact, if it weren't for Michael, I wouldn't even be a student at Shelton High School. Perhaps the fact that I wasn't accepted at Fairfield Prep, which he himself had attended, was an important factor. Some people think that I am some kind of intellectual because I like to read, but when it comes to academics, Michael is a natural. He could beat me by a million miles without even breaking a sweat. But my disappointment at the rejection was major. My parents and the nuns at St. Joseph School took it for granted I would go to Prep. All of us were surprised when the rejection letter came. Dad even blamed Michael because my brother had become something of a discipline problem during his senior year at Prep. I remember that night like it was yesterday. It was after midnight, and I was awakened by a conversation in the kitchen which was right off our bedroom.

I heard Dad's sharp voice: "Yeah, well it had to be because of you."

"But why would they reject him because of me?" Michael pleaded.

"It's simple! Because they don't want another DeMarco at Prep after all of the trouble you got in this year!"

"Will you stop it, God dammit?" Mom cut in, trying to defend Michael. She was always defending him.

Then I heard Michael shout, "Okay! Everything is always my fault! Fine! Blame me! I'm going to bed!" When he came into our room, he slammed the door behind him, and I could tell he was crying. As far as Michael knew, I was still fast asleep. Laying there with my eyes closed, I felt really bad for both of us. He had gotten in trouble because I'm not as smart as he is, and I knew that Dad shouldn't have blamed him. Realizing it was my own fault and not Michael's, I felt silent tears begin to roll down my cheeks.

Michael recently told me that the next morning he went to see the assistant principal, Mr. McGill, at Prep and asked him if he was the reason I got rejected.

"Certainly not, Mr. DeMarco," said Mr. McGill. "That's not the way we operate here. Your little brother's entrance scores weren't high enough. Simple as that. In the meantime, you need to straighten up and fly right in these last weeks of school."

I don't know if Michael flew right, but Dad's plan was for me to go to another somewhat less competitive Catholic high school. Michael had other ideas, though, thank God. He told me how he always wished he had gone to Shelton High School where all his best buddies went, and he felt I was in a similar situation. I knew he was right.

"But Dad won't go for it, and I'm not about to ask him," I complained.

"Don't worry. I'll talk to him for you," he promised.

I wasn't present for the conversation, and Dad's and Michael's talks seldom went well, but when September came, I was a freshman at Shelton High. Some people think destiny is a lot of hooey, but I really think there's something to it. Not to mention that, despite how he might have treated me when we were younger kids and despite any moodiness or quirkiness, Michael was turning out to be an amazing older brother.

When he pulled the Corvair up to the curb at our house, he did have one more remark.

"I can't believe Novak dropped the fucking ball," he moaned. "He catches everything."

"Well, that was a brutal hit Adamo put on him. Adamo's an assassin."

"Fuck Adamo," Michael said bitterly.

I countered with, "Well, I feel kind of sorry for Novak. He obviously felt bad. Did you see him lying in the end zone with his arms covering his head?"

"Fuck Novak," Michael shot back, and, in a hot second, he was out of the car. End of conversation. As was often the case, he had left me speechless.

I sat in the Corvair, contemplating our relationship as brothers. I remembered what might have been the very first time Michael left me speechless. He must have been fourteen, which would have made me ten. As I was accompanying him on his paper route one Sunday, he dropped a fat newspaper on a customer's doorstep and mumbled, "There's your fuckin' paper, Mr. Williams." I wondered if my ears were playing tricks on me. I had never heard him swear before. Our eyes met for an awkward moment, and then we both burst out laughing. After delivering a paper a few houses later, he muttered, "That fuckin' cheapskate never even tips me." Once again our eyes met. Once again we broke up laughing. When he swore for the third time, mumbling, "I hate delivering these fuckin' papers," he shifted gears. As I was about to giggle, he shut me down, "Don't laugh at me again, Gabe. I swear now, so get fuckin' used to it!"

I guess five years later, I still hadn't gotten completely used to it. After digesting our brief conversation, there was nothing left to do but get out of the car and go up to our room, crash on my bed, and get back to reading *On the Road*. It would take my mind off an otherwise lousy Saturday. When I walked into our bedroom, Michael was out like a light, his mouth half open. He was probably lost in a dream world, hopefully one where his favorite teams always won and where Mickey Mantle hit a home run at every at bat. As I flopped on my bed and flipped open the book, I couldn't concentrate. The image of a disappointed kid, probably not very different from Michael or me, lying in the end zone with his hands covering his face haunted me. I couldn't stop thinking about Daryl Novak.

2

Twenty minutes after the game, Tony Adamo is back at his grocery market on Minerva Street. As he walks in the door, his wife Rose says, "Oh my God, Tony, I listened to the game on WADS. Our Frankie had quite a game, didn't he?"

Tony wraps his strong arms around Rose's waist and lifts her off the floor. "He sure did, baby! He made the game saving hit!"

"Oh, yeah...yes! I heard that. I almost cried...you know, happy tears!"

"I wish you could come see him play, Rose, but somebody's gotta mind the store."

Besides the fresh meat and produce and canned goods that he sells at the market, which his father opened before the Great Depression when he was only seven years old, Tony runs a sideline business, a small bookmaking operation, which is an affiliate of a larger bookmaking establishment out of Bridgeport.

One by one, customers arrive at the store, and within a half hour there are seven or eight guys, toasting Derby with a glass of sambuca — hospitality, Adamo style.

"Here's to our Red Raiders," Tony says, and the group responds, "Salut!"

"You had the best view, Tony," Johnny Consiglio, a 6'5" Derby cop, offers.

"Why do you think I volunteer to be a fuckin' linesman," Tony quips.

The gang bursts into laughter, but the truth is Tony loves being on the chain crew as one of two "rod men" who assist in determining first downs. It makes him feel like he's part of the action. It makes him feel alive.

"Anybody bet against our kids?" asks Dominic Angioletti, a friend from the Marchigian Club, a few blocks away.

"Oh yeah," Tony replies. "There were about a dozen fuckin' stunods. Ansonia and Seymour guys. I'm more than happy to take their dough."

Tony doesn't allow gamblers to bet in favor of Derby for several reasons...because the Red Raiders never lose and because his son is the team's star player and because he doesn't want to jinx his son's team. Tony only entertains bets *against* Derby. Besides, the majority of his income comes from bets he takes on pro sports.

"How about my cousin Enzo?" Dominic asks, "I'll bet my cousin Enzo bet against our team. I'll bet ya that's what my cousin Enzo did, right Tony?"

"That's right," Tony answers. "The only guy in the Valley who's a dumber fuck than you, Dominic, is your cousin Enzo." Tony's joke lands as the gang of men explode in another round of laughter.

The meeting of the group is a kind of brotherhood, a collection of men who are mainly first-generation Americans. Their parents came to the United States from countries like Ireland, Italy, Poland, Czechoslovakia, and the Ukraine, arriving at Ellis Island in New York in search of a better life in America. Tony's customers and friends have surnames like Mongillo and Lungarini, Pietrzak and Ramatowski, O'Callaghan and McTigue, or Zagrebelnyj and Vitko. These particular European families settled down in the Lower Naugatuck Valley in Connecticut, known throughout the state simply as "the Valley." Most of these men are veterans of World War II who fought in Europe or the Pacific. Those of their generation who didn't fight in the War contributed to it on the home front by working in plants that manufactured not only tanks, rifles, ammunition, airplanes and ships, but in small towns like those in the Valley, also items like artillery cartridges, Army pea-coats, airplane engine parts, fuses, and parachutes.

"Where's Frankie going to school next year, Tony?" Johnny Consiglio asks.

"I don't know yet. He doesn't want to go to UCONN because my older boy Anthony goes there, and Frankie wants to make his own mark. You know what I mean?"

"I know," a short, stocky man with thick glasses says in a high-pitched voice, "but these damn kids think we're made of fuckin' money. If they don't get a scholarship, how do they expect us to pay these college tuitions?"

"No shit! Don't forget. I got three boys," Tony says. "When Anthony is a senior, my youngest will be a college freshman, so that makes three tuitions for me to worry about at the same time, but I'll figure it out. I don't wanna see any one of my guys end up in Vietnam, capice?"

College is in the future not only for Frankie Adamo but also for most of the boys who played in the Derby-Seymour game that morning because their parents, who in many cases didn't have such an opportunity, have drummed into their heads that a post-secondary education is crucial for success in life. Also, while not usually explicitly expressed, enrollment in college means a draft deferment for four years, helping young men to avoid fighting in what is, day by day, becoming a progressively more unpopular war being fought in the Southeast Asian country of Vietnam.

On this day, though, thoughts of war are the furthest thing from the minds of the players. This was a victorious day for one Valley town over another. Along with Derby and Seymour, the other two Valley towns of Shelton and Ansonia comprise a football hotbed in the state. After the big game, Frankie Adamo and his fellow Derby players shower in the old white-washed, cinder block field house at Ryan Field, named for the legendary coach, "Nuggy" Ryan. Then, along with their teen fans, the team makes its way through the neighborhoods of Derby in a festive motorcade, beeping their horns and hooting and hollering out of their car windows in celebration of their big win. The parade of cars noisily makes an intentional detour over the Shelton-Derby Bridge, crossing over the Housatonic River, and turns left onto Howe Avenue, Shelton's main drag, disturbing the peaceful afternoon. With windows rolled down, and players and fans leaning half out of their cars, they roll slowly down Howe Avenue, with the cheerleaders in the first two cars leading the way and the players and fans echoing, "We're from Derby/We're from Derby...and no one could be prouder/and no one could be prouder...and if you don't believe us/and if you don't believe us...we'll yell a little louder/we'll yell a little louder!" Even though Derby has reigned victorious over Seymour, not Shelton, on this autumn morning, the message to Shelton is clear: "You're next!" Thanksgiving Day, only a few weeks away, will tell that tale.

The Derby convoy pulls onto Route 8, making its way to Main Street in Ansonia, whose team they had beaten just three weeks before, just to rub it in. The motorcade finally reaches its destination, the parking lot of Duchess Drive-In, the local hang-out for all of the Valley towns, located in Ansonia, only a few hundred yards from the Derby border with Seymour about a mile to the north and Shelton about the same distance to the south. The Derby players are joined by dozens of their fellow schoolmates and quite a few adult fans from Seymour as well, making for a busy lunch hour at Duchess. The players and fans jostle their way into a crowded vestibule and line up at one of two windows where they place their orders. Knowing the game is over, the grill men busily throw successive "twenty-fours" — rows of sizzling hamburger patties — on the grill while toasting and dressing soft, round buns; the fry man, after having put pounds of potatoes through steel gadgets that peeled and cut them, fills the deep sizzling fryers with multiple baskets of french fries, then rapidly scoops the golden potatoes into small and large bags; the drink men, having made certain the milkshake and soda machines are filled, are ready for action.

The biggest orders are placed by the players, fresh from victory, who bring with them voracious appetites. Each of the two window men listen to the orders, call out the drinks — "one chocolate milkshake and one large Coke" — and then with their own athletic deftness, shake open a white paper bag and, in just a few fluid steps, snatch two double cheeseburgers from the meat bin and two large fries, while calculating the price in their heads before arriving back to the customer. The window men take pride in being able to move customers quickly out the door, and, in a way, they put on a show of their own. Occasionally, a customer questions whether their addition is correct, in which case, the window man uses the adding machine on the cash register to double check his numbers. Usually correct, the window man takes further pleasure in his arithmetic skills.

The students from both schools mingle and eat outside in the parking lot, using the hoods and trunks of their cars as dining tables. Fans and admirers, young and old, call out to Frankie Adamo, "Nice tackle, Frankie!" and "You really stuck it to him, Adamo!" and "You saved the game, Frankie!" and "Novak will be having nightmares about you tonight, Frankie!" Frankie squints his black olive eyes and purses his thin lips in a confident smile in response to each plaudit. Leaning against the hood of his candy apple red 1965 Pontiac Lemans, a gift from his father after an auspicious gambling venture, Frankie basks in the glory of their admiration. Looking handsome and relaxed in his varsity letter jacket, the white "D" set against a field of red wool and punctuated with a gold football pin, Frankie holds a bacon double cheeseburger in his right hand while reaching into a white paper bag to stuff some french fries in his mouth with his left. The high school girls like Frankie's confidence and whisper furtively to each other about him as they watch him take long sips of a large chocolate shake. While it had been his bone crushing "hit" that had made Novak cough up the ball, it isn't lost on anyone who saw the game that Frankie had also run for 134 yards on offense en route to bullying his way into the end zone for all four Derby scores. Frankie, although deceptively quick, doesn't have lightning speed. He is fond of saying, "When I can't run past other players, I run over them!"

There is no motorcade for the Seymour players. No celebration. No merrymaking. After a heartbreaking loss like this one, none are in a celebratory mood. And no one is harder on himself than Daryl Novak who feels personally responsible for the emotional loss. After the team arrives back at Seymour High School and hits the showers, Ben Andrews asks Novak if he wants to go over to his house for a sandwich. Novak just shakes his head, droplets of water spraying from his hair which is still wet from a shower, and gloomily mumbles, "Naw, I don't feel like it, Benny." Andrews calls out, "See ya later, then?" to which Novak simply shrugs. Andrews soberly watches Novak as he crosses the high school parking lot, gets in his beat up VW Bug, and drives off.

Daryl Novak's parents had not attended the game. Though a fan, Walter Novak, who drives a semi for Old Dominion Freight Line, is out of state with a delivery and won't be back until mid-week. When he calls home on Sunday morning, his first question will be about the outcome of the big game. Helen Novak, a homemaker and mother like Rose Adamo, had also not attended the game. While she is proud of Daryl's many athletic accomplishments, it isn't her custom to be in attendance at Daryl's games. She doesn't understand football, and she worries that he will get injured. Daryl's one sibling, Susanna, now a freshman at Seymour High School, was indeed at the game, but her reason for being there had nothing to do with being a sports fan and everything to do with the beginning of a new and exciting social life as a high school student. So it was, then, that at the moment when Frankie Adamo put the game saving "hit" on Daryl Novak, Susanna, though in attendance, had not seen the play. She was too busy circling the field with her girlfriends with the express purpose of being seen in her latest outfit, which included wide bell bottom jeans, a suede fringed jacket, a chocolate corduroy cap with a wide brim, and rose colored, wire-rimmed round glasses, recreating a look she had seen her favorite model, Twiggy, wear in a magazine spread.

At the same time that Frankie Adamo and his fellow Derby players are basking in the glory of their victory, Daryl Novak pulls his Bug up to the curb in front of the Novaks' small, grey ranch style house in Seymour. Upon entering the house, Daryl's mother asks him what he would like her to make him for lunch. "Nothin'," he mutters. "I don't feel like eating, Mom."

"But, Daryl, you must be hungry," Helen responds. "After a game like that, you must be starved."

"Naw, Mom, don't worry about me," Daryl says, and continues to his bedroom.

Helen Novak worries about her son who is, for the most part, a deeply introspective individual. *He never talks about how he's feeling,* she thinks to herself. Daryl grabs a spiral notebook and a pencil and falls onto his bed. Replaying Seymour's final offensive play over and over again in his mind and on paper, Daryl is deeply troubled by what he feels had been his failure to score in a clutch situation. He has let down his teammates, coaches, and fans. For the next hour, he draws out a series of Xes and Oes, page after page, diagramming various pass routes he could have run that might have assisted him in avoiding a collision with Adamo. He rips each page out, one by one, crumpling it and throwing it on the floor until his rug is dotted with crinkled up balls of paper. Finally, spent physically and emotionally, a tired and distraught Daryl lays his cheek on the notebook as if it were a pillow as sleep grants his troubled mind, finally, to rest.

3

For a girl like Susanna Novak, getting ready to go to a dance on a Saturday night requires careful planning and preparation. At 4:47, a little more than four hours after Daryl's big game against Derby ended, the phone rings at the Novak home. Helen answers, finding it is for Susie.

"Yes, Sally. One moment, please. Susie!" Helen calls, "Telephone!"

Susie's best friend Sally Jablonsky and she make plans for the dance that night. "Yes, Sally, my mom says Daryl is going to take us there and pick us up at the end of the night...yes, that's right, Mary Jane is going to walk over here, and then we'll pick you up around 7:45, okay? No don't worry, I'll talk to Daryl because I don't want to be late either. Right. Right on! It's going to be totally groovy!"

The sound of the phone ringing and of Susie's subsequent chatter wake Daryl from his nap. He can hear the incessant sound of Susie's voice, but Daryl is so groggy he is unable to process the words she is saying. Daryl moans, pounds a flat palm down on his mattress, and rubs his hand across his cheek. He feels a spiral indentation, the result of his cheek resting against the edge of his notebook as he slept.

Hearing him stir, Helen Novak peeks into Daryl's bedroom. "Oh Daryl, what are all those papers on your floor? I cleaned this morning."

"Sorry, Mom," he says with a yawn. "I was...just...just drawing up some plays. I'll pick everything up. Just give me a sec, okay? Does she have to gab like that? She's so loud."

"She's just excited about the dance. Now, I expect you to follow through and clean up the floor. By the way, Daryl, speaking of the dance in Derby, are you going tonight?"

"Oh yeah, Mom, that's exactly what I'm gonna do. I'm gonna go to the dance in Derby after I helped them beat us in the game this morning."

"I am sorry that your team lost, Daryl, but there's no need to be so fresh. In any case, I need you to drop Susie and her friends at the Derby Community Center later."

"Aw, Mom, I have stuff to do. Can't one of her friends' parents take them?" Daryl moans.

"Daryl, it will only take you a few minutes. You can do this for her. The Reillys took them last week, and the Jablonskys the week before. You know I don't like to drive in the dark, especially with all those crazy kids and their hotrods on the road. And I'll need you to bring them home after the dance."

"Mom," Daryl erupts, "you're kidding me, right? I mean, you're really kidding, right? After today's game and everything, I have to be Susie's taxi service for the night? This is absurd! Why does she get everything she wants, Mom? I'm just asking. Why do you spoil her?"

"Daryl, I do not spoil her. I simply told her she could go to the dance," Helen explains, trying to remain calm. "She bought some new outfits, and she's very excited to dress up and go out tonight. It'll only take you a short while to drop them off and bring them home. Please, Daryl, just do this for me, just this once," Helen pleads.

It is always "this once," Daryl thinks to himself. Whenever his mother resorts to almost begging, he inevitably weakens, which Helen well knows.

With an exasperated sigh, Daryl surrenders, "Okay, Mom. Okay. You win. And Susie wins, as usual. Susie *always* wins. I'm the only person who doesn't ever win!" He slaps both palms on his mattress and storms out of the room.

Susanna Marie Novak, known to her family as *Susie* and to her friends simply as *Sue,* is a product of the styles and fads of a cross section of society known as "the hippies." By the time Susie was in seventh grade, she had already begun to buy into the mod clothing styles and the music that characterized the hippie movement, which the media began to call a "countercultural revolution." Madison Avenue made it easy for Susie by analyzing, producing, marketing, and selling every nuance of the culture in magazines, commercials, and department stores across the country.

Oblivious to the conversation that has just taken place between her mother and brother, Susie continues her conversation on the phone with Sally.

"Have you heard the Hollies' new song, Sally? 'Carrie Ann'?"

"Oh yes, I love it!"

"Wait! I'm going to play it!" Stretching the black, curly phone wire to its limit from the hallway into her bedroom, Susie grabs a forty-five, places it on the padded turntable of her Motorola record player, and carefully places the needle onto the edge of the record. Dancing back into the hallway to the Hollies' new hit song while wrapping herself in the wire, Susie asks, "Who do you think is dreamier, Sally, Allen Clarke or Graham Nash? I like Graham best."

"Me too. Graham Nash is so gorgeous. What? Okay, Mom," and with a deep sigh, Sally says, "Sue, I have to get off the phone. My mom says I'm not supposed to monopolize it. I'll see you tonight at 7:45."

Hanging up the phone, Susie hears Daryl moan, "Mom, does she have to blast those songs all afternoon?"

Rushing out of Daryl's room and past her daughter, Helen says, in almost a whisper, "Susie, how many times do I have to tell you not to play your music so loud?"

"Okay, I'll turn it down. One sec," Susie replies.

Returning to her room, Susie shuts her door, grabs a half dozen of her favorite forty-fives from her desk and stacks them on the record player spindle. Then, moving rhythmically to the beat of the music, she begins to take clothes out of her closet, analyzing them one at a time and then throwing a veritable wardrobe of mini-skirts and dresses, along with bell bottom pants and peasant blouses across her bed as she contemplates what she will wear to the dance. Rummaging through the top drawer of her dresser, Susie begins to throw a variety of colored tights on top of the assortment of outfits. She is as obsessed with the fashions of the time period as she is with its rock stars. With every ounce of her being, Susie imagines herself becoming a famous model or maybe a fashion designer and dreams of, one day, hanging out in the boutiques and discotheques of Carnaby Street in London with her favorite British pop stars, as if wishes are real...as if dreams come true...as if glamorous tomorrows are truly in her future.

Helen enters the room and, seeing the sudden mess, says, "Susanna Marie Novak. How did this room get so messy? It was spotless when I cleaned it this morning while you were at the game. You're as bad as Daryl!"

Besides the array of clothing, Susie's floor is littered with copies of pop magazines. *Teen Beat*, *Tiger Beat*, and *Seventeen* are strewn about, their pages opened to glossy photos of Susie's favorite singers. Alongside the magazines is a copy of *The Lord of the Rings*, which Susie had been reading after the game before abandoning it in favor of her pop magazines, the only print material she is more obsessed with than the Tolkien trilogy.

Responding in a British accent, Susie says, "I simply can't clean now, Mummy dearest. Can't you see I'm about to get ready for the big dance?" Although *The Parent Trap*, starring British film actress Hayley Mills, was her favorite childhood movie, Susie's proclivity to speak with a British accent has more to do with watching interviews on television with singers and musicians, like Graham Nash and other hipsters, who followed the Beatles to America in what became known as the "British Invasion."

Disarmed as always by Susie's theatrics, Helen replies with a moan, "Oh Susie, what am I ever going to do with you? It's lucky your father travels a lot and doesn't see the things you wear when you go out."

To fully resolve the matter, Susie simply kisses her mother on the cheek, and adds, as if she is Princess Anne in the flesh, "And now, Mummy dearest, if you will kindly allow me my privacy. I simply must tell my diary my hopes and dreams for the evening before I get ready for the ball. Please ask the servants not to bother me."

Moments after Helen leaves her daughter's room, shaking her head, Susie picks up a white mini-dress spotted with large pastel polka dots, and she thinks to herself, *this is what the princess shall wear to the ball.* Holding the dress against her body, she whirls around, and then tosses it up into the air, watching it float whimsically, like a fluffy parachute, back onto her bed. Susie then turns to her bureau and stretches a canary yellow headband over her forehead, and looking into her mirror, she dons her new rose colored, round glasses, and utters aloud, "Perfect!"

Daryl doesn't understand Susie, and the older the two of them get, the less effort Daryl puts into trying to understand. Although there is only a three year age difference, from Daryl's perspective, he and Susie might as well have been born a generation apart. While he, of course, enjoys the music of the era, Susie's total submergence into pop culture is beyond his comprehension. He has as little interest in her dreams and goals of London as she has in his exploits on the athletic field.

I was pumped up because I didn't have to work the Saturday night after the Derby-Seymour game. I didn't hate working, but it was kind of hard to watch every kid in the entire Valley descend upon Duchess after a night at a dance or a game, each of them having the time of their lives, while I labored away. Being one of the new guys on the crew, I had to make multiple trips into the parking lot to pick up the garbage that all the slobs threw on the ground. There I'd be with my broom and a garbage can, sweeping empty cups, dirty bags, rolled up hamburger wrappers, and chewed up straws into large piles, then picking up the filthy mess with my bare hands and disposing of it in my rolling garbage can. It was kind of gross to have to pick up half eaten hamburgers, cheeseburgers, and french fries. After lying on the dirty ground for an hour or two, food gets grubby and starts to smell.

The real worst part, though, was being made fun of by kids in the parking lot. Some of them were drunk, and, since I was only fifteen, most of them were a year or more older than I was, so the drunks didn't spare themselves any fun at my expense.

"Hey, broom boy," one of them would say, "you missed a cup." Puzzled, I'd look down on the asphalt where he was pointing, not seeing anything. Then the jerk would toss his cup on the ground. Hilarious.

The crowd the jerk was with typically got a kick out of such treatment. Sometimes a girl in the group with some inkling of kindness in her heart would try to come to my rescue, admonishing the ringleader. "Aw, leave the poor kid alone. He's so cute with his broom and his apron." Exactly how I wanted to be perceived by a pretty girl. Such remarks typically resulted in more laughter.

I found the best thing to do was to keep my trap shut and just get on with my work. Any other reaction would have been futile. It wasn't that I was scared of them. Well, maybe I was a little scared of them since they were older and bigger — and drunker than I was. So, I chose to just move on. On they taunted and laughed, and on I swept.

But on this night, I was free as a bird, and the plan was for my buddy Jeff and me to go to the dance at the Derby Community Center. We had been going there most Saturday nights since last year when we were measly freshmen since Derby ran the dance every Saturday night during the school year, except holidays. Jeff and I could be found at the Derby dance mostly any time there was nothing going on in Shelton. The Derby Community Center is great because it's only a short walk over the Shelton-Derby Bridge, not more than fifteen or twenty minutes from our neighborhood. I don't know who organizes these dances, but Jeff and I like them. The crowd at the dance is a cross section of kids from the entire Valley. The dance always features a live band, and the gym is dimly lit and packed from wall to wall with all kinds of people.

The local DJ from WICC in Ansonia, Ron Roberts, hosts the evening, and when not making one of his "Is everybody having a good time?" announcements from the stage, he circulates through the crowd with his sidekick, a ventriloquist dummy named Herbie Heckler, mingling with the kids. Ron Roberts himself isn't much of a ventriloquist. To make it simple, let's just say that when Herbie talks, Ron's lips move. Mostly, Ron is pretty corny, but he is kind of a local celebrity, so we never mind talking to him. You don't get to talk to a celebrity every day. He'll ask us if we have any questions for Herbie, and no matter what we ask, Herbie's response, in his high, nasally voice, is always, "How the fuck should I know?" which cracks Jeff and me up since most adults we know don't curse like that in our presence. Not a great many Shelton kids attend the Derby dances, but Jeff and I aren't like a great many kids, so we don't care. We like the music and the excitement of the crowd.

Not surprisingly, since it's their home turf, the Derby Football Team is always there, basking in the glory of their latest win, which is easy to do when you never lose. That night, Adamo was moving through the crowd, flanked by the All State lineman, Nickie Grasso, and the quarterback, Foxy Belchak. Other Derby players were milling about in small groups as well. They thought they were big stuff, all decked out in their letter jackets. I'd say most all of them were drunk. Not that they acted very different than usual, but there was a more relaxed vibe to their arrogance, and they seemed to be laughing a lot, like each of them thought the other was the funniest guy on the face of the earth. Adamo strutted through the crowd, with Grasso close by his side, like a bodyguard — as if Adamo needed a bodyguard. Belchak, with his practically platinum blond hair, tagged a few feet behind them. Belchak didn't say much, but he had a crazy look in his eyes, this fearless look, like he'd try anything once...or twice...or more than twice. I tried to steer clear of those guys. You didn't want to accidentally bump into one of them or you might find yourself in a mess of trouble.

I didn't see any of the Seymour players at the dance, but they weren't likely to show up at a dance in Derby after such a heartbreaking loss. I wondered what Daryl Novak and the Seymour players were doing. Obviously, what football players did was none of my business, though. The game was over, the team I was rooting for had lost, and my plan was to ignore, as much as possible, the victors.

Jeff and I typically split up at dances. Each of us would be on the hunt for a girl we might want to dance with. We felt it was better to work independently so as not to focus on the same girl. Actually, Jeff was often on the lookout for a particular girl he liked, Julie Carter, who was a year ahead of us at Shelton High, and he didn't need to work up any courage since they already had sort of a thing going on. Sometimes, Jeff and Julie would enter a dance contest, and it wasn't unusual for them to win. Julie could really groove, and Jeff wasn't too bad himself. The prize was usually a small stack of comic books from Charlton Press in Derby. Big whoop.

On this night, while Jeff was flirting with Julie, a girl I had never seen before captured my attention. Well, she captured more than just my attention. To use Sal Paradise's expression, she was the "gonest" girl I had ever seen. For atmosphere, only about a fifth of the gym's overhead lights were on, and I was mesmerized as I pretty much gaped at her while she moved in and out of light and shadow while goofing around with her friends. Girls goof around different than guys. Dancing around by herself, weaving in and out between her girlfriends, her straight blonde hair swayed back and forth. She was wearing bright lemon colored tights, and a white mini-dress covered with oversized pastel polka dots almost the size of tennis balls. To match her tights, she wore a lemon-colored headband wrapped around her blonde hair, in the style Indians wear in television Westerns. Her doe-like eyes appeared to be even bigger than they really were, if that's possible, because her eye make-up was almost like a clown's, but in this case a very beautiful clown, with what looked like eyelashes that she must have drawn with a make-up pencil or something below her lower eyelids. I had seen Goldie Hawn wear similar eye make-up on "Laugh In," but I never saw, like, a real girl with eye make-up like that. I mean, I'm not going to lie. The eye make-up was kind of outrageous. The whole look was outrageous, but she really pulled it off with elegance and grace. To me, she looked like an exotic, colorful bird. An elegant, delicate, beautiful bird. I also couldn't help noticing that Miss Polka Dots was holding a pair of glasses in her right hand. When she crossed through the light, I could see they were an over-sized pair of wire-rimmed, round glasses with what appeared to be tinted lenses. It was hard to tell what color they were in the semi-darkness. I guessed they probably weren't about poor eyesight but more about style, which seemed to be this girl's middle name. As she bebopped around, giggling and talking with her girlfriends, she playfully alternated between donning the stylish glasses or holding them in an outstretched hand. That's what I mean about girls goofing around. A guy would either keep the glasses on or put them in his pocket. And a guy wouldn't dance around by himself because, if he did, some other guy would probably beat him up. I wondered if she was able to get away with either the shortness of her mini-dress or the exaggerated eye make-up or the round tinted glasses in school. She wouldn't have been able to at my high school, that's for sure. It was a mod style, a kind of hippie look, which was starting to gain popularity, especially at social functions like dances. I didn't really know what to think or say or do; I only knew that I had fallen under some kind of hypnotic spell. It was one of those times in life when you see a girl, and while she comes sharply into focus, the rest of the world becomes a soft blur around her. That hasn't happened to me very often, but when it has, I am done for.

"What's going on, partner?" Jeff's voice, behind me, startled me back to reality. "You look like you've seen a ghost."

"Oh, nothing...nothing...I didn't see a ghost," I replied, still in my own little world. "What's going on with you?"

"Not much. Some older guy asked Julie to dance, but I'll get back to her in a while. But you are definitely looking at someone," he said, sizing up the scene.

"Yeah, I guess I am looking at someone — sort of." I was so out of it, I sounded like a zombie even to myself.

Trying to evaluate my line of vision, he said, "Well, who is it? Snap out of that trance you're in and tell me." He surveyed the wall where I had been gazing. "It's that skinny one with the polka dots and the eyes, isn't it?"

"Yeah," I said. "Yeah, that would be it."

"You like her?" Jeff asked, as if he couldn't tell.

"Yeah," I sighed. "She's a really gone girl."

"There you go, using that beatnik talk again," Jeff complained. "You have to get rid of that book...you read too much."

"That's the best way I can describe how I feel about her," I replied, not taking my eyes off of Miss Polka Dots for a second.

"Well, I'll say this about her. She's flat as a board, but if that's what you like, what the hell." Continuing to analyze her, Jeff whistled and said, "And that's some crazy-ass eye make-up she's got goin' on, man. Here's my advice. Just go ask her to dance, man. You need to make your move."

"But I don't even know who she is. I mean, she doesn't know me," I complained.

"And she's never going to know you unless you ask her to dance. Have some balls. Make a move! I'll catch up to you in a little bit, and you better have asked her when I get back here."

He was right. I needed to make a move. I was never going to win any trophies for talking to girls I didn't know. The band, The Journeymen, launched into a song I liked, "Gloria" by the Rascals. It had a hard driving beat, and I swallowed hard as I approached Miss Polka Dots.

"Hi," I said, "any chance you wanna dance?" I wondered if she could hear the lump in my throat.

She gave me this up-and-down puzzled look and said, "Are you talking to me?" When she saw I was, she just shrugged and said, "Okay," like being asked to dance by an utter stranger was an everyday occurrence.

Her girlfriends giggled as we took a few steps into the crowd of dancers and joined in. *What do they think is so damn funny?* I wondered. I really liked the way she moved. She was delicate and graceful, and her slender, yellow encased legs danced with a light, rhythmical sway to the beat of the music. But there was another thing. As she danced, she closed her eyes and appeared to be lost in the music in a way, to be completely honest, that I personally was...I don't know how to explain it...was way too self-conscious to do. As for me, I was focused on her more than I was on the music. As for her, she was not only dancing to the music, she *was* the music. In one sense, it was really cool. But in another, it wasn't really that cool. See, she seemed so lost that I began to wonder if she was even still aware that she was dancing with me...or that I even existed. *Would you please open your eyes?* I thought to myself, feeling more than a twinge of panic now. Thankfully, she eventually did, and we finally made eye contact. I think I smiled at her because she seemed to smile back, which was a major relief. I was sure captivated by those groovy eyes. As Jimmy Dee, the organ player, belted out "G-L-O-R-I-A" in his raspy voice, I wondered what Miss Polka Dots' real name was. *It would be weird if her name is Gloria,* I thought, which was a pretty stupid thing to be thinking about. What were the chances of that? Sometimes my mind goes to really dumb places. When the song ended, her eyes were wide open, looking at me with a mystical curiosity, and I'm pretty sure I blushed as I said, "Thanks a lot."

"Sure," she said, "any time."

I stood transfixed, thinking, *She talked to me...I'm in love!* Miss Polka Dots returned to her friends who pulled her into a huddle, and I needed to step outside to get some air so I wouldn't pass out. During the last hour of the dance, I felt the need to pretend that I wasn't looking at her, and, boy, did I ever botch that up. Every once in a while, she shot a glance across the gym to where I was standing and gave me that embarrassed, *I know you're looking at me* look. I had accomplished my first goal, which was to dance with her, but now I had become obsessed with a new goal — to dance a slow dance with her. How I was going to pull that off, I had no clue.

Luckily, good old Jeff was there for moral support. "It's no different from before," he said, "you just ask her to dance again. Same like before."

"I know, but it's *different* from before because it's a slow dance," I explained like I was talking to a third grader.

"Oh, don't be a pussy," he said. "Just ask her! The next slow dance, either you go ask her or I'm going to fuckin' drag you over there and ask for you!"

"Maybe she might say yes. When I said, 'thanks for dancing with me,' she said, 'any time.' "

"There you have it," Jeff said. "What do you want? An engraved invitation? Don't be a dipshit all your life. Just ask her."

The pressure was on. It was 9:50, and the dance ended in ten minutes. Most bands made the last song of the night a slow dance, and the Journeymen didn't disappoint.

"Thanks for coming, everyone," said Tom Redd, the lead guitar player. "We're going to end the night with something we think you'll all like."

The band began "You Really Got a Hold on Me" by Smokey Robinson and the Miracles. A real classic, slow but with a nice beat. I could feel Jeff's hand apply pressure to my lower back. "The perfect song, sport. You're up at bat. It's now or never — you know what I mean?"

I don't know if it was the pressure from Jeff, blind courage, or the mystical spell she had cast on me, but I found myself making my way toward Miss Polka Dots and her friends.

"Hi again," I said. "Uhm...I was wondering if...well...like, if you might wanna dance again."

She reacted with the same slightly puzzled look that she had the first time I asked her to dance. She glanced back at her friends, perhaps for reassurance, and then she timidly said, "Yeah...okay."

As before, we made our way into the crowd of dancers, but this time everyone was more or less in an embrace because that's how you do a slow dance. I reached my right hand around and placed it on the small of her back. I took her right hand in my left, our entwined hands pulled in close to our shoulders. By the time we got going, the Journeymen were heading into the second verse.

As I listened to the vocal, I just tried to lose myself in the words and rhythm of the music...which one hundred percent didn't work, because instead, I found myself feeling more than a tad bit self-conscious and concentrating on what my feet were doing. In my mind, I heard myself counting in rhythm to the beat of the tune, saying, *One (step), two (step), three (step), and four (step).* Which, to be honest, was really bizarre because it's not like I'm uncoordinated or never danced before. My mother, who's really into ballroom dancing, used to make me dance with her in the living room all the time because she couldn't get Michael to do it. Not that I minded. Then, Mom was even more thrilled when, in eighth grade, I took ballroom dancing lessons at Sally Jean O'Connor's School of Dance, which is a block and a half away from my house at the Grange Hall. The thing is, the cutest girl in our grade, Colleen Carey, asked me to get three or four guys from the neighborhood to take the class, and Colleen could be very convincing when she wanted to be. I guess, between dancing with my mother at home and taking lessons with Colleen at the Grange Hall, I should have more or less known what end was up. So why was I freaking out? I guess it was just that I was so nervous.

Luckily, before I knew it, I wasn't thinking about steps anymore, thank God, but just *feeling* the music. I was just loving listening to Tom Redd do an almost perfect Smokey Robinson falsetto, and before I knew it, I could feel Miss Polka Dots' head only about a thousandth of an inch from mine. I'm not even exaggerating. My heart practically stopped beating when I felt her headband and her blonde hair sweep ever so slightly across my cheek, kind of like she was brushing dust off my face. The next thing I knew, she let her head rest comfortably on my shoulder, like it was her soft bedroom pillow...like it was nothing unusual...like she was my girlfriend. It was one of those moments when thought leaves you and you act completely on instinct. I let go of her hand and, bringing my left hand around to the hand I already had on her back, I gently pulled her closer to me. She responded in kind by bringing her right hand around the back of my neck and interlocking the fingers of both hands there. It was perfect. Holding her close, I noticed her perfume, and I thought, *She smells like sunflowers and like love.* It was kind of a dumb thing to think because the truth is I didn't actually know what sunflowers smelled like and I had never been in love unless you want to factor in Colleen Carey (but I don't think eighth grade really counts). But, anyway, that's what passed through my mind during those few precious minutes.

I didn't want the song to ever end. Unfortunately, though, the Journeymen had other ideas because the song did end, and they were already packing up their gear. I wish I had been more eloquent, but the only words I could find were, "Well...uhm...you know...thanks again."

"Yeah, thank you, too," she said, looking directly into my soul with curious, truthful eyes like none other that I had ever seen. And that was it. She turned and walked away, but as dozens of kids crossed her path, I thought I saw her do a quick three-sixty as if she wanted to take one more quick look. Me? I just stood there in a stupor as all of the gym lights abruptly switched on, and I was suddenly jolted back to reality, which was about the last place I wanted to be at that moment. One moment I was holding her in my arms to the romantic sounds of Smokey Robinson in a world of magical dim light and darkness, and the next moment I was swept up in a herd of kids pushing their way out of the gym. I didn't know how or when or if I would see her again, but I had to figure it out.

As Jeff and I filed out of the double doors onto Fifth Street, I felt myself frantically perusing the crowd, trying to locate her, but there were too many people jammed together with kids piling into cars and horns beeping. Souped up cars with loud motors slowly rolled by. Most people were probably heading to Duchess, but Jeff and I didn't want to hitchhike or walk that far, so he pushed for the Derby Pizza Palace, only a block away. I wasn't crazy about their Greek style pizza with its thick crust, probably because I'm Italian.

As we turned on Elizabeth Street heading for Main, Jeff commented, "Your new girlfriend is real cute even though she's flat chested. What's her name?"

"I have no clue," I said.

"What do you mean you have no clue?" he barked sarcastically. "How could you dance close with a cute girl like that and not ask her name?"

"Because I'm stupid," I responded. "I'm an idiot. That's why! One minute I had my arms around her and it was amazing, and the next minute I was at a loss for words. I'm such an ignoramus!"

"Ignoramus? Okay, Shakespeare. You and your big words. Well, let me clue you in on something bigger than big words, pal. A girl doesn't dance that close to a guy unless she likes him."

"Huh," I uttered in a kind of intellectual and thoughtful way, like I had just been given the secret to unlocking the universe. Jeff usually made a lot of sense.

"Don't worry about it, partner. If she was here this week, she'll be back. We'll just keep an eye out for her every Saturday night."

"How come I never saw her before tonight?" I asked dejectedly.

"Just maybe she was here but you didn't notice," he said.

"Yeah, maybe," I said, wondering how I wouldn't have noticed.

"Chin up, my friend. There's a solution to this problem, and I'm going to help you with it. But next time, ask her for her name and number, ya dumb ass, will ya?"

Daryl and his teammates sit on the hoods and trunks of their running cars in pairs and small groups in a woodsy clearing behind Seymour High School, sipping on and chugging cans of icy Budweiser. The boys sulk over the loss as the radio from one of their cars blares the latest Top 40 hits. It is a somber gathering. They cause no trouble and, except for the sound of their music, make very little noise. They just want to hang out together. Daryl has consumed nine beers when he looks at his wristwatch and sees that it is 9:50, time to get Susie.

"Oh, shit! I gotta go. Okay, guys, life sucks but I have to go get my little sister now," he complains.

Ben Andrews says, "Wait, Daryl, I'm starved, man. How about dropping me off at Duchess while you bring her home?"

"Yeah, me too," Willie Jupin, a linebacker on the team, chimes in.

"I'm coming too," Victor Zagrebalny, the team's fullback, yells.

"Whoa! Whoa! What the fuck is this? It's a Bug not a bus," Novak's speech is slurred now. "And besides, I'm almost late now as it is."

But when he gets to the car, the three teammates pile in too. All four of the boys are feeling no pain. Daryl wheels down Great Hill Road on his way to Derby. Jupin and Zagrabelny, cramped in the back seat, sing along with the Turtles whose latest hit "Happy Together" is playing on the radio.

"Guys! Guys!" Novak calls out. "Shut the fuck up, will ya? Let me think. I can't leave Susie standin' out there alone. Christ, she's only a fourteen year old kid, ya know? My mother shouldn't even let her go to these fuckin' dances. Susie thinks she's on Ban'stand or Hullabaloo or one of those other dumb shows. And if one of those Derby pricks hits on her, I'll kick their fuckin' ass!"

Ben Andrews interrupts as Daryl pulls on to Route 8, almost as if he hadn't heard anything Daryl said. "You're gonna drop us off at Duchess, right, Daryl? I really need some food bad!"

"Wait...wai'! Okay...okay...listen," Daryl responds, his speech slurring badly now as he tries pathetically to formulate a game plan. "I know...I know. I gotta...gotta go there first cuz...cuz it's already a little after 10. What I'll do is...we'll swing by the community center and I'll tell her to walk...to walk to Du...Dushess with her friends. It's not that far. Then I'll meet her there and take her home. You guys can get out and get a bite to eat, and then I'll come back to get ya after I bring her home. How's that sound?"

"Yeah, that'll be cool, Daryl. That's cool," says Andrews, who is riding shotgun. "But could ya hurry the fuck up? I'm gonna die if I don't eat somethin' soon."

When Daryl reaches the Derby Community Center, the traffic is thick. Parents are picking up younger kids, while teen boys with cars loaded with their friends are headed to one or the other of two usual post-dance hotspots — River Restaurant for pizza or Duchess for burgers and fries. Daryl spots Susie standing on the corner of Elizabeth Street and Fifth Street across from the Derby Green with Sally and Mary Jane. He pulls up in the VW and rolls his window down.

"Hey, Susie," he calls, "over here!"

Before he can get another word out, sparing no sarcasm, Susie asks, "How are we supposed to fit in your car with the entire football team in it, Daryl?"

"Don't be a smart aleck, Susie," Daryl replies. "You're not gettin' in the car yet."

"What do you mean, we're not getting in the car *yet*? Mom said..." and then she shifts gears, "Daryl Walter Novak! Are you drunk?"

"I said, don' be a smart aleck, Susie. Now listen to me. Aw, Susie! You still have that eye make-up on! I told you to wipe it off when I dropped you off. Yer not a hippie, ya know. Yer just a kid!"

"You can't tell me how to wear make-up, Daryl!"

"Ok...ok...calm down, will ya? Now, listen, for once in yer life, will ya? Here's what we're gonna do."

After Daryl explains the plan, Susie says in exasperation, "You've got to be kidding me, Daryl. You can't make us walk to Duchess. I'm going to a phone booth and calling Mom right now!"

"Susie, for Christ sake, yer really startin' to piss me off now! Why do you have to make everything harder than it is? Don't call mom! She don't like to drive at night, you know that! It'll only take you twenty minutes to get there, and I'll be waitin' for ya when you arrive. Just do what I'm tellin' ya, will ya, for once in yer fuckin' life?"

"Daryl! You know you're not supposed to use that language with me," Susie says with a smugness reserved only for sisters to use on their big brothers.

With that, Daryl shifts into first, leaving Susie and her friends behind, as the VW becomes part of the stream of cars, horns honking and music blasting.

"He's gonna be in trouble when I tell my mother and father about this," Susie promises. "Oh well, I guess we're walking to Duchess."

Susie and her friends start to walk up Elizabeth Street past the Derby Library. Mary Jane and Sally begin talking about the dance, but Susie is quiet...pensive. She doesn't like it when Daryl is mean to her, especially in front of her friends, and she doesn't like that he drinks. She also finds herself thinking about the slow dance she had had with a complete stranger, whoever he was. When they reach the Armory, Sally breaks away from Susie and Mary Jane, runs over to the enormous, steel World War I cannon on the lawn of the historic stone building and begins to climb up the barrel of the cannon.

"Sue! Mary Jane!" Sally yells. "Look at me!"

"What are you doing, you nut?" Mary Jane shouts, as Sally, hanging upside down, fires rounds of laughter at them from the silver cannon barrel, like a monkey hanging from a great limb of a tree.

"I couldn't resist, I've always wanted to do this," Sally yells back.

Sally lets herself fall from the cannon onto the grass, now completely overcome with laughter. The Armory sits at the corner of a major intersection where Elizabeth Street becomes Atwater Avenue. The three girls cautiously look both ways, then cross the street, holding hands on their way to the sidewalk across from the Armory. As they walk past the big Victorian houses that line Atwater Avenue, once the homes of Derby's most successful industrialists, they chatter away.

"That dance was incredible, wasn't it, girls?" Mary Jane says.

"It would have been incredible if someone asked me to dance," Sally replies, which then causes her to focus on Susie. "Sue is the lucky one who got asked to dance, weren't you Sue? So, tell us. Who was that cute, skinny guy you danced with tonight anyway? What's his name and what high school does he go to? Derby?"

"Yeah, we saw you were getting kind of cozy with him during that last dance," Mary Jane teases, and both girls segue, back and forth, into a volley of giggles.

"I don't know," replies Susie with a dazed sincerity.

"Sue, what can you possibly mean, you don't know?" Mary Jane asks disappointedly. "Didn't he tell you his name?"

"No, he didn't," Susie says.

"Boys are so weird," remarks Sally. "Aren't they weird, Mary Jane?"

"Stupid and weird, right Sue?" Mary Jane responds. Not receiving a reply, she waves her open hand in front of Susie's eyes, and then says more loudly, "I said, boys are stupid and weird, right Sue?"

"Oh," says Susie, startled, as if having been woken up from a deep sleep. "Yes...I...I guess so." She is feeling more than a touch of melancholy at the thought of the cute, gentle boy with whom she had enjoyed a slow dance.

As the three girls approach Division Street, they only have about ten more minutes to walk before arriving at Duchess. Turning right on Division, they start down the steep, winding hill, at the bottom of which will be Pershing Drive. Walking down the right side of the road, Sally says, "In Girl Scouts we learned that if there's no sidewalk you should walk on the left side of the road, so you're walking toward the oncoming traffic. C'mon girls," she squeals and sprints across the street to the other side of the road, screaming with more laughter. A moment later Mary Jane follows suit and dashes across the road right before the big bend.

"C'mon, Sue! What're you waiting for?" Sally shouts, "You're supposed to be on this side of the road. Be a good Girl Scout!"

"Okay," Susie yells back. "Here I come!"

As Susie begins to trot calmly across the road, still thinking of her mystery dance, out of the darkness she suddenly sees luminous car headlights, rolling around the bend in arcing parallel beams. Blinded by the stark white light, Susie freezes in the middle of the road. The driver straight arms the steering wheel with his left arm, punches his horn with his right, and slams his foot down hard on his brake pedal. The screeching brakes and droning horn pierce the quiet night in a dolorous alarm as he sees a girl in a polka dot dress illuminated in the darkness.

4

Michael DeMarco is used to being swamped by a 10:00 wave of teens after a dance or a game. He has, after all, been working at Duchess since the fall of 1964 when the Moscowicz family opened the drive-in on Pershing Drive in Ansonia adjacent to the train tracks which run alongside the Naugatuck River. Herman Moscowicz had handpicked Howie Millea to be the manager of the first Duchess Drive-In. Like Michael, Howie had gotten involved in the food business at only sixteen, working for the Moscowicz family at their hot dog stand in Bridgeport in the late 1950s. Michael, in turn, had been one of Howie's early hires. Howie had liked the fact that Michael was a student at his alma mater, Fairfield Prep. Howie had gone on to Fairfield University and had become a science teacher in nearby Trumbull, but Herman Moscowicz kept him interested in the food business, promising him a future career where Howie could become not only a manager but an owner — an opportunity which would allow Howie to earn an income a school teacher could only dream about. Michael, an education major at Southern Connecticut State College, dreams of a similar fate. He imagines beginning a teaching career and then being scooped up by Howie or by Herman Moscowicz himself to take over a new Duchess store. It's no secret that Herman Moscowicz is planning to build more Duchess Drive-In stores across the state, and Michael often thinks, *Maybe I'll be the next Howie Millea.*

Adept at all facets of the business, Michael had begun as a drink man, and moved up the chain to fry man, grill man, and, beginning when he was a senior in high school, a window man, which brings with it the authority of an assistant manager when he works on a night crew. Michael takes great pride in how quickly and efficiently he can fill an order, cracking open a small, medium, or large white paper bag, depending on the size of the order, and filling it in just a few adroit motions. Great with numbers, he adds all orders in his head, and when questioned, Michael is never wrong.

For Michael, getting ready for an influx of customers is like getting ready for a big game. He feels a similar rush of excitement. On the night after the big Derby-Seymour game, once the dinner hour rush ends, it is a quiet night for Michael and his crew, his cousin Tomaso DeMarco, Kevin Binkowski, and Les Wilson. Growing up, Michael had a penchant for bestowing nicknames on neighborhood kids, and that practice has continued in his working life at Duchess. And so it is that Michael's cousin Tomaso, a notorious prankster, has become known to the crew as "Tommy Trouble," compliments of Michael, and sixteen year old Kevin Binkowski, has become known as "Bink," because it amuses Michael to have dubbed him so. Michael hasn't bestowed a nickname on Les Wilson, probably because Les is Michael's senior by almost twenty years. The younger employees think Les might be a homosexual, although in 1967, they know almost nothing about the subject. Sometimes one of the bolder kids will tease Les and say, "Well, we all know you're a little strange," to which Les will reply in a dramatic drawl, "Hey, baby — don't knock it until you try it!" Michael likes Les, and he is keenly aware that working with Les is his only real experience of interacting with a homosexual, at least that he knows of. Les also lives in the Ansonia Olsen Drive projects, the same as all of his black coworkers. In fact, most black families in the Valley reside in Ansonia at what is more formally known as the Riverside Apartments on Olsen Drive, an 11-building complex of 160 government-subsidized housing units, constructed in 1963. Across the nation, such housing projects subtly but effectively segregate black families from the middle-class white families of the suburbs.

At 9:45, Michael says, "Okay, guys, it's almost game time. Tommy Trouble, throw two twenty-fours on the grill, Les, let's get a couple of baskets of potatoes in the fryers, and Bink, make sure all of the drink machines are filled and ready to go."

By 10:00, cars are already rolling into the parking lot. Not only the usual family cars, which parents have allowed their teens to use for the night, but muscle cars souped up by gearheads — GTOs, Mustangs, Chargers, Stingrays — begin pulling into what just moments before had been rows of parallel white lines, designating vacant spaces. These are cars filled with groups of boys or girls, and cars with lovebirds, the girls practically sitting on their boyfriends' laps. On a weekend night when there are no high school events, these same cars might show off and cruise by, driving around the building slowly, and ten or fifteen minutes later cruise by again. After a dance like the one tonight, though, everyone is famished.

The teen customers who arrive on this night began as young customers with their families when the Moscowiczes opened the place three years ago. For residents of the Lower Naugatuck Valley, Duchess Drive-In had brought a new excitement to the region. With hamburgers costing only $.20 and french fries only $.15, a night out at Duchess meant Mom didn't have to cook, Dad didn't have to break the bank, and the kids enjoyed a special treat. Now, these kids had grown into customers in their teens who had their own income to spend. Like McDonald's, which the Moscowicz family has modeled Duchess after, there is no dining room. After having their orders filled, customers make their way to their cars, which become mobile dining rooms. Like drive-in movies where car interiors are transformed into mobile living rooms, the car dining experience is completely viable.

It is the good fortune of the crew that, with a vestibule filled with raucous Valley teenagers, Howie Millea himself happened to be driving by with his wife Antoinette, on their way back from a dinner dance at the Ansonia Armory. Howie, decked out in a pinstriped, three piece suit, throws an apron on and opens the second window. Working together, Howie and Michael move customers out of the vestibule and into the parking lot at lightning speed. By 10:30, things have calmed down considerably.

"Thanks, Howie," Michael says, "that was a big help."

"That's how we operate here," Howie replies. "You're good, Michael. Really good! Nice work, Les...Tomaso. And Bink, you're getting better all the time."

"Thanks, Howie," Bink says, blushing.

"I have to go, though. I left Antoinette out in the car. She's going to give me hell."

After Howie departs, Bink asks Michael a question. "One of the guys told me Howie used to be a teacher. Is that right, Michael?"

"Yup," Michael replies. "But I figure, even before he started teaching, he always knew he was going to run this store."

"How long did he teach?"

"I think he told me three years, at Madison Middle School in Trumbull."

"Where did Howie grow up?"

"You're full of questions tonight, aren't you, Bink?" Michael remarks ironically. "He grew up in Bridgeport. He invited me and some of the guys over to his parents' house about a year ago for a pick-up basketball game in the driveway. Howie's mom and dad are from Ireland. They both have thick Irish brogues. It was fun listening to them talk."

"How did they feel about him leaving teaching and taking over this store?"

"No idea, Bink, but he obviously did it. And there's no doubt in my mind he's making more money here with lots more to come because somehow he's in the process of becoming some kind of part owner in the company."

"Wow," Bink says. "It looks like he's going to be a big success."

"Dig it," Michael replied, "but how about if you make a big success of yourself by going out and cleaning the lot, Mr. Chatterbox? I'll bet all those kids left a hell of a mess."

Cars are now driving out of the lot, as it nears 11:00. When Ben Andrews and his fellow teammates come in for a second helping of food, Ben asks Michael if there is anything left.

"You're Ben Andrews, aren't you?" Michael asks.

"Yup, that's me," Ben replies.

"My little brother and I were at the game this morning. You and Novak played a great game. And that was a great pass you threw him on your last play. I wish he had been able to hold on. We really wanted you guys to win."

"Thanks a lot, man. I appreciate that. Daryl's outside but he's flipping out right now because his kid sister, I don't know, like, got lost somewhere. She was supposed to meet us here a half hour ago."

"Well, hopefully she isn't too lost." Then grabbing a large bag, Michael throws the remaining food — five cheeseburgers and three french fries into it and adds, "You guys can have this food. I just closed out the cash register for the night. Besides, we would have just thrown it out."

"Oh wow," Andrews replies. "Thanks, man!"

Making their way out of the vestibule, Andrews' teammates jokingly grab for the bag of food as they push through the glass doors.

Growing more sober, Daryl Novak glances down at his wristwatch and, seeing that it's 10:40, he worries, *Where the fuck can Susie be? It shouldn't have taken her more than a half hour to walk here, a half hour at the most!*

"Daryl, you still hungry?" Ben asks. "The head guy in there just gave us a bag of food...for free."

"No man. I'm too freaked out to eat anything. Susie should have been here a long time ago. Okay, I don't get it. What the fuck is going on?"

"What do you think we should do?" Ben asks, stuffing a handful of french fries into his mouth.

Daryl bitingly snaps back, "I gotta go fuckin' find her, that's what I think *we* should do!" Ben is mostly unfazed, having witnessed Daryl's moodiness on many occasions.

"What about us? The place is about to close. You can't leave us here now. How will we get back to our cars?"

"Yeah, right. Shit. You guys will have to come with me," Daryl says, squinting his eyes, trying to formulate a good plan. "When we find them, we'll just have to somehow stuff everyone into my car. That'll be an interesting fuckin' trick."

The four boys pile into the VW, and Daryl speeds out of the Duchess parking lot. As Michael DeMarco heads into the vestibule to lock the doors for the night, he hears the sound of a broken muffler and looks up to see Daryl Novak's Volkswagen Bug fly out of the parking lot and onto Pershing Drive on two wheels.

5

Driving down to the light, Daryl readies himself to turn right at the bottom of the Division Street hill, but the road is blocked off by three large orange and white striped sawhorses.

Seeing the reflection of flashing red lights against the houses above the bend, Ben says, "I wonder what the fuck happened up there. Must be a car accident. I guess you'll have to go straight onto Route 8 and get off in downtown Derby."

Daryl speeds straight to Route 8, gets off Exit 15, and turns left onto Main Street. He drives past the Derby Community Center and heads toward the Armory and Atwater Avenue, the route the girls would have walked. The streets are completely deserted except for a middle aged drunk reeling unsteadily on the opposite side of the street.

"Fuck," Daryl explodes. "I'm telling you guys, when I get my hands on Susie, she's really going to get it. Fuck! She's so spoiled! This really takes the cake."

When Daryl gets to the light at the intersection of Atwater and the top of Division, he would have turned right, but there is another set of barriers, detouring traffic in other directions.

"Okay, guys, I don't know what to do. My mother is going to wig out," Daryl blurts out. "I'm going to drop you guys off back in the woods and go home and see if Susie somehow got a ride home. She seemed pissed at me. It would be just like her to do that. Mother fucker!"

Tony Adamo Sr. is playing poker at the Adriatic Marchigian Club, which, ironically, is not even a full block from the Derby Community Center where his son Frankie attended a dance earlier. As he sips beer from a tall pilsner, Tony is in a dark mood, but not because he isn't winning. It's a few minutes after 11:00, and Tony is up about $75.00. His Italian compatriots are giving him space. He is a man with a short fuse, and he has already expressed his ire at how the night has turned out. Saturday is usually Tony's date night with his girlfriend.

Since he was only a small child, Frankie has had a vague sense of Tony's dalliances. When Frankie was eight years old, he remembers that one night after dinner his father got up, grabbed his hat and coat from the closet near the door of the second floor apartment, and said, "I'm going out. Don't wait up for me."

"What do you mean you're going out?" his wife Rose asked with a measure of anxiety. "Going out where?"

"Don't you worry about where I go or what I do, Rose," Tony had responded sharply. "Just worry about where *you* go and what *you* do! I'll worry about me and you worry about you, capice?"

Even then, little Frankie understood that when Tony ended a sentence by asking if the other person understood, the smartest thing to do was not to question him. Rose, in fact, never questioned Tony again when he went out. She never knew where he went, although she did know he spent a lot of time at the Club, playing cards and drinking with his buddies. Otherwise, she preferred not knowing. Rose didn't want to make waves. Tony liked it that way. He felt everyone should know their place and their role. His role was to provide a living and pay the bills. Her role was to cook and clean and take care of the three boys. Rose had never written a check or used a credit card. Tony liked being in control of everything.

Tonight, Tony doesn't feel in control. He is used to a certain routine on Saturday nights. A nice dinner with his girlfriend in a New Haven restaurant, and then a ride down to the Debonair Motel on the water in West Haven. A little diversion from a long week of running both a store and an illegal gambling operation, which brings with it its own pressures.

When he arrived at the Club at 7:30, he approached the bar and addressed the handful of guys, "Hey, guys. What's up?" and then looked at the bartender, "Mario, pour me a tall one, will you? Budweiser." Tony headed to the wooden phone booth near the restrooms. After only a few minutes, Tony returned to the bar.

"Fuck," he exclaimed, sitting on a tall stool.

"Whatsa matter, Tony?" asked a skinny, bald headed guy with a paper-thin mustache a few stools away.

"My girlfriend can't go out tonight," Tony responded. "She don't feel good. What bullshit."

"Oh, yeah, that's right," said a fat guy with a button down cap to Tony's left. "Tony goes out with his girlfriend on Saturday nights."

Tony gave the fat guy a dirty look. "Shut the fuck up, Dominic, before I get pissed off."

"Hey, easy...easy, Tony," Dominic replied. "Madonna mia, I was just fuckin' teasin' ya."

"Yeah, well now I'm not going to get a blowjob tonight, and I was planning on it, so fuck you."

"Right, we understand," Dominic said, walking over to Tony and putting his hand on Tony's shoulder supportively. "But listen, we have a good card game every Saturday night. You know that, Tony. Join us. Maybe you'll win some money. And maybe you'll go home with a few more lire than you arrived with, eh?"

Winning a few dollars has only lightened Tony's mood a little. He doesn't like any routine disrupted, especially his Saturday night routine. Tony doesn't bounce back well from setbacks.

At 11:22, there is an assertive knock at the Novak front door, waking Helen Novak with a start. She blinks her eyes and realizes that, while watching the eleven o'clock news, she had fallen asleep on the chintz couch, something she never does unless she knows everyone is home, safe and sound. Disoriented, she pulls herself up from the couch and nervously begins to tie her robe, angry with herself for having fallen asleep. She feels like she has neglected her motherly duties in some way. Arriving at the door, she switches on the porch light and, looking through the peephole, she sees a police officer standing on the stoop. Helen opens the door and says anxiously, "I'm sorry, Officer, I was asleep. Is there something I can help you with? Is everything alright?"

"Good evening...sorry to wake you, Ma'am. Are you Helen Novak — the mother of Susanna Novak?" the tall policeman asks soberly. He has only had to deliver such a message once before in his fifteen year career. It is an assignment he had hoped never to draw again.

"Yes...yes...that's right. Is everything alright?" Helen asks again, her voice cracking as she speaks. She glances at her wristwatch and thinks that Susanna should have been home by now.

"Mrs. Novak, may I come in for a moment? My name is Sergeant Dalton from the Ansonia Police Department, and I'm afraid I have some very bad news for you."

Helen says, "Of course...please..." and she steps aside so the police officer can step into her living room. As Sergeant Dalton begins to explain, "The reason I'm visiting so late, regrettably, is because..." Helen feels suddenly disoriented. She can only process snippets and phrases of his explanation: "walking down Division Street"..."hit by a car"..."drunk driver"..."rushed to Griffin Hospital"..."traumatic brain injury"..."pronounced dead on arrival." She suddenly feels smothered, like the walls are closing in on her. Thoughts flash alarmingly through her mind: *Where is Daryl? Why didn't he bring Susie home like he said he would? Where is he right now? He should have had Susie home an hour ago! Why is my husband away now? I hate when he travels for work! What am I going to do?*

"Mrs. Novak? Mrs. Novak?" Sergeant Dalton says, "Do you understand what I've said?"

A trembling Helen says, "I need to sit down." Dalton guides her to an upholstered chair as she suddenly cries out, "Oh my God... Oh my God! This can't be happening! Tell me this isn't true! What am I going to do?" Her body begins to heave as she emits spasmodic sobs.

"Mrs. Novak, Susanna was with two friends, Mary Jane Reilly and Sally Jablonsky, so we have an unofficial I.D. on her, but I'm sorry to say we're going to need you to come to Griffin Hospital to make it official. Is your husband home, Mrs. Novak?"

"No, he's asleep at a truck stop somewhere...somewhere between, between here and Florida." Trying to remember his schedule, she says, "He's not due home until Tuesday."

"Mrs. Novak, I know this must be terribly hard, but I'm afraid I need you to come to Griffin Hospital with me right away," Sergeant Dalton says, trying to be as sensitive and as helpful as possible.

"Yes...yes...let me just get ready. But, Officer, do you...have you... seen my son? Where is my son Daryl?"

"We don't know, Ma'am, the two girls said your son was supposed to drive them home, but there was some kind of mix-up, and they were walking to Duchess. By the time we got there, the place was closed and locked up. The parking lot was vacant. The only ones left were the employees. The fellow in charge said he thought Daryl was outside the place just before closing. He said one of Daryl's friends told him your daughter was lost or missing, he wasn't sure. Mrs. Novak? Are you able to understand what I'm telling you?"

Once again startled, as if she had just been awakened from a deep sleep for the second time of the night, Helen responds, "Yes...yes, Officer. But I...I..."

"Mrs. Novak, I'm so sorry about this. I can only imagine how upset you must be. But we must get an official I.D. Since your husband and son aren't available, I will need you to come with me."

"I...I....yes...let me...give me a minute to get...to get dressed," Helen says, her voice growing louder and more and more hysterical.

"Alright, Mrs. Novak. Try as best you can to calm yourself down. I will wait at the door until you're ready."

The card players hear the phone at the bar ring. Tony looks at his new Bulova gold watch. It is 11:22. His frustration that the game will be interrupted is palpable.

"Who the fuck is calling here at this hour?" the dealer, chewing on a stogie, wonders out loud, and then he shouts, "Dominic, you're light. Ante-up, ya cheap bastard."

Dominic pushes a half dollar into the center of the table. "Oh, fuck you, ya prick. I was just about to ante-up."

"Yeah, you been light all night," the dealer complains.

"Like I said — fuck you," Dominic coughs out.

"Hey, Tony," the bartender yells from across the room. "For you, your wife."

"What the fuck could she want at this hour?" Tony mumbles, getting out of his chair. "Deal me out of this one."

"Whataya want?" Tony growls into the black phone receiver.

"Tony," she says emotionally. "Thank God you're there. I didn't know where to call, and the Club was the only place I could think of. Thank God you're there!"

"Okay, thank God I'm here," Tony parrots sarcastically. "How many times ya gonna say that? What the fuck is goin' on? Are the kids all okay?"

He listens to the trembling voice on the wire. "Something really bad happened, Tony. The Ansonia police just called. Frankie got in a bad accident. He's okay, but a girl got killed, Tony. They said they gotta lock Frankie up until he sees a judge in the morning. They want us to come talk to them at the station right away. I'm gonna have a nervous breakdown, Tony!"

"Jesus Christ! What else could go fucking wrong tonight?" Tony asks mindlessly, as if only talking to himself. "Okay...okay...let me think. You stay put at home, Rose. I'll handle this," and he slams the phone back on the hook.

"Tony?" Rose says. "Tony?" but she hears only a static buzz on the other end of the line, and she is once again silenced.

When he arrives back at the table, Dominic asks, "What was that about, Tony? Rose find out about your girlfriend?"

"Fuck you, asshole," Tony responds, gathering up his winnings and his jacket, and, without another word, he heads aggressively for the exit.

"Tony!" Dominic calls to him. "C'mon, Tony, I was just fuckin' kiddin'. Can't ya ever take a joke? C'mon, Tony...Tony!"

When Daryl arrives home at 11:26, the door is locked and the lights are out. He unlocks the door. "Mom?" he calls, walking through the house, frantically flicking on light switches. "Susie? Mom? Susie? Is anybody home? Where are you guys?" He hears the pitch of his voice rising as he calls out, "What's going on here?"

Daryl flies down the basement stairs and swings open the door to the garage, where, to his dismay, he finds his mother's car. *Where can Mom possibly be?* he asks himself. Beating his fists on the hood of the car, Daryl shouts at the top of his lungs, "Mom! Susie! What the fuck is going on here?"

Not knowing what to do, Daryl exits the garage, bumps into two metal garbage cans, upending them, and yells, "Fuck!" as one of the cans rolls down the driveway, clanking against the asphalt. He ignores it, and continues around the house perimeter to the front door, steps onto the stoop, and helplessly looks up and down the street. Finally, Daryl sits on the step and buries his head in his arms.

Five minutes after leaving the Club, Tony bursts into the Ansonia Police Station. He sees Frankie, hunched over on a bench against the wall, his face buried in the palms of his hands. Tony knows most of the Ansonia policemen, and they know him, having placed many a bet at the market.

"What the fuck is going on, Danny?" Tony asks the officer at the desk.

As the policeman explains the events of the night, Frankie sits upright and then leans his head against the wall behind him, wondering how this could have possibly happened to him. Upset and confused, Frankie tunes into bits and pieces of the hushed explanation. "He hit her at the curve on the Division Street hill"..."beer cans all over the floor of his Lemans"..."manslaughter charges"... "appear before a judge in the morning"..."post bail"..."set a court date"..."you'll need a good lawyer"..."spend the night in jail."

"Danny, you're not really fucking telling me, I hope, that you're going to lock my kid up," Tony angrily says.

"I have no choice, Tony. I have to follow the law. You must know that!"

"Can I talk to him privately, at least?" Tony asks.

As Tony approaches him, Frankie slowly rises to his feet. He is sober now. He falls into his father's arms. "I'm so...so sorry, Dad," Frankie cries. "I didn't mean for this to happen. She just, like, froze in the middle of the road, and I couldn't...couldn't stop in time. It was an accident!"

"Of course you didn't mean for it to happen, and *of course* it - was - an - accident," Tony says in a vexed staccato. "What the fuck else would it have been?" Then Tony places his strong hands on Frankie's biceps, stands him up straight, and firmly whispers into Frankie's ear. "Stand up straight and be a man, son."

The policeman shows Tony and Frankie to a small office. "Okay," Tony says, "What the fuck happened?"

Frankie explains about how two of the guys from River Restaurant bought the team six cases of beer, about the drinking party in the high school parking lot, about cruising around streets above Pershing Drive, and about not being able to stop in time to avoid hitting the girl with the polka dot dress on the curve of Division Street.

Tony, irritably stands up, shakes his head, and says, "You really fucked up this time, Frankie!"

"I know, Dad, but like I said, it was an accident."

"We don't need these kinds of fuckin' accidents, capice?" Tony shouts, kicking a small, waste paper basket across the room. "I don't know how the fuck I'm gonna get your sorry ass out of this one! In the meantime, you get to sit in a jail cell tonight and tomorrow and think about how fuckin' stupid you are!"

The next hours are completely surreal to Helen Novak as she finds herself trapped in a sterile, white nightmare. Being held by the officer in an upright position as he escorts her into the white world of the hospital. Entering the stark white room and seeing the gurney with her baby's fragile body prone upon it, covered in a white sheet. Watching in frozen horror as a man in a white hospital coat pulls back the immaculate sheet, revealing Susie's colorless face. Collapsing onto the polished hospital floor, her knees stinging as they make hard contact with the linoleum. Doubling over and holding her stomach and hearing herself cry out in a guttural, animal sound.

Sergeant Dalton and the hospital staff have heard such a cry on very rare occasions. It is the white, primal scream of a mother's grief at the loss of a precious child.

She hears someone whisper, "You better take her out into the hallway. In fact, it would be better to put her in one of the examining rooms for privacy." The police officer and a nurse help Helen to her feet and out of the room.

Helen's mind races: *Lord, please help me. Please, Lord? Where could Daryl possibly be? How could my husband make me go through this alone? How will I ever recover from the loss of my baby? Not my baby, God! Please, not Susie! Why? What did I ever do to deserve this?*

These disturbing thoughts collide in the deepest recesses of Helen's mind as her caretakers seat her in a chair in an examining room. "There, you just relax here for a moment," she hears one of them say. Everything is a blur. Helen feels that her eyesight is failing her.

A moment later, Helen senses someone leaning close to her and she hears a soft voice, "Mrs. Novak? Mrs. Novak, if you don't mind, I'm going to give you something for your emotions. We're going to have a police officer bring you home, but I'd like to give you five milligrams of Valium to take when you get there. It will calm you down, and it should help you to sleep. Is that alright with you, Mrs. Novak? Do you hear me, Mrs. Novak? Is that alright with you?"

"Yes...yes," Helen replies, completely numb now, as if she has already taken the Valium.

While driving home, Sergeant Dalton asks, "Is there any way at all to contact your husband tonight, Mrs. Novak?"

"No." Helen seems confused. "Not until...not until he calls me in the morning around 8:00. Not until then."

"Okay, Mrs. Novak. Well, when you talk to him, if there's anything we can do to help him understand what happened, please tell him to call the Ansonia Police Station. In fact, there are details that we need to go over with both your husband and you, but they can wait. You've been through enough tonight."

"Yes, Officer...I don't...I don't think I can take any more tonight," she says, as rivulets of tears roll down her cheeks. She makes no attempt to wipe them dry.

When he drops Helen at her door at 12:42, Daryl is sitting on the front stoop, his arms wrapped around his shins and his head resting on his bony knees. Daryl jumps to his feet. "Mom...Mom? Where were you? Mom, I've been waiting for you. Why are you with a policeman, Mom? What happened? Is there some kind of trouble?"

Mrs. Novak's knees give out for the second time that evening despite the fact that Sergeant Dalton is trying his best to support her right arm. One knee hits the narrow flagstone walkway that Walter Novak had laid two years before, then the other, as she sobs, "Oh my God, Daryl! Oh Daryl! What are we going to do? What am I going to do?"

As Dalton attempts to get Mrs. Novak to her feet, Daryl remains helpless and immobile. Making eye contact with Daryl, Sergeant Dalton says assertively, "I'm very sorry to tell you, young man, that your sister was killed in an accident tonight. Your mother has been through a very difficult evening. You need to be strong right now and take care of your mother. Do you think you can do that?"

At 12:52, Bob Goldman is awakened from a sound sleep when his phone rings. He reaches for the receiver in the dark, fumbling it in the process.

"Yes," Bob utters with a yawn. It is not the first time a client has woken Bob in the middle of the night.

"Bob, this is Tony Adamo. I'm sorry to wake you up, but one of my kids is in bad fuckin' trouble. Frankie hit a girl with his car and killed her a few hours ago."

"Where is Frankie now?" Bob asks.

"The police got him locked up in Ansonia."

"Okay...uhm...meet me there in about fifteen or twenty minutes."

Bob's wife stirs in the darkness and whispers. "Who was that?"

"Tony Adamo. His son killed a girl with his car. I'll fill you in when I get back from the police station."

"Oh, no. That's terrible."

"Yes. It certainly is."

Tony and Bob have known each other for twenty-five years. Both are graduates of Derby High School, Class of 1942. After high school, Bob went on to Yale and then Duke Law, and Tony went to work in a factory before enlisting in the Air Force in the summer of 1943. Tony went on to see front line action in the European theater while Bob was completing his legal studies. At the end of the War, Tony joined his father in the grocery business; Bob began his law practice at his father's office.

Bob is the smartest lawyer I know, Tony thinks, hoping he'll have answers to his current dilemma. Tony sees almost everything as his current dilemma.

When Bob arrives at the police station, he sees Tony waiting for him, illuminated by a globe shaped lamp outside the front door where he puffs on a cigarette. The two men head inside and are shown to Frankie's cell.

Upon hearing the clank of the key in the lock, Frankie is roused from a restless sleep. "Get your ass up," Tony orders. "I need you to talk to Attorney Goldman."

A police officer sets up two folding chairs for Bob and Tony, and Frankie sits up on his bed and faces them. His face is pale, and his eyes are bloodshot.

"How are you doing?" Bob asks Frankie. "You don't look like you're feeling too well. Are you sure you're alright?"

Relieved to hear kind words, Frankie replies, "I'm doing okay, I guess."

"Obviously, you both realize we have a serious case here," Bob continues, "but let's start by asking Frankie a few questions. Tell me what happened tonight, Frankie." He grabs a legal pad and a fountain pen from his briefcase.

"What happened?" Frankie mumbles.

"You heard the man," Tony interjects imperiously.

"Yes, start at the beginning," Bob urges. "You went to the dance, right? Where did you go when you left the house to go to the dance?"

"To the parking lot at the high school."

"Who was there and what did you do there?"

"The guys...you know...the guys on...on the...the team," Frankie says reluctantly.

"All of the guys?"

"Uhm...yeah...pretty much."

"And then, Frankie?"

"We had some cases of beer...Belchak's uncle got 'em for us. We just wanted to celebrate. You know...it was a big win."

"Yes, I know. What time did you arrive at the dance?" Bob asks.

"I dunno. 8:30. Maybe a little later."

"By the time the accident happened, the alcohol should have worn off. Do you feel you were still drunk?"

Frankie and Tony make eye contact, and Tony's eyes command Frankie to tell the rest of the story.

"Well, we decided to go to Duchess after the dance, but I still had a partial case of beer in my trunk...so...we drove around for a little while... you know...just looping back and forth from...you know, from the high school and then back down by Duchess...back and forth three or four times...and while we were doing that, we knocked down...I mean, we drank a few more beers. We didn't mean for anything...bad to happen."

"And describe the accident to me. What happened?"

"I dunno. I was just driving — just driving down the hill to Duchess like any other night...and I came around the curve...and this girl was kind of jogging...and...and she just stops running and stands still...she just...just, like, freezes and I felt like she looked right into my eyes. I don't know. It all happened so fast, but I felt like she looked right through me. I tried to stop. I...I slammed on my brakes...hard...but I...I couldn't get the car to stop in time." Frankie shakes his head and buries his face in his hands. Looking back into Attorney Goldman's eyes, Frankie feels he has been heard, somehow, in a non-judgmental way, which he appreciates.

"Did the police ask you if you had been drinking?"

"Well, it was pretty obvious," Frankie says. "There were empties all over the floor in the back seat."

"Did they ask any other questions?"

"No...they said something like, 'You guys have obviously been drinking,' and that was basically it."

As Frankie drops his head dejectedly once more, Bob offers, "Okay, Frankie. I can see you're upset. This is what I want you to do. Under no conditions are you to talk to any police officer or anyone at all without me being present. Anybody asks you any questions, and you say, 'You need to talk to my lawyer.' "

Tony interrupts, "What's the deal, Bob?"

"Here's the story. Frankie, I'm sorry to tell you that you're going to have to stay here in this cell until Monday morning when we will appear before the Court of Common Pleas at the Ansonia Courthouse. I expect you'll be charged with Misconduct with a Motor Vehicle because of the beer cans and your alleged drunkenness. It's considered a second-degree felony by law. Tony, bail will be set Monday morning, probably at about a thousand dollars."

"Are you tellin' me, Bob, that you're going to let my kid sit in jail for two fuckin' nights? Can't you fix this thing?"

"There are laws we have no control over, Tony."

"Jesus Christ," Tony blurts out in irritation. "Okay...but let's get to the fuckin' point — what are we looking at here, Bob?"

"Worst case scenario — loss of license, a year in prison, and a ten thousand dollar fine." Bob purses his lips, inhaling and then exhaling slowly.

Hearing this information, Frankie feels disoriented. His head is spinning.

"You said 'worst case scenario,' " Tony says. "What's the best case scenario?"

"Best case? We get the charge reduced by proving that there isn't enough evidence to show that Frankie was drunk. Of course, we will also argue that the victim crossed the street in an irresponsible fashion. Then there's the third case scenario — you plead guilty, we go for a suspended sentence, you pay a smaller fine, and maybe Frankie is assigned community service for six months to a year."

A glum Frankie stares at the floor, shaking his head.

"What about school and everything? College?" Tony asks.

"Well, that's an important point, and it's one we will build our case upon," Bob says. "Frankie is a first time offender, a star high school athlete with an important college future on the horizon, a responsible student — reasons that a jail sentence isn't an appropriate consequence."

Tony sighs. "I see. When will the trial happen?"

"Not for at least six months...maybe a year, to give us time to build our case," Bob replies. "In the meantime, Frankie goes to school, studies hard, continues to succeed in sports, and applies to colleges. Oh, I think it's best that Frankie only drives if absolutely necessary. We don't need any other issues. And most important, Frankie stays sober going forward, starting immediately."

"Did ya hear what Attorney Goldman said, Frankie? We don't need no more issues. And we didn't fuckin' need this one either, you stupid shit!"

"Hey Tony, easy. You need to ease up on the kid," Bob says, as Frankie covers his ears with his palms, tears streaming down his cheeks.

"Don't tell me to ease up, Bob...the only thing I need you to do is make this whole thing go the fuck away, capice?"

6

The phone rings in the Novak hallway on Sunday morning. Hearing it ring and ring and ring, Daryl stirs in bed and moans. He wishes it would stop. *Mom,* he thinks in his somnolent state, *answer the phone, please.* The incessant ringing continues. Daryl rolls over in bed and sees 8:07 on his alarm clock. He realizes that he is still in his street clothes, except for his black Chuck Taylor sneakers. He must have collapsed on the bed last night. *Mom, please,* he again thinks to himself, and then, after what seems an interminable number of rings, it stops. Daryl, relieved, exhales deeply. He stretches his arms and his legs and tries to sleep for a while more. A moment after he closes his eyes, the ringing begins again. "Fuck," Daryl mutters, dragging his gangly body up from the bed and stumbling into the hallway. He sees his mother lying asleep on the couch, also fully clothed. The Valium has done its work, and she remains oblivious to the noise of the ringing.

With trembling hands, Daryl picks up the nagging phone receiver. "Hullo," he mumbles in an exhausted baritone.

"Daryl? You sound tired. Did I wake you up?" he hears his father's voice say.

"Uhm...no...I mean, I dunno. Maybe. I think I was just resting my eyes...but maybe I dozed off."

"Daryl, I was driving all day and all night. How did yesterday's game go? Did we win?" Walter Novak asks hopefully.

The phone table in the hallway is right across from Susie's bedroom. Daryl's eyes suddenly become transfixed on the big teddy bear sitting on Susie's bed surrounded by layers of Susie's clothes, strips of refracted light from the partially open blinds shining on its fur and the nearby fashions.

"Daryl? Are you listening? I asked how the game went."

"Oh, yeah. Sorry Dad. It...uhm...it didn't go too good, Dad. They beat us by a touchdown."

"Aww, damn," Walter responds. "Well, I hope you're not too upset, son. It's been a great season, and remember, while it might feel important today, it's still only a game. Where's your mother?"

"She's...uhm...she's still sleeping."

"Sleeping? Why is that? She's never asleep past 7:00. Is she sick?"

"Not exactly sick, Dad."

"Well what then? Wake her up."

"I don't think that's a good...uh...listen, Dad, I don't think I should wake her up right now."

Daryl feels as if he's drowning in an ocean of anxiety. He realizes he's going to have to break the news to his father, something he hadn't counted on.

"Uhm, Dad, listen…" He realizes he can't find the words.

"Daryl? Daryl? Are you there? What the hell is going on?"

"Yeah...sorry. Yeah...yeah, I'm here. So, yeah Dad. Uhm...like, we got some real rough news last night. Ya see, Susie...Susie...she was in an accident...and…"

"An accident? What kind of accident? Was she injured? Is she in the hospital? What happened?"

Feeling pummeled by the barrage of questions, Daryl can barely think.

"Dad...Dad...listen...slow down. Please slow down!" Daryl hears his own voice rising in panic.

"Well either tell me what happened, Daryl, or put your mother on the phone *right now*!"

Daryl knows his mother will be too distraught to deal with delivering the news to his father.

"Okay, Dad. I don't really know how to say this, Dad...but Susie, ya see...Susie was hit by a car last night after the dance in Derby...and she was...she was..."

"She was *what*?" Walter asks with blaring impatience.

Daryl hears himself choke out in barely a whisper, "She was...she was killed, Dad."

Daryl hears heavy breathing on the other end of the phone. Hyperventilating, Walter finally says, "Put your mother on the phone, Daryl!"

"Dad...she's really...uhm...I don't know exactly how to explain how she is. She's...she's...real upset. And she took some kind of medicine they gave her. I don't...what I mean is, I don't think she'll be able to talk without completely unraveling. You better come home right away, though."

Walter immediately calls his dispatcher. "Oh Jesus, Walter, I don't even know what to say. I'm so sorry," the dispatcher offers. "Let me get right to work on this. One way or another, I'll figure out a plan to get you there as soon as humanly possible."

On Sunday morning just after 10:00, I sat on the metal guard rail at the entrance to Route 8, reading *On the Road*. Well, actually, I was hitchhiking to work, but at the moment no cars seemed to be getting on the highway. It's good to have a book in your pocket at moments like these so you have something to do when there's nothing else to do except vegetate. At least that's how I feel. One of the reasons I was reading *On the Road* for, like, the third time, is because just like the author, Jack Kerouac, I am a hitchhiker. In the novel, the main character, Sal Paradise, is supposed to more or less be Jack Kerouac. At least, I think that's the deal. What a cool name Sal Paradise is. Anyway, Sal Paradise travels back and forth across the vast United States of America several times, from New York — mainly to Denver,

San Francisco, Los Angeles and eventually even to Mexico. He goes in various ways, hitchhiking being one. Sal also takes buses and a 1949 Hudson (what a sharp car) as well, but early on in his journey he does a lot of hitchhiking. Like Sal and his best pal Dean, I dream of one day taking off with my best buddy Jeff and meeting up with lots of wild and unusual people, not to mention all kinds of pretty girls. Just, basically, having a blast.

I can't take full credit for my hitchhiking or give Jack Kerouac too much credit either. I have to give Michael most of the credit. Because I was just copying him like always. Look at it this way: Michael played Little League and then so did I. Michael went into Scouting and I followed suit. Michael took clarinet and saxophone lessons and, before I knew it, so did I. Michael's favorite pro sports teams and his favorite athletes became my favorites. Older kids would address me as "Little DeMarco," kind of meaning "Little Michael," and sometimes adults would accidentally address me as "Michael." Obviously, I would correct them: "It's Gabriel," I'd say politely. Eventually it was just easier to let them get my name wrong. Sometimes you feel like you're nothing but a little copycat. But getting back to my main point — I started hitchhiking because Michael hitchhiked before me.

Just to change the subject from hitchhiking for one second, though, I will never forget that last February on my fifteenth birthday the first thing my father said to me was that I needed to get a job by the time I was sixteen. I kind of grinned at him — you know, that grin that says, *You're kidding, right?* — but when Dad asked out loud, "What the hell are you grinning at?" I realized it wasn't a joke. Of course, I had had a paper route for three years. That was a job. It was a snap, though. With only twenty-four papers, I could run downtown at 3:00 to get my papers by the pharmacy, flirt with Jody Riordan for an hour and a half, then run the mile or so that covered my route, and still be on time for dinner at 5:00. Being late for dinner at our house was a bad idea.

I wasn't too worried because I figured I had a year, but I didn't even end up making it to sixteen. Five months before my birthday, Michael told Dad, Mom, and me at dinner that Howie Millea, the manager of Duchess, had asked him what he thought about me beginning working a couple of shifts per week and being paid "under the table" even though I was underage. After Michael explained, I felt myself under the scrutiny of three pairs of eyes. It's not like I hadn't wanted to work at Duchess practically since Michael had started working there when the joint opened. So I popped a morsel of medium rare steak in my mouth, said "okay" and that was that. It was time to get rid of the paper route and be more grown up.

But how was I going to get to Duchess? That's my real point. I guess that one of the oddest things about our family is that before Michael and I got our licenses, getting to and from our destinations was his and my problem to figure out. At fifteen, I was already a pretty experienced hitchhiker. And while it was clearly an explicit rule that we had to have jobs by the time we were sixteen, another family rule, unwritten and unspoken, goes something like this — get a job but do *not* ask your parents for a ride to work. My mother is a very nervous and unsteady driver, plus she doesn't like driving on the highway. And Dad, well, that's where the unwritten rule comes in. You just know he is not to be asked to drive you anywhere after a long day of work as a plumbing contractor. Some things I guess are just understood. That doesn't mean I never asked Michael for a ride to work. He and I often worked the same shift, and when we didn't, he would take me to Duchess or bring me home at the end of the night if he didn't have anything better to do. Essentially, Michael learned early on and I had learned from him that if we wanted to get to an out-of-town game, to a dance, to Duchess, or to just about anywhere at all, it was probably going to mean the power of the thumb.

That morning, I had been alternating between reading and thumbing a ride every time a car drove by, which wasn't often. I was doing more reading than hitchhiking. I closed my copy of *On the Road* and looked at my watch. It was 10:20, and it looked like I was going to be late for work. But just in the nick of time, a neighborhood lady, Mrs. Erwin, drove by.

When she pulled over, I jumped in her car, and said, "Hi, Mrs. Erwin. Thanks for stopping for me."

She was just a little lady with glasses and white hair. She was probably about a hundred and ten years old, and she was wearing a navy blue Sunday dress, but not because it was Sunday. She dressed like that every day because when her husband, old Mr. Erwin, used to throw us kids off their lawn where we liked to play touch football, I'd see her hovering near the screen door in similar dresses. She probably went to bed in one of those dresses.

"Do your parents know you're hitchhiking, Gabriel?" she asked.

"I'm not sure," I replied. "My mother is at church and my father's sleeping. I didn't want to bother him after he worked so hard all week." Both were lies, but I didn't want her to think Mom and Dad were lousy parents. Sometimes the most sensible thing to do is to lie, even though it means breaking a commandment.

"You won't tell them, will you?" I asked. Of course, both of my parents knew I hitchhiked, but it was easier to just play along with old Mrs. Erwin.

"Well...alright...but hitchhiking doesn't seem like a very good idea to me, Gabriel. You just be careful who you take a ride from. Some people are reckless drivers, especially some of these teenagers with their hotrods. Heavens, these days you have to be really careful."

She pulled into the Duchess parking lot, and I got out of her sedan. "That's so true, Mrs. Erwin. A lot of kids are crazy drivers, if you know what I mean. Well, thanks a million for the ride. I really appreciate it."

At 10:25, Walter pulls into a rest stop and calls home again. Helen is now awake and has been informed that Walter knows about the accident.

When she lifts the receiver and hears Walter's voice, Helen feels a temporary sense of relief.

"Helen, Daryl told me about..."

Interrupting, Helen relapses into heaving sobs. "Oh, Walter, what are we going to do? I can't do this. I need you to...to...I need you to help me!"

A helpless Daryl listens from his room. He and his mother haven't exchanged a word all morning.

"I know, Helen. I understand," says Walter, his voice also breaking as he tries to console her. "I called the dispatcher after talking to Daryl, and I am already on my way home. I figure that I can be back in Seymour by maybe 2:30 or 3:00, depending on traffic."

"Oh thank God, Walter. I don't know what I'm going to do. Please try to get here as soon as possible!"

"I will," Walter chokes out. "I will."

Old Mrs. Erwin had dropped me off at the store a half hour before the 11:00 lunch hour. Just in time. All the guys on the crew call Duchess a store because it isn't exactly a restaurant since there is no inside dining. Luckily, as only a drink man, I didn't have a lot of preparation like the other guys. I just had to make sure the shake machine was filled, the gas tanks for the soda machines weren't low, and plenty of crushed ice was in the bin below the soda spigots.

I wasn't surprised to see that Karl Fischer, who was always stirring up some kind of trouble, was in something of a debate with Lenny Singleton. Both were working the grill that day. In this case, the two adult men were arguing whether the newly appointed Heavyweight Boxing Champion, Joe Frazier, could beat the great Muhammad Ali, who had, months before, been stripped of his boxing title because he had refused to submit to the military draft.

Muhammad Ali had said: "Why should they ask me to put on a uniform and go 10,000 miles from home and drop bombs and bullets on brown people in Vietnam while so-called Negro people in Louisville are treated like dogs and denied simple human rights? No I'm not going 10,000 miles from home to help murder and burn another poor nation simply to continue the domination of white slave masters of the darker people the world over."

That kind of talk made him a hero to lots of black people, like Lenny Singleton, and even to plenty of white kids like me. We didn't completely understand what he was talking about, but we liked the way he said it if that makes any sense, which it probably doesn't. Such outspokenness also made Muhammad Ali wildly unpopular with a lot of adult men who apparently didn't like the way he said it, like Karl Fischer — and like my father, for that matter. Ali had already rendered himself unpopular with adult men when, in February of 1964, the young, brash, twenty-two year old gold medalist, after winning the Heavyweight title from the seemingly invincible Sonny Liston, announced that he was declaring himself a member of the Nation of Islam and changing his name from Cassius Clay to Muhammad Ali.

"Cassius Clay is a slave name. I didn't choose it and I don't want it. I am Muhammad Ali, a free name – it means 'beloved of God,' and I insist people use it when people speak to me," he had said, and with that statement, he shocked the world even more than with his unexpected victory over Liston.

The big deal was that hardly any American knew what the Nation of Islam was, and I personally hadn't ever heard of a name quite like Muhammad Ali except maybe in story books. Personally, at the time, I was only 12 years old, so all of the hoopla was way over my head. I didn't know what to think of it because people don't go changing their name every day, even now. Mainly, I listened to my father lash out at

Muhammad Ali, and I assumed, at the time, that Dad knew what the real score was. When you're a little kid, you trust your dad to know what's what.

Since the day he won the championship, Ali had also referred to himself as "the Greatest," which also didn't go over tremendously well with guys like my dad. Previous sports greats who were negroes, guys like Joe Louis and Willie Mays, had been quiet, humble men. The truth is, white athletes were the same way. Guys like Mickey Mantle and Johnny Unites. They don't run around telling everyone they're the greatest, even though they are. Muhammad Ali was a different story when he came onto the scene. He was a new kind of pro athlete. He wasn't afraid to say how good he was, he had the skills to back it up, and he was entertaining in the process. It kind of made me ask myself if a white athlete bragged about himself in the same way, if guys like my dad would have the same negative reaction.

By the time I entered high school, though, Ali had become hands down my favorite professional athlete, and he was super popular with most every sports fan my age, including and especially my brother Michael and my pal Jeff. I guess there's something about being a boy that makes you like to watch two guys beat each other up. We were just sorry Ali wasn't going to be allowed to box at a time when he was entering his prime, and maybe never again.

Like I said, just about every white adult man I knew thought Ali had a big mouth, which he kind of did, but kids like us admired him for refusing to participate in the military draft, even though we never said so to our parents. While we might not have known about the ins and outs of the Vietnam War, we watched the long-haired, freaky protesters on the nightly news, and in our guts, we knew the protesters were right. For Muhammad Ali to sacrifice his boxing title, millions of dollars, and perhaps his entire boxing career for a cause really spoke to us. Ali's dazzling athletic skills, his electric charisma, and his pre-fight theatrics certainly hadn't hurt his popularity with us either. We only hoped he'd get an opportunity to show them off again.

Karl Fischer and Lenny Singleton were unpacking the hamburger meat and organizing the patties in stacks of twenty-four — because that's how many burgers are usually cooked at one time — on the shelves of the walk-in refrigerator doors.

"I tell ya, Lenny," Karl was saying as I was filling up the shake machine, "Clay wouldn't be any match for Joe Frazier. Frazier would murder him."

Karl has a pot belly and not only are his eyes usually bloodshot but so are his cheeks. He speaks with a noticeable lisp, and if you get too close to him, you're liable to be spat upon, something I personally try to avoid at all costs, so I always keep my distance from him.

"Bullshit, Fischer," Lenny replied, never making eye contact with Karl. "And his name ain't Clay no more. It's Muhammad Ali. Get with the times."

"Okay, Lenny, his name is Muhammad Ali, whatever kind of name that is...and whatever you want me to call him is fine with me. But think of Frazier. He's a slugger." As I listened to Karl's severe lisp, I figured that he had been lisping since he was a small child...that lispers developed the speech impediment when they first began speaking and never broke out of it. Karl continued, "More like a Joe Louis, and you know, Lenny, that there's no way Clay...I mean no way...Ali...could have beaten the great Joe Louis. You must know that, right?"

"I don't know shit, man." Lenny was obviously irritated. About ten years Karl's junior, Lenny was not of the generation that idolized the great Joe Louis. Lenny was hip, Lenny was "now," and Muhammad Ali was his champion and his people's champion. Shaking his head, Lenny punctuated his comment with, "Ain't no man alive can touch Ali, Fischer. Not then and not now. He is too fast...too agile. He knows how to dance away from fighters like Frazier and Louis, and they ain't never able to lay a glove on him. Ain't you never seen the man fight?"

"Yeah, that's what I mean," Karl responded, as he wiped the bloody residue from the raw meat off of his hands with a towel, "always dancing like a girl. Why doesn't he plant his feet and fight like a man? Anyways, that fuckin' draft dodger is never even gonna get a chance to step into the ring with anyone again, never mind Frazier."

"I hope you ain't callin' my champion no draft dodger, my man, and you best not be calling him a girl," Lenny fired back, his eyes now wide and menacing.

"I'm just kidding about that, Lenny. You know I'm kidding. You can take a joke, right, Lenny, because..."

Lenny just talked right over him. "Cuz, my man, Muhammad Ali way too smart to let himself be a punching bag for some kinda Joe Frazier or, for that matter, for some Joe Louis. And he ain't no draft dodger neither. So just get that straight in your fat head." Lenny turned away and started adeptly throwing burger patties on the grill in vertical lines, strongly indicating that the conversation was over.

Karl didn't want to ruffle Lenny's feathers. He certainly showed Lenny more respect and deference than he would have shown any of us younger guys, so he followed Lenny's lead and started toasting buns without another word. Karl kept glancing at Lenny as they worked, but Lenny didn't look back at him. Lenny just shut him out, ignoring him like he was vapor. The contrast between the two men was stark. While Karl was about 5'6" and shaped like a dumpy, worn out egg, at 6'2", Lenny had a powerful presence and resembled a professional athlete in stature and physique.

Howie came out of his office with a newspaper and said to no one in particular, "What a shame about that little girl getting killed last night, huh?"

"Whataya talkin' about, Howie? What little girl?" Lenny asked.

"That Seymour football player — what's his name — his sister got hit by a car on Division Street, right around the corner above the gas station. Traumatic brain injury. Ironically, the driver was that Derby kid, Frankie Adamo. I guess he was drunk. What a shame. She had her whole life in front of her."

Lenny asked, "Who told you this, Howie?"

"It's on the front page of the *New Haven Register*," said Howie. "Feel free to take a look."

Howie laid the register out on the tray where the grill men dressed the hamburgers, and all five guys on the crew gathered around in a circle. The headline read, "Seymour Freshman Killed in Accident." As Lenny slowly began to read the article, my eyes scanned the two accompanying photos. One was of Frankie Adamo's Lemans with two police cars and an ambulance next to it. The other was a school picture of a young girl with the caption: Susanna Marie Novak. I couldn't believe what I was seeing. *Miss Polka Dots*, I said to myself in disbelief. I suddenly felt dizzy and unsteady on my feet, like after a crazy carnival ride. Afraid I was going to cry, I escaped from the group and headed toward the back sink. I needed to just breathe for a minute or two.

One of the guys, Kevin Binkowski, must have noticed me slip away because he followed me to the back sink.

"You okay, Gabriel?" he asked with concern. Kevin had only been working at Duchess a month longer than me, so we were both the new kids at work. He's kind of a dorky Derby kid who we call "Bink." Well, Michael started that. Anyway, I wished Bink hadn't noticed I was upset, but, still, it was nice of him to check on me.

"Yeah, sure," I said. "I'm okay. It's just seeing someone so young being killed just kind of got to me...that's all."

Howie yelled, "Okay, fellas, that's sad news, I know, but let's get to work. It's 11:00 so we're going to unlock the doors. Man your stations."

"Oh, okay, Gabe," Bink said. "Well, if you need anything, let me know."

Driving on I-95, Walter is struggling to hold himself together.

Crossing from Delaware into New Jersey, he has the radio on in a futile attempt to silence the emotional noise in his head. Unable to get reception on a station that plays music of his liking, Walter endures the popular music of a Top 40 rock station even though it's not helping accomplish his purpose. It reminds him of hearing Susanna spin records in her room. He feels sorry, in his present state of mind, for having ordered her to turn down the volume on so many occasions.

The 11:30 news comes on, and Walter mindlessly listens to the same stories that play on the news every day in what feels like an endless loop — reports about civil rights and war protests across the nation. His thoughts are elsewhere. Fretting about how the scene will play out when he arrives home, he knows he has to be the strong one...the rock...for Helen. He contemplates the challenges of being a husband and father. He feels like one day he was a young carefree guy, marrying his high school sweetheart, and the next day he was a homeowner, a breadwinner, and the parent of two teenagers. And now this.

The radio news report seems to reel him in from the treadmill of discursive thought he is on when he hears, "This week in Vietnam — 227 American soldiers were killed in action, 1320 were wounded, 12 are missing."

Following the news report, a fast talking DJ seizes the air waves. "Hi everybody, all over America, this is your Cousin Brucie, and it's the WABC Party Go-Go from New York! Hey, look at this one. This was a Pick Hit not too long ago. Last week number fourteen, it jumps to number two on the Billboard charts. Number two! The Mamas and the Papas hit, 'Dedicated to the One I Love.' You're gonna like this one, my dear cousins!"

Unlike most of the latest songs Walter has heard on the radio, this one is familiar. While he feels, somehow, that he's heard it before, he realizes it wasn't this rendition. *Was it a black girls' group,* he wonders, *or was it a men's group?* He likes this newer version, finding the singer's rich alto voice along with the background harmonies pleasing.

At the same time, listening to the pop song following the Vietnam casualty report makes Walter feel even more emotional. Despite having served his country in the Navy during World War II as well as trying to support the current war effort in Vietnam, Walter knows he has, in recent months, found it harder and harder to stomach the reports about casualties. He feels deeply within that, unlike World War II, he doesn't understand the true reason for this war and what week by week seems like a senseless loss of young lives.

Droplets of tears spill, involuntarily, from the corners of his eyes and onto his work pants. Walter thinks to himself, *The casualties of war I can understand, whether I like it or not. I've lived through it. But, Dear God, how am I supposed to understand the loss of our innocent baby? Please tell me, God, how can this be?*

The late morning started out slowly. My job was to wrap trays of hamburgers and cheeseburgers as Lenny and Karl sent them up and to get any drinks that Howie or Craig Betts called out.

As I began wrapping a tray of twenty-four hamburgers and placing them in the warm bin, I was trying to comprehend the shocking news. I had just seen her last night. I had danced with her — twice. It wasn't even twenty-four hours since I felt her head on my shoulder and her arms around my neck. I could almost still smell her perfume. How could I ever forget that moment or the beautiful, delicate girl?

I'm not going to lie. It wasn't my best lunch hour ever. Not being able to concentrate, I made several mistakes on drink orders. Rush hour at Duchess can get really hectic, and sometimes people's patience grows thin, especially people like Howie and Craig Betts.

"C'mon, man, I need you to wrap these hamburgers faster," Betts said, as he stopped taking orders to wrap a dozen burgers. He wrapped twice as fast as I did even when my head was clear.

When a second customer complained to Howie that his drink

order was wrong — in this case, that he had gotten a Coke when he had ordered a root beer — Howie turned to me and gave me a dirty look while abruptly pouring the Coke down the drain and slamming the empty cup down on the counter next to the soda machine. Scowling at me he said, softly but sternly, "You need to get your act together, Gabriel. That's the second screw up of the afternoon."

"Yeah, I know. Sorry, Howie," I whispered apologetically.

The window men hated it when they had to stop the process of filling an order to correct someone else's mistake.

At 1:00 p.m. things started to slow down, and Howie said, "Gabriel, you're not yourself today. What's wrong?"

"Nothing, Howie. I'm fine," I responded.

I wasn't going to tell him that I knew who Susanna Novak was... that I had danced with her the night before...that I had hardly slept the previous night because "You Really Got a Hold on Me" played over and over again in my mind...that I imagined her in my arms all night.

"Yeah? Well, you don't seem fine to me. Why don't you go out and give the parking lot a sweep?"

Usually I didn't look forward to sweeping the lot, but today it was a chance to breathe and clear my head a little. The lot was a hot mess. As I began sweeping the litter, I tried to wrap my brain around the idea that the girl I had danced with was dead. I hadn't had much experience with death. There was a guy, Robbie Lobdell, that hung out with Michael for a while a few years ago who was recently killed in Vietnam, but I never really had any contact with Robbie. After Robbie got arrested for stealing a car, my father forbade Michael to hang out with him anymore. There was also Michael's best friend Paulie's father, Gino. He had had a heart attack when I was in ninth grade, but I didn't feel like I actually knew Gino that well because he hardly ever said anything to me. The hardest one was a neighborhood kid, Arty Miklos, who was killed a year ago in a car crash. Like Susanna, it was hard to believe that a kid was dead. But Susanna's death was hitting me a lot harder than Arty, who was a few years older than me. As I weaved my way between cars, sweeping the debris into the middle of the lot where I could pick it up, I felt dizzy. I just kept playing the name in my mind over and over again: Susanna Novak...Susanna Novak... Susanna Novak. Grabbing handfuls of trash and depositing them in the large, grey garbage can, I pictured her in my mind, with her bright tights and her polka dot mini-dress and her far out, mod look — not quite like anyone I knew. More like a TV star than some local girl. It was super hard to think that I was never again going to see someone who I had hoped to get to know, that I hoped maybe even to have as a girlfriend. *What will happen to Frankie Adamo?* I wondered. *How must Daryl Novak be feeling?*

When I came back into the store from outside, Howie asked me what time I was scheduled for. He had to know it was 6:30 since he composed the schedule himself each week, but I politely replied, "6:30."

"You know what?" he said, his lips pursed, analyzing me with troubled eyes, like I was a pathetic loser or something. "I think we'll let you go early. It's slow now, and when things get busy, you're not going to be much help to us anyway. You're out of it for some reason. Call your brother or someone and see if you can get a ride home."

"Yeah, sure...okay, Howie. Sure. Okay, I'll do that."

When Walter arrives home at 2:47, Helen falls into his arms at the door. He guides her to the couch, where together they sit. Helen's parents, who have come to comfort her, are nearby. Walter holds Helen in his strong arms for a long time as she sobs. Grandma and Grandpa Comcowicz feel helpless, and Walter himself, though trying to be strong, can't hold back his own tears, which stream over his unshaven face. Helen and Walter are united in the rawest form of grief they have ever known. They don't speak because words will not help.

Grandpa Comcowicz whispers to Walter, "We'll give the two of you a little privacy now. This has been hard on Helen's mother...and on me too. We all lost our precious, baby girl."

Daryl watches this display of family support from his bedroom doorway and then withdraws and falls onto his bed, alone with his own grief. He grabs his pillow and wraps it tightly around his head in a futile attempt to escape his parents' sobbing.

Although Howie had hurt my feelings a little, I was happy to be sprung, but I didn't call anyone for a ride because normally in daylight I would hitchhike like usual. Today, though, I decided to walk. It would only take me about a half hour to forty-five minutes. Rather than walking on the shoulder of Route 8, though, I made my way to the corner of Pershing Drive and Division Street and took a right by the Texaco station, climbing the Division Street hill to see if I could determine the location where Adamo had hit Susanna Novak. When I got to mid-way up the hill, I saw one possible link to the accident. Right at the curve, there were skid marks from car tires, like the ones my cousin Tomaso had often made with his Chevelle just to show off. I stopped and shook my head as I contemplated Frankie Adamo trying to skid to a stop in an effort to avoid hitting Susanna Novak.

I also found what I thought was another clue. On the side of road, I spotted what looked like a piece of glass. I picked it up and saw that it was a partially rounded fragment of rose colored glass. *This must be a broken lens from the glasses she was wearing at the dance,* I thought. I looked around, like somebody might be watching me...like I was a thief or something, and then stuffed it into the pocket of my jeans.

After five or ten minutes, I continued on because you can only stare at skid marks for so long no matter how upset you are. As I took a left on Atwater Avenue and headed for downtown Derby, I wondered why Susanna Novak would have been walking down Division Street so late at night. There wasn't even a sidewalk. The accident probably took place around the time Jeff and I had finished our food at Derby Pizza.

I felt I needed to talk to someone, and the only person I could think of to discuss the matter with was Jeff since he was the only other person in my world who even knew who Susanna Novak was.

Eventually, after their tears are spent, Walter takes Helen into the kitchen and helps her try to eat something. Relatives and friends, having read about the accident in the newspaper, have stopped by with more food than the Novaks can eat in a week. As they have called and visited, Helen has been unable to talk about Susie or the accident. They assure her that they are here for her when she is ready to talk. Helen tells Walter how wonderful people have been, and then she explains what she knows about the accident, including the call from the police station, and the awful experience of having to go to Griffin and identify Susie's lifeless body, something, Helen says, she doesn't think she will ever recover from. She shares with Walter, in fact, that she can't imagine herself ever feeling any happiness again. After hearing what Helen knows of the accident, Walter calls Daryl into the kitchen.

"Sit down," Walter says to Daryl.

Daryl sits at the round kitchen table where the family of four had shared so many nightly meals, where Walter had helped Daryl make his Pinewood Derby cars for Cub Scouts, where Helen had read stories and recited poems to his sister and him, where the four of them had enjoyed informal talks with each other in twos and threes and fours.

They each have their own chair. Walter and Helen are across from each other, and Daryl gingerly sits in his chair across from the vacant chair that had been Susie's.

"Daryl," Walter begins tentatively. "Your mother told me you were supposed to pick up Susie after the dance. Why was she walking?"

Daryl recounts the events of the night, truthfully, even the fact that he and his teammates were drinking and intoxicated.

"I just...I was late because I...I lost track of time. And I didn't want to leave her standing alone in downtown Derby...because...because she...well, she's too young to be at those dances anyway."

Helen's eyes widen at the judgmental implications of Daryl's remark.

"And then what?" Walter asks in as controlled a manner as he is able to muster.

"And then...and then...like I said...I had Ben and a couple guys, you know...in the...the car still because they wanted food, but like I also said I was late, so I told Susie to walk to Duchess where I'd meet her because there wasn't room for seven of us in the Bug. It's just a short walk...maybe, you know, like, twenty minutes. I figured, with the other girls there, she'd be fine...but I didn't think about there being no sidewalk on Division Street...and I...and...I don't know...I..."

Helen's eyes suddenly grow wide and wild. Horrified by Daryl's explanation, she presses her flat palms onto the surface of the table hard, her white knuckles pressing against her taught skin, and pushes herself into a standing position while almost tripping over her chair in the process.

"So, if it wasn't for your drunken behavior," she begins, tears again streaming down her cheeks, "if it wasn't...if it wasn't for your self-absorbed, childish, drunken behavior...over...over losing a *ridiculous* football game...if it wasn't for that...if it wasn't for...for *you*...your sister would still be...our Susie would still be alive! Oh Daryl...Daryl!" And Helen unsteadily races out of the kitchen.

Walter pursues Helen but not before pausing to give Daryl a look aflame with contempt and disappointment. Deep in thought, Daryl sits at the table in solitude for a few minutes, and then he angrily grabs onto the bottom of the table surface and purposely upends it, sending the bowls of soup, silverware, and drinking glasses crashing to the floor. Grabbing his hat, coat, and shoes, Daryl sprints out to the

VW where he flees the nightmare that is currently the Novak family's reality.

As he turns the key in the ignition, Daryl sees his father at the storm door shouting, "Daryl! Daryl! Get back here now! Daryl!"

7

As I crossed over the Shelton-Derby Bridge at around 2:15, I wondered if Jeff was home. For Jeff, though, home could mean 52 Kneen Street in Shelton or 18 Mclaughlin Terrace in Derby. Jeff was the only kid I knew whose parents were divorced. It happened when he was only a year old. His father lives in another state now, and Jeff barely knows the guy. It's actually a subject he doesn't talk about much because dwelling on the negatives isn't Jeff's thing. Anyway, growing up, Jeff and his mother sometimes lived with Jeff's grandmother and grandfather, Mr. and Mrs. Bailey, who live five minutes from my house, and sometimes they didn't. Jeff and I have been friends since we were about five or six. When he was in fifth grade, Jeff's mom purchased a house on the hill in East Derby. It's strange to divide Derby into geographic regions because it's one of the smallest towns in Connecticut, but everyone who lives in the Valley calls the area where Mclaughlin Terrace is East Derby.

I never knew from one year to the next whether Jeff would be living with his mother on the hill in East Derby or with Gramma and Grampa Bailey here in Shelton, or even why. As a freshman, he had attended Derby High School, and this year, beginning in September, he was at Shelton High with me because he was back living with his grandparents.

I really needed to talk this out with someone, and I figured he was my best option because if he hadn't literally pushed me, I might never have asked Susanna to dance. When I got to the Kneen Street homestead, I circled to the back door where the kitchen was and rapped my closed knuckles gently on one of the windowpanes. You want to knock politely at the homes of old people.

Mrs. Bailey pushed the lacy curtains aside to see who it was, and then opened the door. I could smell something delicious through the open door. Her kitchen always smelled like she had just finished baking cookies.

"Hi ya, Gabriel," she said warmly. Mrs. Bailey is a real nice lady.

"Hi, Mrs. Bailey...Jeff home?" I asked.

"No, he said he was going to visit a girl. Now let me see...what did he say her name was? Julie something," she said, trying to remember.

"Oh, it must be Julie Carter."

"Exactly! That's it, Julie Carter." She smiled as if she was amused.

"Yeah, I guess he likes her."

"Oh, you boys and your girls," she teased, giggling. I laughed with her — not just to be polite but because her laugh cracked me up.

"Okay," I sighed, "well, if he gets home before dinner, would you please ask him to give me a call?"

"Sure, Gabriel, happy to do that."

Now what was I going to do? There wasn't anyone at home I felt comfortable discussing this with. I wasn't going to talk to my father about it. It wasn't that he and I didn't talk, but after observing a great many arguments between Dad and Michael, I had learned to only discuss what I would call "safe subjects" with my dad. Talking to Michael was kind of out. He was a good brother when it came to helping me to get places and building my confidence about things like sports and girls and making sure I was going to the right high school, but he wasn't big on serious discussions unless maybe they were about sports. I guess my mother would understand, but it was super complicated to explain. I mean, let's face it. I didn't even know Susanna Novak.

When I got home, Michael wasn't there nor was my dad.

"Aren't you home early?" my mother asked as she went about putting spices on a small pork roast.

"Yeah, it was slow, so Howie let me go. That's how it is sometimes."

"How did you get home?" she asked.

"Oh, I just walked."

"Wasn't there anyone who could take you home?"

"It was a nice day, so I felt like walking."

"What are you going to do now?"

"I don't know. I'm not in the mood to do anything. I think I'll just lay down and read for a while."

"You don't look right. Are you sure you're not sick?" she asked, putting her hand on my forehead.

She has this magic way of knowing if you have a fever just by feeling your head. No thermometer is needed. A special mom power, apparently.

I just looked at her for the verdict, and, after holding her hand there for about fifteen seconds, she finally said, "No fever."

"See, I told you, Mom, I'm fine." I sounded a little too whiny.

"Are you sure you're telling me the truth?" she asked.

"Of course," I replied.

"Let me see," she said. Then she put her two hands on my face and squeezed the bridge of my nose with her thumbs.

It's another one of her magic powers. Since I was a little kid, she always told me that if the skin on my nose turned white when she squeezed, it meant I was lying. It's kind of a joke between us, I guess. She was even smiling in her unique, playful way as she squeezed, but I still wondered if, like feeling a fever, her hands were a human lie detector device too.

"Is it white?" I asked, a little worried. My nose was starting to hurt from being squeezed too hard.

"Hmmm," she said with a loving smile. "Just a little. I think you might be telling me a little white lie."

"Can I go lie down now?"

"Yes, you *may* go lie down. But you know you can talk to me about anything, right?"

"I know, Mom."

"What do I always tell you? You know you'll always be my...what?"

"Mom, please don't."

"Let me hear it...my what?"

"Your...baby." I felt a little dumb, but I had to say it or she would have been real disappointed. And then she pointed to her cheek, which was her signal for me to give her a kiss, which, of course, I did, because what else was I supposed to do? Even though I couldn't bring myself to tell her about Susanna, it was nice knowing I had a mom who I could talk to if I wanted to. It's just there's some stuff that's hard to talk to your mom about.

Flopping on my twin bed, I cracked open *On the Road*, but I couldn't concentrate. After laying there like a vegetable for about a half hour, I dozed off. The phone abruptly roused me from my sleep.

"Yes, Jeff, he's here. I'll get him," I heard my mother say.

When I picked up the phone, I said, "Hey, man, can you meet me at the playground in a few minutes?"

"Yeah, sure. Is anything up?" he asked.

"Yeah, kind of."

"Okay, I'll be right down there. I'll bring my basketball."

"Yeah, good. See you in a few."

Sitting on a picnic bench next to what was a poor excuse for a basketball court — it was only a paved area with one hoop — I saw Jeff approaching, dribbling the ball as he walked. When he was about fifteen feet from me, he brought the orange ball to his chest and threw me a pass.

"What's going on, brother? Anything interesting? My day was interesting, that's for sure. I spent the afternoon with Julie in her basement. Her parents were home, so we had to be careful...catch my drift? But we made out a lot, and she let me pull her blouse out of her jeans and feel her tits. It was nice, man."

"Yeah...yeah...it sounds nice," I responded. "Listen, I have to tell you..."

"I don't know if you ever noticed," he interrupted, "but Julie has quite a set. Real nice."

"Yeah...yeah, I noticed. Listen, I *really* need to tell you something important."

"Okay, easy does it, pal. What's the deal?"

"Did you hear about the accident?" I asked.

"What're you talking about? What accident?"

"Last night...after the dance...Daryl Novak's sister got killed. Frankie Adamo hit her with his car. She's dead!"

"Wow! That's too bad," Jeff said. "You look pretty upset. I mean, it's not like we know Daryl Novak or anything. Is his sister someone we're supposed to know?"

I just shrugged. "Daryl Novak's sister is...is Miss Polka Dots."

"You're shittin' me."

I just shook my head helplessly.

"Oh, man...that's a bummer. That's a real fuckin' bummer. Well, I guess the good thing is you didn't really know her, right? I mean, sort of, but not really. You know what I mean?"

I knew he was trying to be helpful, but trying to be helpful and actually being helpful aren't always the same thing. He probably didn't know what to say. I knew I wouldn't have known what to say if the tables were reversed.

"Listen, Gabe, why don't we play a game of one-on-one. Maybe it'll take your mind off of everything that's going on. Maybe I'll even let you beat me for a change."

We stepped out on the court, and he gave me the ball first. As I drove to the hoop, attempting to lay the ball up, he stuffed me, retrieved the loose ball, and dribbled out to the foul line. He fired up a jump shot — swish. Jeff could really shoot. We always played "winner's out," so he went back to the foul line and tossed me the ball and said, "check." No sooner had I handed it back to him that he faked right, took three dribbles to the left, and swished a second jump shot.

Neither my head nor my heart were in the game. I found myself questioning why I was playing basketball at a time like this. As he made his way to the foul line, I rolled the ball to him and said, "Listen, I can't do this right now."

"Can't do what?" he said. "We're just playin', man. Don't worry, I'll ease up on you."

"No, it's not that. I just can't do this. I...I can't. I gotta go. You wouldn't understand. I'll see you in school or somewhere."

Making my way across the playground, I heard Jeff call, "Hey, what don't I understand? Where ya goin', man?"

I didn't answer and I didn't look back. I took big strides, moving across the playground with purpose, but my truth was, I had nowhere to go and no one to talk to. I had no idea who I even was.

"Gabe! C'mon, man! I understand! Where ya going?" he called once more, but he didn't follow me.

As I rounded the far side of the building, my mind was fixated on one thought and only one thought. *The pretty girl I danced with last night is dead. The girl with the polka dot dress, the headband, the hippie eye make-up, and the round glasses is dead. Susanna Novak is dead!*

8

Jeff never asked about Susanna's accident again. I guess I couldn't blame him. He probably didn't know what to say, and it was morbid to talk about anyway. There was really no one to talk to about it. But on Wednesday night the subject sort of came up at the dinner table.

"They should hang that Derby kid who killed that young girl," my father blurted out, unexpectedly.

"Oh, so awful," my mother interjected. "That poor little girl. Her parents must be devastated. I don't know how I would ever cope with such a thing."

"You guys know that kid?" Dad asked. I couldn't find any words.

After a brief moment, Michael said, "Not really. I mean, yes and no. Everyone knows who he is. We've seen him play football, and he comes in Duchess a lot, but I don't know him personally."

"Well, they should hang the bastard," my father replied.

It was rough listening to my father carry on like that. It was even rougher acting like I didn't really have any feelings about it. After that, though, there was no further discussion in our household about the tragic death of Susanna Novak. Not that death was much of a topic of discussion anyway. When I was nine years old, my grandmother died, and my mom decided not to have me attend the wake or the funeral. I'm guessing she thought I was too young. I was just shipped off to a babysitter, and no mention of Nonna Alberino's death was ever made. I had been to Paulie's father's wake a year ago because my mother felt that, as a freshman in high school, it was a good way to expose me to death, being that I had no strong emotional attachment to Gino. But even though she made me go, she never talked to me about it, but the truth is, seeing the dead body in the casket kind of spooked me out.

A day later, on Monday night, Michael surprised me when he said, "You're awfully close-mouthed. Something wrong?"

"No, nothing's wrong," I said, as if I suddenly thought Michael had lost his marbles.

"Don't be a wise ass. I think you're just acting really weird," he replied, "not like your normal self."

Perhaps a little too defensively, I said, "No, I'm my normal self, whatever *normal* is." Michael just kind of squinted at me as if he didn't recognize me, and I buried my face in my book, trying to look normal.

On Tuesday, Susanna's obituary appeared in the *Evening Sentinel.* I didn't typically read obituaries, but I needed to read this one. After my dad was through with the paper, I asked, "Mind if I read the sports page?" and I took the paper into my room where I had privacy because Michael was working. Leaning over the paper, I read the obituary over and over again, maybe, like, a couple billion times, hoping it would give me some insight into who Susanna really was.

Susanna Marie Novak, age 14, died due to injuries sustained in an accident on October 21st. Susanna was born on July 12, 1953 at Griffin Hospital in Derby to Walter and Helen Novak of Seymour. Susanna was a freshman at Seymour High School and was a member of the French Club, the Home Economics Club, and the Dance Club. She loved fashion, music, poetry, and dance.

Besides her parents, Susanna is survived by her older brother Daryl, her paternal grandparents, David and Barbara Novak, as well as her maternal grandparents, Robert and Dorothy Comcowicz.

Visiting hours will take place at the Ralph E. Hull Funeral Home, 161 West Church Street in Seymour between 4:00 and 7:00 p.m. on Thursday, October 26th. A mass of Christian burial will take place at 10:00 a.m. on Friday, October 27th at St. Peter and St. Paul Ukrainian Catholic Church, 105 Clifton Avenue, Ansonia.

It didn't really say much. I wasn't surprised to see that she liked fashion. She was probably the most fashionable girl on the planet who wasn't already famous. She liked music. Made sense — we all did. I wondered what she did in the Home Economics Club. That was, like, cooking and sewing. Maybe she was learning to sew her own clothes, but her outfit Saturday night didn't look like it was any homemade job, but how would I know anyway? I wondered if she went to church and what it was like to go to a Ukrainian Church. The Mass had recently changed from Latin to English, due to the Second Vatican Council a few years ago. Go figure, just when I can understand the Mass, I stop going to church. But I wondered about Susanna's church and if the priest said the Mass in Ukrainian. If he did, did she understand it? Susanna and I probably had a few things in common. For one, we both had older brothers. I wondered if she and Daryl fought sometimes like Michael and I do. I wondered if Daryl was good to her like Michael has been to me in recent years. I imagined Daryl was very protective of his little sister. *I'll bet he wouldn't let anyone mess with her*, I thought to myself. I wondered what Susanna's parents and grandparents were like. I could picture the Novaks spending Sundays and holidays with the grandparents, like us, except all the adults spoke Ukrainian or whatever instead of Italian, which my aunts and uncles and grandparents speak every Sunday. I pictured Susanna, like me, not understanding a word of it, but, like me, still somehow being comfortable hearing it, like soothing background music. I tried to guess what bands she liked. She must have liked the Beatles. Who doesn't? But who else did she like? The Stones? Did she like the Motown sound as much as I do? How about the Rascals? Did Susanna like sports like I do? She must have loved watching her brother play football and basketball and baseball.

She had to be proud of being the little sister of maybe one the best all-time athletes ever to come out of the Valley.

I created all kinds of stories and scenarios in my mind about Susanna. Things that may or may not have been true. It was an attempt to connect the dots, a hope of finding things that she and I may have had in common. The bad news is I would never know the answers to any of these questions. There would never be any way to find out if Susanna and I had anything at all in common. She said "yes," though, when I asked her to dance. Twice. Even a slow dance. And when we started dancing, she was the one who rested her head on my shoulder. I didn't make her do it. So, there must have been something about me that she had liked or none of that would have happened. Jeff had even said it.

I grabbed a scissors and cut out the obituary, and then I rolled the *Sentinel* up and threw it in the garbage. Folding the column of newsprint into thirds, I tucked it neatly into my wallet, safe and sound, where no one else would see it.

It was at that moment that I made a big decision. It was probably the craziest thing I had ever decided to do up until that point in my life. Not that I'm the world's craziest person or anything, but I felt an overwhelming compulsion to go to Susanna's funeral on Friday. I just had to figure out how I was going to pull that off since obviously my parents didn't even know that I knew Susanna, so I wasn't about to ask for permission. I couldn't exactly skip school, because if my father ever found out, it would be lights out for me. No, skipping wasn't an option. A good idea suddenly hatched in my bird nest of a brain, though. Earlier in the year I had overslept and checked in tardy to school. I was only a half hour late, but there were no consequences. The main office secretary just said, "Can I help you, Gabriel?" I responded, "Yes, I'm late for school." She looked at the clock and said, "8:05," wrote it down, and asked, "Reason?" I faked embarrassment and replied, "Reason? Oh, I overslept." And as she made a note of it, in her nasally voice, she said, "O-ver-slept." And that was basically it.

I had to formulate more of a plan, though. For instance, I would need to get dressed early and act like I was going to school. When I met Jeff, I would tell him that I was going into school late. I wasn't sure whether I would tell him where I was going. It might be best not to. I would need to decide if I was going to walk or hitchhike to St. Peter and St. Paul Church. It might be better to walk. I might be more likely to be seen by people my parents knew if I got on Route 8 and hitchhiked. If I walked the right streets on my way to Ansonia, I might be more inconspicuous. Of course, with the funeral at 10:00, I would be walking into school a lot later than 8:05, so I was probably going to need a better alibi.

The night before Susanna's funeral was my parents' bowling night, and Michael was working, so I was home alone. I decided it would be smart to alter part of my plan. I gave Jeff a ring.

"Hey, what's up?" he said.

"Nothin' much," I responded. "I just wanted to give you a buzz and tell you that I have a sore throat, so I'm going to stay home from school tomorrow."

"Oh, okay, partner. I'll have to survive the day without you, not that I'm in any of those brainiac classes you take. I hope you feel better."

In the morning, I did everything as usual. When I left the house at 7:15, my parents didn't notice anything out of the ordinary. Michael wasn't even awake since his first college class in New Haven wasn't until the early afternoon. I just needed to avoid running into Jeff. When I got to Prospect, the street he would be walking on, I furtively looked in the direction of Mrs. Bailey's house, and seeing no one, trotted across the street heading downtown to Canal Street and the railroad tracks. I got that far without running into any kids from school. I walked alongside the tracks to the bridge and headed toward Derby, walking underneath the girders and cement of the old bridge. As I headed over the Housatonic toward downtown Derby, I worried about being seen by someone my family knew — or worse yet, my father himself if he drove by to a little joint called JoAnn's where he liked to stop for breakfast. *He's probably not out of bed yet,* I thought, knowing Dad and Mom were usually awake until after midnight so they weren't exactly early risers. Running my hand gently across the cement barrier as I walked, I kept my head turned away from the road, as if looking down into the river. When I passed the river, I just had to stay away from Main Street and Elizabeth Street where all the businesses were. I took side streets, but there was no guarantee that was safe. All of my DeMarco relatives lived in Derby, and that meant, including spouses, about fourteen aunts and uncles, not to mention almost twenty first cousins. It would be a miracle if I reached my destination undetected, but I was going to try.

Walking on Olivia Street, parallel to Elizabeth Street, I passed the back side of the Derby Community Center, remembering the magic of last Saturday night. I began to feel a little emotional, which didn't surprise me. Instead of making my way to Atwater Avenue, I followed Seymour Avenue, which ran parallel to Atwater, slanting toward Griffin Hospital. *Strange that I'm on a street called Seymour Avenue,* I thought, *since this is Derby but Susanna and Daryl are from Seymour.* I wondered what happened when the ambulance brought Susanna to Griffin Hospital on Saturday night. *Did she look awful? Was there blood? What would it have been like to be there when they brought her in?*

I had time to kill because it wasn't even 8:30 yet, and the funeral didn't start until 10:00. I took a left past Griffin Hospital, and I made my way up to Osbornedale Park, which is across the road from Derby High School and Ryan Field, where Adamo had caused Novak to drop the pass that might have changed the history of Valley football had Novak held on to it. And now, Adamo's and Novak's lives had collided in another way. I felt really bad for Novak. First the game, and now this. I even felt bad for Adamo. I mean, he was probably an alright guy, maybe a little too conceited, but I'm sure he hadn't meant to hit

Susanna. What would become of him now? I didn't agree with my dad that they should hang him.

I walked up the drive into the small state park and I made my way to a picnic bench in the stone pavilion next to the pond with its shimmering water. Jeff, my cousin Tomaso, and I had ice skated on this pond many times. In fact, it was probably the place where my father had first put me on skates when I was a dumb little kid, still one of my earliest memories. This area was beautiful in every season. The autumn leaves, which were beginning to fall from the trees, floating gently to the grassy expanses below, reminded me of watercolor paintings I had seen — splashes of gold everywhere. There was no one at the park except for some old guy across the other side of the pond who was walking a little dog. I reached into my back pocket and took Jack Kerouac out and tried to kill some time. Thankfully, I was able to focus for a while. Absorbed in my reading, I didn't notice that the old man and his dog had made their way around to my side of the pond.

"Taking a holiday from school?" the old guy called out to me. His dog simultaneously began to bark at me, a high pitched, annoying yelp. I continued to read, wishing that they would both mind their own business. I wasn't bothering them.

"Did you hear me, young man?"

I looked up. "I'm sorry, I was reading. Were you talking to me, sir?" I asked politely.

"Yes, I was, young man," he said. "I asked if you were taking a holiday from school. A fair question, no?"

I had to think fast. "Oh yes, sir, that *is* a fair question. No, not a holiday. I'm going to a funeral down the road. A friend of mine died, but it doesn't start until 10:00, so I had my mom drop me off here for a little while."

"Not that little girl from Seymour?" he asked, his tone now a little more sensitive.

"Yes," I answered, "I'm sorry to say that's the one."

"What a tragic thing that was," he said. "You say she was a friend of yours?"

"Yes, we were really good friends. We grew up together, and we were in some of the same classes together at Seymour High School. She was one the nicest people I've ever met. Actually, Susanna Novak was one of my very best friends." In telling these lies, I felt my eyes well up with tears. I guess I was feeling emotional about what might have been...what I wish had been. Somehow, I willed the tears from running down my cheeks.

The old man couldn't help but notice. "Well, I'm very sorry for your loss, young man. I'm sure she was a very nice girl. You seem to be a very nice boy as well. Good luck to you."

As he moved on up the dirt road that led further into the park, I wiped the corners of my eyes with the backs of my index fingers. I might not have been telling the complete truth, but sometimes maybe there's a morsel of truth in the way we wish things had been. In any case, despite the fictional nature of most of what I said, it was the best talk I had had about Susanna's death with anyone so far.

At 9:15, I decided I'd make my way to the church. Ironically, St. Peter and St. Paul Church was only around the corner from Division Street where the accident had taken place, not even a five minute walk. I approached the church from the opposite direction because of the secretive nature of my trip. St. Peter and St. Paul was an older brick structure, probably at least a hundred years old, with one large dome and four smaller domes topped off with gold crosses. The other Catholic churches I was familiar with didn't have domes; they just had steeples, and only one. This church looked more something — more exotic.

I decided not to get too close to the church. I hung outside of Williams Plumbing Supply, which was about fifty yards away. *I hope Dad doesn't get his supplies here. With my luck, he'll show up here any minute,* I worried. The parking lot and the curbsides had already begun filling up with cars. I couldn't believe the number of high school kids who were ascending the stairs of the old church. Every kid from Seymour High School must have been there.

My heart began to beat faster when the long, black hearse and limousine pulled up in front of the church. Six males of varying ages approached the hearse. A man in a black dress coat, the funeral director, I guess, guided the group of men in extracting the coffin with its gleaming red wood and brass handles out of the back of the vehicle and led them toward the stone steps. It was hard to believe Susanna was in that box. I recognized Daryl Novak as he got out of the limousine. Daryl and a man I assumed to be his father each took a woman's arms, his mother's, and helped her to walk in the direction of the coffin. While the men looked shell shocked, Mrs. Novak was obviously having even a rougher time. Her face projected deep pain and despair, even from half a football field away. The pallbearers made their way to the top of the church steps, and, followed by the Novaks, disappeared through the heavy wooden doors.

Now, with no one left outside on the street, I slowly walked down to the church. I wanted to go in, but I felt paralyzed. What was I doing? What made me think I belonged here? I sat down on the lower stone steps, feeling more loss and more *lost* than I'd ever felt. After all, the real truth was that Susanna and I didn't even know each other. What right did I have to mourn her death? What right did I have to be at her funeral? For one thing, I was the only Shelton kid there. For another, even though I had gone to a Catholic elementary school, I hadn't been to church in about a year, mainly because of laziness, which must be a sin. After giving the matter some thought, though, I realized that I had taken a big chance to come here, and I wasn't out of the woods yet either, so I needed to keep my wits about me. Deciding it was worth the risk, I stood up and headed up the stairs. I pulled open the door furthest to the left and seeing that it was a standing-room-only affair, I reached into the holy water font, blessed myself, because that's what you're supposed to do, and leaned against the nearby wall. With so many people there, especially kids, no one would notice me.

The Mass was well underway when I entered. At that moment, a bald headed priest was at the lectern, giving one of the readings. He announced, "A reading from the Book of Ecclesiastes." He had a strong accent, probably Ukrainian, as he spoke and read:

For everything there is a season, and a time for every matter under heaven: a time to be born, and a time to die; a time to plant, and a time to pluck up what is planted; a time to kill, and a time to heal; a time to break down, and a time to build up; a time to weep, and a time to laugh; a time to mourn, and a time to dance; a time to throw away stones, and a time to gather stones together; a time to embrace, and a time to refrain from embracing; a time to seek, and a time to lose; a time to keep, and a time to throw away; a time to tear, and a time to sew; a time to keep silence, and a time to speak; a time to love, and a time to hate; a time for war, and a time for peace.

Listening carefully as he read, I realized that it sounded a lot like one of my favorite songs by the Byrds: "Turn, Turn, Turn." I hadn't realized the song was based on a Bible reading. I wondered if the song was also one of Susanna's favorites. *It must have been*, I figured. As organ music played and the priest sang, I imagined sitting in Susanna's basement with her and spinning our favorite songs on a record player. With that scenario playing itself out in my head, I found myself reaching into my pocket, reaching for my wallet. I reached into it and pulled out the remnant of Susanna's rose colored lens and held it tightly, making sure the sharp broken part didn't cut my palm. It was my souvenir of our dance together, and I cherished it. My mind continued to drift on a river of thoughts of Susanna, who still seemed so real to me, that I hardly even heard the second reading, but just the drone of the priest's voice echoing somewhere out in space. The second round of organ music brought my attention back to the altar.

The priest, preparing to read the gospel, said: "The Lord be with you," to which the congregation responded, "And also with you." Then he said, "A reading from the Holy Gospel according to John:

Jesus answered the Jews and said to them:
Amen, amen, I say to you, whoever hears my word
and believes in the One who sent me
has eternal life and will not come to condemnation,
but has passed from death to life…"

As the monotone voice of the priest rang throughout the church in broken English, I began to zone out again. I couldn't help asking myself, *Why did Susanna's funeral have to be so boring too?* Upon finishing the reading of the Gospel, the priest kissed the Bible and said, "This is the word of the Lord," and everyone responded, "Thanks be to God." The priest then went on to express his condolences to the Novak family, saying what a nice little girl Susanna had been and how she always came to church and received the sacraments, and he told everyone that was the reason why we all didn't need to be sad, because Susanna showed she believed in the One who sent Jesus, and it was the reason she now has eternal life, and all that standard junk that priests say. It didn't help me. In fact, I was starting to get angry because I realized that he didn't know Susanna even as well as I did. He didn't have one specific thing to say about her except that she went to church and believed in God. I'll bet he didn't even know what she looked like or that she was beautiful or that she liked mod clothes. I thought to myself, *She probably didn't go to church because she believed in the One who sent Jesus, but instead because her parents made her, the way mine used to make me until they finally gave up.* The fact was that this priest almost definitely didn't know a single thing about what Susanna believed or didn't believe, and I was feeling that he had no right to tell hundreds of people that he did.

Through my irritation, I heard the priest say that two of Susanna's friends were now going to recite a poem. I saw two familiar faces approach the pulpit. They were the two girls who were giggling when I asked Susanna to dance. The first, a freckle-faced redhead, said, "Uhm, we want to thank Mrs. Novak for letting us borrow Sue's book of poems by Emily Dickinson, who was her favorite poet. We found this poem in the book, and we just want to recite it because, well, because Sue liked poetry so much." You could tell the freckly-faced girl was a bundle of nervous emotions just by the lost look on her face. She recited half the poem, and the taller dark-haired girl recited the second half. They had the poem typed on a piece of paper, and as each girl read, her hands shook pretty much uncontrollably.

Because I could not stop for Death –
He kindly stopped for me –
The Carriage held but just Ourselves –
And Immortality.

We slowly drove – He knew no haste
And I had put away
My labor and my leisure too,
For His Civility –

We passed the School, where Children strove
At Recess – in the Ring –
We passed the Fields of Gazing Grain –
We passed the Setting Sun –

Or rather – He passed Us –
The Dews drew quivering and Chill –
For only Gossamer, my Gown –
My Tippet – only Tulle –

We paused before a House that seemed
A Swelling of the Ground –
The Roof was scarcely visible –
The Cornice – in the Ground –

Since then – 'tis Centuries – and yet
Feels shorter than the Day
I first surmised the Horses' Heads
Were toward Eternity –

I'm not sure I understood it, but the opening words, "Because I could not stop for Death, he kindly stopped for me" struck some kind of incomprehensible chord in me. I would remember it and find a copy of the poem myself to remember Susanna by as soon as possible.

The mass continued as I had remembered it with the Offertory, the Consecration, the Communion, and the Closing Prayers. I mean, I was an altar boy when I was a little younger. During most of it, I found myself staring up at the intricate stained glass windows and the many paintings with pictures of saints in colorful flowing robes. Something about the style of the art, oddly, was different from the ones in my church.

When the pallbearers brought the coffin down the center aisle to the back of the church and the Ukrainian priest began to recite the closing prayers, I remember smelling the distinct aroma of incense and hearing Mrs. Novak's intermittent sobs echoing as Daryl and Mr. Novak held on to her. It was hard to listen to her cry and not feel really bad. When the pallbearers took the coffin out of the main doors of the church, I was the first one out of the left hand doors, but lots of people flowed out behind me as well as from the far right doors. As the Novaks made their way down the stairs, I saw Daryl kind of look up at the late morning clouds and then survey the crowd around him. It seemed strange, but as he perused the crowd, I felt like our eyes met. It must have been my imagination.

It was getting late, so I decided to walk down to Pershing Drive and take a chance and hitchhike back to Shelton. Luckily, a guy in a pickup truck which was loaded with wooden step ladders picked me up within the first few minutes. He must have been a painter. Sitting in his truck, I realized that I was still holding the lens of Susanna's glasses in my left hand. I pulled out my wallet and tried to slip it in unobtrusively. Luckily, the painter didn't notice. When he asked me where I had been, I told the truth, except that I repeated my lie about Susanna and me being close friends. He was so moved by my story that he delivered me right to the front doors of Shelton High School. What a good guy.

When I walked into the main office, the secretary asked me, "Can I help you, Gabriel?"

"Yes, Mrs. Petz," I said. "I'm tardy."

"It's 11:22. I'd say you're very tardy," she said curtly.

"Yes, I'm sorry I'm so late."

She wrote my name and 11:22 down on her notepad, and then she said, "Reason?"

"I overslept," I said.

Looking over her glasses, Mrs. Petz did a double take. "Why didn't your parents wake you up?"

"It's kind of funny, but they didn't even realize I was still asleep," I explained, "because it's something that almost never happens. Actually, usually I'm out of the house right before they even get up because, the thing is, they're both big night owls, you see. By 9:00 this morning, my father was off to work, and my mother was out at the grocery store, and I was still fast asleep in my bedroom. They didn't even realize it because, you know, why would they? So they don't even know I'm late for school because they were gone before I got up. Isn't that funny?"

"Hilarious," she replied, sarcastically. "Well, it sounds to me like you must be something of a night owl yourself or you wouldn't have overslept so badly. Perhaps you need to get to bed earlier at night.

This better not happen again, Gabriel, or you'll be telling your story to Mr. Martin," she said. Mr. Martin is our assistant principal — a hard-nosed but fair guy. I wondered if he would have bought my alibi.

"Yes, Ma'am. I think that's exactly what I need to do. Don't worry, though. You won't see me arrive late to school again. Not a chance."

She handed me a yellow tardy slip to show my teachers, and I was on my way. *Whew*, I thought, leaving the office, *that was a close call.* Now I just had to figure out how I was going to explain being in school to Jeff since I already told him I was sick. Boy, lying could really get a guy in a picklc, but going to the funeral was an important step for me. My next move would be to figure out when I was going to get to the library to look up the poem Susanna's friends had read that morning. "Because I could not stop for Death, He kindly stopped for me." I needed to understand. I just had to get a copy of that poem.

9

While I had been less than impressed by the words of the priest at the funeral, I was so obsessed with the poem Susanna's friends had read that I had trouble sleeping that night. Poems aren't always easy to understand, so doing a little research can help. The next day, on Saturday morning, I took a walk to the Plumb Memorial Library to see what I could find out. Probably the most historic and most beautiful building in Shelton, the Plumb is a place I really like to hang out at, which is not something I broadcast to all my friends.

I had heard of Emily Dickinson, but I had never gotten into poetry. Maybe Emily Dickinson would change that. I went to the author card file and searched her name. I quickly found a half dozen possibilities. I grabbed one of the small pencils on top of the oak file cabinet and a small square of scrap paper, and I wrote down the first three call numbers: 811.01Dic, 812.32Dic, 812.91Dic. Then I made my way to the 800s. The aromatic shelves smelled of old books. I found the books without a problem: *Poems of Emily Dickinson* — that was a start; *The Essential Emily Dickinson* — even better; and *The Complete Poems of Emily Dickinson* — bingo! I made my way to a table and picked up a volume with shiny gold lettering on the cover and spine. It looked more official than the others. On the back cover, I saw a blurb about Emily Dickinson:

> Emily Dickinson, the "Belle of Amherst," is one of the most highly-regarded poets ever to write. In America, perhaps only Walt Whitman is her equal in legend and in degree of influence.

> Dickinson, the famous recluse dressed in white, secretly produced an enormous canon of poetry while locked in her room and refusing visitor after visitor. Her personal life and its mysteries have sometimes overshadowed her achievements in poetry and her extraordinary innovations in poetic form, to the dismay of some scholars.

I was immediately intrigued. A recluse. A life of mystery. It made me want to know more. I found the poem in two of the three volumes, but my problem was there was no explanation of the poem, which is what I needed. I approached the librarian behind the counter, a short, older woman with white hair so thin I could see her scalp, which didn't particularly thrill me. "Pardon me, Ma'am," I whispered, because that's how you talk in a library, "but I have a question I'm hoping you can answer."

"I'll try, young man," she honked in a voice which seemed to come completely through her nose. She did not whisper. There must have been a rule that the librarian could speak in a full voice, but no one else could.

"Yes, I am looking at some volumes of Emily Dickinson's poetry, but what I'm basically looking for is an explanation of one of her poems."

"You mean a scholarly analysis, I think," she said, telling me what I meant.

"Oh, is that what I mean?" I sounded clueless even to myself.

"Yes, indeed. We probably wouldn't have anything like that, being a small library, but let me look."

I followed behind her as she waddled over to the chest of drawers where I had begun. She flipped through the same section of the drawer with what seemed like great efficiency, as if she had been flipping cards her entire adult life, which she probably had. Then she turned to me, and said, "As I assumed, young man, we don't have anything like that.

You'd probably need to go to a bigger city library — Bridgeport or New Haven."

"Oh, okay," I said.

"Do you know that you can use your Plumb card there to borrow a book?" she asked. I responded that I did not know that. "And when you are finished with the book, you can bring it here and we will return it to the city where you borrowed it."

"Oh wow, that's cool," I said. She gave me that look adults give kids when we use words like "cool."

I was grateful for the information, though, and politely thanked her and went about the business of returning the three books to their shelf, but not before I copied the poem into a notebook I had brought. Exiting the library, I thought to myself, *I have nothing to do. I'll go to New Haven now.* I thought I'd hitchhike, but it was a cold day. I decided to try something I had never done before — take the bus to New Haven. I had often passed by the bus stop on Howe Avenue, very near the Boys Club. I waited outside a seedy looking package store for the bus to arrive even though I didn't know what its schedule was. After about a half hour, it arrived. I got on and asked the driver if he was going to New Haven.

"Yes, my young friend, that's our destination," he replied.

"How much?" I asked.

"Sixty cents," he said.

Not bad, I thought, and I handed him two quarters and a dime, noticing that no one else was on the bus.

No sooner had I taken my seat on the long bus that I began to think of Michael. The bus kind of made me think of something he had done as a mere tenth grader, just like me. Strictly legendary. As a student at Fairfield Prep, because there was no school bus from Shelton to Fairfield, Michael needed to carpool with either upperclassmen or with Fairfield University students because Prep is about twenty miles away from Shelton. Not exactly right around the corner. Despite wanting Michael to go to Prep, Dad apparently had no intention of driving him there. As a sophomore, Michael had somehow irritated the guy who drove him to and from Prep, so much so that the jerk threw Michael out of his car. For the remainder of the year, instead of finding another ride, Michael hitchhiked back and forth to Fairfield every day. Seriously! I don't know if a conversation ever took place about it between Michael and Dad, but if it did, it was probably a conversation I would have preferred not to be in on, which was what most of their conversations were. To make it simple, they didn't get along that famously.

So, every morning, Michael made his way down the same embankment right next to old Mrs. Erwin's house, leading to the Route 8 underpass, and he stood on the shoulder of the highway with his thumb in the air. Knowing Michael as I did, I can only imagine him heading down that path, sliding along slick ice or sludgy mud or sopping wet leaves, depending on the season, and mumbling to himself as he descended the hill to begin his journey — because Michael was famous for talking to himself. It was probably just a series of almost incoherent swear words. Something like, "Mother fucker. What the fuck am I doing? This fucking path can go fuck itself!" Such a soliloquy would have continued on the highway below as Michael undoubtedly cursed out drivers who zoomed by without picking him up. One of the few things I didn't copy from Michael was his specialty — using colorful language.

He told me that it sometimes took him two or three rides to get to Fairfield. He might be dropped off near I-95 in Bridgeport, and then again at the bottom of North Benson Road in Fairfield where Prep was located, but still a mile away. In each case, it was back to thumbing the next leg of the journey. At the end of the school day, it was the same routine, only in reverse. He and I didn't talk about it much but one day I asked him if he was ever late to school. "Never," he replied. Unreal!

Michael's accomplishment truly should be in the Guinness Book of

World Records. I tried to look up hitchhiking records at the Plumb, but I couldn't find a related category. I found things like Longest Distance Hitchhiked (Bill Heid from Andrews Park, Michigan, 673,200 km), Furthest Point Hitchhiked on the Globe North (Nordkapp, North Norway) or South (Buenos Aires, Argentina), Longest Distance Hitchhiked in 24 Hours (1742.4 km), Most Hitchhikers Picked Up by a Driver (a Jim Sanderson picked up over 7500) — things like that. But there didn't seem to be a category for Michael. What about records for the Kid Who Hitchhiked the Most Consecutive Days to School or the Kid Who Hitchhiked the Furthest Distance to School or, better yet, the Kid Who Hitchhiked the Furthest Distance to School Without Ever Being Late? I've never heard of such an accomplishment, and in my opinion, Michael deserves a prize.

When we passed by Yale Bowl, I awakened from my daydream about Michael, and perused the seats around me. The bus had made several stops along the way, and I now counted fourteen passengers. Interestingly, I noticed that I was one of only two white people on the bus. The other was an old guy who was either drunk or homeless or both. Not that it was any of my business.

I didn't know where the New Haven Library was, and I hoped, after making a long trip like this, I would find what I was looking for. We arrived at a block where there was a gigantic green across from three towering churches with park benches interspersed along diagonal walkways. I headed to the front of the bus.

"This where I get off?" I asked the driver.

"You betcha," he replied with a kind smile.

"Can you tell me where the library is?" I asked.

He pointed with his big, right hand. "You see that big ol' brick building with the white columns on the other side o' the green? That's the one. And the bus goes back to Shelton at 1:30 and at 4:30," he added. I thanked him. I was glad I asked him, or I would have had to ask a complete stranger on the street.

Walking across the green, I wondered what it must be like to live in a bigger city like New Haven. I saw a lot of negroes pass by, more than I had ever seen in one area, and I thought about how in the Valley, most of the black people lived in Ansonia for reasons that I didn't really understand. You almost never see a black person in Shelton, Derby, or Seymour. At Shelton High School, there are maybe seven or eight black kids, all of whom come from three families, the Howards, the Robinsons, and the Whites. That suddenly struck me as almost funny, or at least odd — a black family called the Whites. I remembered Muhammad Ali talking about getting rid of the name Clay, which he called a slave owner's name. I remembered a history teacher saying that slaves had only a first name until the end of the Civil War, and then, needing a last name as free men, they were given the last names of their owners. *Were White and Howard and Robinson slave owners' names?* I wondered. I realized, if it weren't for working at Duchess, besides Gerry Howard in my history class, I probably wouldn't know a single black person.

I walked up the granite steps of the historic building and saw a wide banner hanging over the door — New Haven Free Public Library — and the word free grabbed me. While I felt grateful to live in a country that was free, where slavery once existed but no longer did, lately I'd found myself asking a lot of questions, like: Why were there so many black people in Ansonia and so few in Shelton, Derby, and Seymour? Why did my dad seem to hate black people so much, always calling them "niggers" when talking about them? Why did Muhammad Ali talk about black people in Louisville being treated like dogs? Was that true? And just a little while ago — why did the black people on the bus outnumber the white people twelve to two? At the moment it occurred to me, though, that the word free on the banner maybe just meant I was walking into a building where I could borrow books for free.

The interior of the library must have been ten times the size of the Plumb. There were quite a few people searching for books and reading at tables. I asked a librarian where the card catalogue was, and she pointed me in the right direction. Again, I went to the author cabinet and searched Dickinson, now finding dozens of cards. I wrote down call numbers for a bunch of them, but upon finding them, I had a decision to make. I didn't want to get back to Shelton too late, so I couldn't exactly do the research in New Haven. I also didn't want to take out a stack of books, which might require some explaining at home, but rather just one book, not too conspicuous, which would tell me what the poem meant. Moving across the shelves, I found a book that fit my size requirement called, *Emily Dickinson: A Collection of Critical Essays*. I thumbed to the back of the book, to see if there was an index. There wasn't. Then I flipped to the table of contents in the front and saw, "Chapter 5: An Analysis of I Could Not Stop for Death." Bang! I was glad I had learned to use the library when I was a younger kid. It was almost too easy.

I brought it to the checkout counter and handed the librarian my card. She could have been the Shelton librarian's sister. Same height. Same white hair, although thankfully I couldn't see this one's scalp.

"You're from Shelton, I see," she commented in her old lady voice.

"Yes, Ma'am," I replied.

"Make sure you return the book by the due date, a week from today," she ordered.

"Yes, Ma'am, will do."

I should have said, "Yes, Sarge, will do," because she could have been a drill sergeant with her attitude. On the way back to the bus stop, I passed by a luncheonette called Maxim's and got an order of french fries and a Coke to go. I needed to run to catch the 1:30 bus. I made it just in time and was happy to see the familiar face of the nice bus driver. I gave him another sixty cents and took a seat. By the time I finished my food, we were halfway home. I thought to myself, *I'll wait to read the explanation until I can write notes on the pad where I had copied the poem.*

Arriving in Shelton, I headed for Moscardini's, which was a half block away from the bus stop, diagonally across the street from the Boys Club. It would be a good place to look at my book. If any of the kids asked, I would tell them I was working on a homework assignment. The place had become known to everyone simply as "Mosci's." It looks like any normal small luncheonette, with a long, high counter and chrome swivel stools with red tops along the right wall, a glass enclosed phone booth opposite the counter, and wooden booths in the back. Behind the booths there's a rickety magazine rack, a jukebox, and two pinball machines. The thing about it that maybe isn't normal is, somehow, the customers are almost exclusively teen boys, who listen to records, scan magazines and newspapers, and play pinball for hours. It's rare to see an adult man enter Mosci's, and never an adult woman. Kids don't like the idea of their girlfriends going to Mosci's either, so only the most daring girls enter the place, and we're supposed to think of those who do as some kind of whores, but I personally always find myself wondering if they really are.

I was still hungry. I asked Stanley Moscardini to make me a hamburger and a vanilla shake. Duchess's twenty cent hamburgers had their appeal, I guess, but a hamburger from Mosci's was serious. Mosci's is owned by skinny, gray haired Stanley, who I guess to be about sixty, and his younger brother Lou, whose age is hard to pinpoint because he sports a crew cut but has snow white hair. Lou is clearly the younger of the two, though. Lou is also built like a linebacker — solid.

As I made my way to one of the four booths in the back of the store, Aretha Franklin was wailing out "Respect" on the jukebox. *Phenomenal song,* I thought. I mean, who has a better voice than Aretha? Nobody. There weren't many guys there. An older kid was in the phone booth, probably talking to a girl because what else would he be doing in a phone booth? I noticed he was smiling, which is what I'd be doing if I was talking to a girl. There were two guys at the pinball machines, and there was one guy thumbing through a detective magazine in a nearby booth. He was probably just looking at the pictures, though, which featured many shots of shapely ladies in sexy dresses and even only underwear. None of the guys ever bought the magazines but only looked at them. Me too. I knew all of these guys, but none of them were friends of mine.

I pulled out my notebook from the library and got underway with my research. As I readied myself to get to work, one of the guys at the pinball machine, Clutch Kichinko, slammed his fists on the glass top, and yelled, "Tilt? Fuck! That's bullshit!"

From the grill behind the counter where he was making my burger, Stanley called to him in a trembling voice, "Hey, Clutch, now don't go hitting the machine like that! You'll break it! And you watch your language in here!"

"But the machine tilted, and I lost my game," Clutch replied.

"That's because...because you kids shake the machine too hard."

"It's because these machines suck, Stanley. You guys need to get some new fuckin' machines." Clutch's buddy was dying trying to hold in his laughter.

Stanley's whole body was trembling now. "That's it, Clutch! If you...if you swear one more time, I'm gonna throw you guys out!"

"Oh yeah, sure you will, Stanley. Just chill out," Clutch shot back, and he and his friend burst into laughter.

I felt sorry for Stanley. The guys who hung out there showed him no respect. If Lou had been on duty, it would have been a different story. He wouldn't have taken any guff from the two idiots and probably would have grabbed them firmly by their arms or the scruffs of their necks and escorted them to the door. Nobody messes with Lou.

Stanley brought me my burger and shake. I said softly to him, "Don't let those guys get to you, Stanley. They're jerks." Stanley just shook his head and walked back to the counter.

Ready to plunge into the book and find out what the poem meant, I flipped to the right chapter and grabbed my pen. I drew a vertical line right next to where I had jotted down the poem, so I would have a second column to make notes, a study technique that my World History teacher, Mr. Waleski, had taught us. There was a lot in the poem, and it made me think as I began to write down the interpretation:

> Because I could not stop for Death -
> He kindly stopped for me -
> The Carriage held but just Ourselves -
> And Immortality.

• First line - The speaker didn't know she was going to die. *How could Susanna have known?*

• Death capitalized - personifying the word. Death portrayed as gentleman suitor who takes speaker for a ride in his carriage. *I had just learned the word suitor reading* The Taming of the Shrew *in English class. Death had beaten me to being Susanna's suitor.*

• When speaker says "Ourselves" - suggests a relationship between her and Death, as if something important will happen between them. *Would something important have happened between Susanna and me after the dance if the accident never happened?*

• "Immortality" - means speaker feels there is eternal life. *Did Susanna believe in eternal life? I didn't know if I did.*

> We slowly drove - He knew no haste
> And I had put away
> My labor and my leisure too,
> For His Civility -

• "Slowly drove"..."no haste" - the speaker is <u>patiently</u> taken from her earthly life. *To me, it seemed like Susanna was abruptly taken from her life. Maybe I didn't understand.*

• "Had put away my labor and my leisure"...shows willingness to go with Death. Speaker has come to terms with her mortality. *This blew me away. It was hard to imagine Susanna being willing to die.*

We passed the School, where Children strove
At Recess - in the Ring -
We passed the Fields of Gazing Grain -
We passed the Setting Sun -

• Speaker - given a few moments to look back on her childhood. *What had Susanna's childhood been like? Had it been happy?*

• "Grain" - represents prime of her life. *She was definitely in her prime all right, up until the accident.*

• "Setting sun" - represents passing from her earthly life to eternal life. *A sunset would never be the same again for me.*

Or rather - He passed us -
The Dews drew quivering and chill -
For only Gossamer, my Gown -
My Tippet - only Tulle -

• Tone of poem shifts. With sun having set, speaker feels suddenly cold. She becomes aware she is underdressed for Death. *Right! I thought of her in her mod outfit. The image of her dying in that dress was awful.*

We paused before a House that seemed
A Swelling of the Ground -
The Roof was scarcely visible -
The Cornice - in the Ground -

• "House" - "Swelling of the ground" is her disappointing earthly grave. *It hurt to think of how disappointed she must be.*

Since then - 'tis Centuries - and yet
Feels shorter than the Day
I first surmised the Horses' Heads
Were toward Eternity -

• Centuries pass / life goes on without her...but, to her, it seems only a short time ago when Death, having appeared to her as a gentleman, seduced her and then left her alone in the cold, dark, damp grave. *He was no gentleman in my opinion. I would never treat a girl badly, and I would never have abandoned Susanna!*

I realized that, while making my notes, I was so absorbed in what I was doing that I had left my burger and shake untouched. I bit into the burger. It was cold, but I was still hungry. When I looked up, the place was empty except for Stanley. I didn't even notice the other kids walk out. With a sigh, I continued to eat my cold hamburger and drink my warm shake, while looking down at my notes and reflecting on what I had written. I thought to myself, *this poem and these notes will be something I will keep always to remember Susanna by.*

Looking up, I was surprised to see Jeff walk through the doors. He lifted his head, acknowledging me with a nod. As he approached the booth, I shut the notebook.

"What you up to, partner?" he asked.

"Nothing. I was just working on a homework assignment." I put the book on top of my notebook for extra security.

"I should do some homework someday." He picked up the book. "Emily Dickinson. Looks very exciting. I just stopped in to call Julie. There's only one phone at my grandmother's. No privacy. Know what I mean?"

"Yeah, I can relate."

"Things really got exciting at Julie's last night."

"I'm sure," I grinned at him.

"You could use a little excitement in your life."

If he only knew, I thought...but he was oblivious.

"Hey! Earth to Gabriel. You completely zoned out."

"Oh...sorry, I'm still here. Uh...I'm just shot from working on this homework. I think I'm going to head home and take a nap."

"That's cool. Like I said, I have to call Julie anyway. I'll catch up to you later."

I stopped at the counter to pay Stanley as Jeff stepped into the phone booth and shut the bifold door. "Thanks a lot, Stanley," I said. *Poor Stanley,* I thought.

I walked out onto Howe Avenue, and I decided to head to the Plumb and return the book in the drop box so no one at home would know I had it. I wasn't ready for any questions, although it might have been nice if one of my parents or Michael got a clue that I wasn't doing so great. I mean, basically, I was pretty deeply in mourning. I mean, I was kind of coming apart at the seams, if I want to be truthful, and nobody even noticed.

10

Two school days after the funeral, Coach Flaherty isn't too worried about Daryl. *After all, the kid needs time to grieve,* he rationalizes. But when a third, a fourth, and even a fifth day pass and Daryl is still missing in action, the coach really starts to panic. He is, in one sense, concerned for Daryl's emotional health, but, in another sense, the team is 7-1, and they have a big showdown with Shelton in a week before they face Naugatuck on Thanksgiving. Daryl is key to the success of the team in these games, especially against the formidable Shelton Gaels, also 7-1.

Coach Flaherty, a Boston native, has completely turned the program around after coming to Seymour four years ago. The Yellowjackets have gone from being a substandard team in the early '60s to being an important presence in the Housatonic League. Of course, having two superbly talented athletes like Novak and Andrews hasn't hurt at all. *But,* Flaherty thinks to himself, *having one without the other isn't going to quite cut it.*

He pulls Andrews aside at practice. "How's your buddy doing?" he asks the quarterback.

"I don't know, Coach," Andrews replies. "I've been calling him, but he just says he doesn't feel like talking. I mean, he's not the biggest talker I ever met anyway, but he's acting really odd. I even stopped by, and he more or less told me to go away."

Digesting Andrews' comments, Coach Flaherty says, "Yeah, well losing a family member is rough. Especially one so young."

At home, more than living together, the Novaks are existing

together. With the exception of Susie, they have always been very much of a taciturn family. But the recent lack of conversation, the current quiet in the house, has a different feel to it for Daryl. Since their talk in the kitchen, Daryl feels a chasm between himself and his mother that he has never before experienced. She is not only silent but emotionally absent. Walter has noticed it too, but he simply looks on, helplessly. It's a life of mundane exchanges that do no more than give information. "Daryl, there's food in the oven"..."Daryl didn't take the garbage out; I'll have to do it"..."Walter, would you stop at the store and pick up a dozen eggs?" Real conversations have ceased to exist in the Novak family. Genuine warmth is a thing of the past. Each member of the family lives in an isolated cubicle of his or her own invention.

I thought going to Susanna's funeral might have been helpful to me, but in the following days I found myself feeling really sad. Nothing seemed to lift me out of my funk, not reading or listening to music or playing basketball, and people were starting to notice. Michael and I were on the work schedule for Monday night, just a few nights after the funeral, and on the ride there, he began to question me again.

"I know I asked you the other day why you're acting so weird, and you said you were fine," Michael began, "but something is really not right with you."

"What're you talking about?"

"You know what the fuck I'm talking about. I'm talking about the way you've been moping around lately. Something isn't right, even though you won't admit it for some reason."

"False! I'm perfectly fine, and I don't have any idea what you mean." I wondered if he bought what I was saying.

"Listen, no one knows you better than I do. Shit, man, I've lived in the same room with you for fifteen years, and something screwy is going on with you. I don't know what the fuck it is, but I know something's up."

What is this? I thought, *an interrogation by the FBI?* I just wanted him to lay off. I just wanted to live in my own private world and not answer any questions.

Beginning on the Monday after Susie's funeral, Daryl dresses for school each day and leaves the house, never arriving at his destination. The school hasn't called, believing him to be in mourning, but on the following Monday, more than a week after the funeral, Mrs. Novak receives a call from the principal's secretary asking for the family to come in for a meeting.

"What do you mean he hasn't been in school?" Helen asks in a pained voice. "He gets up and leaves for school every morning."

"He may be leaving for school," the secretary replies, "but he isn't arriving here."

Once more, Walter is out of state for work, so Helen will have to face this crisis alone. She wonders how much strength God expects her to have. When she tells Daryl about the meeting, he is defensive.

"I don't want to go to any meeting, Mom," he argues, childishly.

"But where have you been going every morning?" she asks.

"I don't know. Nowhere. Just driving around. There's nowhere to go...and no point to anything," Daryl mumbles.

"Well, you're going to this meeting tomorrow morning at 8:30," Helen responds hotly. "Are you going to continue to make my life miserable?"

Daryl is, once again, deeply wounded by his mother's words. Their first conversation in a little more than a week hasn't gone well.

Michael could read me like a book, and I didn't like it. If that wasn't bad enough, so could Lenny Singleton who was the grill man that night. I think he noticed that there was tension between me and Michael because at one point in the night, after I had run down to the basement to connect new gas tanks for the soda machines, when I came back up the stairs, Lenny summoned me over to the big stainless steel sink where he was washing a round bun tray. I thought it was odd, though, because it was early to be washing a tray.

"What's goin' on, brother?" he asked.

"Nothing much," I said.

"Yo, my man, I was thinkin' about you just last night, because our champ, Muhammad Ali, was on the Johnny Carson show. Did you watch, brother?" Knowing I was a big fan, Lenny liked talking about Muhammad Ali with me.

"Oh no, I'm in bed by then."

"Oh, right...right...good man. Well, Lenny was thinkin' about you anyways because the Champ started sparrin' with Johnny and I near about laughed myself to death. You know how he clowns around? I thought, my man Gabe would dig this. Funny shit, man. Ali's not only the greatest boxer I ever saw, but that cat is one of the funniest dudes anywhere. He'll be champ again soon...no worries about that."

"I hope so." I liked listening to Lenny call people cats and use other jive talk. I wondered if black people had picked up talk like that from beatniks or if it was the other way around.

"So what else is goin' on, brother?"

I just shrugged. "I don't know...nothing, I guess."

"Oh, you can't fool me, my man. Lenny knows when somethin' ain't quite right."

"What do you mean?" I asked.

"What I mean is you ain't your normal effervescent self. And there is most definitely something not cool between you and tonight's boss man." I liked how Lenny liked to sprinkle big words into our conversations.

"Michael, you mean?" I responded, figuring that's what he was implying.

"Right on, my man."

"Is it that noticeable?"

"Sweet Jesus, it sure is."

"Well…I don't know. I'm just struggling with a girl problem, but I don't want to talk to him about it, so he's not completely thrilled with me right now."

"I see…I see. I have had a few of them kind of problems myself. Women can most indubitably make us men go round and round and lose our minds…that's for damn sure…but we have to keep our wits about us, bro. Catch my drift? If you need any advice about women, you just let Lenny know. I got *lots* of experiences with the ladies if you know what I mean. I'm willing to bet all the tea in China that you're stuck on some lovely young lady!"

If he only knew, I thought to myself, but except for Jeff, nobody knew.

"Thanks, Lenny…I appreciate it." And I did appreciate it. The only thing was, even someone with a lot of experience with women couldn't help me with my problem.

When Tuesday morning arrives, Helen is proactive, waking Daryl at 7:00 and supervising his getting ready. His resentment is palpable, but he cooperates.

When they arrive at school, they are awaited by Mr. Lanzieri, the principal, Mrs. Blevins, Daryl's guidance counselor, and Coach Flaherty.

"I think we all know why we're here, Daryl," Mr. Lanzieri begins.

Staring at the floor, Daryl remains silent.

"We know you must be upset at the loss of your sister," Mrs. Blevins adds, trying too hard for Daryl's liking. "But the best thing to do is get back to the real world. And we're here to help you do just that. Running away from life isn't the best way to deal with your grief, sweetie."

"And the guys on the team really miss you, Daryl," the coach interjects.

Without looking up, Daryl sighs but continues to remain silent.

"What do you have to say, Daryl?" asks Mr. Lanzieri. "It's okay to tell us how you're really feeling."

Daryl merely shakes his head and shrugs.

"It doesn't seem like Daryl is comfortable talking right now," Mrs. Blevins says.

Ignoring Mrs. Blevins, Coach Flaherty pushes forward, "Well, listen Daryl, how about you come to practice this afternoon and get back in the swing of things? Like I said, the guys miss you, and we got a big game coming up with Shelton on Saturday. We're going to need you. Then, tomorrow, you come back to school, and everything will start getting back to normal."

Looking up on the word *normal*, as if the word itself has woken Daryl from a deep sleep, he asks with a puzzled expression, "What's normal?"

The adults find themselves at a momentary loss for words.

Slowly and gently, Mr. Lanzieri responds. "Daryl, I know you and your family have been through a lot. More than any family should have to contend with. But normal is coming back to school, being with your friends. Normal is getting ready for college. Normal is playing sports...especially football."

Like the word *normal*, the word *football* jolts Daryl. With a deep sigh, he says, "Okay, I'll be normal if that's what you want. I'll start coming to school again…but I...uhm...I'm not playing football anymore."

Daryl's remarks leave the adults in the room in stunned silence. Then Coach Flaherty, unable to control his emotions, pierces the uncomfortable stillness. "Why would you say that Daryl? I mean, really — why would you ever say that? You're the finest athlete on the team...the best in the Valley...and one of...one of the best in the state. A coach only gets a kid like you once or twice in his career. You understand, I hope, that several college coaches are writing to me about you. The University of New Hampshire...Wake Forest... Northeastern...others. When the season ends in a few weeks, there will be more inquiries about you. For Christ's sake, Daryl, if your grades were a smidge better, I could get you into Harvard or Yale. A college scholarship is in your future, Daryl, and believe me, while that may not be normal for everyone, it is normal for you!" The crescendo and the edge in Coach Flaherty's voice has caused concern for the other adults in the room. Their eyes suggest to Coach Flaherty that perhaps he has gone too far. After a beat, feeling defeated, he says, "Listen, Daryl...I'm sorry. I just don't...I don't understand why you feel the way you feel."

Daryl slowly rises from the oak office chair he is sitting in. "I feel the way I feel," he says, glancing down sideways at his mother, "because football is...let's just say...football...is...ridiculous. So here's the deal," he continues soberly, "I'll be in school tomorrow and for the rest of the year, but I won't be playing football…or any sport for that matter."

"Now listen, Daryl," Mr. Lanzieri begins to say.

But Daryl almost mechanically raises his arm and, with his flat palm, signals the principal to stop talking. "Look," he says, unemotionally, "no disrespect to you, Mr. Lanzieri, but I'm not doin' this anymore. I told you what I'll do and what I won't do. You'll see me in school tomorrow, but right now I gotta get outta here." Having made his point, Daryl darts out of the office in giant strides, leaving the four bewildered adults staring at each other in silence.

As Daryl approaches the exit doors, Ben Andrews and another fellow player turn the corner.

"Hey, Daryl," Ben says. "What's up, man? You coming to practice today?"

Daryl stops in his tracks, momentarily startled by the greeting, but then, without a word, resumes his departure from the building, bursting out the door and into the cool morning air.

11

When Thanksgiving arrived, Derby was still undefeated. Seymour had given them a big scare, but Michael and I had high hopes for our hometown team. The Derby-Shelton game was a storied rivalry, although for the last seven or eight years, the stories had had a happy ending for Derby and a sad one for Shelton. I think the last time Shelton won on Thanksgiving was in 1776! Last year, I had snuck onto the field, and I was standing nearby to an assistant coach, Coach Cappiello, a typing teacher, who was praying that Shelton would score. As Derby slaughtered Shelton, Coach Cappiello kept repeating, "Please, God...let our kids score! Please!" What can you expect from a typing teacher? The problem as I see it is I don't actually think God cares who wins a football game. In fact, I'd bet my life on it.

This year I hoped the Shelton coaching staff would do more coaching and less praying. Once again, we were at Derby's Ryan Field, and the place was so packed that we had to stand on the hill above the Derby bleachers, practically in the woods. And we weren't the only ones. Derby raced onto the field, swarming into their traditional pre-game whirlwind with Adamo, the last one out, catapulting high into the air and landing on top of the circular red and white mass. The pathetic Derby band could hardly be heard playing their fight song as the crowd went bananas. Shelton had a much better band than Derby, but that didn't amount to much in the world of what was important to the crowd. If you don't win, who cares if you have seven tubas with the letters S-H-E-L-T-O-N spelled out on the circular bells of the big gold instruments? Michael even remarked, "Look how big those tuba players are. They should be on the team."

Michael and I had reasons to be optimistic. Derby had a big line, but our Shelton line was huge. All of them were well over two hundred pounds — like, probably averaging 230. Manny Masucci and Tim Mendick were giants, the size of NFL linemen. I'm not sure either of them were great athletes, probably not, but they were sure big. Dennis Quinn and Jimmy Gallo weren't as tall, but they were wide, bulky bodies, to say the least. Dennis, a neighborhood kid, once told me the way to gain weight is to stuff yourself with a lot of food and then lay down and do nothing all day. I'm not so sure that's the recipe for being a great football player, though. Billy Romelis was tall and muscular. Our skill players were good too, especially Danny Mueller. Danny was only a year ahead of me in school, and we had gone to St. Joseph School together. I'll never forget the day that Sister Mary Andrew, during music class, made Danny sit on the floor and then grabbed him by his Elvis Presley hairdo and rammed his head into the stage because he was talking when she was teaching the baritones their harmony. Danny found out that you don't mess with Sister Mary Andrew. It goes without saying that Danny never talked again while Sister was teaching harmonies.

But back to football, Danny had run wild in a close victory against Seymour just two weeks before. In Seymour's defense, though, they had been devastated not only by their loss to Derby but especially by the loss of Daryl Novak, who had stopped showing up to practice. Apparently, from what we had heard, Novak had just up and quit the team. People said that the coach and just about everyone else had tried to talk to him, but the word at Duchess and around the Valley was that the kid had just shut down. I didn't really know what to make of that except to say when I heard about it, I thought, he must be majorly bummed out about his sister's death. Anyway, Seymour without Daryl Novak just wasn't Seymour. He and Ben Andrews were the perfect tandem, unmatched by any other in the recent history of high school football. Seymour had played hard against Shelton, but Andrews didn't have that superstar to pass the ball to, and Mueller simply played an inspired game.

What was interesting about that game, though, was that, even without Daryl, Seymour managed to jump out to a 21-0 halftime lead over Shelton. It was looking bleak, but as I watched the Shelton team come running out of the locker room at the end of halftime, Mueller's dad intercepted Danny as he was trotting by and started to beat on his chest with his right fist while grabbing onto Danny's face mask with his left. "What's the matter with you?" his father screamed in a gruff voice. "What in Christ is the matter with you? Do something! Will ya do something?" I could see Danny's eyes through the hard, plastic mask of his orange helmet. He looked shocked — shocked and horrified. I felt awful for him. It's a well known fact in town that Danny's dad is a drunk. Sometimes when Jeff and I and some of the neighborhood kids are playing hoop on the playground, it's not unusual to see Mr. Mueller staggering by, probably after more than a few drinks at a downtown bar. I guess everybody has their problems. And after Mr. Mueller's antics, Seymour had a problem of their own named Danny Mueller. Danny ran for four touchdowns in the second half using speed, agility, and finesse...not to mention the fact that he was probably feeling a lot of bottled up anger because of his dad's halftime antics. One second there was a would-be tackler right in front of Danny, and the next second Danny was in the end zone. He was a beautiful looking athlete, not unlike Daryl Novak, even though they played different positions.

While we thought of Frankie Adamo as a hard-nosed Jim Brown kind of runner, Danny Mueller's style of play was more like the great Gale Sayers who was one of my personal favorite athletes in any sport. I mean, a few years ago, Sayers scored six touchdowns in a single game against the 49ers, which is an NFL record, matched only by Dub Jones in 1951, whoever Dub Jones was. Danny wouldn't have the kind of game he had in Seymour on Thanksgiving morning, though, nor would he resemble Gale Sayers in any manner, shape, or form. Maybe Big Sal Costanzo knew the way to stop Shelton was to shut down Mueller. Maybe Danny's father hadn't given him a "motivational talk" this time like the one I had witnessed in Seymour. The truth is, Michael was becoming so frustrated with how ineffective Danny was that I almost had to hold him back for fear he would walk onto the field and grab Danny's face mask and start yelling at him like Mr. Mueller had done in Seymour. I wouldn't put such behavior past Michael, and he's not even a drunk.

Frankie Adamo, on the other hand, had his usual stellar game, running for 128 hard-earned yards and both of Derby's two touchdowns. On one score, Adamo ran right into my friend, big Dennis Quinn, knocked him on his rear end, and bounced off Dennis into the end zone. *Nice tackle, Dennis,* I said to myself. Derby ended up winning the game 15-6, which seems close, but the score didn't really indicate how not so close the game was. For the most part, Derby rendered Danny Mueller and Shelton completely ineffective, not even allowing one first down. Shelton had just one big play, actually. At the end of the second quarter, with Derby ahead 7-0, the Shelton fullback, a junior named Billy Montelli, took the handoff on the Shelton 42 yard line and burst through the center of the line with nothing between himself and the goal line except daylight. Either something broke down in Derby's defense or that big Shelton line got temporarily inspired and opened a hole as big as the Grand Canyon. Let me just put it this way — I could have even scored that touchdown. I think it was the only touchdown Montelli had scored all season. In fact, used as a blocking back for Mueller, Montelli hardly ever even touched the ball. Maybe it was the element of surprise. Give the ball to a kid who never gets the ball. The Shelton kicker missed the extra point, and the score at the half was 7-6, which felt pretty good to Michael and me. He even bought me a hotdog at halftime.

Derby came out after halftime, marched down the field in a series of eleven plays, and scored their second touchdown when Adamo banged his way into the end zone from the 2 yard line. They went for the two point conversion, and this time Adamo took a lateral on a patented Derby end sweep, and the score was 15-6, which is how it would end up. The rest of the game was a defensive struggle with neither team giving away an inch.

Like Seymour, Shelton finished the season at 8-2. So did Ansonia, having only been beaten by Derby and Shelton. It seemed like the only teams that could beat Valley high school teams were each other. I mean, here's the deal — football is a way of life in the Lower Naugatuck Valley. The big newspapers around the state in New Haven, Bridgeport, Hartford, Danbury and New London (and probably other cities) pool their resources to create a weekly Writers' Top Ten Poll, and the writers always have their eye on the Valley. Derby had been the preseason number one team, and, after beating a Seymour team with two of the best football players in the state and almost completely shutting down a strong Shelton team, Derby finished the season as the state champion.

Not surprisingly, the loss spoiled Michael's Thanksgiving dinner, and it didn't do much for mine either. He said nothing during the meal. He just wolfed down his turkey, and then he took off in the Corvair immediately after dinner. Who knows where he went? Who ever knew? Of course, I was still preoccupied with the accident. In the few weeks since the funeral when I worked at Duchess, Daryl Novak was always around, sitting in his beat up VW Bug in the parking lot. Big Alfred Bridges, our nighttime bouncer, complained that he had to send him on his way lots of times because he was just hanging out, listening to music on his radio.

I remember Alfred coming in from the lot the night before Thanksgiving and saying to Michael, "I hadda throw that Seymour boy off the lot again. Why's he not playin' football no more?"

"After his sister got killed, he just quit everything," Michael replied. "I guess he's too upset." I heard Michael's patented sarcasm in his voice.

Alfred shook his head, "A shame. I seen that boy play, and he was real good!"

"Dig it," agreed Michael.

When Alfred would give Daryl the heave-ho, Daryl would shift his Bug into first and chug out of the parking lot slowly, but soon he'd be back, circling the building, and then drive right back onto Pershing Drive. Ten or fifteen minutes later, he'd drive right back in. That wasn't so unusual, though. Lots of guys cruised up and down Pershing Drive, between Duchess and the Bradlees Plaza or Valley Bowl, which are right across from each other. Sometimes when Jeff and I hang out with my cousin Tomaso, who has his license, we do the same thing. We drive into the Bradlees Plaza and swing by Friendly's to see if we know any of the waitresses, cross the road to the Valley Bowl lot, and then we drive through the Duchess lot to see who's hanging around there. It's a way to kill time.

The weird thing I started to notice about Daryl Novak's cruising is he seemed to be all alone. Who cruised alone? Where were his friends, Ben Andrews and the other Seymour football players? Daryl, it seemed, had become a loner overnight. When he came to the window, I noticed something else. He always looked out of it, like he was completely drunk...or high. With bloodshot eyes and a glazed look on his face, he'd say, "How about a large fry and a chocolate shake, guys?" I would try hard to make it look like I didn't even notice him, but I don't know how successful I was because once in a while we'd make eye contact. Not like he had a problem or anything. I wondered if he and I had actually made eye contact at Susanna's funeral like I thought we had, and, if so, did he remember seeing me?

On the Tuesday after Thanksgiving, it was really slow as closing time approached. Karl Fischer was in the back at the big sink, washing the trays, and Craig Betts had slipped into the office to count the cash. Cleaning the lot had been a piece of cake, and I had just finished wiping down the stainless steel on the fryers and soda machines, and, with ten minutes until we were officially closed, there was nothing left for me to do. To pass the time, I pulled out *On the Road*, which I was three-quarters of the way through, opened the book on the counter, and began reading.

After a few minutes, I heard someone say, "Yo, anybody workin' here?" It was Novak.

"Oh, sorry," I said, startled. "Yeah we're working. There's not much left, though, because we're about to close."

"Whatcha got, man?"

I looked in the bin. "Looks like we have one hamburger, one cheeseburger, and a few bags of fries."

Slurring some of his words, he said, "O-kay, Dushess, bag it up. I'll take it all. And pour me a large root beer, too."

I knew how to ring up an order, and Craig Betts was busy, so I decided to take care of it myself.

When I put the order on the counter, Novak asked, "What do I owe you?"

"Free of charge," I said. When he gave me a surprised look, I added, "We were just going to throw it out, anyway." I had seen Michael do the same thing on countless occasions when we worked together, but it was bold of me, not even being of official working age, to make such a decision. *If Craig Betts comes out of the office right now, it's going to be awkward,* I thought.

"Thanks, Dushess. Yer a good kid! You can go read your book now. Maybe I'll see ya around sometime."

As I watched Daryl exit the vestibule my eyes followed him as he walked across the parking lot to his car. Thinking of how sad Susanna's death had made me, I could only imagine how Daryl must be feeling. Craig Betts burst out of the office. He was a guy who always walked like he had somewhere to be that was way more important than where anyone else had to be. "It's 11:00. Time to lock the doors," Betts called out. In one fluid motion, he hoisted his butt up onto the counter, slid through the window opening, and then locked the two doors in the vestibule. Making the same sliding motion in reverse, his feet hit the floor on the inside of the store, and he said, "You all set, DeMarco?" not even making eye contact with me. I hated people who called me by my last name. Craig Betts never addressed me as Gabriel, and unless he was ordering me around or yelling at me, he never looked at me.

"Yeah, I've cleaned up everything."

"What a dull night," he responded, heading into the office. "Well, give the parking lot a quick look and pick up anything that might be left out there, and then you can shove off."

He was too self-absorbed to realize I didn't have a ride. Often, Michael or my cousin Tomaso worked the same shift as me, so I was usually all set for a ride home. And even when we weren't working the same shift, while I might have had to hitchhike to work, Michael was usually hanging out at the end of the night, so I was covered on the back end. If Michael wasn't working the shift or hanging out, there was usually someone else I could ask for a ride, where it didn't seem like too much of an inconvenience. Tonight, though, was different. I didn't like Craig Betts, and none of us liked the usually drunk Karl Fischer. Besides, both Betts and Fischer weren't going my way. So when I was all set, I just yelled "good night" at the back door. Neither of them responded. I was sure hoping Michael would drive through, but no luck. My only option was to hitchhike home.

I looked at my watch. 11:10. I had never hitchhiked at night by myself. As I walked down Pershing Drive, I started thinking that the technique I had used probably wasn't going to work too well in the dark. The thing is, a successful hitchhiker needs to be something of an actor. First and foremost, you want to look like someone the driver wouldn't totally hate picking up. So, the first thing to do is to scope out who's behind the wheel and look like someone that particular driver might be willing to stop for, especially if it's a lady. In that case, and with all adults, you just want to basically look like a nice kid, which isn't too hard for me because, frankly, that's what I am. You just flash this kind of wholesome, innocent look on your face to assure the adult driver that you're not a murderer or anything like that. It's important to try to make eye contact and plead with your eyes. Pleading with your eyes is key. It also helps if you hold your thumb kind of high in the air even though doing so makes you look like a big geek, because if you hold it way down low, the adult will probably think you look like too much of a punk. If the driver is another teen, then it's okay to hold your thumb down low because he might think you look cool. It's all about knowing who's behind the wheel and creating the right perception. Still, lots of people just pass you by trying to pretend they don't see you no matter how much you plead with your eyes and no matter how high you hold up your thumb. They don't fool me with that, though. When they pass me by, depending on how soon I need to get to my destination or how sick and tired I am of hitchhiking, I often turn toward the rear end of the car, now distancing itself from me and throw my arms up in frustration, hoping they'll see me through a cloud of exhaust fumes. Sometimes, I'll even call out something, like, "Are you so great and I'm such a loser that you can't even pick me up?" I'm guessing Michael would get more to the point and call out something more interesting like, "Well, you can just go fuck yourself!" I'm almost sure that's what he'd say.

I have been picked up by all kinds of people, not just your run of the mill adult. I'll never, for the rest of my life, forget hitchhiking to Duchess and being picked up by a beautiful girl with long, strawberry blonde hair that ended at her shoulders in round curls. She was maybe seventeen years old and driving this amazing old pickup truck — maybe like a 1950-something Chevy truck. For me, it was love at first sight. Her leather sandals sat on the seat between us. She had on a mini-dress with a pattern of little purple flowers, and she sat way forward on the spacious seat because her perfect feet barely reached the gas pedal, the brake, and the clutch. I was sure fascinated as she maneuvered the shift on the big steering column from one gear to another like she was driving in the Indianapolis 500. Many times after, hitchhiking from the same spot, I hoped that she would come by in that old truck again, but she never did. I began to think I was suffering from delusions and that I had never been picked up by such a beautiful girl, but that's how it is with girls. One minute they're in your life, and the next minute they're out.

There was also the time Jeff and I were hitchhiking to a dance at the Huntington Grange, and we got picked up by a souped up Mustang with three kids in it. We piled in with the one in the back. I immediately smelled something strange. They were passing around a paper bag with airplane glue in it, taking turns sniffing the stuff. On top of that, they were also passing around a bottle of Seagrams 7. They offered us a swig or a sniff, but Jeff and I politely declined. I think I got high just from being in the car. The driver sped at what must have been close to a hundred miles an hour along the narrow, winding roads of Shelton Avenue to Huntington while simultaneously gulping down mouthfuls of whiskey or grabbing quick breaths of gluey fumes from the paper bag. The last person you want to be picked up by when hitchhiking is a guy who's sniffing glue and drinking whiskey at the same time. I was sure Jeff and I were going to die that night.

My immediate problem was that a driver probably wasn't going to see my pleading eyes on a dark night. When I got down to the Bradlees Plaza, I stuck my thumb out and hoped for the best. Because it was too dark to read during the lull between cars passing by, I just let my mind wander to wherever it felt like going. I don't know about anybody else, but my mind has a mind of its own. I could see the giant Bradlees red letters illuminating the night, and I remembered being a little kid and going to the big department store with my parents. I would try to work up the courage to ask my dad if I could have a dime to put in the gum machine that dispensed little plastic containers with cheap toys in them. I guess I had been scared to ask Dad because he typically remarked that the little toys were just junk, which was the truth, but he usually gave me the dime anyway. I also remembered that when Michael had first begun working at Duchess at sixteen, he used to often come home with records by the Beatles and some other top groups that he bought at Bradlees. It was always exciting to see what new 45 Michael would show up with and to listen to the A side, which was always a hit song, and then listen to the B side, which, in the case of the Beatles was also usually a hit, but for other groups was typically some unknown song, sometimes good and sometimes not so good.

Quite a few cars zoomed by like I wasn't even there, and, after ten or fifteen minutes, it wasn't looking promising. Suddenly, it started to rain, which I was not expecting. *Oh, just perfect,* I thought to myself. Hitchhiking in the rain is absolutely no fun at all, but you just kind of hang in there and deal with it. It wasn't the first time, and I knew it wouldn't be the last. In just a matter of a few minutes, my hair was sopping wet and flat against my head and my sweatshirt was drenched. Finally, a VW Bug with what appeared to be a broken muffler began to slow and pull over by the shoulder of the road. I was a little nervous because I wasn't used to hitching this late at night, especially by myself.

As I got into the car, I said to the driver, "Hi, thanks for stopping, I really appreciate it."

"Yo, Dushess," I heard the driver bellow. "It's my little buddy who gave me free food. Thanks, man...I was so starved, I wolfed it down in about point two seconds." There sat Daryl Novak behind the wheel chugging beer from a very large brown bottle. Pulling the bottle out of his mouth, he belched and asked, "Where to?"

While I had seen him in our lot in his Bug, I wasn't expecting him to be heading on Route 8 toward Shelton, so it hadn't occurred to me that it might be him. I was just happy someone stopped, though. I was still pretty stunned to be sitting next to the great Daryl Novak in his junker of a car. Sitting there in a ragged army jacket and a button down cap, he shifted into first and continued sucking on the bottle as he moved into second, third, and beyond. It was the biggest bottle of beer I had ever seen. It must have been at least a quart bottle, if not a two quart bottle, which seemed unusual to me since I had never seen anyone drink out of anything but a normal twelve ounce can or bottle.

"Uhm...I'm going home...to...to...Shelton," I stammered, "Just off of Exit 14. Maybe a minute off the exit. If that's not too far. I mean, if that's okay with you."

"Yeah, don't worry about it, Dushess. You look a little wet there, buddy," Novak said with a chuckle, and then he took another gulp.

"Yeah, I guess I am," I said with a laugh. "Thank God you picked me up, but listen, I don't want to make you go out of your way," I said. "If you were only going to Exit 15, you can drop me off in downtown Derby, and I can walk the rest of the way. I guess I can't get much wetter than I already am. I mean...I think you live in Seymour, right?"

"Yeah, that's right, Dushess, I live in Seymour, but don't you sweat it. I ain't got nowhere fuckin' special to be, and, besides, I don't let good kids like you walk in the rain," he said as the Bug barked its way onto Route 8.

"Oh, okay," I responded. "I really appreciate that."

"That's nice, Dushess. I'm glad you appreciate it," he said, with a hint of sarcasm. He seemed to be amused by me. Pushing the bottle toward me, he said, "Now shut up and take a swig of this. It'll do ya some good." As he pushed the bottle into my chest, I could see the Ballantine's label with its signature three rings.

"Who me? Oh, no thanks. I don't really...I don't....drink...but I appreciate the offer."

"You don't drink?" he responded, raising his eyebrows. "Hmmm, we're gonna have to do somethin' about that one, Dushess." He shook his head, as if it was some kind of malady...as if there was actually something to do about someone who doesn't drink. And with that, he started chugging down more beer. It was hard to tell if he could see the road in front of him beyond the thick, round base of the glass bottle. I found myself worrying if we'd make it to Shelton safely.

He sped down the ramp of Exit 14 without braking at all, or so it seemed. At the bottom of the ramp, he skidded to a short stop just shy of the light, and then, looking straight ahead, he asked, "Lef' or right, Dushess?"

"Oh, yeah...either," I said, with some confusion. "I mean, you can go either way, but...uhm...I guess maybe the quickest route is to take a right and then a quick left."

Giving the quickest route probably wasn't the best idea because the quick left was on to the bottom of Maltby Street, which is probably the steepest hill in Shelton. That meant he had to downshift to a lower gear to get the momentum to take the hill. Not being in a state of mind to react quickly, it was a challenge for him.

"This is quite a fuckin' hill, Dushess. The ol' Bug is jus' about gonna make it."

Another block and we arrived at my house. "Thanks a lot," I said as I opened the door and stepped out of the Bug. "It was really nice of you to go out of your way to give me a lift home."

"Yeah, don't worry about it. No big thing. Anyways, one good turn deserves another. Nex' time, you're gonna have to help me drink this beer, though. And thanks for the free food, Dushess."

"Oh, yeah...yeah," I replied. "Yeah, definitely...definitely." I have an annoying habit of repeating myself when I'm nervous. "Well, thanks...thanks again."

And as he drove away, I worried that the unmuffled sound of his engine would wake up the entire neighborhood. As I coughed from inhaling in the exhaust fumes, I felt a little dizzy, but I think it was more than just the carbon monoxide. Had I just been given a ride by and talked to the great Daryl Novak? Let me put it this way. Playing on our school JV basketball team, I am sometimes on the court with seniors who are major athletes in Shelton. The thing is, outside of practice, those guys wouldn't give me the right time of day. Most of them would have probably driven by me if I was hitchhiking in the middle of a blizzard. And another thing is, not to be crude, but none of those guys could fit in Daryl Novak's jockstrap. And here was Daryl who not only picked me up but really talked to me, almost like we knew each other, and who called me by a nickname, almost like we were friends, and who invited me to drink some of his beer, and who thanked me for giving him some lousy food we were just going to throw out anyway. Oh yeah….and just before he took off, he told me next time I was going to have to help drink the beer. *Hmmm,* I thought. *Next time. Would there really be a next time?*

12

Thanksgiving and Christmas came and went. Our family had the usual routine. We went to our grandparents' house both on Christmas Eve night and Christmas Day. Well, except on Christmas Eve, Michael was not in attendance. Several years before, he had found other ways to occupy himself on Christmas Eve, whatever they were. In fact, at about sixteen, Michael had even begun to remove himself from Sunday gatherings at our grandparents' house, which in an Italian family like ours is a regular thing. It started with an early morning disappearing act. When everyone rolled out of bed late on a Sunday morning, Michael was nowhere to be found, and we didn't see him until early or mid-evening. I was surprised that no conflict ensued because, while he was in high school, Michael and our dad were always going at it. I could still tell from my father's facial expressions and body language, though, that he didn't like Michael not visiting with the grandparents one little bit, although Michael still joined us on Christmas afternoon at Nonna and Grampa's.

I myself continue to still be in attendance every Sunday and on all holidays, including midnight mass, which quite honestly is getting old even for me. An important function of being a younger brother is sometimes you have to pick up the slack and make up for the sins of your older sibling. At least that was the role I played and continue to play in our family. On holidays, tables are put end to end to create the longest dining table I've ever sat at. The traditional meal begins with a delicious Italian Wedding Soup and ends with sfogliatella and other pastries baked by our Aunt Sofia. In between is a sumptuous Italian meal. All told, there are usually nearly fifty of us on Christmas Day, including aunts, uncles, cousins, and Grampa and Nonna, the latter of whom doesn't speak a word of English. Grampa speaks a little.

For some reason, Grampa seems to like me. He and I have had our own little routine for the last three years or so. Each Sunday, after parking the car on the street, we walk up the long incline of the asphalt driveway to the back door. Weather permitting, white haired Grampa will be sitting in a lawn chair next to the ramshackle garage, clad in baggy trousers, t-shirt and suspenders, and his old Fedora hat, with a pipe dangling from his lips. Upon seeing us, I am the only one he addresses.

"Hey, Alberini," he calls, addressing me by a variation of my mother's maiden name, Alberino. I think it means "Little Alberino." Maybe he thinks I look like her or take after her, and I kind of think, for unknown reasons, he likes that.

"Hi Gramp," I reply, kissing him on his stubbly cheek as a sign of love and respect — and because my father will murder me if I don't.

"Tell-a me, Alberini," he asks, "you got a girl-a-friend?"

"Oh yeah, Gramp, I've got two," I tease back.

"Ahhhh, you little som-a-na-beetch," he growls, and bursts into gravelly laughter.

The language of the day on Sundays and holidays, though, is Italian, which I assume the adults speak so that my grandparents feel included in the conversation. Oddly, Michael and I haven't ever picked up our family's native language.

Christmas had fallen on a Monday that year, and the next night, I found myself on the night crew at Duchess with Michael and Karl Fischer. Our cousin Tomaso, who started working at Duchess a year before me, was hanging around that night. My Uncle Marcello and my Aunt Lucia, who are both older than my dad, had been born in Italy, so they named Tomaso something real Italian, but we usually just called him "Tommy Trouble." Of course, Michael, the master of nicknames, bestowed that name on him because Tomaso is always pulling a prank of one kind or another when we least expect it. Anyway, it's completely normal for an employee to be hanging out in the parking lot because Duchess is, after all, the Valley hangout for about a zillion and seventy-five kids. It's also a regular thing for an employee to come into the store and B.S. with us when things are slow. By the same token, if we get slammed at night — like, if an away-team bus pulls in after a basketball game, any employees in the parking lot will come to the rescue, helping to dress hamburger buns, get drinks, and cook "specials." Duchess is, in that sense, a brotherhood.

Anyway, the point is, Tommy Trouble, whose brain is always stirring the pot and thinking of ways to play practical jokes on people, was hanging out that night. There must have been a full moon because between mischievous Tommy Trouble, intoxicated Karl Fischer, and what was to come at closing time, it was a wild ride for me. It started when I was reaching down to the shelves below the soda machine to get some new sleeves of drink cups, and Tommy Trouble snuck up behind me with the ketchup squirter, lifted the paper Duchess hat off my head and plopped a hamburger bun-sized dab into my hair. I was ticked.

"You jerk," I moaned, wiping the red goo off of my head and onto my apron. I grabbed handfuls of ice and began rolling them into hard balls. Tomaso began to emit that throaty laugh of his as he backed out beyond the grill to the back door. He knew he was in trouble.

"You assholes better knock it off," Karl warned, as if we were going to listen to anything he said.

Tomaso is a stocky guy, a big target, and as he got near the back door, I hurled an ice ball at him full force. He ducked and it splatted against the door. That sent us both into a fit of laughter because neither of us could believe I missed at such close range. Now Tomaso backed completely out of the door, and I followed in hot pursuit. Running around the building, I chucked the second ice ball at him, hitting his big body squarely in the back. Bullseye! There was a border of snow around the parking lot from a storm the week before, and Tommy Trouble and I began to make snowballs and fire them at each other while circling the building, in spite of the customers in the lot. Strategically maneuvering around the building, we continued pelting each other with the hard, white ammunition. Michael allowed our antics to go on for about ten or fifteen minutes, and then he came to the back door and ordered us back in. Tomaso and I entered the building laughing and out of breath.

Michael said, "You two need to stop the horseplay now, before you regret it."

"We were just having a little fun," Tomaso said sheepishly.

"A little too much fun," Michael shot back sternly. "You're always having a little too much fun. If Howie popped in, he'd get rid of both of you, and it would be your own damned faults."

The presence of a customer at the window interrupted the conversation, although Tommy Trouble was not going to challenge Michael because he looks up to my brother almost as much as I do. The customer at the window was Daryl Novak. He was still around just about every night — or at least every night that I worked. Still alone in his Bug doing and thinking God knows what. Still being sent on his way by Big Alfred who wasn't on tonight. Simply, Daryl was still a mystery to all of us.

Even though he was around all the time, the last time Daryl had spoken to me was the night he had picked me up hitchhiking, about a month before. Maybe he didn't want anyone to know we knew each other. That was probably best, actually.

On this night, after ordering and paying for his food and drink, Daryl remarked, "Nice snowball fight, guys," and then he nodded toward me. "I think the skinny kid won."

"Thanks," I said, my cheeks feeling warmth rise into them.

After Daryl left the building, Michael remarked, "That guy is really kooked out now," shaking his head. "Gave up sports and everything. It's too bad. He was so good."

"Yeah," Karl chimed in. "What a waste of humanity."

"Aw, leave the kid alone," I defensively offered. "He's alright."

"Why?" Tomaso asked. "Do you know him or something?"

"How would I know him?" I responded defensively. "It's just that he's not bothering anybody, so I think people should lay off him. He just got a tough break, that's all."

"Ooooh-kay," Tomaso said exaggeratedly, and Michael's eyes and mine met briefly. He squinted at me again, with that same judgmental gaze he gave me the day after Susanna's accident.

With a deep sigh, I said, "I need to cook up another basket of fries, which should get us through closing," and I turned away from them.

Things got stirred up again at about 10:30 when a guy about nineteen or twenty came in. Tommy Trouble and I were talking by the shake machine, Karl was reading the sports page of the Daily News by the grill, and Michael was in the back office, starting to count the money and close out for the night.

Upon seeing the long-haired guy at the counter, Karl crossed his arms up on the high counter over the grill, and said, with exaggerated politeness, "May we help you, miss?" The kid gave Karl a dirty look.

"Boys," Karl almost sang, "would you tell the window man there's a pretty girl at the window who wants to be waited on?"

Shaking his head in disgust, the kid pushed away from the counter and burst through the exit back out into the parking lot. He must have decided Karl wasn't worth getting himself arrested for.

"That wasn't cool, Karl," Tomaso said.

"Why not?" Karl asked, with the same patronizing tone he had addressed the kid. "When I see a pretty girl, I try to be nice to her."

"You knew it wasn't a girl, Karl," Tomaso pushed forward. "If the kid wants to wear his hair long, that's his business. Lots of guys have long hair nowadays, you know that."

When Tomaso isn't pranking somebody, he can really stand up for what he thinks is right. He and I might have worn our hair longer, but our high schools have dress codes. I guessed that the guy at the window was a few years out of high school, like Michael.

"Yeah," said Karl, his tone now becoming belligerent. "Well these fuckin' hippies can kiss my German ass."

"Okay, Karl," Tomaso replied, "let's all just calm down, man."

We knew Karl had probably had at least one beer too many before he arrived at work, which was how it often was with him.

"Fuck you, DeMarco! How about if I kick your ass?"

Wow, he's completely soused, I thought to myself.

"Hey, Karl," I said. "Cool down, man."

"Fuck you, too, you skinny fucker," Karl continued, saliva shooting out of his mouth as he lisped his next threat. "I'll kick your fat cousin's ass and yours too." *Where was Michael?* I wondered. Karl looked like a trapped animal, with his unshaven face, his drooling mouth, and his bloodshot, demented eyes.

"You DeMarcos think you're so fuckin' great! How about I take on all three of you at once?" He staggered from the grill, getting much closer to us, his spit now spraying onto our clothes. "Get your brother and let's go out in the parking lot, and I'll show you fuckin' guineas how a real man fights!" I was stunned. My father had told us about how he had been called a guinea when he was a kid, but I had never heard anyone use the word against someone my age...against me.

Miraculously, the office door sprang open. Like the Archangel Michael himself, my brother's tall, powerful frame filled the doorway. The only thing that was missing was the sword.

"What's going on out here, guys?" Michael asked, glaring at the three of us. Then the glare shifted to a deeply serious expression where, with squinted eyes, he looked not only puzzled in the moment, but also utterly confused as if suddenly observing something he would never, ever be able to comprehend...a look that left no doubt in anyone's mind that Michael didn't like what he didn't understand. Not one little bit.

"Uhm," Tomaso hesitated. "I guess we were having a little disagreement."

"Oh, yeah? Are we all okay here, Karl?" Michael asked with an intensity and an assertiveness that really grabbed your attention.

"Yeah, we're just Jim fuckin' Dandy."

With that, Karl abruptly picked up a big burger tray, lifted it over his head, and staggered toward the back sink. He might have had second thoughts about messing with Michael.

"What the hell was that all about?" Michael asked Tomaso.

"Nothing," Tomaso said. "It's not important. It was stupid."

"Okay," Michael said. "Crazy night. Anyway, it's already a little after 11:00. I'm going to lock the doors and finish in the office. Gabe, you better go out and give the parking lot a last pick-up."

I passed Karl at the sink, dancing by him sideways in the tight space, as I headed for the back door. We didn't make eye contact. I grabbed a garbage can and pushed through the door. There wasn't much debris in the lot. It had been such a slow night, and I had hit the lot earlier. After rolling across the lot and picking up a half dozen or so cups and bags, I made my way to the dumpster in the back corner near the railroad tracks.

I jumped when a loud voice broke the quiet of the night. "Hey, Dushess, when are you going to give me some free food again?" It was Daryl. He was standing on the very top of a stationary cargo car on one of the train tracks, holding another large bottle of beer. He took a big gulp and called again, "Dushess, come up here and help me drink this beer, man!" The top of the car must have been almost twenty feet above me. He kicked at a powdery white mound of snow, causing his own man-made avalanche to fall on me. The cold snow stung my face and bare arms, since I only had a short-sleeved white work shirt on. *I should have put my coat on,* I thought to myself.

I found myself running toward the track. "Daryl what the hell are you doing up there? Get down! You'll get arrested...or fall off and kill yourself."

"Aww...c'mon, Dushess," he slurred. "Don' be a...a chicken shit all your life. Come up here an' have a snort with me."

"Daryl," I reasoned, "please come down from there. If anyone sees you, they're gonna call the cops, and you'll end up in jail."

"Okay, Dushess, yer probly right. Jus' hold this while I climb down the ladder," and, without further warning, he tossed his beer bottle high into the air like it was a juggling pin. In a futile effort to catch it, I looked up, but it disappeared above the parking lot lights into the black sky. At the last second, I ducked my head, like that would have helped if it had landed on me, and the bottle hit the gravel between the heavy wooden railway ties, shattering into millions of brown shards just a few feet away.

"Awww fuck, Dushess, ya broke it. I hope you don't play football cuz you got lousy han's."

"Daryl," I pleaded, "please come down. I'm trying to help you. This is nuts. You're acting crazy!"

"Yeah, ah'm actin' crazy. Yer right, I'll come down." And he grabbed the rungs of the steel ladder on the side of the car, climbing down and skipping rungs, like a long, tall monkey. He jumped backwards off the final rung and miraculously, although unsteadily, landed on his feet.

"Why'd ya break my beer bottle, Dushess?" he asked with sadness in his voice. "Now I don' have nothin' left to drink."

He ran over to another track, and started to walk on a steel rail, stretching his arms out horizontally and balancing himself like a tightrope walker. "C'mon, Dushess. Le's go for a walk. Follow me."

I began to trot alongside him next to the opposite rail. "This is a really bad idea, Daryl. I think a train comes by on one of these tracks in a few minutes." It was true. Every night at about 11:15, a passenger train from the New Haven Railroad passed behind the store. I had heard and seen it many nights when I was doing the lot.

"Yeah, well don' you worry about me, Dushess. I'm fine," he said, still doing his circus act, one foot or the other slipping off and then stumbling outside or inside of the track. Just as I had thought, we could now hear the train whistle, maybe only a minute or two away.

"Get off the track!" I shouted. It felt a little like I was harassing him, but I don't think it's harassment if you're trying to save some crazy, drunk person's life. His ears were deaf to me, anyway, as his unsteady tightrope act continued.

Still running and kind of skipping sideways alongside him, I cried, "Get off the track! This is insane, Daryl! You're going to get yourself fucking killed!"

"Don' worry about that! That won' matter to anybody, Dushess," he yelled, looking down at his unsteady feet on the rail.

The bright, round headlight on the locomotive now came into view in the distance. "What do you mean it doesn't matter, Daryl?" I screamed, "Of course it *fucking* matters. It matters to me! How about that? It matters to me — do you hear that? Get off the track!"

The train whistle was now screaming louder than I was. I wasn't sure if it was a standard, routine whistle, or if the train engineer saw us on the track and was sending out a warning. Either way, the monster wasn't slowing down.

I could hear the ominous sound of the whistle, wailing and shrieking its warning of impending doom, but the locomotive obviously wasn't going to stop. With a feverish wave of panic, I felt helpless. I yelled one last time, punctuating each word: "Get! Off! The! Fucking! Track!" Then, instinct just took over, and I barreled across the rail from my side onto the track and drove my shoulder into Daryl's mid-section, just the way I had seen Adamo hit him weeks before. Miraculously, I somehow knocked Daryl completely off balance, and both of us went tumbling into a mound of snow outside of the track. Within seconds the passenger train passed by us and continued on its way.

Startled, we sat on the icy ground, out of breath and staring at each other. "Nice tackle, Dushess," Daryl said quietly, as if he had somehow come to his senses. "Maybe you *could* play football. I mean, you ain't no Adamo, but tha' was still a pretty good fuckin' tackle, man," he said quietly.

"Yeah, well you almost got us both killed," I said angrily, and I felt my cheeks moist with what must have been tears, which I began to wipe away on my sleeve.

"Thanks, Dushess. You saved my life, man. I owe ya another one. I really do. Except, I'm real sorry to tell you this, man, but...uhm...it... isn't really worth savin'." His plaintive tone cut me.

"Listen, Daryl," I said, shaking my head and delivering the words slowly because I was out of breath. "What are you...what are you even...talking about? Of course it's worth saving."

"Gabe!" I heard Michael yell from the back door of the store.

I stood up, and, trying to catch my breath said, "Listen, Daryl. Now I need you to listen to me really good. I really have to go. Promise me you'll stop acting crazy and you'll go home and sober up...just promise me that."

He sat there calmly, like a little kid, in the snow and the gravel and smiled at me and said, "Sure, Dushess, you got it, buddy. Nothin' else crazy tonight." I couldn't believe this guy.

"*Gabriel,*" Michael yelled again, more sternly than before.

"I'm sorry...but I really gotta go now, Daryl," I said apologetically.

"That's cool, Dushess. Don' be sorry. You go. Like I said, I owe ya one. Make that two."

We had probably traveled fifty yards down the train track. Running back to the building, I saw Michael and Tomaso at the door. Trying to act natural, I shot a stream of questions at them, "We all set? Did Fischer go home? That guy's nuts, isn't he? I mean he's always a little crazy, but when he's drunk like this, he's certifiable!"

"Where the fuck were you?" Tomaso asked.

"Oh, I was just looking at some of these old railroad cars that are parked on the tracks," I lied. "It's practically a railroad museum, isn't it?"

Tomaso eyed me up and down skeptically, "How did your jeans get all wet?"

"Oh, they *are* wet, aren't they? I didn't even notice. I was so absorbed in looking at the construction of the cars that I tripped over one of the rails and fell into a mound of snow. Fascinating how they build these monstrosities." I hoped they bought my story.

"Monstrosities, huh? Since when have you been interested in train cars?" Michael asked, suspiciously.

"Since just recently. I was reading about them in our Britannicas at home. The history of the railroad is really interesting stuff. And important too. Anyway, back to Fischer. He's really crazy, isn't he?"

Michael gave me that look again. "I'm beginning to think *you're* crazy. In fact, sometimes I think you're a little fucked up in the head, and if nobody minds my saying so, this was a really fucked up night. You two goofballs are lucky you have me to keep an eye on you. Let's go home. Tomaso, we'll see you this weekend."

As we drove down Pershing Drive, I thought to myself that what Daryl said was true. I had sort of saved his life. It made me sad to think that I wasn't there to save his sister's life too. I should have introduced myself that night and asked her if she and her friends wanted to grab a bite to eat with me and Jeff. Who knows what might have happened if I had been with Susanna on Division Street that night? I might have been able to make a difference in the outcome the same as I had just done with Daryl.

"I hate to wake you up from your dream, Screwball, but we're home." Michael turned the car off and pulled the key out of the ignition. He tossed the towel that he had been wiping the fog off the windshield with into the back seat. The heat didn't work in the Corvair, so that meant the defroster didn't do its job either. And for some reason gas fumes often permeated the interior of the car, so we had to drive, even in winter, with the windows cracked open. I had been so lost in thought, I hadn't even been aware of the fogged up windshield or the frigid temperature or the fumes.

"Oh sorry," I said.

"What were you dreaming about? Trains?" he asked, with more than a hint of sarcasm.

"No. Not trains," I said embarrassedly. "Something else."

"Something you want to tell me about?"

"Uhm...well...do you mind if I ask you a question?"

"Nope," he said, "go for it."

"Have you ever saved anyone's life?"

"Not that I remember," he replied, "and I don't think it's exactly the kind of thing I would forget. Why? You planning on saving somebody's life anytime soon?"

"No," I said, hoping he didn't detect the uncertainty in my voice. "Nothing like that. I guess it was just a dopey dream I was having."

"Yeah, well it's too cold to talk about dopey dreams out here in this shit box. Let's go inside where it's warm. In the meantime, if you ever save anybody's life, make sure I'm the first to know. I'll even call the *Evening Sentinel* and make sure it gets on the front page. And besides, I want to catch the sports report on Channel 8 before the news ends."

He climbed up the stairs to our second floor apartment, his long legs taking them two at a time. Trudging slowly behind, I thought, *I guess saving lives isn't something Michael would understand about.*

13

Since Tuesday, I had been having restless nights of sleep. Of course, I couldn't seem to get my encounter with Daryl and the train out of my mind. Who wouldn't be bothered by that? Getting such an inside look at his reckless behavior scared the heck out of me. On top of that, I was bummed out by Karl Fischer. Being drunk and picking a fight with all three of us DeMarcos was no way for an adult to act. *What drove a person to drink so much and behave like that?* I wondered. More than that, though, it really troubled me that he called us *guineas*. I knew if I told my dad the story, he'd probably go straight to Duchess and have a few choice words for Karl. Maybe more than just words actually. At the same time, I questioned how my dad could get so angry when someone called an Italian a *guinea* yet seem to feel it was perfectly fine to call black people *niggers* when talking about them. The weird thing is that's what he calls black people when talking about them as a group, but when he's talking about individual black people, it's kind of a different story. For instance, I remember recently, he mentioned a young black guy who works at the plumbing supply house. "Jimmy at Manzi's Plumbing Supply is such a good kid," Dad said. I guess I'm coming to the age when you realize not everything your parents say or do makes sense.

On the Sunday after New Year's Day, the All State Team was published in the papers around the state. Since our dad only subscribed to the *Evening Sentinel*, which didn't have a Sunday edition, Michael and I had to wait to find out who made All State until we got to work at 10:30. We both made a beeline for The *New Haven Register* in

Howie's office. There, on the front page of the sports section, were two pictures, one below the other, of the offensive and defensive teams. Below the photos were biographical blurbs on each All State player, and below those, a list of players named "second team" and "honorable mention." We leaned over the sports page and studied the pictures first. Eleven players in each picture stood proudly in their uniforms, their numbers emblazoned on their jerseys and their right arms wrapped firmly around their helmets. What glory! A glory a distance runner like me could only imagine. On offense, three players from the state championship Derby team had made it: the big tight end, Trent Stanley; the center, Nickie Grasso; and, not surprisingly, the halfback, Frankie Adamo. Four Derby players were named to the defensive team: Roderick Zubek at guard; Tommy Ciaburri at defensive back; and again Nickie Grasso at tackle and Frankie Adamo at linebacker. *Wow,* I thought, *little Derby garnered seven spots on the coveted All State first team, and Adamo and Grasso made it on both offense and defense.* The only other Valley player to make the first team was Seymour's quarterback, Ben Andrews. Shelton's Danny Mueller made the second team, as well as two more Derby players, one Ansonia player, and one Seymour player. Several more Valley players were cited as honorable mentions.

Walking out of the office, Michael muttered, "It's too bad about Novak. He should have been in this photo." Daryl, ironically, was the only current athlete who had made the All State team as a junior.

"Yeah," I chimed in. "Novak should have made it."

"I didn't say he should have made it," Michael clarified. "I meant he shouldn't have quit the team, in which case he *obviously* would have made it. Any moron would know that. Instead, the guy's wasting his fucking life."

I'm not going to lie. Implying that I was a moron hurt a little.

"I mean, he was so good, and he only missed the last two games of the season because of...well, stuff," I said. "I think he should have made it anyway."

"Give me a fucking break," Michael said. "You're so far out in left field, it isn't even funny."

"Well," Lenny Singleton, overhearing the exchange, interjected, "that boy is a little messed up in the head after everythin'. Whatcha gonna do?"

"I wouldn't put it that way," I replied. "He's just...he's just upset."

"How would you know?" Michael asked, growing more and more irritated with me with each passing remark. "What are you now, a mind reader? The Amazing Kreskin?"

Ouch! I needed to learn to keep my big mouth shut. "Not a mind reader. I just know I'd be super upset under the same circumstances, wouldn't you?"

Michael shrugged. "I guess so, but I hope I wouldn't let everything go down the toilet. I mean, even though his sister is gone, this kid has everything to live for. Life goes on, ya know? He could have had a full boat to a lot of great colleges, but instead all he does is cruises up and down Pershing Drive...drunk...or...or high...or whatever the fuck he is."

Michael's highly critical remarks bugged me. Although irritated, I decided to get on with my morning set-up and not pursue the conversation any further. It wasn't likely I was going to win a debate with Michael anyway.

I heard Lenny Singleton say, "Too bad the boy ain't playin' basketball neither cuz I seen him play against Ansonia last year, and he pretty much did whatever he felt like. He ain't no showboat or nothin' like that, but he sure enough gets the job done."

"Speaking of," said Lance Jefferson, who was on Ansonia's team, "we play Seymour on Friday night."

With sudden curiosity, Howie jumped into the conversation. "Oh yeah? What's your record and what's Seymour's record?" As the boss, he was probably too busy running the store to stay on top of local high school teams.

"We're 2-1, and I'm not sure, but I think Seymour is 0-3," Lance answered. Lance is not only animated and energetic, he's also handsome and smart. *He should be on TV,* I thought.

"I'll bet you that Seymour beats you on Tuesday," Howie challenged.

"Fat chance, Howie," Lance laughed. "Those white boys can't run with us, and they can't rebound with us neither."

"I'll still bet you Seymour beats you," Howie repeated with an annoying confidence.

Lance looked confused. He was new at Duchess, and he didn't know how to interpret what Howie said. He didn't know if Howie just meant a gentleman's bet or if Howie meant he wanted to bet real money.

So with an innocent look in his eyes, he just asked, "What do you mean, Howie?"

"I mean I'll bet you five bucks Seymour beats you guys," Howie said, smiling and offering his right hand to Lance.

I've noticed this about Howie since beginning to work at the place in September. He loves to bet, no matter how big or small the wager. I feel that, in some way, he likes showing you that he knows something you don't. Weird. In this case, I'm guessing he had no idea who was the better team, but it was his way of showing a sense of superiority. If he lost, big deal. What was five dollars to the great Howie Millea, who was well on his way to becoming a wealthy man? But to Lance Jefferson, five bucks meant a tankful of gas or maybe two or three lunches in the Ansonia school cafeteria. And besides, it felt wrong that a thirty-something year old guy would set up a bet with a high school kid. I made eye contact with Lance, squinting my eyelids and subtly shaking my head, as if to say: "Stay away from it, Lance." But Lance's school spirit and pride in himself and his teammates made the bet irresistible.

"You got it, Howie." Lance smiled, grabbed Howie's hand firmly, and shook it.

It was a typical lunch hour, hectic and fast-paced. I was getting good at my jobs. I could slide two sodas out from under the spigots while moving two more empty cups in with hardly any waste, and then cap the two full cups while the others were still pouring. I could carry five large milkshakes — two in each hand with the fifth trapped in the middle — to the counter from the shake machine which was back near the grill without ever dropping a single one.

At 5:00, a few other guys came in to transition to the night shift. Among them was Will Granger, who had only recently returned from the Army after a tour of Vietnam, having been drafted two years ago. Michael and Will are about the same age, and they had worked together when the place opened. Michael was less than enthused about Will's return. He described Will as a sarcastic needler. Howie, on the other hand, was *definitely* enthused about Will's return.

I've noticed that when Howie interacts with Will, he does so with eyes of admiration, as if, for the first time, he is seeing a famous actor or a star athlete. Will is neither. But he also isn't the sarcastic needler Michael had remembered. Well, I'd say we're all sarcastic, but he's no more of a needler than anybody else, and less than a lot of guys, including Howie himself. Will mostly treats everyone with respect. I don't know what he was like before he left for the military because I was only thirteen, but he had, perhaps, grown up while he was away. He is a super good looking, charismatic twenty-something year old who is a bundle of energy, always in motion. Will routinely carries on conversations while wiping counters clean or refilling sleeves of drink cups or taking the scooper and tossing the fries around to see if they look fresh enough to sell to the customers. Talk about productive. No wonder Howie likes him.

Will is also honest. Or maybe a better way to say it is that he is a true realist. For instance, during a recent slow night at Duchess, we got into a talk about Vietnam. Some of the guys were asking him questions that night, and I was really struck by what he had to say.

"You guys think war is like that John Wayne and Audie Murphy hero bullshit you've seen in movies, but that's not it at all. Let me straighten you all out. No American soldier is running at an enemy battalion, throwing hand grenades to save his men while the enemy riddles him with machine gun bullets. Shit, you can't even see the enemy in Nam. You don't even know who they are. It's not like they're wearing uniforms like us. They're all dressed like Chinese peasants. You're in the middle of the jungle, and when all of a sudden fuckin' machine gun fire comes spraying at you from all directions, it's a race to see who can dig the deepest hole to stay alive. No heroes. Just guys scared out of their fuckin' minds, some of them praying and some of them crying and some of them pissing their pants."

"Wow," I said. "I didn't realize it was like that."

"Well, now you know. That's how it is, and you can take that to the bank," Will replied. "When I got back to the States, I still had three months left. And guess where they assigned me. To an Air Force base in Arizona to clean up litter and garbage on the grounds, like I was the new fuckin' kid working here. Wrap your brain around that one — cleaning up garbage in sweltering heat. That's the thanks I got for risking my life for my country. When my time was up and I flew back home, before I got off the plane, I took a change of clothes into the restroom, took off my uniform and put on my civies. I left the uniform in a bag next to the toilet. When I got off the plane, my father was disappointed not to see me in uniform, but I was all fuckin' done, believe me."

Hearing Will's explanation, I could understand how a guy could get cynical. I began to realize that life isn't everything we see in the movies...or everything we learn in school...or even everything our parents tell us. It appeared that sometimes the truth is something other than what we have been fed. My early impression was that I liked Will, and I liked his brand of stark honesty. Michael came around about Will too. Besides, Will was a good guy to like. By the end of the summer, Howie would be busy opening another store in Bridgeport, and Will would be the new manager of our store.

On this particular Sunday, Howie told the crew that Karl Fischer had called in sick, and he asked if anyone could work the night shift. It meant "working through," meaning you worked a twelve hour shift, eleven to eleven. I wasn't personally interested. My seven hour shift had been plenty for me. When no one volunteered, Michael, forever loyal to Duchess and Howie, said, "I'll cover it."

Howie said, "Great. Thanks, Michael. You don't mind working the grill, do you?" and without waiting for an answer, he continued, "So Will is in charge and on the window. Michael on the grill, and Bink will be on fries and drinks."

Michael didn't seem to mind. Anyway, it's just the way it was. Even though Will only returned to work a few months before and Michael had been steady here during the two years while Will was away, Will was clearly Howie's main man. As things started to pick up for supper hour, Michael pulled me aside and asked me how I would get home. I told him I didn't mind hitchhiking, and I didn't. If it wasn't for the oncoming rush, which would last well past my 6:00 departure time, he would have taken me home and come back.

I finished my last hour, and then unobtrusively slipped out the back door. Secretly, I hoped crazy Daryl Novak would come by and pick me up again. Even though he was a little nuts, I couldn't help but like the kid. Beyond the drunkenness and the off the wall behavior, I knew there was something really special about him. Just a feeling I had in my gut. And I hadn't forgotten Susanna by a long shot. I began to walk down Pershing Drive, making no attempt to hitchhike yet, but instead looking over my shoulder to see if maybe that beat-up Bug of his might rattle by. What a bomb that car was. When I got down to the Bradlees Plaza, I could see that it wasn't meant to be. Resigned that you can't just wish something into reality, I finally stuck out my thumb and waited to be picked up. Luckily, it wasn't terribly cold.

After about fifty thousand cars raced by me like I didn't even exist, a middle aged guy in a station wagon finally pulled over.

I gave my standard, "Thanks for stopping," as I got in his car. "I thought I was never going to get a ride."

"I'm in a little bit of a hurry, but I don't mind helping you out. Where are you going?"

"Just the first exit in Shelton."

"Sounds good. I'm on my way to a meeting in Bridgeport, so how about if I drop you off at the top of the exit? Exit 14, right?"

"Yes, right. That'd be great."

As we drove, he asked, "You go to Shelton High?"

"Yup," I responded.

"You like football?" He must have inferred by my physique that I didn't *play* football. I nodded that I did. "Did you see the All State team in the paper today?" he continued. "All those Derby players. Little Derby. Unreal, right?"

I smiled and nodded. "Yeah, it is. A few different breaks, though, and Seymour might have been the state champion."

"Yeah...well, I saw that game, and it was a good one. That Novak kid played one helluva game. Too bad he didn't catch that pass at the end. Then that...that awful accident. His little sister. What a tragic thing."

"Yeah," I said. "It was terrible. A lot of us knew those kids. We used to see each other at Duchess where I work and at, you know, dances. We're pretty freaked out."

There was no more time for talk, though. I thanked him when he pulled over at the exit. As I headed down the ramp on foot, my brain was going two-forty. Like racing lights running through the marquee of my mind, two names flashed over and over again: Daryl and Susanna...Daryl...Susanna...Daryl...Susanna...Daryl...

14

Daryl seemed to have suddenly disappeared. I missed him, and I wondered where he was and what he did with himself when he wasn't cruising and drinking. On the Wednesday after the All State team had appeared in the paper, Michael and I were on the schedule with a new grill man they were breaking in, a nineteen year old kid from the projects named George Barnes who everyone called "Poobie." Poobie was a relative of Big Alfred's, which is probably how he got the job. I was grateful that we wouldn't have to deal with Karl Fischer even if Poobie was a rookie. For some reason, Poobie had miraculously skipped the bottom rung, which was to be a drink man, like me, who picked up the garbage in the parking lot. I think he had some prior experience cooking. Big Alfred was out in the parking lot when Michael and I arrived at work. Except for Friday and Saturday nights, you never knew when Alfred would be working or when he wouldn't. Sometimes, I was beginning to think Howie let Alfred work whenever he wanted.

I had mixed emotions about Alfred being on because, on the one hand, Daryl couldn't cause any drama with Alfred there, which was good, but on the other hand, I actually really wanted to see Daryl. And not only because I kind of liked the kid, but also because my curiosity and my own personal sense of loss caused me to care about him. I didn't know if I had any right to feel loss, but the reality was that I did feel it.

As was sometimes the case, Big Alfred brought two of his five kids with him to work, and this was one of those nights. I'll bet his wife tells him, "I'll take care of the little three, but you'll have to take the big two." Like usual, it was Tyrone and Trina, who are about twelve and ten. Completing Alfred's entourage that night was Buster Brookes, a muscle bound kid with thick, black rimmed, Coke bottle glasses. I don't know how old Buster is, exactly, or what grade he's in, but he is often with Alfred, probably as backup in case some drunk kid in the lot thinks he's a tough guy. Not that Alfred needs backup. Alfred's kids either circle the building with him and Buster or hang out in the vestibule where it's warmer. They never cause any trouble, so no one minds. What's interesting about Alfred is that, for some reason, he really likes me. I am totally unsure what I did to earn his affection, but it's fairly obvious. He kind of looks at me the way Howie looks at Will Granger. Following their dad's lead, Alfred's kids like me too, and they fall all over themselves saying hi to me.

Around 9:30, Alfred took a break and was talking with Michael and Buster about the upcoming Super Bowl and the Oakland Raiders' chances against the mighty Green Bay Packers. The Packers had recently broken my heart for the second year in a row when they won the NFL Championship by beating my favorite team, the Dallas Cowboys, 21-17 in what is now known as "the Ice Bowl" in Green Bay. I like Dallas' slick silver and white uniforms with the blue and white star on the sides of their silver helmets. I like the way the offensive line often shifts in unison before the ball is snapped. I like that one of their stars is "Bullet" Bob Hayes, the 1964 Olympic Gold Medalist in the 100 meter dash, making him the fastest man on earth. Mainly, though, I think liking the Cowboys has something to do with becoming my own person instead of always liking and doing what Michael likes and does.

I was half listening to the conversation while going about my job tasks.

"Oakland isn't any match for the Packers," my brother pointed out.

"Get outta town, Michael," Buster argued, bellowing out a sarcastic laugh. "The Raiders are the baddest team ever!"

"I think Buster got a point," Alfred added, squinting his eyes. "They score lotsa points — buckets fulla points. I think more points than everybody else this year. That quarterback, Daryle — I can't say his las' name — but he got a great arm, and that receiver with the German las' name — I can' say that one neither, but he is *so* good."

Buster, a little too excited by Alfred's input, said, "Tha's right, Big Alfred...tha's right!"

Alfred was talking about the great tandem of quarterback Daryle Lamonica and receiver Fred Biletnikoff. I immediately thought of Andrews and Novak, who were to Connecticut high school football what Lamonica and Biletnikoff were to the American Football League. It also hit me that Daryl had the same first name as the great Raider quarterback, just a slightly different spelling.

Filling up the ice bin and then wiping down the grates under the soda spouts, I noticed Trina leaning over the counter at the window, obviously staring at me.

I turned to her and smiled. "Everything okay there, Trina?"

"Mmmm, mmmm," she exclaimed, like she just finished an ice cream sundae. "Gabriel, lemme just say – you...*is*...*pretty*."

"Uh, pardon me?" I replied, confused by her remark.

"I'm jus' sayin' how pretty you is, Gabriel," Trina continued. "Not like my cousin Poobie back there behind that grill. Poobie jus' pitiful." And she made a face as if her parents made her eat a vegetable she hated.

I didn't quite know how to respond. A ten year old girl appeared to have a crush on me.

"Daddy?" Trina called, interrupting Alfred's and Buster's sports debate with Michael. "Ain't Gabriel pretty, Daddy?"

"I don' know if I wanna call Gabriel pretty, Trina, but I will say one thing for him. Gabriel is the best white boy I know."

I felt myself blush. I had a lot of respect for Alfred, and I was flattered by the compliment, despite still not knowing how I had earned it.

"The real question, Trina, ain't whether Gabriel is pretty, but whether your Daddy is pretty. You think your Daddy is pretty, Trina?" Alfred cooed in the sweetest voice he could muster up. He can be quite an actor.

"Oh, Daddy," Trina said, blushing and bursting into a bubbly laugh as if Alfred's was the silliest and funniest question she had ever heard.

"I will tell you the answer then, Miss Trina Johnson, since most obviously you don' know it. The answer is, 'Yes, Daddy, you are the prettiest in the whole world!'" Alfred emphasized each and every word. "And do you know why? That's because your daddy was born with ridiculous good looks — jus' like a movie star or...or, better yet, jus' like the great Muhammad Ali."

Trina practically screamed in laughter at this remark. It was almost as if the entertaining Muhammad Ali himself was in the room.

"Now, Trina, jus' look at your cousin Poobie leanin' over the grill there, and you tell me who is handsomest — Poobie Barnes or your gorgeous Daddy?" *Boy,* I thought, *Poobie is sure getting it from all sides.* It seemed like Poobie could really take it, though. He shook his head, flashed a good natured smile, and went back to scraping down the grill.

A customer came to the window, which was a signal for everyone to get back to work. Alfred and Buster headed back out into the parking lot, and as he made his rounds, Trina and Tyrone trailed them. I could hear Trina's bubbly laugh as they disappeared around the back side of the building.

Alfred made his way back inside about fifteen minutes later and said, "Michael, ain't much happenin'. I think I may as well take off an' put these children to bed. Especially Trina before she goes and laughs herself half to death," which only caused another fit of laughter to pour out of Trina.

"Sounds good to me, Alfred," Michael replied. "Whatever you think is best."

"Oh, but before I go, I talked to that Seymour boy a few minutes ago," Alfred shifted gears. "What's his name?"

"Novak?" I asked.

"Tha's right, Novak," Alfred continued. "I was throwing him off the lot like I always do, but he asked me can he talk to you, Gabriel. I tol' him I would check with you."

Scowling, Michael asked, "What the hell would Daryl Novak want to talk to you about?"

"How should I know?" I said. "You sure he wanted to talk to me, Alfred?" I asked, playing innocent.

"Well, he didn't know the name of the boy he was talkin' about, but he said, the skinny white boy who always got a book in his pocket, and we all know that's you, Gabriel. It ain't Michael, and it sure as hell ain't Poobie. I don't even know if the school learned Poobie how to read yet." There went Alfred, busting them on Poobie, who just smiled his warm, affable smile.

"Can I see what he wants?" I asked Michael, who grimaced.

"What could he possibly want to talk to you about?" Michael complained. "Would you go out there with him, Alfred?"

"Okay," said Big Alfred, "I'll keep an eye on them before I take off, but he don' really seem like no kinda troublemaker. I been sendin' that boy on his way for weeks, but truth is, besides maybe being a little drunk or a little high, he ain't no kinda problem. He's always polite, and says, 'Okay sorry, Alfred' and 'whatever you say, Alfred' and 'no problem, Alfred.' "

With a deep sigh, Michael said, "Okay, go talk to the guy then."

When I walked out the back door, Daryl's Bug was one of the few cars in the lot. It was running, probably to keep the heater going on this frigid early January evening. I headed for the driver's side, but Daryl waved me to the passenger side, mouthing, "Get in."

I opened the door and sat down. "What's up, Daryl? How you been doing?" I could see Alfred across the lot. He was keeping his distance, giving us space.

"Up and down," he said. "Mos-ly down, which probly isn't a surprise to you." He was obviously drunk again, as usual. I could see a partially full, big bottle of Ballantine Beer on the floor in front of his seat and an empty between the two seats right behind the stick shift. He wasn't drinking from it at the moment. He probably didn't want to be seen drinking by Big Alfred.

"I can only talk to you for a few minutes, Daryl," I explained. "My brother won't let me stay out here long."

"Oh, that tall guy is your brother?" he asked, and I nodded. "You'd never know it, Dushess, you two guys don't even look alike."

"So, how can I help you?" I asked in earnest.

"I don' know. I don' need any help. I just wanted to thank you for...you know...for saving my life," he said. "You really did, Dushess, and I want to thank you. Yer a really good kid, ya know what I mean, buddy?"

Alfred, satisfied that we seemed to be having a calm conversation, headed out onto the shoulder of Pershing Drive and started walking with Buster and the kids back to the projects, I assumed. It had never occurred to me that Alfred walked back and forth to work, but there he was in all of his mammoth glory, walking under the yellow streetlights on the shoulder of Pershing Drive with his children and his friend in his watchful care.

It felt uncomfortable being thanked for saving Daryl's life. "I was just trying to be helpful, Daryl. I mean, I wasn't going to stand by and let you get yourself run over by a train, ya know? But I really have to get back in, so if..."

"Wait a sec, Dushess...jus' wait a second," he said. "I was jus' wonderin' if you and I could get together an' talk sometime. I don' have anybody to talk to lately...and I jus' thought...well, you know...I thought...maybe we could jus' talk sometime."

"I'm not a psychologist, Daryl. I don't think I'm the right person to..."

"I don' want a psychologist," he said, "Jus' a friend. Whataya say, Dushess, one friend to another?" How could I say no?

"Okay, how about Friday night? I'll tell my parents I'm going out with my buddy."

He picked up his bottle and took a big gulp. "Perfect, Dushess... perfect!"

"Only one condition," I warned. "You need to be sober. If you're drinking, I won't go."

"Okay...okay, Dushess, you got a deal. Sober it is," he promised.

We made plans for him to pick me up at the bottom of Exit 14 at 6:30 on Friday. Heading back into the store, I watched Daryl drive out of the parking lot and on to Pershing Drive, his broken muffler crying out in pain. When I arrived back inside, I found myself once more under the scrutiny of my older brother.

"So, what did he want?" Michael asked.

"Oh, nothing much," I replied. "I recently thumbed a ride home from work, and he picked me up. He just wanted to know if I needed a ride tonight, but I told him you were my brother, and you and I would be going home together."

At least some of my explanation was true, but it was hard to look Michael in the eye when I wasn't really being totally honest. I held his gaze, though, and I hoped nothing gave me away.

Michael shook his head. "He could have asked that at the window."

"Yeah," I said, "he could have. But he didn't. He's a little shy, I think. And kind of troubled."

"Yeah, like I didn't fucking notice," Michael replied, not making any attempt to hide his annoyance with me. I stood, watching him shuffle toward the back and into the office.

Getting tangled up with the Novaks hadn't made my life get any simpler, that's for sure. In fact, I'm pretty sure that, since the night I danced with Susanna, I had lied more times than I had in my entire life. And knowing Daryl was getting more and more sticky, causing me to become an even more creative liar. It was lucky I didn't go to church anymore because some annoying priest would have really had a field day with me in the confessional, telling me what an awful sinner I was. But I really hated lying to Michael because, the thing is, Michael is the kind of guy who pretty much always tells you the truth, even if you don't want to hear it. Still, I knew I couldn't resist taking Daryl up on his invitation. There was just something about him that I really liked. My plan was to keep the date with him on Friday and say whatever I had to say to make it happen. I'd figure Michael out later.

15

Choosing Friday night to hang out with Daryl was a no-brainer for me because Jeff was no longer available on Fridays which had become "Julie Carter Night" for him. Julie's parents went bowling on Friday nights, he had told me, so she and Jeff had the house to themselves. Jeff would swing by after Julie's parents left at 6:45 and slip out into the night before they arrived home at 9:30. During the weeks since the accident, Jeff and I hadn't talked about it again, but what he did talk about, incessantly, was his progress with Julie. First it was how he had felt up her breasts. *He's miles ahead of me right there,* I thought. Then it was how he had taken her blouse and bra off, and they had made out with her naked from the waist up. Did I say he was miles ahead of me yet? Then it was how he had reached down her pants, in the back...and then in the front. I mean, how do you even have the guts to do that? By now, they were having full fledged sex. *I'm so far behind,* I realized, *it's ridiculously embarrassing!* Because Julie was a year older than us, I guess she was ready to do stuff that most girls I had kissed — all one of them — weren't ready to do. Let me sum up my experience in a nutshell. Like I said, I have only kissed one girl, and here's how it happened. The only relationship I have had ended in November of last year when I got shot down by Lenore Ott. Her friend told me the bad news at my locker. Before walking away, the friend asked, "You never even kissed her?" in utter disbelief. That made me feel just great. The next day, I called up Doreen Grutadario and asked her to go to the movies with me because I had heard she was "fast on the draw." It was true. Doreen made out with me for the entire movie. That was the first and last time I have kissed a girl. Pathetic, I know. Anyway, Jeff had made it around the bases while I was barely headed for first. Either way, having Friday nights to spend alone was a nice break from "Confessions of a Teenage Sex Addict."

The only problem would be making up a lie to tell my parents. I obviously couldn't tell them I was hanging out with Daryl Novak. Lying was something I seemed to be doing more and more since the accident, and I was getting good at it, which was beginning to worry me a little. There are some things that you don't want to be too good at. I remember that when I was in eighth grade, Father McMahon took all the boys into a classroom and gave us a talk about the birds and the bees. Explaining the allure of kissing and touching, he warned, "One thing leads to another, and then it's too late and you're in more trouble than you can handle." I was now learning that, just like kissing and touching, one lie leads to another, but I was in too deep to turn back now. I'd tell my parents that Jeff and I were going somewhere... maybe to Valley Bowl or somewhere like that.

Tonight would be an adventure, but I hoped not too much of an adventure. I was having trouble wrapping my brain around everything that had happened, and I was really puzzled about how I had gotten to this point — hanging out with the great Daryl Novak. Well, I guess he wasn't doing too great anymore, but I hoped I could help a little because he was a pretty good kid when he wasn't drunk and running head on at locomotives. *Daryl had better be sober like we talked about,* I thought, *or I'm not going.*

I was waiting at the bottom of Exit 14 under the Route 8 overpass as promised. It was a bitterly cold night, and my face and ears were frozen and probably a deep purple by now. He was late, so I tried to stand near the streetlight and read my book. It's lucky I like reading or I'd be bored out of my gourd any time there is nothing to do or I have to wait around for someone or for something to start. I heard Daryl coming down the ramp. He pulled over, and I jumped in the car.

"Hi Daryl," I said in my most cheerful voice. I wanted to discover as quickly as possible if he was sober. I scanned the car as furtively as possible for any quart sized beer bottles. None were visible.

"Good to see you, Duchess, what's happenin'?" His words weren't slurred, which was a good sign. "Whataya doing?" he asked. "Getting ready to write a book report?"

I looked down into my lap and saw my book, which I was still holding. With an embarrassed laugh, I said, "No, I was just passing time until you got here." And I reached under my butt and stuffed the dog-eared book into my back pocket.

"Whataya reading?" Daryl asked as he swung the Bug around the curve and got back on Route 8, heading back toward Ansonia.

"Uhm...nothing much...it's called *On the Road*," I replied, hoping I could change the subject as soon as possible.

"Is that the same book I saw you reading a few weeks ago at Duchess when you gave me the free food?"

"Yeah, actually, it is. Not that it takes me a million years to read a book or anything. I finished it about a week after that night, but I started it again."

"You...started...it...again," he said, echoing my words. "Why would anybody read something they already read?"

How shall I put it? He was befuddled. "It's hard to explain. Maybe I'm addicted to reading this book because this is, like, my fourth time reading it." I was attempting to be humorous, but Daryl didn't bite.

"Fourth time," he repeated in disbelief. "We're going to have to do something about that, Duchess." There he went again, acting like there was something wrong with me. First it was that I don't drink and this time it was that I like to read.

"Okay, then, if it's so good, tell me what it's about."

"Oh, uhm...let's see. I guess it's not really about anything exactly," I said. "It's just a couple of guys, traveling across country...getting from place to place...hitchhiking...or however."

"Wow! You're an interesting kid, Duchess. Here I am, somebody who tries not to read if I can possibly help it, and you're reading a book that isn't about anything for the fourth time," he said with a chuckle. "Go figure. Who wrote it, Duchess?"

"Uhm...Jack Kerouac," I replied. "He's considered a pretty important author, actually, and this book, even though it isn't really about anything is considered a pretty significant book."

"Oh, significant is it?" I thought he might have been mocking me. It seemed like further clarification was needed.

"Yeah...well Jack Kerouac was a member of a group that were known as 'the beat writers.' You've heard of beatniks, right? Yeah, well, like that. You know, like Maynard G. Krebs on the *Dobie Gillis Show*, only more serious, sort of. I don't mean that beatniks are serious...I just mean they're not silly like Maynard G. Krebs." I was rambling now. "I'm not sure, but I think Kerouac might have kind of been responsible for coming up with the term beatnik. He was pretty out there. They say, in his original manuscript, Kerouac typed it without ever starting a new paragraph...and without ever indenting...on a continuous scroll, or something like that. Of course, I guess the publisher decided it had to have paragraphs and chapters, so they edited it that way. And they obviously weren't going to publish and sell it as a scroll. But think of it, two hundred and fifty pages without a single indentation. Isn't that wild?" I asked, realizing I had gotten a little carried away and thinking how odd I must sound.

Daryl nodded, "Oh yeah, Duchess, that's just about the wildest thing I've ever heard of." His sarcastic tone erased any doubts about whether he was mocking me.

"You don't have to be facetious about it."

"Fa-what?" he asked, chuckling.

"Never mind." There wasn't any point in pushing it. I could take a little razzing.

He didn't get off the Pershing Drive exit, which was just fine with me because if people I knew and worked with at Duchess saw me with him, they'd probably wonder what I was doing with him. I guess we had exhausted Jack Kerouac because we now sat in silence until he popped an 8 track in his tape player. He had the same set-up Michael had in the Corvair, with the tape player on a chrome, metal rack under the dash right below the glove compartment. You could unplug it, slide it out, and put it in the trunk when you parked the car, so no one would steal it.

"Aw, man, outta sight! I love this song," I said excitedly. It was "How Can I Be Sure" by the Young Rascals. "My brother has this tape in his car. The Rascals are one of my favorite groups. I think Felix Cavaliere has an amazing voice, don't you?"

"Felix who?" he asked, puzzled.

"The lead singer," I said.

"You know who the lead singer of the Rascals is?"

"Of course."

"Hold your wild fuckin' horses. You can name the lead singers of different rock groups?"

"More or less."

"Okay, how about the Lovin' Spoonful?"

"Easy — John Sebastian."

"How about the Guess Who?"

"Burton Cummings...another amazing voice. I'd put him in the same league with Felix Cavaliere."

"Please don't tell me you know who the other fuckin' guys in the band are."

"Well, let's see...the Guess Who? Uhm...Will Evankovich and Derek Sharp on guitars, Rudy Sarzo on bass, Garry Peterson on drums, and, uhm, Lenny Shaw on keyboard and woodwinds." It wasn't fair. I was just showing off now.

"How about...oh, never mind. So, you're, like, a walking rock 'n roll encyclopedia, huh Duchess? Me myself, I just like listening to the music. Ever fuckin' hear of that?" he said, still sarcastic toward me. "I don't necessarily pay attention to who the lead singers or the guys in the band are, except for, you know, like the Beatles or the Stones. For all I fuckin' know, I might not even know who they are if it weren't for the fact that Susie is constantly talking about..."

He suddenly became silent. I realized by Susie, he meant Susanna, and the mention of her name startled both of us. I hadn't heard him speak of her before. And he and I both realized he had just talked about her in the present tense.

After a brief pause, I decided to go for it. "Susanna liked the Beatles, huh?"

After about ten seconds, his mood having grown suddenly dark, Daryl inhaled deeply and mumbled, "I don't talk about Susie, man."

"Oh, okay," I said. "No offense, I was just making conversation."

He turned off at Exit 18 and headed toward Seymour.

"Where we going, Daryl?" I asked.

"Ice skating," he said.

Baffled, I asked myself, *How do we go ice skating without skates?* Moments later, he pulled down a dirt road that led into the dark woods. Sure enough, at the end of the dirt road was a small pond, frozen over from the frigid weather. Daryl got out and yelled, "Let's skate, Duchess!" Reluctantly, I followed him. He trotted across the frosty grass and leaves to the frozen pond, and he jumped on the ice with only his sneakers, landing on his feet, and like a surfer, Daryl glided about ten yards toward the center. I couldn't help but notice how incredibly agile he was in the process. He repeated the movement, lifting his feet into a slippery run on the ice before gliding a similar distance. "Wheeee," he called out. His voice echoed in the frigid air against the tall evergreens. "C'mon, let's get goin' Duchess...*Duchess...Duchess.* It's winter...*winter...winter.* Let's skate... *skate...skate.*"

I walked unsteadily onto the ice. "You sure this is safe?"

"Yeah, man, but don't tiptoe around like a fuckin' candy ass. You gotta run and glide, like me...*like me...me*," he called out, the sound of his shouting still echoing within the boundaries of the wintery cavern, as he demonstrated. I tried again to imitate his moves. "That's better... *better...better*," he called from across the small pond. And then I made a third attempt. "Now you're getting the hang of it." We alternated between gliding and standing on the pond and talking.

"So, you don't play football, right, Duchess? I mean, you're kind of scrawny, but we got a few scrawny guys like you on our team," he said.

"No, I tried it last year. I went to the first day of a double session practice," I explained. "But when I went home for lunch, I decided to lie down for a few minutes before going back, and I fell asleep. So I missed the afternoon session...and then I...I don't know...well, I never went back. It would have been too embarrassing."

He broke out into a belly laugh. "That's quite a story, Duchess. That's rough. You didn't make it through even one full day of practice," and he continued to laugh as if it was the funniest thing he had ever heard. "So, you don't play any sports?"

"No, I do. This past fall, I ran Cross Country," I said.

"Cross Country?" he said with a smirk, "That's not a sport. That's just agony. You just run long distances, right? Like miles and miles, right? Who would do that? It's insanity."

"Yeah, I guess it's a little crazy, but I liked it okay. Running helps me think."

"I'm trying *not* to think," he said with emphasis. "Well, were you any good at it, Duchess?"

"Actually," I replied with a measure of pride, "I was the best runner on the team. In fact, I broke the course record, which everyone said was pretty good considering I'm only a sophomore."

"Hold it right there. Let me get this straight now, Duchess. You hold a school record in Shelton?"

I nodded in the affirmative.

"Well, fuckin' A, man! I'm impressed, Duchess. Any other sports?"

"Yeah, I also play basketball. Last year I was on the freshman team, and now I'm on the JV team."

"You get any playing time, Duchess?" he asked, now genuinely interested.

"Last year, very little, but this year a lot more. Sometimes I even start at point guard."

I explained to Daryl that the Shelton High School head coach had seen me play in eighth grade and was upset when I told him I planned to attend Fairfield Prep. The coach urged me to change my plans and come to Shelton. But then when that's the way it actually worked out, I found myself warming the bench on the freshman team. Things were looking up now, though.

"Whoa, I'll say it again, Duchess. Fuckin' A! You might have some potential after all. After you told me you read books that aren't about anything four times, I was worried about you," and, again, he chuckled. It was the happiest I had seen him.

Suddenly feeling playful, I gave him a good hard push, and he slid backwards swinging his arms like he was in a swimming pool doing the backstroke, and then fell on his butt.

"Okay, Duchess, you're going to get it now," he warned, and the next half hour turned into a game of the two of us trying to upend the other, running and sliding and pushing and gliding. I'm afraid that between his size and agility, I got the worst of it. Finally, we were sitting on the ice, our pants sopping wet from falling and sliding across the surface of the pond. But we were laughing like two ten year olds.

Since we had been talking about sports, I decided to go down another kind of slippery path. "How come you stopped playing sports, Daryl?"

"I don't really talk about that," he said.

I knew I was pushing now. "No, it's just that I used to love to watch you play football. I mean, nobody was better than you. And even though I only saw you play basketball against Shelton, I follow the box scores in the *Sentinel*, and I saw, last year, that you scored double figures in, like...well, like every game from what I could tell. You must have averaged 16 or 18 points a game as only a junior. And you made All League, didn't you? Imagine how phenomenal you would have done this year. All State probably. They say you're a heck of a baseball player too. I'll bet you could really hit the..."

"That's enough, man...*man...man!* Cut it...*cut it...cut it!"* he yelled, his volume and its eerie echo startling me into silence. "Did it ever occur to you...did it ever occur to *anybody* that I'm not just an athlete... that I'm a person? That's all anybody ever says about me ever since... ever since I was just a little...a little..."

"Hey, listen, Daryl, I didn't mean to…"

"Fuck you...*you...you!* Like I said, I don't fuckin' talk about that shit anymore, man." He got up and started walking off the ice.

Following, I called, "Hey, Daryl, wait! Daryl? You said you wanted to talk, right? Isn't that what you said?"

He went right to the Bug and started it up, the round headlights blinding me as I hurried behind him. I was afraid he was going to leave me there, and I had no idea where we were. Luckily, he stayed put, his car idling as loudly as ever.

I opened the door and got in. "I didn't mean to upset you, Daryl. I was just talking because...you know...that's why we got together... because *you* said you needed a friend to talk to...so I'm just trying to be a friend. That's all."

"No, it's cool, Duchess. Talking about sports makes me fly off the handle. And sometimes, I don't know...I just get a little down because... because I didn't want to...to give up sports."

"Well, why did you, then?"

"It's personal man. I can't talk about that."

"Okay, well, do you mind if I ask you a different question, then?"

He just sat there and shrugged, so I went for it. "What happened to Ben Andrews and your friends from the team? Can you talk about that? I used to see you and Andrews and those other guys at Duchess all the time."

He reached across me and opened the glove compartment. He pulled out a wrinkled, brown paper bag, and then he reached into it and pulled out a small piece of paper, which he started to crease in several accordion-like folds.

"Uhm, what are you doing, Daryl?" I asked suspiciously.

He reached into the bag a second time, taking out a few fingers full of a dark green substance, which he carefully sprinkled into the paper.

"Uhm...Daryl, is that marijuana?" I asked.

"I prefer to call it *weed*," he said.

"Daryl, I told you hanging out only worked if you were sober."

"I'm sober. I just need to relax a little. Keep talkin', Duchess."

I weighed the situation carefully. If I could keep the conversation going, it might be good for him. If we got arrested for possession of marijuana, my life was as good as over. I decided that keeping the conversation going was worth the risk. "I was asking you what happened to Andrews and your friends, Daryl."

"We still see each other in school, and they're okay to me. But I pushed them away, I guess. And they think I'm fucked up...or something like that, which is probably true. Anyway, I don't really give a shit what they think. I don't need those guys."

"Oh...so you don't really have any friends anymore?" I asked.

"Only you, Duchess." He adeptly twisted the ends of the joint and then he struck a match and lit it.

I felt flattered that he considered us friends. "You know I have a name," I said to him. "It's Gabriel."

I saw the furrows above his eyebrows as he contemplated what I had just told him. "If it's all the same to you, I'd like to just call you Duchess," he replied. Then he took a long drag on the joint, holding the smoke inside his lungs for what seemed like a long time before releasing it.

He offered the joint to me, "Here try this, Duchess. It's really good stuff."

"No thanks, Daryl. I don't smoke pot either."

"Of course you don't," he said, shaking his head. "You read books four times...and you run miles and miles...and you memorize the names of rock stars, but you don't smoke or drink. Oh, and I noticed something else. You don't really swear much, do you?"

"Not if I can help it."

"Why's that?" he asked.

"I don't know exactly. It's just a choice, I guess."

"And sometimes you use big words."

"Well, I think it's because I like to read. I recently read an article in Reader's Digest — my parents get it — which was called 'The Power of Words.' The article talks about how highly successful people have good vocabularies, and it says the best way to acquire a good vocabulary is to read, which I do naturally, so I figure it just rubs off a little."

"Okay, Duchess. The perfect person. He reads. He runs. He's a walking encyclopedia. He never swears. And he uses big fuckin' words."

"None of those are terrible things, Daryl." The sweet pungent smell of the weed was pervasive in the small space. "Am I going to smell like this when I get home? Because if I do, I don't know how I'll explain it."

"It shouldn't be too bad, but I wouldn't get too close to anyone. And you might want to wash those clothes yourself," he suggested.

"So, what else you wanna talk about, Daryl?" I said, exasperated.

"You pick a subject," he said, as he continued to smoke. It appeared that he was becoming more relaxed, which was probably a good thing.

"Can I ask you a question about your sister?" I asked.

"I don't know about that one."

"I heard you call her Susie. Is that what everyone called her?"

"No, just our family. To everyone else, just Sue." Now gaining some momentum, he continued, "And my mom? When she's real mad at Susie, she calls her...she *called* her Susanna," he said, fixing his error in verb tense. He obviously had trouble thinking of her in the past tense. I could understand that.

"Were you close?" I asked.

"Once we might have been close, when we were kids, maybe, but not so much in recent years. I treated her lousy," he said sadly. "Oh, I remember what a cute little kid she was. She used to come to my Little League games, you know, and if a player hit a homer, whoever retrieved the ball would get a free ice cream bar if they turned it in. Susie would call to me, 'Hit a home run, Daryl! Hit a home run!' in her little cartoony voice."

"And did you?" I asked.

"More than a few. And then if some other bratty kid beat her to the ball, she would bust out crying," he remembered.

"Yeah, that's kind of a funny story...and kind of a nice one too," I said.

"Yeah." We sat in silence for a good long while. He smoked, and I chilled out. It was one of those silences when you don't know what to say next. Finally, I found myself compelled to share something. "Daryl, can I tell you something?"

"Go for it, Duchess," he said.

As I began, I wondered if my brain was being affected by the smoke in the car. I spoke very slowly and carefully. "Daryl, this...this may...may surprise you...but...but I met your sister...I met — Susanna — the night...the night of the accident."

He turned to me, suddenly more alert and attentive than he had been a few moments ago.

I continued. "Yeah. Truth. I was at the dance at the Derby Community Center. I saw her there...and...and I danced with her...twice. She was a beautiful girl. I hope you don't mind, but that's what happened."

He squinted and smiled like the light had dawned on him. "I get it, Duchess. You had a crush on my little sister. On Susie. That makes a lot of sense. No, I don't mind. After all, like I just said, you're the perfect person."

I had no words.

"Then I went and ruined it all for you, didn't I?"

"How do you mean?" I asked, puzzled.

"I mean...I killed her." His voice broke with emotion.

"Daryl, what are you talking about? Adamo was driving the car," I said, trying to clear up his apparent confusion.

"You might know a lot of fuckin' things, Duchess...about authors who write without starting new paragraphs and other useless shit, but what you don't know is this — if I wasn't such a fuck-up, Susie would still be alive and you'd probably be dancing with her again."

"Daryl, I'm feeling really confused. I don't understand."

"It's basic math, Duchess. I was supposed to drive her home from that dance, but I let her down. I had the guys with me, so I made her walk to Duchess. The whole thing was my fault, not Frankie Adamo's. Do I have to fuckin' spell it out for you?" Fat tears began rolling down his cheeks now.

"Aw, geez, Daryl," I said. "Don't blame yourself for something like that. You couldn't know what would happen."

He snuffed the joint out. "Let's get the fuck outta here, Duchess. I'm tired of talking." He wiped the tears away on the sleeves of his army jacket.

It was 10:15. "Yeah, it might be best," I said. "I need to be home by 11:00."

We drove in silence, and he got off on Pershing Drive. Was he going to Duchess? I hoped not. But he headed towards downtown Ansonia. He turned on Main Street and pulled up to a curb next to some dark stores. He jumped out of the car and entered a door between a luncheonette and a bakery. I watched him ascend a flight of stairs in a dimly lit hallway. I had no idea where he was going. He was back in a few minutes with a bag.

"What's that?" I asked.

"I need a drink," he said. I could see now that it was another jumbo beer bottle.

"Where did you get that?" I asked.

"It's not who ya are, Duchess, it's who ya know."

He took off down Main Street, and he turned right on Bridge Street and then a left on Pershing Drive. "I'm gonna just stop and get a burger," he said. "That weed gave me the munchies."

Oh no, I thought. *This isn't good,* but I could see he was determined. He pulled into a space at Duchess and pushed the bottle into my chest and said, "Hold this."

Thankfully, he pulled the front of the car into the space, so people passing by only saw the back of my head. As I waited, I could see that Kevin Binkowski was cleaning the lot. I prayed he wouldn't see me. All I needed was Bink to walk over to the Bug and see me holding a giant beer bottle like it was a baby or something. Daryl wasn't long. Before I knew it, he was back in the car. I handed him his bottle back. In exchange, he handed me a bag with a burger, fry, and a Coke in it.

"I thought you'd be hungry too after all that sliding on the ice."

"Thanks," I said.

He waved off the thanks, grabbed the bottle back from me, and started to chug it.

"Hey, put that down! Someone will see us. None of this is supposed to be happening, Daryl. We made an agreement that you'd be sober."

"For most of the night I was," he said. "But don't worry, you're going home now."

"Aren't you?" I asked.

"Not by a long shot, Duchess. I have 'miles to go before I sleep.' I think that's from a book. Look it up."

And he pulled out of the space. I hung my head down low as he circled the lot. I think Tommy Trouble was working and I especially didn't want to be seen by him.

He headed down Pershing Drive, alternating between eating his burger and then putting it in his lap and gulping down beer. As we passed the Bradlees Plaza, he made his way toward the long, curving ramp which led onto Route 8 South toward Shelton. As we got closer to the end of the ramp, we could see two police cars with lights flashing. They were pulling cars over.

"Oh fuck! A spot check," Daryl moaned. He pushed the beer bottle into my chest and ordered. "Throw this fuckin' thing out the window! Far!"

"What?" I said, panicking.

"Wake the fuck up, Duchess!" he yelled at the top of his lungs. "Throw it over the guard rails. Throw the fucker!"

Following orders, I quickly rolled down the window, and, with the neck of the bottle in my left hand and a short flick of my wrist, I flung it as hard as I could, sending it like a boomerang into the night. And just in the nick of time. I could see a police officer flagging us over to the shoulder with a flashlight. Had he seen me throw the bottle?

Daryl rolled down the window as the officer looked into the car, blinding me with his long flashlight.

"How you boys doing tonight?" he asked.

"We're doing good, officer," Daryl replied politely.

"Where you coming from, boys?" the officer asked.

"We were at an ice skating party with some good friends," Daryl offered. *Oh God,* I thought, *please don't ask us to see our skates.*

"You boys been drinking?" he asked.

"No, sir," Daryl said. "We don't drink, do we, Gabriel?"

"No, sir, we don't," I said.

"And where are you off to now?" he asked Daryl.

"Shelton. I'm going to drop my buddy Gabriel home because he has an 11:00 curfew, don't you, Gabe?"

"Right," I replied.

It seemed like the time to say as little as possible. The officer flashed his light around the car, and seeing nothing, he said, "You better do something about that muffler, son."

"Yes, I'm getting that fixed soon." Daryl had an answer for everything. He must have been practicing lying like me.

"Okay, boys, you can go on your way. Drive carefully."

As we pulled away, Daryl said, smiling, "Nice throw, Duchess. Like I said, maybe you do have some potential. But every time I have a good bottle of beer, you end up ruining it." We both chuckled.

"I don't want to say anything, but that was a close call," I said with a sigh of relief.

"Woohoo," he sang out, and then he flicked his wrist, imitating the way I had thrown the bottle out the window, and we both broke up. I mean, I don't know if I have ever cracked up like that.

"I'll say this," I continued, through my convulsive laughter. "Life is never dull with you, is it?"

"You can say that again," he replied, so carried away by his laughter now that tears were streaming down his cheeks. It was one of those moments when something strikes you *and* someone else so funny that it kind of makes you bond with the other person. Anyway, the only other person I ever remember sharing this feeling with is Michael.

As the volley of laughter between us subsided, he sped down the exit ramp, turned right at the light, and then took the quick left onto Maltby Street hill faster than anybody should make that turn. After getting over the initial shock of the reckless turn he had made, I felt kind of flattered that he remembered the way to my house.

"Okay, Daryl, well it was a fun night, mostly." I got out of the car, ready to shut the door and head up the stairs to our apartment.

"Fun for me too. See you around."

"Yeah, sure. Oh, and thanks for the food. I was hungry too."

"That's payback for the free food you gave me that night. I don't know how I'm going to pay you back for saving my life, but I'll figure something out eventually. I pay all my debts, Duchess."

I pushed the door shut and made my way around the car. He rolled down his window. "Hey," he called and then after pausing, softly said, "It's good to have a friend again. Take care...Gabe." Standing curbside, I watched him drive off into the night. Hearing him genuinely call me by my real name surprised me a little. It kind of boggled my mind that he even called me his friend. *Daryl Novak* called *me* his friend. He shared some pretty heavy things with me that night, and we laughed a lot, just like real friends. It felt really good.

16

Before I knew it, we were past the middle of January, and there was a ton of excitement in the air because of a nationally televised college basketball game, touted as "the Game of Century," between the number one ranked UCLA Bruins and the number two ranked University of Houston Cougars. Both teams had marquee players in Lew Alcindor for the Bruins and Elvin Hayes, known as the Big E, for the Cougars. Michael told me that Hayes, along with another teammate, were the first two black guys ever to play for Houston. It was hard to believe that black players were so new to any American university. UCLA had won the national championship three of the last four years, and they were riding a two and a half year, forty-seven game winning streak. Kind of the Derby High School of college basketball. Unbelievable! Houston, also undefeated this season, suffered their last loss, ironically, to the Bruins a year ago in the semi-finals of the NCAA tournament. The guys at Duchess wanted to get some betting going, but no one was stupid enough to bet against UCLA. No one, that is, except Michael. I know he bet with Will and with the always-willing-to-bet Howie, and maybe others. *God only knows how much money he might lose,* I thought. But when Elvin Hayes responded to a pro-Houston crowd chanting "Big E...Big E...Big E" with a remarkable 39 point performance, leading his team to a two point win which ended the Bruins' long win streak, Michael suddenly wasn't looking that stupid anymore.

So happy was he, in fact, that the next afternoon, as Mom was preparing our Sunday dinner, Michael made an announcement. As I was snacking on a piece of Italian bread with Mom's incredible meat sauce on it, Michael burst into the room and said, "I want everyone to know that from now on you are to call me the Big M."

"What're you talking about?" I asked.

"What I'm talking about is, Elvin Hayes is known as the Big E, and from now on I want to be known as the Big M, so I'd appreciate it if you all address me that way."

"You're crazy," our mother remarked with a baffled smile.

"No I'm not," he argued, good-naturedly, "and for your further information, from now on, you are to be known as the Big C." Our mother's name is Cecelia. Mom blushed, and both she and I were charmed by Michael's energy and enthusiasm. He was obviously feeling high because he had picked the winner of the Game of the Century and won a ton of money in the process.

Let me just say that Michael is the only guy I've ever known who gave himself a nickname. Most of the time, Michael was giving nicknames to other kids, like Bink or Tommy Trouble or kids in the neighborhood, like Fish and Mouse and Sparky. In this case, the nickname stuck, and, in no time at all, everyone we knew was calling him the Big M. The Big M didn't dub me the big anything, though. I was maybe not big enough in size or importance. I ended up thinking of myself as the Little G anyway.

The next time I saw Daryl was at Duchess the following Tuesday night. He came to the window at about 9:30 p.m. Will Granger asked, "What'll it be?" and Daryl ordered eleven coffees. Will teased, "Got a gang with you tonight?" to which Daryl responded, "No, it's for the guys at Charlton Press." Charlton Press was just down the road on the corner of Pershing Drive and Division diagonally across from the Texaco station. Daryl had a list of how each coffee should be made — black, dark, light and sweet, etc. — which Will handed to me, since I was the drink man. As I prepared the coffees, Will, always personable, initiated a conversation with Daryl.

"You work at Charlton Press now?" Not that Will knew Daryl personally, but everyone pretty much knew who Daryl was.

"Yup," Daryl answered, "the 3:00 to 11:00 shift. Today's my first night. My old man told me I had to get a job and pay for my own car insurance or it would be the end of driving for me. No other choice I guess."

"Your dad paid for it up until now?" Will asked, making some small talk.

"Yeah...and he gave me an allowance because...you know...I used to play three sports, so between school and practice and games, there wasn't much time for me to get a job. But, uhm, now I have the time."

I was surprised that Daryl brought up sports, and I found myself marveling at how openly he was sharing. I brought the coffees to the counter carefully in three cardboard trays. When I reached the counter, Will rang up the order and I made eye contact with Daryl. "What's up?" Daryl said, almost as if we didn't know each other. We apparently weren't going to let on that we were friends. I saw that his eyes were bloodshot and wondered if he was drinking or smoking weed on the job. I wondered what he did at Charlton Press. Nothing too important, I supposed. Probably just a gofer.

Will thanked him and walked away from the window, and Daryl gave me a look and a nod that I felt said, "We'll catch up to each other." I hoped it said that.

Charlton Press is owned by probably the richest family, not only in Derby, but in the entire Valley — the San Marini family. Everyone knows about them. God, they own half of Derby. My dad told me they own pretty much the whole Derby side of Pershing Drive, including the Bradlees Plaza, the Valley Bowl, and Charlton Press. Their house on the corner of Atwater and Division at the crest of the hill looks like an Italian villa. When passing it, you feel like you should genuflect and bless yourself. It occurred to me that the San Marini villa is not more than a few hundred feet from where Susanna had been struck by Adamo's Lemans.

For a few weeks, I only saw Daryl in his capacity as a Charlton Press employee. He worked Monday through Friday nights, and I didn't always work on Saturdays or Sundays, but when I worked on a weeknight, seeing each other was now a given. He started bringing us magazines and comic books that were printed at the Press. He'd place his orders for eleven coffees, which must have covered the entire second shift, and he'd drop a half dozen magazines on the counter. The comic books were mostly recognizable, like *Archie*, *Beetle Bailey*, and *Little Lulu*, all of which I had been familiar with for most of my life. Others were obscure car and nudie magazines — nothing like *Car and Driver* or *Motor Trend* or *Playboy* or *Penthouse*, but names like *Corvette Fever*, *Auto Round-Up*, *Black Silk Stockings*, and *Girls on Parade*. They featured lots of photos of cars or girls — or cars *and* girls — on what seemed like cheap, high gloss paper. Not the greatest, but it gave us guys something to pass the time during the last hour of work, presuming our cleaning was done.

Soon, February blew in, and two nights before my sixteenth birthday, the Big M and I went to see Derby play basketball in the state tournament. They were not nearly as good in basketball as they had been in football. In fact, at 10-8, they were the lowest seeded team in their classification, and in this first tournament game, they had drawn the number one seed, Kolbe Cathedral, an all boys' Catholic school in Bridgeport. It was no secret that Kolbe recruited black players from Bridgeport. Among them was the current best player in the state, Trevor Rogers, an unbelievably good wing player who could shoot the eyes out of the basket or go inside and jump over everyone if needed. Derby, on the other hand, was mainly a carbon copy of their football team with only two players who were strictly basketball specialists. Unlike football season, Michael and I weren't there in hopes that Derby would lose but just because we wanted to see the great Rogers play. Also, one of our co-workers, Robbie Latella, was an important player for Derby. Robbie is shorter than me, and he isn't particularly fast on the court or a great jumper, but he is one of the best shooters I have ever seen. I mean, he hardly ever misses. His hand-eye coordination is totally unbelievable. Here's the thing — if you pitch coins against the wall with Robbie when things are slow at work, you had better be prepared to lose some dough. If you want to win a stuffed animal at the baseball pitching booth at a local carnival, just ask Robbie to throw the balls for you. One night, a group of us were at the local Holy Rosary Food Fest in Ansonia, which featured carnival games, and parents got in line asking Robbie to win their kids stuffed animals. Robbie couldn't miss. Eventually the manager of the carnival came by and pretty much pleaded with him not to continue to play. It was fun seeing the carnival manager squirm.

The Derby-Kolbe game took place at Naugatuck High School, a neutral court, not that that was going to help Derby. The place was packed. Wall to wall people on both sides. Standing room only. When the Kolbe team entered the court for warmups, their side of the stands went berserk. The first five players, starting with Rogers, dunked the ball in the lay-up drill, sending their fans into an insane frenzy. Michael and I made eye contact, eyes that said, "This isn't going to be bad; it's going to be ugly!"

We were surprised to see that our friend Robbie didn't start, and even more surprised to see that, as the game progressed, he saw very little action. Derby's starters were the three football All Staters, Nickie Grasso, Trent Stanley, and Frankie Adamo at point guard. Joining them were Marvin Williamson, another solid football player and probably the only black kid in Derby, and finally Zack Kowalski, who was the only true basketball player on the floor for the Red Raiders. As the game unfolded, Michael and I couldn't believe our eyes as Derby intimidated and bullied the Kolbe team. It started to look more like a football game than a basketball game, and that was a style of play Kolbe was having trouble with, no matter how many of their guys dunked. At one point, a Kolbe player responded with a rough foul, cutting Marvin Williamson's feet out from under him, causing the high jumping Williamson to hit the deck with a hard thud. The Derby fans around us freaked. Angie Garuffi, a big Derby lineman, jumped over our third row seats onto the court, as if to defend his gridiron teammate. Several Derby students had to hold him back. As Marvin headed to the foul line, we could see Nickie Grasso put a muscular arm around the Kolbe player who had committed the foul and bring his right index finger up to the player's nose, probably telling him what was going to happen to him the next time he fouled one of the Derby players. I felt sorry for the Kolbe kid.

At halftime, Derby was only down, incredibly, by two. With a minute and a half left, the score was tied. Michael and I couldn't believe what we were seeing. Was Derby going to actually knock off the number one seed and end the career of the best player in the state with a loss? Rogers had other ideas, though. With his teammates rendered ineffective, especially inside the bucket, Rogers took over, swishing four long range shots in the closing ninety seconds to secure the win by eight points. One after another from way downtown: Bang! Bang! Bang! Bang! Derby's upset bid had been foiled, but, for me, it was the most exciting high school basketball game I had ever seen.

Frankie Adamo had done a fine job at point guard, scoring thirteen points and feeding his fellow players for eleven assists, having perhaps his best game ever. I wondered what it must be like for the Frankie Adamos, and for that matter the Daryl Novaks, of the world, to excel at every sport they tried. Robbie Latella and the Derby kids tell a story about Adamo as a junior. He was walking back from baseball practice and passing the track team as they were working out. He and Grasso stopped and watched the javelin throwers work on their technique. The muscular Adamo walked over to one of the boys and said, "Lemme see that thing." Having never touched a javelin in his life, Frankie trotted, taking the ten or twelve steps he had observed the throwers take, and then he launched the aluminum spear up into the air, sending it soaring just below the white clouds until it landed, point down, in the grass, a throw farther than any current varsity track athlete had achieved during his career. Some said the throw would have been a new school record if Frankie had been on the team and the throw had happened during a meet. They say he flashed his classic arrogant smile at the dumbfounded track athletes and headed to the locker room.

As for me, I guess I had been in the process of making my mark as a distance runner, but that's about endurance, not about skill exactly. And it certainly isn't a glamour sport like football or basketball. Yes, I was a junior varsity player on our basketball team and, while I started some games, there was no certainty that I would eventually be a varsity player. This season, there were guys in my class who were already dressing varsity, so I was basically behind them. Would I ever play in a game against the likes of a Trevor Rogers? And, if so, would I show I could be competitive against that level of competition as Adamo had been tonight? Were guys like Adamo and Novak born with an absurd skill level at everything, or was it something they developed over time? *It must be nice,* I thought on the way out to the Corvair, *to be a legend in your own time.* And then reality hit me — Daryl and Frankie were now both parties to a different Valley legend that brought with it no glamour.

When we got into the car and slammed the doors, the Big M, befuddled, shook his head and said, "Well they almost pulled off the fucking upset. Just when you thought their heads couldn't get any bigger."

"That was some game," I replied. "Robbie hardly got to play."

"Kolbe would have shut Robbie down completely," Michael said. "He can't handle their speed or their pressure. Derby's coach had a good strategy. Play a football game out there and see what you come away with. Let's go see what's happenin' at Duchess."

It was only about a fifteen minute ride to Ansonia. It was a crisp

February night, so Michael had to intermittently wipe the frost off the inside of the windshield, and I thought the gas fumes in the car would asphyxiate us. We both rolled our windows part way down so we could breathe. The Corvair is a real classic. When we pulled into the parking lot, things were already cooking. Ansonia High had played in a tournament game as well and their fans already filled the vestibule. The Derby fans were arriving as we were. Will, Tommy Trouble, Bink, and Les Wilson were on, leaving them with only one true window man. In a jam, Tomaso could have taken the second window, but it wasn't really his bag.

"Let's go in and lend a hand," Michael said as he jumped out of the car and made a beeline for the back door. He loved Duchess and lived for moments like these. I followed the Big M in like his obedient puppy dog. He opened the second window, and I helped get drinks, along with Bink, for Michael and Will. The rush lasted for more than a half hour. Soon, the Derby players themselves walked in, having achieved what they undoubtedly considered a moral victory. Normally, you're supposed to feel bad when you lose a game. But, in this case, Derby should have gotten blown out. They had the best team in the state on the ropes, and, if not for the heroics of a blue chip player who was being recruited by Division I colleges, Derby might have won. Grasso, Stanley, Williamson, Belchak, and Adamo entered the vestibule as if they were English royalty. Robbie, Zack Kowalski, and the other non-football players seemed a little more humble. Fans were congratulating the team just as if they had won. Remarks like, "Nice game guys"..."You deserved to win it"..."Rogers won't forget you guys anytime soon" echoed throughout the glass enclosed space. I marveled at the good fortune of the Derby players. They seemed to win even when they lost.

When the rush subsided, Will said, "Thanks, fellas. We would have been buried without you."

Robbie soon came in the back door, and we gave the crew a verbal replay of the game. He wasn't even upset that he didn't see much action. A quiet, unassuming guy, Robbie still had two years of high school in front of him. At about 10:45, Michael decided we should head home, so we made our way to the car. As we approached the Corvair, the Derby players were parked right next to it. Grasso and Belchak were sitting on the hood of a Dodge Dart talking to one girl, and Frankie was leaning against the front passenger door of the Big M's Corvair, talking to two other giggling girls.

When I reached the door, Frankie was obviously in my way, so I timidly said, "Uhm, excuse me. I just need to get in our car."

"No problem, man," Frankie said, almost not looking at me, and then he took a few steps, the two girls scooting along with him.

"By the way," I offered. "We saw the game tonight. You played a real nice one."

Hearing my compliment, he now made eye contact with me, smiled his winning smile, and replied, "Thanks, I really appreciate that, Duchess."

It was eerie to hear him address me in the same way Daryl always did. What were the chances of that? I guess people were so used to seeing us working that it wasn't all that unusual to associate us with the name of the place, but it was still super strange. I realized that it was the first time Frankie Adamo and I had ever said a word to each other.

What I also realized was that, since the accident, I never saw Frankie driving anymore. The Dodge Dart they were just hanging out near was obviously not his. He drove that beautiful Lemans. These days, he was always a passenger in Grasso's or Belchak's cars while prior to the accident, it was usually the other way around.

As we drove away, I said, "Hey, Big M, you ever notice that we never see Frankie driving his Lemans anymore?"

"Yeah, the word on the street is that his lawyer told him not to drive until after the trial. He doesn't need any new traffic violations."

"Oh, yeah, that makes sense," I said.

"Dig it," he said. "I don't think we'll see him driving for a very long time. I also hear he isn't drinking anymore. Trying to keep his nose clean before the trial is in full swing."

"You think he'll get convicted of a crime?" I asked.

"I hope not. He's got his whole life in front of him, and he's not a bad kid really. I'm willing to bet he feels pretty bad about what happened. Accidents happen, but who the fuck knows what the future will bring?"

The Big M was a good guy. In fact, it hit me smack between the eyes that he was a better person than me. I personally wasn't as quick to let Frankie Adamo off the hook or forgive him. I didn't like the way he was casually joking around with the two stupid, giggling girls. Not at all. I wondered if he even cared that he had run down poor Susanna only a few months before. It sure didn't seem so. I thought to myself, *Who knows if Frankie even feels any guilt over what he did?* Or to use Michael's expression, *Who the fuck knows?*

17

The only time I saw Daryl during the rest of wintertime was when I worked on weeknights. He continued to come by for coffees for the crew on the Charlton Press night shift. In the process, he became a little more familiar with some of the guys who worked at Duchess, especially with the magnetic Will Granger. Will is so socially gifted that just about everyone who comes in contact with him likes him. Even businessmen who come to the window — guys in grey suits and little gold tie-clips on their maroon neckties — try to steal Will away from Duchess. Truth! "When are you going to come work for me?" they'll ask Will, never asking if he has any post high school education, which he doesn't. Will just laughs it off in his own good natured way. "You need me like you need a hole in the head," he'll joke and then flash that million dollar smile of his. And there doesn't seem to be a woman between sixteen and sixty who doesn't shamelessly flirt with Will. It makes you kind of wish you were him. Well, except for the older ladies. Since sex is one of the most talked about topics at work, Will likes to razz the other guys about it. A common greeting from Will goes something like this: "What's up, Gabe? Gettin' much?" which for me is kind of an absurd question since I still obviously have neither any sexual experience nor a girlfriend to be "gettin' much" from. But with another guy — a guy with a girlfriend — it might get a little more graphic. After the initial greeting, Will might get closer to the guy and almost whisper: "You bangin' your girlfriend yet?" Some kids try to avoid answering the question because their relationship with girls hasn't progressed to that stage yet. In such cases, Will will add, "I hope so...because if you aren't, somebody else is." Personally, I don't know what to think about that one. Let's just say I hope Will is wrong.

Such is the cynical perspective held by Will who is a married man. I'm going to cut him some slack, though, because maybe there are good reasons for his cynicism. From what I've heard, when he returned from Vietnam, Will came home to a pregnant wife. The problem was that the last time he had seen his wife was more than a year before. Will and his wife are still married, but he has an active sex life outside of his marriage, which he makes no secret of. Some guys brag about their sexual escapades. Some exaggerate or manufacture sexual experiences. Not in Will's case, apparently. Howie likes to tell a story about how he once doubted that Will was getting all the action he claimed, until one day Will walked into Howie's office and dropped a stack of sexy Polaroid snapshots on his desk. Howie tells the story with an admiration for Will that I find myself questioning, considering the lessons on sex, love, and marriage that I have been brought up with. It sounds a little gross, I guess. But I still like Will a lot. I just can't help it. Anyway, nobody's perfect.

When March arrived, I was working on the same crew as Will when Daryl came to the window at the usual 9:30 time. Will was spraying polish on and meticulously wiping down the stainless steel counters, giving them a gleaming sheen, when he turned around and saw Daryl.

He offered his standard greeting, "Hey, Daryl, what's up, buddy? Gettin' much?"

"About the same as usual, Will," Daryl offered with irony.

"Too bad," Will offered sympathetically. "Got your list?" Daryl laid it on the counter, and Will handed it to me.

"Hi Daryl," I said.

"What's up, Duchess?" he responded.

"Hey! How come he gets to be called Duchess?" Will asked good-naturedly. "Is Gabe the new owner or something?"

Daryl shrugged. "Naw, just kind of an inside joke, right Gabe?"

"Right," I said. It was only the third time he had called me by my first name since our outing on the pond in Seymour, which was more than a month ago.

Changing the subject, Will said, "Hey Daryl, I've been meaning to ask. Where'd ya get your hands on that military-issue jacket?"

"Oh, this beat up rag? My cousin who is in the Army and stationed in Korea got it for me." The coat was indeed beat up. I hadn't seen Daryl wear anything else except at the Derby game and the funeral. It looked like Daryl slept in it.

Military clothing has become something of a trend. You see lots of guys and girls in bell bottom jeans and a military shirt or jacket. Kind of a hippie thing. I am realizing, in a way, it is a subtle protest against the war. Sometimes you find yourself looking and thinking a little like the hippies, even though you're not really one of them. The World War II veterans like my father don't like seeing kids in military apparel, nor do they like anything that hippies say or do.

"Oh okay," Will replied, "but let me give you a word of advice. Don't follow in your cousin's footsteps. Be smart. Stay out of the military."

Obviously puzzled, Daryl wasn't sure why Will was offering this sober advice, but I certainly knew why. But Will is a complex guy. Between surviving the horrors of what he and so many felt was a pointless war and returning home to a wife who had been unfaithful, he had been through a lot. While I didn't approve of everything he did, I also found it kind of hard to judge him. I still feel he has a lot of good in him.

After ringing up Daryl's order, Will said goodbye to Daryl and headed toward the back of the store. I brought over the cardboard trays with the coffees, and Daryl and I had a few minutes to talk.

"What's new, Duchess?" he asked.

"Nothing at all."

"We have to get together again sometime, maybe slide around on a pond or drive through a spot check or run on some railroad tracks," he said, trying to be funny.

"I don't think the pond is frozen solid anymore, and, if you don't mind, I'd rather not do either of the last two," I offered.

"Okay...but really, let's connect some time. I could use some Duchess time again."

"You name it," I said.

"Well, it would have to be a Saturday or Sunday since I work every weeknight."

"Okay," I said. "Let me check the upcoming schedules for the next few weeks and see when I'm not working."

"You got it, Duchess. I'll look forward to it." Before he picked up the tray, he flicked his wrist in that bottle throwing motion of mine, and we both cracked up again. As Daryl exited the store, Will came up behind me, holding a new can of stainless steel polish.

"What's so funny?" Will asked.

Still laughing, I replied, "Oh, nothing...nothing. It's just...just kind of an inside joke."

"You and Novak seem to have a lot of inside jokes," he said with skepticism.

"Kind of," I said, trying to suppress the laughter. "It's hard to explain. Just something only he and I would understand."

Will gave me a baffled look like he didn't know what to say, then finally, he advised, "Well, tell him not to join the military or nobody's going to be laughing anymore." And he began spraying down the silver counters again.

A few days later, at the end of the day when I walked out of the building after school, I was surprised to find Jeff waiting for me right beyond all the buses. It was just past the middle of our sophomore year, and Jeff was attending his third Valley high school, which if you ask me was kind of unusual. After spending his entire freshman year at

Derby High School, he had transferred to Shelton at the beginning of our sophomore year, and now he was attending a technical high school in Ansonia.

When our eyes met, I smiled. "What the hell are you doing here? Didn't you go to school today?"

"Nope," he replied, "it's a holiday at Emmett O'Brien Tech today."

"What holiday is that?" I asked.

"It's Jeff Takes a Holiday Day," and we both cracked up.

As we walked down Perry Hill Road toward downtown Shelton, we talked about the upcoming baseball season and the Yankees' playoff hopes. We grew up in a world of Yankee fans, but their glory years had ended shortly before our high school years. Unbelievably, between 1947 and 1964, the Yankees won the American League Pennant fifteen times and the World Series ten times, making them the greatest dynasty in the history of pro sports. All that in only seventeen years. Amazing. It was simply an unreal level of success that I don't personally think will ever be matched. Except that it kind of happened before I was actually a sports fan. It figures. Now in the spring of 1968, despite our hopes, they were a sub-par team. The great Mickey Mantle was still playing, but injuries and age had gotten the best of him.

"My brother will be sad when Mantle retires," I said.

"Don't I know it. Nobody loves the Mick more than the Big M, but I'm a close second."

When we reached the corner of Center Street, Jeff opened the glass door of Kushner's Drug Store and took a seat at the soda counter. While Jeff was a student at Shelton High, we always stopped there on our way home from school. It was automatic. He ordered a cherry Coke, and I ordered my favorite, a vanilla soda with milk. Johnny O'Connor, a recent grad who worked the counter, would say, "Same thing, fellas?" practically while dispensing the drinks. Kushner's was closer to the high school than Mosci's and had a completely different vibe. For one thing, it was cleaner. It also wasn't a hangout — no pinball machines, no jukebox, and no sexy magazines. We finished our drinks, making a bubbly, slurping sound through our straws as we always had, and we headed out the door.

"So, I wanna tell you something," Jeff said as we headed further along down Center Street.

"What's up?" I asked.

"I've been talking to a Marine recruiter at school. I'm joining up."

I was stunned, "You're what? Joining up? How can you join up? You're only sixteen!"

"He said I can join as soon as I turn seventeen, which is at the end of May, in case you forgot, Shakespeare." Even though Jeff and I were in the tenth grade, while I had just turned sixteen, he would turn seventeen in May because he had stayed back in an early grade.

I was completely rocked, considering the constant stream of news about anti-war protests, not to mention the fact that I had heard a firsthand, cynical but truthful account from Will about the way it was in Vietnam.

"But...you won't be finished with high school yet."

"The Sarge told me no problem...the Marines will set me up to take a high school equivalency exam and get me my diploma. He told me not to sweat that."

"The Sarge?"

"Sergeant Higgins, the recruiter."

I was running out of arguments. "But nobody enlists anymore. Somebody needs to tell the Sarge that. Maybe you haven't heard that we're fighting an insane war in Vietnam," I said sarcastically. "Why would you...why would *anybody* want to end up in Vietnam?"

I had gotten carried away, I knew, but I couldn't help thinking about Will's description of life in Vietnam. I almost blurted it out, but I thought better of it, sparing Jeff the ugly details.

"The Sarge told me that they...uhm...let's see...that they don't... wait...that they *can't* send anybody to Vietnam until they're eighteen, and since I won't be eighteen for another year, by that time, he told me I'll already have been assigned somewhere else, making it highly doubtful that I'll receive orders to go to Nam. And if they send me and I have to shoot a few gooks, then that's what I'll have to do."

I had heard others use these derogatory labels, shortening the name of the country to *Nam* and calling its people *gooks*, just like the Japanese were called *Japs* during World War II, but hearing Jeff talk like this bugged me. He must have heard the recruiter use this language. *The Power of Words,* I thought. I was practically speechless. We walked in silence to the main intersection and waited at the crosswalk to turn right and head home up Coram Avenue.

As we passed Fowler School where Jeff and I had met as little kids on the playground, the long grassy lawn in front of the tan, brick building held many memories, like memories of pick up football games — sometimes two-on-two or three-on-three. I would usually play quarterback and throw the long ball to Jeff. He had great hands and caught a pass thrown anywhere near him, making me look good. When I wanted to improve my status in Babe Ruth Baseball from bench warmer to starter, Jeff helped me improve on my hitting form on the lawn of Fowler School, because hitting a baseball was something else he excelled at. The truth was that the only sport I could compete with him in was basketball. I got to thinking of how just the two of us would stand at opposite ends of the lawn, throwing high pops to each other. I would inevitably throw an errant ball up on the third story roof of the building. That left us no other choice but to scale the low part of the brick building above which was a flat roof and a window with a broken lock. Like thieves in the night, we would enter the building and climb our way up to the roof above the third floor to retrieve our ball. While we caused no harm to the building, if we had been caught, we would probably have been arrested for breaking and entering, something that would have gone over real big with my dad.

We approached the corner, which was home to an ancient Maple tree. The biggest tree in the neighborhood, it had massive roots that accommodated a half dozen neighborhood boys who would sit and drink Giant Colas from the local grocer on a hot summer day. There was a system of seniority at the tree, and we younger boys would have to get up if Michael and the older guys showed up. Jeff and I each took a seat on a root.

"Well before you officially sign up or anything, you need to really think about this," I offered.

"Too late, Shakespeare. It's official. I already signed on the dotted line."

"I just don't understand why you're doing this," I moaned.

"I don't know," he said, sullenly. "Things kind of suck at home. I hate my mother's boyfriend. He's a real dick. Everything sucks. I just need to get out of here, and joining the Marines is one way to do it. Haven't you ever just wanted to book? You know, to just fuckin' get away from everything?"

"Well, yeah. Of course. But not by joining the Marines."

Jeff's eyes reflected his disappointment at my negative reaction. It made me think about our friendship. In our neighborhood, we were part of a big group of boys, but Jeff and I really started to bond, apart from the bigger group, in the middle school grades when we developed both a sports rivalry as well as a mutual crush on a neighborhood girl, Noreen Kozlowski. Jeff "dated" her before we entered eighth grade, and I "dated" her before ninth. Our games of one-on-one were fierce, but we remained friends no matter who won. And Noreen? Well, whichever one of us she showed affection for was the object of green envy from the other, yet somehow it didn't change our closeness. But our bond really became unbreakable in ninth grade when the neighborhood guys began drinking before dances and night games. Mikey Casella would steal homemade wine from his grampa's basement, and the guys would congregate behind the big stone wall on High Street and pass the gallon jug around. I didn't want to participate, which the group generally didn't like. Jeff stuck by me, though. "If you don't drink, then I don't drink, partner," he assured me. And that was that. How can you not appreciate that kind of friend?

And sure, maybe I didn't approve of his sexual relationship with Julie, but maybe that was some kind of repressed jealousy or maybe even a psychological problem I had. I had also felt abandoned because he had been spending so much time with her. As he left me at the corner of Maltby Street and headed to his grandmother's house, I realized that no one had a perfect family and that everyone had problems. It hit me smack between the eyes that Jeff had problems that he didn't usually talk about. That isn't his style. He signed up for the Marines because he was unhappy at home. I realized that my last two years of high school were going to be really difficult without Jeff. As I stood at the corner, watching him walk up Prospect Avenue in the distance, my throat felt as if I had swallowed something whole, something hard, and it wouldn't go down. I found myself wondering if he could get me an Army coat like Daryl's. It would serve a dual purpose. I'd wear it as my own personal protest against the war in Vietnam, but also as a tribute to my friend, my *best* friend who might end up there.

18

As I considered any family problems Jeff may have been facing, I began to think of my own. I knew then, and I know now, that my family is far from perfect, even if Dad and Mom try to pretend it is. Memories of arguments between them as well as between Dad and Michael replayed in my mind. Dinnertime in our house, especially when Michael was in high school, often erupted into an hour of arguing and hollering. I mean, usually Dad would start yelling at Michael for some reason, like because he didn't get all As on his report card, Mom would yell at Dad for yelling at Michael, and before you knew it, everyone except me was yelling. Kids don't like to see their parents fight, and Michael and I are no exceptions. I remember being eleven years old and witnessing a particularly hostile fight between our parents one Sunday. I don't even remember what it was about or how it got going, but, in the midst of the heated quarrel, Michael left the table and bolted out the door. Mom yelled at my father, "See? Damn you! See what you did?" Dad was at the door in a flash, yelling for all the world to hear, "Get back here, Michael! God dammit! You get back here right now!" Echoing through the neighborhood, Dad's words not only went unheeded by Michael but they also further fueled the argument with our mother. Feeling lost and alone, I copied Michael, like I always did at that age, and flew out the door as he had moments before. I found Michael at the big Maple at the corner of Fowler School. At this time of day, there were no other kids at the tree, especially on a Sunday — just a very wounded Michael. I sat down on a mammoth root near him, but he didn't make eye contact with me and neither of us spoke. Sometimes, the deepest connections happen when nothing is being said...when, without a look or a word, you know you occupy the same head space as someone else. Finally, he got up and headed back to Maltby Street. I followed about ten feet behind him because, I mean, I knew my place, and, after arriving home, no one spoke of that argument ever again. It seemed our parents had the presence of mind to leave well enough alone.

As the month of March arrived, we started to get some relief from the biting cold temperatures, but the sides of the roads still had lingering strips of dirty snow and ice. Basketball season had come to an end. It had been a good one for me. Having emerged as the starting point guard on the JV squad for the entire second half of the season made me feel like I was in good shape for the future. Some of the guys on the team poked fun at me during the season, addressing me as Gabriel Ruggerio, which was the last name of our JV coach. I didn't mind the ribbing, though, because if you want to survive in a world of guys and sports, you have to be able dish it out as well as take it. Or at the very least, take it. Track practices had begun. Feeling like I needed a break, I was considering not going out for Track, but when Coach McMahon got wind of my reluctance, he waited for me outside my English class to convince me to participate. He and I didn't know each other, but he had heard about my Cross Country success. It felt pretty good to be recruited by a coach. Life seemed to be going pretty great for me, actually, yet I was still experiencing a prevailing sense of anxiety and loss. I didn't know why I still hadn't gotten over Susanna... and I continued to be linked to her brother and his problems. The truth was that I was more than linked to Daryl, I was drawn to him, like a moth to a flame. How did I get myself into this mess?

We made plans to get together in mid-March on a Saturday. It was the earliest time we could find to meet up. The plan would be a little different this time. The Big M and his friends were going on a little field trip to a dance club in Brewster, New York. The reason for such an excursion was that the drinking age in New York is only eighteen while in Connecticut it's twenty-one, and Michael and his pals were all a year or two shy of twenty-one at the time. It wasn't that they couldn't find a few dives in the Valley that would serve them, but only dives where there were no girls. They'd be meeting up at Duchess at 6:30 to allow themselves plenty of time to get to Brewster. Personally, I still didn't get what everyone's fascination with getting drunk was.

Since I had worked the daytime shift, I told Daryl that I would kind of hang out at Duchess after work, and he could pick me up at about 6:45. By that time Michael and company would be well on their way to Brewster. That only left me with breaking my plans with Jeff, which would take some creativity on my part. He and I were planning to go to the dance at the Derby Community Center. The last time we had been there was the night of Susanna's accident. The fact was that after Susanna's death, I found it hard to go to the Derby Community Center, so I had been making up excuses not to. Besides, he and I were able to go to other dances at Shelton High School or the Huntington Grange Hall in the rural part of Shelton. So all I needed to do was come up with a new excuse, something I was getting better and better at. I decided to call him from the Duchess phone and tell him I had a big homework assignment due for Monday, a research paper, and I didn't want to wait until Sunday to get the thing done. What a lie that was. "O-kay," Jeff said, a hint of skepticism in his tone, "let's shoot to go next week then." I hated to lie to him, but I felt a massive urgency to hang with Daryl. Hopefully, my friendship with Jeff would weather this minor deception like it had other challenges.

Michael pulled the mighty Corvair into Duchess around 6:15. Having just gotten off work, I was standing alongside the red and white tile building wolfing down a cheeseburger and talking to his three buddies. Two were guys Michael had grown up with in Shelton and the other one he had met at Duchess, all former star athletes from Derby and Shelton. I wasn't completely surprised to see the fourth,

Will Granger himself, pull in a few seconds after Michael. Interestingly, Will and Michael were growing closer and closer all the time. I could only assume that Will left his wife alone on nights like these while he went out carousing. The Big M walked over to us, and said, "Do you need a ride home? It's kind of on our way, but I don't know how we'll fit six of us in the car."

"No sweat," I replied. "I'll get home. You never need to worry about me."

At 6:30, all five guys piled into Will's hot Camaro, not the Corvair, and they were off on their adventure.

I was left alone to wait for Daryl, which I didn't mind at all. If it had been a little later, there would have been some good people watching to keep me occupied, but since it was a little early for kids to be cruising by, I just sat on the curb and continued reading my latest book, which is how I fly. Daryl arrived promptly at 6:45. I was happy that Michael had left on time. When Daryl got to my side of the building, he nodded to me. I ran over to his Bug and hopped in, hopefully unseen by the night crew.

"How's it going, Daryl?" I said.

"What's up, Duchess? Still reading that beatnik book?" he asked. He was sarcastic, but his speech wasn't slurred, which was good news.

"No, no," I laughed. "I think I'm done with *On the Road* for a while. This is something else."

"Is this one also about nothing?"

"No, it's about something. It's called *Slaughterhouse Five* by an amazing author named Kurt Vonnegut — an anti-war novel…really entertaining and thought provoking."

"Oh, thought provoking, is it?" For some reason, he liked to bust them on me when it came to reading.

"Yes, and it's even funny. Vonnegut cracks me up."

"An anti-war novel is *funny*?"

"Well, it's satirical."

"Satirical? Okay, let me ask you something, Duchess. Are you reading this book for school? Please say you are."

"Sorry...I hate to break your heart, but just my own pleasure."

"And do you read your assigned readings in your English class? Because I certainly don't if I can avoid it."

"Of course, I read them. Last month we read *A Separate Peace*, which is also kind of an anti-war novel. Only not satirical. Not funny at all. I really liked that one because it's about kids like us. And now we're reading *A Midsummer Night's Dream*."

"Shakespeare, right?"

"Yes, *A Midsummer Night's Dream* is by Shakespeare."

"And, let me guess. You like it, right?"

"Oh yeah. It's pretty funny. Well, obviously, Shakespeare was totally brilliant."

"You're really out there, ya know. I don't know any kid who likes reading Shakespeare."

"Well, you might call me the exception to the rule. I know most kids don't like Shakespeare, but I do. I mean, I read my first Shakespearean play when I was in seventh grade."

"Of course you did."

I decided I should quit while I was ahead, if you want to call where I was *ahead*. "Okay, enough with the sarcasm. Maybe we should just change the subject." As we were talking, I noticed that Daryl took a right on Pershing Drive, heading away from Derby, and now we were driving through downtown Ansonia. "Where are we going?" I asked.

"Since it's not dark yet, I thought we'd go over to Nolan Field and shoot some hoops," he replied.

I liked that idea, and he sounded sober, which I also liked. Nolan Field was Ansonia's home field, a complex which featured not only football and baseball fields, but also outdoor basketball courts.

"You and I are going to shoot some hoops? Just...just the two of us?" I asked.

"No, not just the two of us. I've also invited the New York Knicks," Daryl joked. "Of course just the two of us. Do you see anybody else? We're about to see what you're made of, Duchess." It might as well have been the legendary Oscar Robertson telling me he wanted to see what I was made of.

As I gazed at the horizon, I could see that the sun was almost down, so we'd have to hurry unless we planned to play in the dark. Not that Jeff and I hadn't often played at nightfall at the playground in our neighborhood. It was now nearing 7:00, and the purple horizon offered some lingering light as Daryl pulled the Bug into a space by the courts. He reached behind my seat and grabbed a ball, jumped out of the car, and trotted on to the court. He took a shot and the ball went right through the iron. I would say it swished, but there were no nets on the hoops. The city would have to replace them before the summer leagues started up in June. I chased down his rebound and took a shot, it rattled in and out of the rim. He rebounded the ball and threw it back to me.

"You get one more practice shot, big guy," he said. "Then we play before it gets dark. We probably don't even have twenty minutes."

I took another shot, missing again, and then he bounced it back to me and said, "I'll give you the ball first."

I seldom played one-on-one with anyone older than me. Mostly, I played Jeff, who was my age and who was a good match for me. Probably the last time I had played against an older kid was about a year ago against Michael. Unlike Michael, I had never been an all-star anything as a kid. But the summer before eighth grade, I began to realize that while I was short, I was also quick on my feet and coordinated. One afternoon after school, I was shooting some hoops at the Boys Club all by myself when Michael walked into the gym, took a few shots, and then asked me if I wanted to play one-on-one. I was pretty psyched because I couldn't remember the last time he had wanted to play anything with me. What Michael may not have been expecting was that I had developed a competitive edge, something I had never demonstrated when I was younger, and I quickly found myself lost in the spirit of the game. When I saw that I might be able to beat him, I went for blood. I outhustled him to every loose ball, and he couldn't match my quickness when I drove to the basket. Of course, he had a big height advantage. He would back me close to the hoop and shoot over me. I fought hard, though, and the final score was 21-19, my first, true win ever over my big brother — at anything. After I scored the last basket and called out "game" in victory, Michael picked up the ball, threw it angrily against the wall with all his might, and stormed out of the gym without another word. As I said, Michael took his sports seriously. I never beat Michael again at any game — not basketball, not ping pong, not pool. When I was ahead, he always seemed to make a last ditch comeback and win the game. It was better that way.

Playing against Daryl was going to be another matter. He slid his arms out of his Army jacket and tossed it past the faded out-of-bounds lines. I followed suit with my jacket. I soon realized that, while he may have abandoned his high school sports career, he hadn't lost anything. I was completely overmatched. First I found out that Daryl was no kind of hotdog. Nothing too fancy. Just an extremely effective player with great fundamental skills. He dribbled the ball at least as well as I did — no, better actually — and he was equally quick. But, like Michael, he had a five inch height advantage. What he also had that Michael didn't have so much were great fakes and moves under the hoop, and he fooled me each and every time, resulting in absurdly easy baskets. Then, should I even mention that he could both dribble and lay the ball in equally well with either hand? *Fabulous,* I thought, *the guy's ambidextrous.* I never knew if he was going to drive right or left. I was a southpaw, and I almost always went to my strong side, which Daryl quickly figured out, stopping me again and again. And, boy, could he ever shoot from long range. I began to think, *Geez, does this kid ever miss?* It was insane. One moment he'd drop in a twenty-five foot jumper, and the next he would fake the same shot, and then drive to the hoop. The game ended just as the final glimpses of daylight disappeared into the night — the score: Daryl - 21, Gabriel - 7. A massacre!

On the winning point, he threw the ball hard into my chest and called out, "Nice game!"

"You killed me," I said, weakly.

"Not at all." He seemed puzzled by my self-criticism as he looked directly through me with curious, truthful eyes, and for a split second, it felt just like when I had made eye contact with Susanna after we slow danced. And then he stunned me by adding with a level of sincerity I have maybe never encountered with another guy, "You're gonna be a good player, Duchess. I'm impressed."

And that was that. No gloating, no bragging, no razzing. Just a compliment. Roger, over, and out. Then he just skipped by his coat, picking it up in one fluid motion, and headed for the car. I followed behind, suddenly feeling good about myself after being obliterated by the best athlete in the Valley. As we drove away, I found myself imagining what would have happened if he had played for Seymour in the recent season. They would have made the state tournament for sure. There's no doubt Daryl would have been All Valley and All League, and probably even All State as well. Then I thought to myself, if he lived in Derby when the Red Raiders almost upset the great Trevor Rogers and his Kolbe Cathedral teammates, a player like Daryl might have made the difference for Derby. Unlike the Derby players, he was as much a basketball player as he was a football player. I wasn't going to verbalize that to him, though. To suggest to a player from one Valley town that he would have helped another Valley team win was practically sacrilege.

Despite losing, I felt the night was off to a good start. Daryl was sober, and we had done something normal. Noticing that he was now getting on Route 8 South, I asked, "Where to now?"

"You'll see," he said, popping a tape into his player. A good song came on, "Homeward Bound" by Simon and Garfunkel. Oh man, I love them. The mellow acoustic guitar playing, the perfect harmonies, Art Garfunkel's unbelievable range, and Paul Simon's amazing ability to write a song that makes you feel...I don't even know how to describe it...feel something profound.

I found myself grooving to the song, and I began to gently beat out the slow, steady beat on Daryl's dashboard the way I often did on the dash of Michael's Corvair. Daryl didn't seem to mind at all. In fact, he appeared to be enjoying it. On the last verse, he kind of shocked me when he began to sing along with the tape. He sang kind of flat, actually, but what he lacked in musical talent, he made up for in passion. I mean, I'm not going to lie — Daryl was so into it, it surprised me. At the same time, something about his singing was sort of so free that it made me lose any inhibition I might have had. I joined in, and together, the two of us belted out the last chorus of the song, as Paul Simon's guitar reverently brought the song to a close.

When the song ended, Daryl ejected the tape, and without saying a word, he somehow signaled to me not to say anything. It was like he needed a moment of silence.

"Homeward Bound" is a song that makes you really feel what it's like to be alone. I know for sure that I often feel like I'm alone on this planet. Considering the passionate way Daryl had sung along, I guessed that he felt alone as well. I thought to myself, *Maybe Daryl and I are drawn to each other because we both feel so alone.*

After about a minute, he broke the silence. "Way ta go, Duchess. You might have missed your calling."

"What calling?"

"You should be the lead singer of a rock group," he teased.

"Who me? Get outta town."

"No really! You're a good singer, man. But now let's see how smart you really are. Name the two guys singing on that track? If you can do that, you're the smartest dude on earth," he said with a sly smile.

"Okay, now I know you're ragging on me," I said, feeling my cheeks tense into an ironic smirk. "Obviously, we both know who they are. Everyone knows who they are."

"Right on, Duchess! And that's the smartest fuckin' thing you said since I picked you up." Daryl busted out laughing — a genuine, hearty laugh that made me crack up just to hear it.

He seemed truly happy, which made me feel good. He got off at Exit 18, Division Street in Derby. It was the street Susanna had been killed on. *Why was he getting off here?* I asked myself, worried. He didn't turn on Division Street, which was a relief, but went straight toward Derby High School. But why there? Daryl pulled his car into the vacant Ryan Field parking lot, jumped out, and yelled, "Let's go, Duchess!"

I wondered if our friendship was made up of him leading the way and barking out orders for me to follow, which if that was the case, was fine since he was older and everything like that. Besides, being Michael's younger brother, I had a lot of experience as a follower. The gate to the football field was closed and padlocked. Evaluating the scene, Daryl suddenly grabbed on to the chain link fence and climbed it in two or three easy steps, grabbing onto the upper bar, sort of vaulting over the top, and then landing with uncanny agility on his feet on the other side. We stared at each other from opposite sides of the fence.

"What's going on, Daryl?" I asked, cautiously.

"Let's go, Duchess, you can scale a fence. You're athletic."

"We're not supposed to be on the field at night, Daryl. That's why the gate is locked."

"Oh I know why the gate is locked, *Gab-ri-el*," he replied, exaggerating my name mockingly and then heading down the black asphalt walkway determinedly. "But here's the thing," he called out as he walked away from me, "you don't need to always do what you're supposed to do."

I was left with a decision to make. Would I stay put and keep an eye on him from my side of the fence? Would I walk back to the car and wait for him? Or would I follow him into who knew what kind of trouble on the other side of the fence? Something about my friendship with Daryl always seemed to cause me to choose the riskier option. I wrapped my fingers into the metal links and, with a lot more effort than Daryl had exerted, I managed to climb up and over to the other side. He was walking out onto the field, right through the end zone where he had dropped the pass in the crucial game against Derby. He stopped for a moment and looked around the end zone, searching as if he had lost something there. I watched him walk out onto the field. He assumed a position — a wide receiver position — around the 9 or 10 yard line and began to run slowly from left to right, horizontally, on the field, as if in motion. Then he called out in a mumbled baritone, "Hut one...hut two...hut..." which echoed in the darkness, and he ran the pass route he had run on Seymour's final play of the game, recreating the play just as if the other players were around him. He rolled off the imaginary would-be blocker, ran a few more yards along the sideline and then made a razor sharp cut into the center of the end zone, reaching out his hands at the exact spot where Adamo had made the game-saving hit. Then he came to an abrupt stop and began to shake his head like he was deeply troubled. He walked back to his place at the far left of the line of scrimmage and repeated the pass route again. And then he did it again...and again...maybe six or seven times, each time reaching his hands out to catch the imaginary ball, and then stopping and frustratedly shaking his head again. For about fifteen minutes, I helplessly watched him torture himself as he attempted to recreate a past moment that he would never be able to change.

Finally, he lay down in the end zone and put his arms over his head, exactly as he had done when the whistle had blown the play dead on that fateful October morning. I walked into the end zone and gently said, "C'mon, Daryl. We should go." He just shook his head slowly from right to left. "Really, Daryl, c'mon," I urged him. "It's late, and we're not supposed to be here."

I waited and waited, but it looked like he needed to lay there in the dark night. I wasn't sure if he was just thinking or if he was crying because his arms still covered his face. Finally, I surrendered and just sat down right next to him and crossed my legs, as if I was about to meditate or something like that. I guess I was meditating because, since I didn't know what to say, there was nothing else to do. Together we rested, the only sound was Daryl's labored breathing.

After what felt like forever, he broke the silence. "Ya ever feel sad, Duchess?"

I opened my eyes. "Me? Well, yeah...of course I do. I think everyone feels sad sometimes."

"No, but I mean really, really sad. Deeply sad. Fucked up sad. Like you've fallen into a pitch black hole...a...a bottomless hole...and like you're falling and no matter what you do, you can't find a way to break your fall." And now I could tell he was crying. It was a soundless cry, but his breathing was becoming more labored and his chest was heaving. "I'm just sayin', man...not being able to break a fall was never a problem for me before, ya know, Duchess? I guess I'm just not used to it."

It was upsetting to see him so disturbed. The fact that he was sober didn't help. *It would be easier if he was drunk,* I thought to myself.

"Yes, I think I understand," I said. "But listen, Daryl, okay? Uhm... well...maybe I've never felt quite that sad. Now, *please* really listen to this, okay? It was just one game. And it was just one play. You can't take full responsibility for the loss. There were other players...other things people could have done to score or to stop Derby from scoring."

"It's not the fuckin' loss so much, Duchess," he continued. "Here's the thing," he said, pushing himself into a sitting position and facing me. His face was stained with tears. "The thing is...I mean, do you understand that the thing is...it's...it's if I had held on to that fuckin' ball, no matter how hard Adamo hit me, Susie would still be alive now. Don't you get that?"

Wow — I was in a jam, and I wanted to be careful how I responded. "How could you know that, Daryl? There's no way to know that."

"No, but I *do* know it. Listen, Duchess. Do you believe in fate?"

"Oh wow...I don't know. Well, yeah, I mean, I guess I believe in it."

"I think that maybe every action we take leads to our fate. What I mean is, if we just change one little action. Something stupid. Like... like...let's say you eat a hamburger and fries for dinner. After you eat them, your fate plays out in some way. But let's say you didn't eat that stuff. Maybe you eat broccoli. Then maybe your fate turns out different. Does that make sense? I don't know if I'm saying it right...but if you just change one thing — maybe one important thing like dropping a touchdown pass, or...I don't know...even a super unimportant thing like...like eating a stupid, fuckin' hamburger — then things turn out differently. I think dropping the ball was...I think it was...that kind of thing. Maybe if I caught the fuckin' ball, maybe then my fate changes, and maybe then...maybe Susie doesn't die. You get me?"

As we stared into each other's eyes, I don't think I had ever felt more connected with anyone in my life. The look in his eyes was...I don't know how to describe it. Naked, I guess. I didn't know Daryl went this deep, and I didn't really know what to say to help him. I wasn't sure if he was right or wrong about fate. Suddenly, we heard an adult's voice yell, "Hey you kids, you're not supposed to be on the field at night. I'm going to call the cops!" A man who appeared to be in a bathrobe was standing under his porch light directly across the street. He re-entered his house, and the screen door slammed shut behind him.

"Shit," Daryl said. He jumped up and made a mad dash to the fence with me trailing closely behind, he took the fence as easily as he had on the way in, and I lagged behind him. We reached the car, and Daryl sped out of the parking lot. As we drove down Chatfield Street, Daryl zoomed down the hill and turned onto Route 8 South again, and then got off Exit 15, which took us on to Route 34 as if we were going to New Haven. I had no idea where he was headed, and I had no words.

About a mile or two toward New Haven, Daryl pulled into St. Peter's Cemetery. He found his way to a narrow driveway in a confusing maze of many narrow driveways and finally stopped. "Wait here," he said, and he bolted out of the car and trotted down a shallow incline of grass. *Wait here?* I said to myself. *How can I wait here?* I got out and followed behind him into the darkness. Being there creeped me out a little. He plopped himself down in front of a tombstone. I knelt down on one knee next to Daryl, laying my palm gently on his shoulder, and whispered softly, "C'mon, man...I don't think we're supposed to be here either. We're gonna get in trouble."

"Yeah, okay, Duchess, just give me a sec." He reached into the deep pocket of his Army jacket and pulled out his brown bag, took out a rolling paper and began to roll a joint.

"Daryl," I pleaded. "This is a bad idea...a really horrendous idea. If we get caught here and you're smoking pot, we'll get arrested for sure."

"I just need to relax a little," he said, sprinkling the pungent weed onto the paper.

Once again, I gave in. Respecting his sadness and the solemn moment we were sharing, I refrained from badgering him any further. I sat next to him in silent resignation as he smoked. After about five minutes, I drew closer to the tombstone in the darkness so that I could see what it said. I could make out the words:

Susanna Marie Novak
Born July 12, 1953 – Died October 21, 1967
Earth has one angel less, and Heaven one angel more

"Don't bother looking too close," Daryl muttered, after releasing the smoke from his lungs. "She ain't here."

"She...what?"

"She's not here. I come here all the time...hoping...you know... just...I don't know...for a sign."

"What kind of sign?"

He inhaled and held the smoke in again. Then after exhaling, he sighed. "I don't know. A sign of...of forgiveness, I guess. But nothing. What I sense...no, what I *know* in my gut...is that she ain't fuckin' here. I don't know why I even bother."

"Oh." I didn't know what else to say.

"What am I gonna do, Duchess?" There was an unrestrained directness in his tone, stripped away of everything we learn in life to protect ourselves...everything but the deepest, rawest emotion.

"What do you mean?" I asked.

With an eerie expression, he raised his eyebrows and practically whispered, "I don't know what I'm gonna do." And then he kind of bit his lower lip.

Fighting to find the right thing to say, I replied, "Well, you're... you're really upset right now. You need to talk to someone."

"I'm talkin' to *you*, Duchess! Don't you fuckin' get that?" Like an electric shock, his irritation jolted me. He looked down and took a deep hit from the joint.

I took a moment to gather myself and then I said, desperately, "Yes, I do get it. And that's good. But I'm not, like...I'm not a psychologist, Daryl. You must know that. You need to talk to a psychologist or a counselor or a priest or someone who can really help you!"

"I already talked to my guidance counselor at school," he said sarcastically. "She was a big fuckin' help."

"Well, maybe someone else then. How about the priest at St. Peter and St. Paul?"

"Fuck no, man. I haven't been to church since the funeral. That priest can go fuck himself. All priests can just go..." and then he cut himself off and paused for a good, long while. "It's just that...just...I feel so...so bad most of the time. The school year's gonna end soon. I don't know...maybe I'll join the fuckin' Army."

I had a knee jerk reaction to his remark. "Oh no," I said, "no way! I already have one friend who's doing that. Not you too. That's a horrendous idea. You'll end up in Vietnam and you'll probably get yourself killed!"

He turned to me slowly and said in that same soft voice that scared me a minute ago, "That's the general idea, Duchess, if you catch my drift."

A second knee jerk reaction. "If I catch your drift? What the hell is that supposed to mean, Daryl?" I shouted, and I heard my own voice reverberate through the cemetery. He remained silent and just shook his head slowly. Now I was getting angry. "I wanna know! Tell me what you meant by that," I demanded.

In another ghostly whisper, he said, "Don't worry about it, Duchess. Just fuckin' forget I said anything." Wearily, he pulled himself up into a standing position, walked over to the tombstone, and sort of lovingly petted the top of the granite surface. Then I heard him half whisper, "Sorry, Susie," his hushed voice beginning to break, "I'm really...just... really sorry." He was weeping now. It was the second time in less than an hour I had seen Daryl cry, and it was painful to see him so sad. There was really nothing I could do, though, so I just rested calmly in the stillness of his grief.

Wiping his eyes on his sleeve, he turned and headed for the car. Again, I followed closely behind him. I looked at my watch. It was 10:18, time for me to start thinking of going home. He didn't need to be told. He headed back the way we had come on Route 34, and then got on Route 8.

In front of my house, we sat in silence for a short while. Sometimes silence isn't quiet but instead pounds away at your brain, like a siren rising in pitch in the deep recesses of your mind. Finally, I needed to turn off that siren. "I'm really worried about you, Daryl...I mean, *really* worried. You need...I don't know...you need...help."

He practically mumbled a response. "Having a friend like you helps, Gabe."

I was once again moved by hearing him address me by my real name, and now I began to cry. "I'm not enough, Daryl, I don't know how to help you."

"Sure you do. Hanging with you tonight helped me a lot."

I just shook my head.

"You better go in before your mom and dad start worrying about you," he advised me.

"Don't your parents worry about you?" I asked.

"Maybe they used to once upon a time, but not anymore. They've given up. I get it. It doesn't matter. Listen, bud, I'll see ya during the week."

"Okay," I said, wiping my tears on my sleeves. "See ya soon. Take care of yourself."

It had been an emotionally draining night. I wasn't exactly used to someone opening up to me like Daryl had. It's not how most guys are. Jeff or Tommy Trouble or especially Michael aren't ones to spill their guts in emotional heart to heart talks. We either play sports or talk sports or just horse around when we hang out. What was also kind of weird was that Daryl seemed to feel I was helping him, even though I hadn't done a thing, as far as I could tell, to help him in any way. So, I was baffled in more ways than one. As I had done on two previous occasions, I watched him drive away in that bomb of a Bug I was beginning to love. I found myself thinking about something my dad says when describing a situation where he didn't know what to do. "I didn't know whether to shit or go blind," he'll say. I know — gross. That's how I was feeling at the moment, though. I certainly didn't want either of my dad's options. What I did want was to come up with a strategy to get Daryl help, and that was going to take some doing.

19

While my get-together with Daryl had begun pretty well, even though he creamed me in basketball, the night had unfolded in a strange way that left me pretty shook up, for sure. It was hard watching Daryl repeatedly run his pass route in the darkness of Derby's empty football field. And then the cemetery...I don't even know what to say about that. Seeing Susanna's tombstone kind of got to me. And it obviously got to Daryl who must have been visiting it on a regular basis. No one should torment himself like that. It wasn't his fault that Seymour lost the game, and it definitely wasn't his fault that Susanna was killed in the accident. The way he had openly cried in front of me just made me feel closer to him. I mean, I'm not going to lie. I was really starting to love the guy. I didn't know how to help him with his deep feelings of guilt, though, and I was really concerned about him. Maybe I didn't need to worry, though, because I still saw him every time I worked a weeknight, and he basically looked alright as far as I could tell.

A few weeks after that night with Daryl, on a Thursday, I was on the night crew with Will, Les Wilson, and Tommy Trouble who was breaking me in on the grill. Big Alfred came in from the lot and looked rattled. I had never seen him look anything other than cool, calm, and collected. Will, perpetually in motion, was busy cleaning and restocking salt, pepper, straws, and napkins. Les was reading a newspaper, and Tomaso and I were having a conversation by the grill when I noticed the strange look in Big Alfred's eyes.

"What's going on, Alfred?" I asked. "You look, uhm, weird."

"A boy out in the lot just tol' me...he...he say he hear on the radio that some man shot Dr. King a few hours ago. They reportin' that Dr. King is dead." He just shrugged and shook his head as if he himself couldn't believe the words that had just come out of his own mouth.

"Did you hear that?" Tomaso called to Will. "Alfred said that Martin Luther King is dead."

Les and Will rushed over to us with incredulous faces wanting to hear what Alfred knew. Alfred related what the boy had told him — that Dr. King was standing on the balcony of a Memphis motel, that he was hit in the neck by a bullet, and that he was pronounced dead upon arrival at the hospital. The shooter was not found.

"Tell me this isn't true, Alfred baby," Les pleaded. "Please tell me it isn't so!" Les's big eyes began to well up.

"I jus' know what the boy outside tol' me he heard on the radio, Lester," Big Alfred said, shaking his head. "I don' know, for sure, what is true and what ain't true."

"Un-fucking-believable," Will blurted out. "First Kennedy, and now King. This country is so fucked up...it's...it's just...I can't even believe how fucked up this country is." Will walked into the office and pulled the door shut.

I didn't know what to say to Alfred or Les. The news hit me hard, and it obviously hit Will hard, but I couldn't fully comprehend how hard it hit Alfred and Les. I was sort of just beginning to understand the Civil Rights movement because it was a lot to grasp for a kid who didn't really have any close black friends at school and who only heard negative things about the movement at home. There are some things that you just know in your gut, though. In mine, I knew that Dr. King was a modern day hero. For Alfred and Les to lose a leader who was, hopefully, steering their people to a better day was obviously devastating. Maybe black people had come a long way since being freed as slaves, but even I could see that a lot more needed to happen in order for them to be treated as equals. I had observed that Alfred was pretty good at keeping his emotions in check, but Les was a more sensitive kind of guy.

Les is different than the other black guys we work with. First of all, he is very well spoken. So much so, actually, that he corrects us when we're wrong. "Not 'me and Michael are leaving now,' sweetie," he will say to me, "but instead, 'Michael and I are leaving.' " Another difference is he is artistic. He often amazes us by drawing pictures of landscapes and bridges and buildings and faces on the backs of the white paper bags we fill orders with. It makes me wonder why he's shoveling french fries in little bags instead of working as a professional artist. His speech and his gestures are, somehow, more refined and dramatic than anyone I know, white or black. He speaks in a rich baritone voice that sounds like he's a radio or television announcer. One big difference is that I think Les is what my mother calls a "fairy." For instance, when the author Truman Capote appears on television talk shows like the Tonight Show, my mother will say, "I think this guy is a fairy." We guys don't typically use the word "fairy" because using that word sort of makes us sound like we're fairies ourselves. Instead, we say guys like Truman Capote and Les are "queers." I know most of the kids I hang out with at school would have a problem with someone like Les, but knowing him, I think he's a good guy. I guess, either way, Les probably wouldn't like it if he heard us calling him names like these. Maybe guys who are queers are more refined than regular guys. I think that's probably true.

As the night wore on, all of us went about our jobs as best we could. I found myself thinking about the assassination of President Kennedy just a few years before. I was only twelve, a seventh grader, and while walking home from school, I saw one of my classmates, Robert Guttman, who was waiting by a bus at the public middle school near my house. We Catholic school kids got out of school a half hour earlier than the public school kids did, so kids who took the bus had to wait at other schools until dismissal. It was better to be a walker.

"Did you hear?" Robert Guttman said. "The president's been shot!"

"What president?" I asked, puzzled.

"President Kennedy," he said, "President Kennedy has been shot!"

"You're lying, Guttman," I answered, alarmed, but I knew from the freaked out look on his face that he wasn't.

I could hear Guttman yelling, "No, I'm not," as I sprinted home where I found my mother in our living room watching the ongoing story unfold on the news. She looked pale. The two of us sat before the television set grimly listening to a recounting of the shooting and waiting to hear the condition of the president. Much to our sadness and shock, at 2:38 p.m. Walter Cronkite reported live:

"President Kennedy died at 1:00 p.m. Central Standard Time...2:00 Eastern Standard Time, some 38 minutes ago."

I will never forget the feeling I had upon hearing this news. I felt my chest tighten seeing Walter Cronkite, after making the announcement, pause and take off his glasses. He appeared to be fighting back his own tears. He was as rocked as we were. It was the first time I had ever seen a television news reporter show emotion. He seemed like a good man...a sincere man. I turned to my mother who had tears streaming down both cheeks. Embarrassed, she got up and went into our bathroom.

As the news coverage continued, our family stayed glued to the TV. Two days later we watched the alleged assassin, Lee Harvey Oswald, get shot at close range by a man with a handgun named Jack Ruby, and I was certain the world had gone mad. To see this act of violence live made it all the more unnerving. It was the only time I had ever seen a man shot while it was actually happening. I had a keen understanding that I wasn't watching some fictional crime show, but the real thing. Confused beyond hope, I had no idea why someone would want to shoot the President of the United States and even less of an idea why another civilian would shoot the assassin while he was in police custody. I mean, Oswald would have probably gotten the chair anyway.

About a year and a half after President Kennedy was killed, Malcolm X was assassinated. I knew very little about him except that my father and any white man I knew hated him. What Malcolm X was all about was something a kid like me didn't really understand. I was more concerned about playing sports, listening to the latest music, and what girl I had a crush on than racial tensions and black leaders with mysterious names. For me, the only thing that had interested me about Malcolm X was that he seemed to be friendly with Muhammed Ali. I think their friendship had something to do with the fact that they were members of the same religion, but I'm not sure. What had hit me hard, though, was the men who killed Malcolm X were also black. I couldn't even begin to figure that one out. "Good! Let these niggers all kill each other," my father had ranted, which just added to my confusion.

And now, I was still just a kid, and another important leader had been assassinated. Three in less than five years. Two of them black. The news left the crew at Duchess all in a funk, but we had to push through and finish the night. All of us were upset, but Les was completely wrecked emotionally. He left the building several times during the night, and each time when he returned, his eyes seemed more bloodshot and he was becoming noticeably more unsteady on his feet. I often felt that Les, like Karl Fischer, was drunk while at work. Thankfully, he was just a nicer drunk than Fischer.

Tomaso was at the back sink washing some trays, and I was cleaning up and probably staring at Les because I was worried about his condition. "I don't know what we're going to do without Dr. King, honey," he kept saying to me, wiping tears from his eyes in the process. It didn't bother me that Les addressed me as "honey." I was used to it. He used pet names when talking to just about anyone. Well, maybe not Karl Fischer. Let's just say anyone he liked.

Never a man short of words, Les continued while I scraped down the grill, getting ready to run six more hamburgers and six cheeseburgers to put in the bin.

"Things are going to be so bad without Dr. King. Now what are we left with? I will tell you what we're left with, honey. We're left with Huey Newton, Stokely Carmichael, Bobby Seale, and the Black Panthers. And believe me when I tell you, those boys don't play."

"I've seen those guys on the news," I said to Les, "They wear straps with bullets and carry guns, right? My dad hates those guys, but I don't really understand what they're all about."

"What they're all about?" Les repeated. "They are basically about the same things as Dr. King, equal rights for our people — because we don't have equal rights, baby. But unlike Dr. King, who preached non-violence, the Black Panthers feel that if the government doesn't give our people those rights, they will take them using force."

"That sounds scary," I responded.

"It *is* scary, Gabriel honey. I'm afraid we're going to see tremendous violence now. Tre-men-dous violence. And believe me, honey, I've seen violence firsthand. I have seen ugliness when I was a child. I have witnessed sinister acts perpetrated against my people that I simply wouldn't even describe to you because they were so incredibly hideous. Furthermore, I have been the object of violence. I can tell you that. And not just because I am a black man, either, but because of other things that I am. None of us are, after all, just one thing, Gabriel."

At this point, he was starting to lose me, and despite his red, glassy eyes, Les recognized my uncertainty.

"I can see, baby, that you don't have the faintest notion of what I mean. I guess you wouldn't, my innocent lamb. Let's just say that there are many people of all colors that don't like it when people are different than they are. They hate it...they *simply* hate it. I didn't earn these scars on my face just because of the color of my skin."

I looked more closely at Les's battle worn face, lined with four or five crevices — under his chin, on his cheeks, and above his right eyebrow. I had always wondered where they came from. The truth is that since I had begun working at Duchess, I had often found it challenging to look directly at his imperfect face for more than a fleeting glance. I was looking at him now, though — directly at him because I think that's the way you look at someone when they get this real with you.

"These scars were a *gift* to me in 1951 — I will never forget that year, I assure you. Yes, indeed...a gift from some boys who didn't like it at all when someone was different from themselves — ugly people who don't like people like me, white or black, who look for love in... well, who look for love in less conventional ways. Those boys are still around all over the place in 1968, I assure you, Gabriel honey. I had high hopes that Dr. King's work would be the beginning of changing this country on many levels...many, many levels. Civil rights means more than mere race relations. I know you see black folks protesting on the news, but other kinds of people need to join in the fight because discrimination — the ugliness of mankind — extends far, *far* beyond race. I can tell you that. But look at you, you innocent child. You hardly have the slightest idea of what I'm talking about, do you? Old Les wishes that darling boys like you didn't have to see the ugliness of the world, but that just does not seem possible."

All I knew was what I was seeing on television — bits and pieces of civil rights protests on the news where, around the country, black people were protesting, carrying signs that said things like "equal rights for all," "decent housing now," and "stop school segregation," to name a few. I had seen the police sic their dogs and turn hoses on the black protesters. I had seen the protesters carried bodily to paddy wagons. And the most important person whose interpretation of these turbulent events I had heard from was my father, who strongly felt that black people had no right to protest.

I remember when the riots came to New Haven the summer before my sophomore year, my father was particularly concerned about his older sister, my Aunt Vincenza, who lives in New Haven. "If these black bastards do anything to harm my sister, somebody's gonna pay," he warned. "Who the hell do these goddam niggers think they are? Breaking into and looting stores...setting buildings on fire. Just who in Christ do they think they are?" His anger was palpable. But now, I had just heard a different interpretation, from a black man, not too much younger than my dad who was concerned about the unrest and afraid of the greater violence that might follow the death of Dr. King. Les's analysis of the situation made a lot of sense to me. For the first time in my life, I was beginning to realize that my dad's opinions might be wrong.

I was concerned about Les, though. Our conversation removed any doubt that he was drunk. He didn't slur his words like some drunks, but he talked more slowly and deliberately than usual. And his unsteadiness was obvious. He walked away from me toward the deep fryers, saying, "I don't know, honey...I just do *not* know," and he suddenly reeled into the counter near the hotdog fryers and slipped and fell. It was an ugly, awkward spill. I ran to him and asked if he was alright.

"Oh, yes, Gabriel honey, I'm fine. I am just fine. Aren't you a sweetheart to care about old Les like that?" he said, but I could hear in his voice that he wasn't fine.

Will, who was waiting on a customer, heard the thud of Les's body hitting the floor and rushed around behind the grill. He ran back to us and joined me in my concern for Les. When Will made eye contact with me, I could see he knew Les was drunk.

"Hey, listen Les, I'm going to ask Alfred to drive you home. I don't think you're feeling very well. Big Alfred can drive your car and Tomaso can follow him in his and then bring Alfred back."

"I am fine, Will Granger, you silly man," Les sang out in what suddenly was a higher pitched voice. "Don't you understand? I just slipped. I *am* just fine. I can finish the night. Besides...I am saying, be-sides, those boys are needed here."

"No, Les. Gabe and I will be fine. And your apartment isn't even five minutes away, so there's no problem. You go get some rest."

Reluctantly, Les conceded. "Well alrighty, Will, if you think it's best. I am pretty upset about...about losing Dr. King. Maybe resting will be good for me." His voice trembled and his eyes once again welled up.

Shortly after Tomaso and Alfred assisted Les to his car, Daryl appeared at the window for his nightly coffees. It had been about a week and a half since our troubling get together which took us to the Derby football field and the cemetery. While I had felt compelled to seek some kind of help for Daryl, I had failed to come up with a plan.

"What's up, Daryl? Got your list?" Will asked.

"Yup," Daryl replied and set his magazine donation and his list on the white counter. I walked over and picked up the list.

"Hey, Daryl," I said.

"What's going on, Duchess?"

We made eye contact. I shrugged and headed over to the coffee machine. I was still recovering from my conversation with Les and his subsequent fall.

"Did you hear about the assassination?" Will asked.

"Yup," Daryl said somberly. "Somebody's always got a radio playing at the plant, although you can't hear it too well when the presses are running."

"We live in a crazy world, Daryl...a crazy, crazy world," Will said.

"You don't have to tell me," Daryl said in agreement.

When I brought the trays of coffee to Daryl, he and I had a few moments to talk as Will just headed to the back of the store to get something.

"How've you been doing?" I asked in a soft voice.

"Doing okay," he said. "Sorry if I got emotional last time we saw each other."

"You really should talk to someone, Daryl. A teacher...a coach... your parents...someone."

"Sorry, Duchess, but that ain't happenin'. I can't talk to any of them. I can't really talk to anyone...except you, I guess. Sorry about that. If you don't want to bother with me, I'll understand. None of my other friends do."

"No, it's not that, Daryl, it's just that...that..." but I had to clam up because Will returned with a cash box to put some of the money in.

"Yeah, okay, Duchess, I'll see you around. And Will, you too, man."

"Keep the faith, Daryl," Will replied, "although there's not much to have faith in."

"I hear ya," Daryl said.

Of all things to say to Daryl, I thought. If there was anyone who needed faith in something right now, it was Daryl.

Tomaso and Alfred returned and reported that Les seemed okay when they got him back to his apartment. Since I was still the low man on the crew, I needed to go out in the parking lot and do a late night pick up. Alfred joined me and helped. He was good like that and willing to help out a little even if it wasn't in his job description.

"Les took the assassination pretty hard, huh Al?"

"We all takin' it hard, my man. Les is jus' a little more sensitive, if you know what I mean, than most people."

"Yeah, I can see that," I said, as I swept some of the bags, wrappers, and cups into a pile. The lot was messier than most weeknights.

"Well, you know, it's not so bad up here," Alfred continued, "but a lot of us come from the South where it's all different. Before I was Big Alfred, I was just little Alfred, livin' in North Carolina, and I seen the KKK hold their rallies in our town a few times a year. You know what the KKK is, Gabe?"

"Yes, I've heard about it a little. Did they do anything bad?"

"No, jus' a lotta speeches and carryin' on in their white hoods and robes, but it still scared me and my brothers and sisters plenty. Then, when momma throwed my daddy out because of too much drink, she said, 'Well, I ain't stayin' round here with no man on the property,' so she picked up and move all seven of us to Chicago."

"Wow, I think you told me you lived in Chicago, but I didn't know why," I said. "You said you won a Golden Gloves boxing championship in Chicago, didn't you?"

"That's right, Gabriel, but that was some years later. I don't know. You don' feel safe around certain white folks down South. Even some of the boys aroun' your age. Boys in the South ain't like you, Gabriel. You get this feelin' about some of 'em, and you think: before long, this one or that one will be wearing a white hood and a sheet and makin' a lotta noise."

I continued cleaning in silence for a few minutes, digesting what Big Alfred had said. He just followed close by, softly humming a tune I didn't recognize. It sounded like it might've been a church song maybe.

Finally, I asked, "Alfred, can I ask you a question?"

"Shoot, brother. I probably ain't got no answers, but I can try."

"What if you had a friend...and...and what if that friend was really depressed...but that friend didn't have anyone to talk to...and you were worried about your friend. What would you do?"

"Hmmm…that's a tough one. Lemme see now. I guess I would probably go talk to our minister because he's a wise man and always willin' to help any folks that need help."

"Oh," I replied. But I couldn't imagine talking to a priest since I had been away from church for a while, and I didn't like any of the priests I had known at St. Joseph's. And besides, Daryl had made no bones about how he felt about priests at the cemetery.

"I think I know the boy you talkin' about, Gabriel. That Seymour boy, right?"

"Yup," I said, shrugging, not knowing what else to say.

"That boy in a bad way, Gabriel. Even I can see myself, an' I ain't no doctor. I didn't even finish high school. I don' know what white people do to help each other, but I seen black people who tear themselves up with liquor and drugs an' won't let nobody help them. This might not help, but I gotta say it. There's some people you jus' can't help...that you can't save. Tha's jus' how it is. They jus' gonna destroy theirselves and there's nothin' nobody gonna be able to do about it."

I sighed. I knew there was wisdom in what Alfred had just said. And while his words were, in one sense, painfully honest, in another sense, his tone was kind and caring.

I took a deep breath and said, "Well, I'm still going to try."

"I figured as much. Tha's cuz you a good man, Gabriel. I knowed that the first time I talked to you." I looked up and saw that genuine smile of his, a smile that you couldn't help but love the guy for.

Big Alfred's words made me feel good, and they also made me feel like I was on the right track. I smiled back at him and finished picking up the last few bits of debris in the lot.

20

Daryl Novak, Frankie Adamo, and the young men of their generation have only a superficial understanding of the changing times of which they are part and parcel. They are growing up in an era of permissiveness that has already been labeled as the Sexual Revolution, ushered in by a variety of phenomena, from Elvis Presley's gyrating pelvis in the late 1950s to the advent of the Pill in 1960, the latter of which promoted the idea that women have a right to enjoy sex the same as men and, in the process, have the ability to take personal responsibility to protect themselves from pregnancy. Daryl and Frankie, of course, know about Elvis and the Pill, but they don't know the true significance of either. Along with their peers, they have watched married television couples like Ozzie and Harriet and Lucy and Ricky sleep in separate twin beds (suggesting that married couples don't engage in ongoing sexual relations), while getting conflicting messages from the media, from music, and from pop culture that not only do married couples engage in sexual relationships, but it is also commonplace and acceptable for unmarried couples to do so. They witness talk show hosts like David Susskind, Johnny Carson, and Mike Douglas discussing the changing sexual role of women in American culture with their celebrity guests. Daryl and Frankie are seeing nudity in films, where the changing morality is depicted more openly and more graphically than it is on television. Daryl and Frankie have seen Mrs. Robinson seduce her daughter's boyfriend Benjamin in *The Graduate*. They have observed their female classmates secretly passing around *The Harrad Experiment*, a novel about college students being assigned roommates of the opposite sex. And, without a doubt, Daryl and Frankie are cognizant of the hippie movement and its doctrine of free love, promoting the idea that single people should be able to be sexual without any commitment other than what they are feeling at the moment. Daryl and Frankie are not hippies, though, nor are they even aware of the fact that they are deeply in the midst of discovering how they fit into the world of free love and sexual permissiveness. They are too busy growing up and too preoccupied with their own triumphs and failures to fully understand the puzzle of changing sexual mores.

The two high school athletes understand that sexuality in their era is different than it had been during their parents' youth. Based on family conversations about love and marriage, Daryl believes that his mother was a virgin on her wedding night. Frankie believes the same about his mother, although the truth is that Rose Adamo didn't quite make it to her honeymoon night. She gave in to her husband-to-be, Tony, in his car five weeks before their wedding day. Since Tony had been conditioned by his Italian culture to expect a woman to retain her virginity until she was married, he, ultimately, never forgave Rose for being weak. The fact that he pressured Rose into giving in was neither here nor there. Tony's disappointment in Rose was subtle but gnawing and insidious, allowing him, ultimately, to have a justification for his own future infidelities.

Daryl believes his father is a good and decent man, and he doubts that Walter Novak has ever been unfaithful to his mother. Frankie, conversely, is relatively certain that his father has been unfaithful to his mother. He was, after all, at the kitchen table when his father warned his mother not to question his whereabouts, and he has also seen the sexually explicit magazines and reels of sixteen millimeter "blue" films in the basement. Frankie has come to the conclusion that all men cheat on their wives.

I was not only worried about Daryl's mental stability, but I was beginning to worry about my own. I often found myself obsessively dreaming about Susanna. I had a recurring dream that took me back to our slow dance together. I heard "You Really Got a Hold on Me" playing in my mind as I slept, remembering her closeness to me, her head on my shoulder, her hands around my neck, and the scent of sunflowers. I found myself missing Susanna in the depths of my inner being and wishing for her. I even found myself having daydreams about her, creating scenarios in my mind about what might have been. So obsessed was I that I actually found myself reimagining our first encounter:

As the slow dance ends, without releasing her right away, I say, "What's your name?" and she answers softly, "Susanna, but everyone calls me Sue." "My name's Gabriel," I say, following that with, "Would you mind if I call you some time?" "No, I wouldn't mind at all," she says, "I'd like that." With my arms still around her, I hear her telling me her number and me memorizing it because I don't have anything to write with. As we release our hold on each other but not our gaze, Susanna and I slowly back away from each other. We don't stop staring into each other's eyes until we can't walk backwards anymore without smacking into people. The very next day, I am waiting to use the phone booth at Mosci's (because it's almost always in use), and when my turn finally comes, I nervously dial her number. A female adult answers the phone. "Hello?" I say, "May I please speak to Sue?" The adult says, "May I tell her who's calling?" "Oh, yes, please tell her that Gabriel's calling," I reply nervously. In my mind, I think, her mother must be wondering who Gabriel could be. Then I hear Susanna's cheerful voice say, "Hello?" with an encouraging tone that almost smiles at me through the phone wires, assuring me it's all going to be okay.

I was just about to turn sixteen, and I imagined myself driving and having a car with a bench seat. I pictured picking up Sue and her sliding across the seat to the middle and sitting close to me, like I had seen couples do in movies and driving through Duchess. I saw us going on dates to the movies, to dances, to picnics, and even to the prom. I especially wondered what it would be like to kiss her lips. Not that I saw us going farther than that — not like Jeff and Julie Carter. While having sex obviously worked for them, it wasn't quite the way I imagined it for Susanna and me.

Throughout high school, Frankie Adamo has had an on-again off-again relationship with a classmate at school, Lillian Bombace. Knowing each other since grade school at St. Mary's, Frankie and Lillian dated exclusively for the better part of their junior year. Then Frankie hurt Lillian's feelings badly when he told her he needed "more space." Most of their peers didn't understand why Frankie broke up with Lillian. Boys and girls alike perceive Lillian to be the prettiest girl at Derby High School. Lillian's pristine complexion; her nutmeg brown hair, usually worn in a silky ponytail; her petite athletic figure, the model of graceful femininity; her eyes, enormous dark almonds; and her sparkling smile all combine to make her a beautiful girl. But her popularity extends beyond the physical. Lillian is involved in a host of extracurricular activities, and she is kind to every student she encounters. In regard to Frankie, despite his need for space, Lillian is devoted to him and believes she will one day marry him. Frankie has been, after all, Lillian's only sexual partner, and she hopes to keep it that way. She knows Frankie has many fine qualities, and she loves the local celebrity that comes with Frankie's sports exploits. A varsity cheerleader, Lillian also loves cheering for Frankie at football and basketball games. She not only has her eyes on him during games but also in classes at school and at dances and other social gatherings. She is waiting for Frankie — waiting for him to come around...to grow up...to realize that no one will ever love him like she does. Lillian is devoted to being there for Frankie, always. Since the breakup, Lillian has gone to the Adamo cottage on the Housatonic River with Frankie on more than one occasion. It was at the little cottage that Lillian lost her virginity to Frankie a year ago.

The night after the King assassination, Frankie and Lillian are at a party in the basement of Nickie Grasso's house. Nickie's parents are away on a trip to Italy. The entire football and cheerleading squads as well as select other friends are in attendance. It's an unseasonably warm April night. Over a hundred boys and girls are scattered throughout the finished basement and the backyard, mingling and dancing, as records spin on the stereo player and beer flows. Strings of Christmas lights with round multi-colored bulbs give the party a festive atmosphere. Though Nickie has the party well supplied with several kegs of beer, neither Frankie nor Lillian partake — Lillian because she prefers to always be sober and Frankie because of Attorney Goldman's advice to stay away from alcohol after the accident. For Lillian, time is running short. With the school year racing to its end and the likelihood of attending different colleges, Lillian pursues Frankie more aggressively than usual. The two talk and dance throughout the night when Frankie isn't distracted by his friends. Frankie doesn't mind Lillian's attention at all. With the pressures of his legal problems, Frankie is more than willing to allow himself to be distracted by Lillian whose plan is to get Frankie alone before the night is over. While she knows the two can furtively slip away into a room in the Grasso home, she has other ideas. At 9:30, about mid-way into the party, Lillian hands a record to her friend, and says, "Play this, Maryanne." It is the hit song, "Never My Love" by the Association, a favorite that reflects Lillian's feelings for Frankie.

Frankie is in the midst of a conversation with his teammates. Trent Stanley jokes, "Mueller got us back for the Thanksgiving Day game by hitting that three-run triple yesterday. Nice pitch, Foxy!"

The circle breaks into a round of belly laughs, while the guys backslap Stanley, spilling their topped off beers, the suds dripping all over their cups and between their fingers.

"Oh, fuck you, asshole," Foxy says.

"Coach shoulda pitched me," Frankie adds. "I woulda got Mueller out."

"Yeah, right," Foxy replies, "just like you did the night he scored 24 on you in basketball!" Again, bursts of raucous laughter explode from the group in response to Belchak's retort, drawing everyone's attention. Foxy is now the recipient of the backslapping as more beer spatters the grass.

Trent questions, "How the fuck did we ever lose to Shelton during the regular season and then almost beat Kolbe in the tournament?"

"Like Sister Mary Agnes always told us: This is a mystery that will be revealed to us when we are united with our Holy Father in Heaven," Frankie replies, much to the delight of the group.

Lillian runs over to Frankie and grabs him by the arm. "I love this song, Frankie! C'mon, dance with me."

Frankie lets himself be pulled away without a fight, looking back at the guys with a smile and a shrug as they call out, "Whoa, Adamo!"

The couple hold tightly onto each other. During the first refrain, Lillian takes her head off of Frankie's shoulder and gazes into his eyes. Focusing on the song's sweet-sounding melody and heartfelt message, she gazes at Frankie with eyes that ask him, "What makes you think my love for you will ever end?" Lillian is hoping to see into Frankie's soul... to connect with him at the deepest level...to become one with him. Frankie himself, after a few beers too many, is feeling very into Lillian.

Her lips, not more than an inch from his, invite him to kiss them. Frankie doesn't disappoint her. By the middle of the song, Lillian's and Frankie's feet have stopped moving. Only their lips are in motion. They have entered their own private world of intimacy, the crowd around them a soft blur.

Lillian whispers, "Do you have the key to the cottage?"

"You know I always do," Frankie whispers back confidently. "Do you want to go there?"

"You know I always do," she mimics, giggling, and she puts her mouth right next to his ear and whispers in her most seductive voice, "Let's go now."

"Let me tell the guys," he says.

"No. Don't tell the guys," she pleads. "Let's just go. We'll be back in a little while."

On the night after Dr. King was assassinated, Jeff and I decided to hang out at the Boys Club since there were no dances going on. Usually he got together with Julie Carter, but she told him she had something going on. Something seemed strange about that to me, but Jeff didn't seem worried. When we arrived at the Club, Jeff and I headed into the gym and immediately launched into one of our aggressive games of one on one. Jeff was a more accurate shooter than I was, but I was a better ball handler, so he won about half of our contests and I won the other half. On this day, it went down to a deuce game, but he ultimately prevailed. When our games are this close, and they usually are, all rules fly out the window. Either of us will go so far as to tackle the other to stop him from scoring the winning basket. The great thing about our friendship, though, is that no matter who wins or how dirty either of us plays, there are never any hard feelings.

After the game, he and I just shot around for a while and talked. Of course, the first thing he brought up was Julie. "It doesn't matter that Julie couldn't get together tonight because her parents went out last night. And I gotta tell you, pal, we had an amazing time."

"That's good," I said, wishing I could think fast enough to change the subject.

"Yup, first I pulled her sweater off and then we made out for a while. Before you know it, I had her bra off...and then, you know, more making out. And then I undid the top button of her jeans, and before ya know it, I had those off too. We must have made out for a half hour with her just in panties. And then...well, before you know it...well, you probably know what the next step was," he said, boasting, as he pulled the ball out of my hands and took a shot.

Enough with the "before you know its" already, I thought to myself. But I just smiled and said, "Yes, I probably do." Father McMahon was right, one thing does lead to another.

"Yup, it was pretty incredible."

"I'm sure it was," I said. Obviously, I was having difficulty holding up my end of the conversation, and I felt like such a dumbbell.

Of course, I had been hearing guys talk about sex since I was in seventh or eighth grade. We used to hang out with a neighborhood kid two years older than us, Bruce Martin, the local expert at building model cars. Bruce used to go into vivid detail about his sex life. He would describe his girlfriend's naked body to us, spending lots of time talking about her pubic hair. No matter how vividly he described it, I couldn't quite picture it, and I definitely couldn't imagine myself in Bruce's shoes. It wasn't that I had anything against sex exactly, or that I didn't plan to eventually have sex. I did. Eventually. It was just that I wasn't quite ready yet.

Around the time when Frankie and Lillian are arriving at the Adamo cottage, Daryl Novak is driving along the streets of downtown Bridgeport. Street lamps, those that aren't broken, cast light and shadow on the blighted buildings with their boarded up and caged windows.

Daryl is searching for something he can't find in the Valley. Having a job now, it's easier for him to pay for sex than to try to pursue it within the conventional avenue of the high school social network. This is his third trip to Bridgeport since his sister's accident, so he is no newcomer to this sordid business.

Daryl has had one sexual relationship, which lasted from the summer before his senior year until the night of the accident when he shut down to just about everyone, including his longtime girlfriend, Erin Kelly. Erin had lost her virginity to Daryl, but not for almost a year after they had begun dating. She was hoping to save her virginity for her wedding night, but her love for Daryl changed the course she had set for herself. After the accident, Daryl had shut out a heartbroken Erin just as he had Ben Andrews and his other Seymour friends. Her hand-written notes and phone calls went unanswered. Not having the heart to answer any more of Erin's calls, Helen Novak finally asked Erin not to call anymore considering Daryl wouldn't come to the phone.

The small groups of Bridgeport residents who wander the street are black or Puerto Rican, walking together or sitting on the stone steps leading into graffiti smudged apartment buildings. Driving slowly along Fairfield Avenue, Daryl knows this is not the safest place for him to be, but he doesn't care. He stopped caring for his own personal safety the day his sister was killed. On the corner of Fairfield and Main Street, Daryl spies what he thinks he is looking for, three young women standing on the corner. He pulls up to the curb. One of the girls nods to the other two. A Hispanic girl in a black leather waist jacket, a denim mini-skirt, black fishnet stockings, and knee high boots with stiletto heels approaches the Bug. Daryl reaches across the passenger seat and rolls down the window.

"Lookin' for somethin', white boy?" she asks.

Directly under a street lamp, Daryl can see her pretty, young face, adorned with ruby red lipstick and long, false eyelashes.

"Uhm...yeah, actually, I am...what do you have to offer?" Daryl asks.

"Let me see. How about this? I get in your little car, Mr. Gringo, and we take a ride down the road under the I-95 overpass, and you pull over in a dark spot, and, uhm, I'll make you happy."

"How much?" he asks.

"Not too much, sweet boy. Le's jus' say $25."

"Okay, hop in," and Daryl releases the clutch and heads toward the overpass.

As Daryl's Bug reaches a stoplight where I-95 covers the street like a giant concrete canopy, making the darkened streets ever darker, the girl says, "Jus' pull right over there, by the curb, sweet boy," directing Daryl to a spot where she believes they won't be seen or bothered.

Learning about sex from the guys in the neighborhood, like Bruce Martin and Jeff and others, was one thing. Learning about it from my parents was another. When I was just an eighth grader, my parents sat me down and attempted to talk to me about sex.

"Your father and I want to talk to you about the birds and the bees," my mom said. Her face looked as embarrassed as mine felt.

"Uhm...o-kay," I responded, stretching out the "kay" for about a minute and a half. What guy wants to discuss sex with his parents?

"Let's start with this," Dad began in his usual authoritative manner, "tell us what you know."

The first problem, obviously, was that I didn't want to tell Mom and Dad about Bruce Martin's girlfriend's pubic hair. The second problem was I didn't really have the right vocabulary to tell them what I knew. I only knew the words I had heard on the streets, and I'm not going to even say what those words are.

"I can't really do that," I said helplessly.

"Why not?" Dad responded impatiently.

And from there, the conversation rapidly deteriorated — literally swirling down the drain, resulting in extreme embarrassment on my part and frustration and annoyance on theirs.

When I entered high school, my parents began bringing up the subject more and more often, but now they had more to offer about it, and these discussions — or perhaps I should call them lectures — had a central theme: virginity. Or more specifically, the importance of a girl's virginity as it relates to marriage. Here I was, in the midst of the 1960s, in what had already become known as the Sexual Revolution, the era of free love, and I was being lectured about the importance of virginity. Talk about confusing, right?

My father and mother loved to talk about how they met and about their courtship. They met shortly before my father joined the Air Force during World War II. My mother's sister's husband and my father worked together at the American Brass in Ansonia, so Mom's brother-in-law set up a blind date. My dad loved to relate that he asked, "Is she pretty?" and that my uncle replied, "Well, she ain't Betty Grable, but, then again, you ain't Clark Gable." Dad would recall how when Mom came walking down the stairs, the first thing he saw were her boobs. That's about as sexual as Dad gets because he isn't someone to talk about sexy things very much or encourage such talk or behavior.

The truth is, though, that Mom and Dad are, in fact, both very attractive people, first generation Americans, who grew up in an era of big bands and Hollywood glamour and tinsel. They love the music, the films, and the fashion of their era, and dancing remains one of their major pastimes today. They attend dinner dances and balls most weekends, Dad dressed in dapper suits and Mom in fancy dresses or gowns, diamonds and furs. My friends' parents look like, well, like parents, but mine look more like movie stars, especially Mom.

When we were younger kids, Michael and I loved sitting at the kitchen table on Saturday nights while she got ready to go to one of their balls. Mom would set a big round mirror on the table, and Michael and I would sit on either side of her and marvel at how she put her make-up on like we were watching a trapeze artist in the circus. She'd start with some kind of flesh color stuff she rubbed all across her face from her forehead to under her chin and then blend it in with the tips of her fingers. Then she'd start working on her eyes. She had a crazy clamp-like device that she would squeeze onto her eyelashes and hold it there — I guess to curl them up better. Then, there was some kind of make-up pencil to draw lines onto her eyelids. Weird. Finally, she'd finish the job with lipstick and rouge. Michael and I would keep making eye contact, sending each other non-verbal messages, like, "Whoa, look at that clamp on her eyelashes! How does she draw that line on her eyelids so neatly? Look! She's a master of lipstick! Amazing!" The whole time, she recited poems to us by famous poets, like "O Captain! My Captain!" by Walt Whitman as well as poems she had written herself as a teenager. I loved her poems and couldn't believe that my own mother wrote them. Even now when she recites poetry to us, she often speaks of her immigrant father who had died of a heart attack when she was only seven years old. She always says, if he had lived, she feels she would have gotten a college education because, she explains, "My father believed in education." Not that she isn't an amazing mother and homemaker, but in the recitation of her poetry, I can still hear a longing for what might have been. My favorite part of her make-up sessions was when she sang songs to us. She said she used to have a good voice and that once a voice teacher came to her house when she was a kid and told her family she had great talent. Mom's mother was from Italy and didn't really understand English never mind about talent and great voices, but her older sister gave the guy five bucks in advance, and then the dude disappeared for good. When Mom told us that one, I always felt sad, and I wondered if she would've been, like, another Judy Garland if the guy wasn't such a fake. I still hate that guy. One song she always sang that I loved, speaking of the subject of sex, was called "You'd Be Surprised." I still remember some of the words:

She's not so good in a crowd but when you get her alone
You'd be surprised
She isn't much at a dance but then when I take her home
You'd be surprised

At a party or at a ball I got to admit she's nothing at all
But in an easy chair you'd be surprised

I didn't understand exactly what the song meant at the time, but now I think I get it. Except how do the words to that song fit in with these lectures I was getting on women, sex, and virginity? I guess it's like acid rock. Liking it doesn't mean you drop acid.

Anyway, no matter what kind of songs she sang, my parents' marriage is one that has obviously been built on the foundation of my mother's virginity before marriage, apparently the most important thing in any relationship, as they explained to me.

My father warned me. "If a girl has sex with you before you marry her, she'll have sex with *someone else* after you marry her."

Wow! There I was, only fourteen years old, and I was being told that my future wife was probably going to cheat on me. What was I supposed to do with that one?

Mom and Dad also explained that girls deserve to be treated with complete respect, that they aren't sex objects. The importance of a good marriage and of raising a good family was stressed in those talks. I walked away from them knowing the following — it is super important to respect girls, and, if you have pre-marital sex with a girl and then eventually marry her, chances are high that the marriage is doomed. Of course, I still had questions. Knowing now that Mom was a virgin on her wedding night, I wondered if Dad was, but asking him seemed like a bad idea. What it boiled down to, anyway, was that I respected my parents and, ultimately, I didn't doubt what they told me.

So, where does that leave me with members of the opposite sex? Let's just say that I don't have any sex stories to relate, and I don't even know if Michael does, because if he does, he's not saying. I guess that Michael and I both treat girls with respect and even put the ones we especially like up on pedestals like we're supposed to. While I imagined having affectionate moments with Susanna, I imagined nothing more happening between us than kissing. In the meantime, I could have all of the romantic aspirations I wanted to, but none of them would materialize, obviously. A pedestal was the platform on which Susanna would forever remain, in life and in death.

Lillian is one of four girls Frankie has gone all the way with, counting a prostitute his father's brothers, Uncle Steve and Uncle Freddy, had "given" him as a present for his sixteenth birthday. Lillian was his second sexual partner. After he and Lillian broke up, Frankie had two other brief flings with other girls from school, but he wasn't interested in them for anything but one night stands. The last time he had sex was the Friday night before football season with Lillian, even though they were no longer a couple. For Frankie, Lillian still stands out over other girls he has been with. Lillian hopes to never have another sexual partner other than Frankie, the Sexual Revolution and free love notwithstanding.

Arriving at the cottage, Frankie unlocks the door, and Lillian kisses him as soon as he shuts the door. Holding hands they head for the double bed in the main bedroom of the tiny four room cottage. Frankie and Lillian collapse onto the bed as they continue to kiss for a long while. Realizing they have time constraints since she, for one, has a 12:30 curfew, Lillian pushes Frankie away and lifts her powder blue, cotton v-neck sweater up and over her head in one fluid motion. She smiles lovingly at him and lets Frankie unhook and remove her bra. Her breasts fall free and she hugs Frankie before she falls back into his strong arms and resumes kissing him.

As Frankie unbuttons and begins to unzip her pants, Lillian hopes their lovemaking will help Frankie turn the corner. She hopes he will see the light. At the moment when he begins to enter her, she whispers, "Frankie, you have a condom, right?" While she had been on the Pill when she and Frankie were in the thick of their relationship, since the breakup she has discontinued taking it.

"Oh yeah." He lunges over to grab his wallet from his side of the bed, where he retrieves a small foil packet. She waits in anticipation. While she hopes to one day carry Frankie's children, she knows this is not the time. When he is prepared, their young, naked bodies once again join in union with each other.

Moments after Frankie has climaxed, the two lie in silence close to each other, Lillian on her right side, her head contentedly resting in the crook of Frankie's muscular left arm. Her plan so far has gone as she had hoped. Frankie is lying on his back, and he is feeling an uncharacteristic surge of emotion, the result of his sexual release he assumes. But he finds himself thinking about the accident. Most of all, snapshots of a frozen Susanna Novak, staring at him in the middle of the road on Division Street, flash through his mind. Contemplating the fact that he has been responsible for the death of another human being, he feels tears begin to flow from his eyes, and his breathing becomes heavy.

Noticing the change in his breathing, Lillian lifts her head from his arm. "Frankie, are you okay? Frankie...you're crying! What's the matter?"

Frankie shrugs and shakes his head, signaling he doesn't know what to say. Misinterpreting, Lillian is hopeful that Frankie has come to the realization she's been hoping for.

"You know you can always talk to me, Frankie. You know I'm always here for you. Always! You know I love you and...and I always will." Taking a closer look in the semi-darkness, she suddenly feels a little unsettled. "Frankie, please tell me what's the matter."

"I...I just," Frankie swallows hard. "I didn't mean for it to happen." The stream of tears is growing bigger.

"You didn't mean for...for what to happen, Frankie?" Lillian worries that he feels he didn't mean to have sex with her. She worries that he feels guilty because he doesn't love her.

"I didn't mean to hit...Novak's kid sister. I really just didn't...

didn't...mean to hit anyone. You know what I mean? We were just... the guys and me...just celebrating because...we...because we won a big one. I didn't mean for anyone to...to die. I could see her eyes right before I hit her. Fuck! She was so...so young!" Despite his efforts to suppress his crying, his chest begins to heave violently.

"Oh God," Lillian says. "You're talking about the accident. You're upset about the accident!"

"I just didn't mean...didn't mean for..." and Frankie has no more words. Lillian tenderly cradles Frankie's head in both of her arms and holds him close to her heart as she notices that the clock on the night table reads 11:17. *It's getting late,* she thinks to herself. *I need to get home soon, but I need to help Frankie!*

When Daryl drops the girl back at the corner of Fairfield and Main, he asks, "Do you mind if I ask your name?"

"No, I don't mind, sweet boy," she replies with a warm smile, as if grateful that she had been asked the question. "It's Linda. And wha's yours?"

"I'm Daryl," he replies.

"Daryl...cute," she muses.

"And...do you mind if I ask your age, Linda?"

"No, I don't mind if you ask," she replies, with an ironic grin. "But that don't mean I'm gonna tell you. Let's just say, I'm old enough. Well, you be a good boy now, Daryl." She steps out of Daryl's Bug, but before closing the door, the girl says, "Too bad. If the world was a different place, I could really get to like you. Be careful now, cute Daryl. It's a dangerous world out there."

Grabbing a quart of beer from behind his backseat, Daryl flips the cap off with an opener on his keychain as he watches Linda begin to walk, in her heels, back to her friends. Before she reaches the group, Linda stops, turns around, and takes a long look at Daryl. Making eye contact with her, he takes a few big gulps, nods, and then slowly pulls away from the curb.

As Daryl finds his way to the Route 8 connector, he feels more empty than ever. His outing has not helped him. He knows that nothing fills the emptiness. Wondering how old Linda really is, he asks himself, *Is she even older than Susie would be? Not much,* he thinks, answering his own question, and he begins to feel pangs of guilt. Suddenly enveloped in a blanket of depression, Daryl feels his eyes well up with tears. He knows certain things. He knows Linda is right. He knows it is a dangerous world. He knows, more than anything else, that he is inextricably drawn to danger. On the remainder of his drive to Seymour, Daryl pictures in his mind a young girl named Linda, as she lingered on the corner of Fairfield and Main, looking back at him, and he thinks about the time he spent with her.

As Jeff and I lingered on the corner of Maltby and Prospect, he went on more about Julie, and, well, let's just say he talked about the time he spent with her. I wondered what it must be like to be with a girl the way he was with Julie. I wondered when I would be with a girl that way. Finally at 11:30, I told him I had to go, which I did, and we said goodnight.

Heading up the stairs of my house, I still had Susanna on my mind. Thinking about girls and the possibilities of being with them was mind-boggling. The problem was I could think about Susanna all I wanted to or put her on a pedestal all day long and twice on Sunday, but it didn't do me any good. Let's be real — we were two people who didn't know each other when we danced together, and we were never going to know each other. She was just an amazing girl who I danced with one night, no more real, under the circumstances, than a character in a book. Even if the accident hadn't happened, what are the chances we would have ever gotten to know each other or seen each other again? Probably nil. I could make believe or wish all I wanted, but wishing doesn't make something true. I needed to let that sink in if I wanted to keep all my marbles, and believe me, I did. And what was my deal with Daryl? Here was, like, the best athlete in the state, who I was beginning to think of as my buddy. But how would I have ever even known him if he hadn't driven by when I was hitchhiking that night? I hitchhike all the time, and I don't think of everyone who picks me up as my buddy, do I? Add to that — if Susanna hadn't gotten killed, he wouldn't be such a mess and probably wouldn't have any interest in me anyway. I couldn't have been feeling more mixed up.

But there I was — stuck with dreams of a girl I would never know, a friendship with a guy who needed the kind of help I couldn't provide, and serious worries about whether I was off my rocker or not.

21

The night after Jeff and I hung out at the Boys Club, we went to another dance at the Derby Community Center. As freshmen, we had gone almost every week, but a year later, we had now only been to one Derby dance — last October, the night of the fatal accident. I had recently blown Jeff off once to hang out with Daryl, something I wasn't about to do again.

When Jeff and I walk to Derby, we like to find our way there by walking down Canal Street, which is lined with factory buildings, a few still in use, like the Sponge Rubber, but some are vacant, their windows smashed by rocks thrown by kids who apparently have nothing better to do. Under the bridge, two steep metal staircases from each side of the street lead to the sidewalks and roadway above. Jeff and I like to race up the stairs.

As we reached the underside of the bridge, he went to the bottom of one staircase and I went to the other. He yelled "go," and we took off. The slightest misstep running up the stairs would not only mean losing the race but would also mean painful shins if one or the other or both banged into the rusty steel stairs. As usual, Jeff won, because, in truth, he is a little quicker than I am.

When we got to the top, he hopped the guard rail and joined me on my side of the street. "Nice try, partner," he said. "Maybe next time."

"Yeah, well, you're good on stairs, but if you ever want to try me in the two mile run, we'll talk."

"I…do...not...run...deestance races," Jeff replied, making a feeble attempt to imitate a Polish kid we call Johnny Ping Pong who practically lives at the Boys Club. We don't know his real last name, but he recently moved from Poland to Shelton, maybe a year ago. The kid is simply invincible at ping pong. Neither of us have ever won a single game against him, and not for lack of trying. Jeff will play him game after game, but each time, Johnny Ping Pong is the victor. I typically sit in a metal folding chair, having lost several times myself, marveling at Jeff's growing frustration. After three or four losses, Jeff will angrily throw a sand paddle provided by the Club on the floor, and explode, "Oh, yeah, Ping Pong, let's go upstairs to the gym and play one-on-one, then we'll see what ya got!"

Johnny Ping Pong stands there, arms crossed, with his store bought, thick rubber paddle under his left arm, and replies, calmly but smugly, "I do not play baskeetball." I think Jeff may hate Johnny Ping Pong more than Michael hates Derby football.

As we caught our breath from the race and passed from the metal bridge over Canal Street to the concrete bridge over the river, I asked, "Are you still planning to join the Marines?"

"Oh yeah," Jeff said. "That ain't changin'. Like I told you before, I'm all signed up. I don't think I could get out of it now even if I wanted to, which I don't."

"Oh, wow." I didn't quite know what else to say.

"By the way, did you tell the Big M I joined up?"

"Yeah," I said.

"What'd he have to say about it?"

"I don't know. I guess, like me, he was surprised," I said, honestly.

"Hmmm...okay," he said, seemingly disappointed, as we reached the other side of the river. "Let's stop in the Bridge Smoke Shop."

Stopping at the Smoke Shop is a regular thing for us. We head beyond the main magazine rack past the counter, which acts as a divider in the small store. On the back side of the rack is another rack with "girly" magazines. The owner, a heavy set guy with white hair and a cigar stub permanently stuck in his mouth, lets us look for a while before throwing us out. I guess he thinks it's normal and healthy for a couple of teen boys like us to look at pictures of naked women. But I think he also doesn't want adult men who wander behind the divider to be upset that minors are back there.

After Jeff and I had been gawking at magazines for about fifteen minutes, a customer walked in, and the owner called to us. "Hey you kids, get the hell outta there. You're not supposed to be back there... you know that," and Jeff and I left, as we always did, not having purchased anything.

We arrived at the dance at about 8:10. Things were well underway. The band was the Dirty Ol' Men, whose lead singer was Billy Dillon, a recent Shelton High graduate. Billy's hair was now almost shoulder length and he wore a beat up top hat, bell bottom jeans that looked like they hadn't been washed in about seventeen years, and a tie dye t-shirt with the sleeves cut off. The Dirty Ol' Men weren't as good as the Journeymen, who were a few years older and better musicians all around, but Dillon was completely entertaining to watch. He really knew how to play the crowd. The place was as full as ever with dozens of couples dancing to the beat of the music. Jeff spied Julie across the gym and said, "I'll be back in a little bit...maybe."

I was left to wander around alone. In the process, I began to recall the night in October when I had danced with Susanna. I even walked over to the spot where I had observed her unique loveliness and remembered trying to work up the courage to ask her to dance. *What a wimp I was that night,* I thought to myself. A couple was slow dancing right at the spot where Susanna and I had slow danced. I circled the guy and the girl, pretending to look around so as not to be totally obvious. It made me sad, and I wished things had turned out differently. I was suddenly distracted by Frankie Adamo and company. Frankie was, as usual, flanked by Nickie and Foxy. They stopped about twenty feet away and began talking to a group of girls. Two girls talked to Frankie, while three others talked to Nickie or Foxy. I guess it was a case of divide and conquer, although I'm not sure who was dividing and who was conquering. Frankie seemed to be really enjoying the attention. The girls were giggling at everything Frankie said, just like the girls were the night he was leaning against the Big M's Corvair, and he smiled confidently every time he made them laugh. I wished I could hear what he was saying so I'd know if he was really funny or if they were laughing themselves silly because he was a football star. I wondered if he ever felt bad about the accident or if he made jokes about that too. As I watched the girls laughing, in my imagination, I heard Frankie saying, *"If you want to hear something really funny, let me tell you about the night I ran over a skinny girl from Seymour,"* and as he launched into the story, the girls laughed harder and harder, which was exactly what they were doing. Lost in a fantasy of my own making, I stood there, hating Adamo in that moment. All of a sudden, completely out of the blue, another Derby football player, apparently horsing around with his buddies, crashed into me and almost knocked me off of my feet. In the process, the jerk snapped me out of the trance I was lost in, which was lucky or I probably would have gone and picked a fight with Adamo, which would have ended badly for me.

"Oh, sorry, man...sorry, I didn't mean to bump into you," the Derby player said to me, his mouth only inches from my face. I could smell the alcohol on his breath. Then he and the idiots he was with continued on their way, laughing like mad men as they continued across the gym.

Having nothing else to do, I continued to watch Frankie and his fan club interact, my hatred having subsided at least a little now. Suddenly another girl, a very beautiful girl, approached Frankie and tapped him on the shoulder. This one might have been the most beautiful girl I've ever seen, and I'm not even kidding about that. I mean, Susanna was beautiful, but maybe mainly to me. What's that old saying? *Beauty is in the eye of the beholder?* This one was beautiful, I think, to the eye of any beholder in the world. She didn't look happy, not by a long shot, and she seemed to be asking him if she could talk to him privately as she pointed to the hallway. He shrugged and nodded and then followed her as she quickly walked to the double doors that led outside the gym. I'm not usually that nosy, but at this point, I felt so obsessed with Frankie that I followed them, trying to understand what was going on.

I couldn't hear them because the music was blasting, and I needed to stay at least ten feet inside the gym so as not to be noticed. But the beautiful girl's body language suggested to me that she was scolding Frankie. It looked like she was fuming. Maybe she was his girlfriend and was scolding him for flirting with other girls. Frankie didn't seem to have anything to say. Miss Beautiful Girl was doing all the talking. He was just shrugging his shoulders in a sort of apologetic way. Finally, with a very hurt look on her face, Miss Beautiful Girl, obviously incensed, shook her head and walked back into the gym, brushing right past me. The breeze alone almost knocked me over. Her cheeks were scarlet, and I could see she was fighting back tears. She walked over to two girls, spoke to them briefly, and then bolted back to the hallway, the two friends following at her heels. All three whipped past Frankie, who stood there helplessly as Miss Beautiful Girl avoided even looking at him while her perfectly-good-looking-but-not-quite-beautiful friends darted evil glances at him. I didn't know what it was all about, but it sure was quite a drama.

Frankie came back into the gym and left off where he had begun, joking and laughing with the flirting girls, just like that...like he hadn't just had a beautiful girl go nuts on him. The little groups of girls seemed to change places going back and forth from Frankie to Nickie to Foxy. I guess that worked out well because then you could keep saying the same dumb, funny things to a new set of girls who hadn't heard your jokes before. I wondered what it must be like to be a big football star and have girls drawn to you like that. Girls are definitely not drawn to cross-country stars. Actually, as a distance runner, it's hard to think of myself as any kind of star. Maybe I'll make the grade in basketball, which might someday give me a taste of what Frankie, Nickie, and Foxy were enjoying that night. I'm not willing to bet on it, though.

Jeff came back to me, not looking too happy. "What's the matter?" I asked. "No go with Julie?"

"Well, we danced a couple of times, but it's not the same. She's...I don't know...kind of aloof. Then get this. When I asked her if I could come by sometime soon, she said, 'I'm kind of seeing someone else now,' and gives me this 'poor you' look. I was going to tell her I joined the Marines, but now, for all I care, she can go fuck herself!"

"Hey, easy does it," I warned. "Don't get yourself all worked up."

"Yeah, don't get myself all worked up. Right! Okay, I won't get all fuckin' worked up." Jeff is a pretty easy going kid, except for when he isn't pretty easy going.

Now that neither of us was having any fun, I wanted to suggest that we take off, but for some reason I didn't. For the last forty-five minutes of the dance, we just stood near the stage, listening to the band and watching Billy Dillon's antics. He was walking from left to right across the stage, taking giant strides holding not just the microphone, but the whole stand with the mic on it in one hand. I would say he was speaking more than singing the lyrics to the songs with bulging eyes, like he was completely possessed.

"Billy is off the wall," I remarked to Jeff.

"I like him," Jeff replied. "He's cool."

Jeff liked the grungier, hard-core types more than I did. While I liked the Beach Boys or the Four Seasons, Jeff was more into the Animals, the Zombies and the Stones. Despite his interest in the freakier rockers, I knew Jeff wouldn't be growing his hair to his shoulders or wearing a beat up top hat anytime soon since he was about to become a Marine.

When Billy announced that they were about to play the last song, Jeff and I, along with packs of other kids, headed for the exit. When we pushed open the exterior doors, we passed the three football players.

"Hey, what's up, Jeff?" Frankie said. Nickie and Foxy followed suit.

"Hey guys, nice to see ya," Jeff replied.

"Yeah, you too, man."

I'm not going to lie. I was impressed. I guess I realized Jeff knew those guys because of living in Derby and everything, but I had never seen them interact. Jeff and I walked to the corner, trying to decide if it was going to be Italian pizza at River Restaurant or Greek pizza at Derby Pizza, when I heard the familiar rattle of Daryl's Bug. Sure enough, he pulled over to the opposite corner, and, seeing me, waved me over his car.

"Wait a second for me," I said to Jeff, and I jogged diagonally across the street. "Hey, Daryl, what's goin' on?"

"What's goin' on is," he said, "your brother just threatened to kick my ass."

Confused, I asked, "What are you talking about? Michael is working tonight."

Taking a big gulp of beer from his latest supply, he continued, "Exactly! I was vegging in my car at Duchess, minding my own business when he raps on my window. I thought he was going to tell me to leave the lot the way Big Alfred always does, even though Big Al was making his rounds. When I rolled down my window, he says to me, 'I need you to stay away from my brother.' So I'm shocked, ya know? And I say, 'What?' Then he gets super sarcastic and says, 'You heard me, pal! I know he's been hanging around with you, and it's gonna stop now or I'm gonna kick your ass!' He was serious. Then he comes at me even harder and goes — 'Don't make me fuckin' tell you again,' and he walks away."

I inhaled deeply. "Wow! I don't even know how he found out we've hung out."

"Yeah, well, let's just say I don't think I want to tangle with him... not only because he's older and at least my size, but my head isn't in a good space for a fight, especially with a dude as serious about it as he is. And besides, he's your brother."

"Listen, Daryl. I'm going to talk to him...I'll just...I'll....I'm going to have a talk with him, okay?"

"Do what you want, but I thought you might want to know about it." And he drove off.

When I returned to Jeff, my ears were steaming.

"What was that all about?" he asked.

"Don't worry about it."

"Wasn't that Daryl Novak?" he asked. I nodded, and he said, "How do you know him?"

"You know the Derby football players," I replied, maybe a little too sharply.

"Yeah, but remember, I played sports with those guys when I lived in Derby. They're only a year older than me because I stayed back in third grade."

"Okay, well I know Novak from Duchess. He works at Charlton Press and comes in every night for coffee for the night crew." I wasn't exactly lying.

Seeing that I was worked up, Jeff switched gears. "What's it going to be, then, Derby Pizza or River?"

"Neither," I said. "Duchess."

"That's a longer walk, and it's in the opposite direction from home," Jeff complained. "I don't feel like hitchhiking tonight."

"Michael's working. He'll bring us home."

"Okay," Jeff responded, and we headed up Elizabeth Street toward the Armory.

As we walked in silence, it hit me that we were on the same route Susanna must have taken the night of the accident, and it made me think about Frankie. "What do you think the deal is with Adamo?" I asked, a knot tight in my gut.

"What do you mean?"

"What I mean is...I mean...do you ever think it bothers him that he killed Susanna?"

"Uhm...I don't know...I would think it probably does, but how am I supposed to know?"

"Well I watched him tonight and I watched him outside of Duchess a week or two ago, and it doesn't fucking seem like he cares at all!"

"Hold up, partner. You're all steamed up. How do we know what Frankie Adamo thinks or feels? You can't just go by seeing him at a dance or at Duchess."

"Yeah...maybe you're right. But I can wonder if I want."

We remained silent as we walked by the Armory, a place I had been passing by my whole life on the way to and from my grandmother's. Since I was a little kid, I had wondered about the big, silver cannon, with two gigantic wagon type wheels, the barrel extending through a big hole in a flat rectangle of steel that must have been meant to shield the operators from enemy fire. I wondered if it had really been used in battle and how many people had been killed by it. The Derby Green also had four Civil War era cannons displayed, surrounded by a big statue of a tired Union soldier. I didn't really get the reason why cannons, which had probably killed hundreds or even thousands of people, deserved places of honor. Obviously they did, though, because there they were. *Did they have cannons on the greens in Vietnam?* I wondered. I pictured an inscription on a cannon in Saigon — "This cannon killed 10,000 American soldiers." Thinking about it, I worried that Jeff would be killed by some kind of cannon warfare.

By the time we passed the San Marini house and turned on to Division Street, Jeff was chattering away about the Knicks, who had just lost to the Celtics in the Eastern Division semi-final playoffs. It was no shame to be beaten by the mighty Celtics, the second greatest dynasty in pro sports, next to the Yankees. Jeff was rambling on about how he loved Bill Bradley. He fancied himself a Bradley type of player, a small forward who could really shoot the lights out. Jeff was kind of like that, I guess. Mostly, I wasn't really listening as we headed down the Division Street hill. I could see, without a sidewalk to keep her safe, how Susanna could have been killed here, especially in the dark night, especially with a reckless driver. I felt my heart race as we walked around the curve. I also found myself thinking about Michael threatening Daryl. It wasn't the first time my brother had felt compelled to protect me. When I was in grade school, he had come to my assistance any time an older kid bothered me. When I was about ten, Andy Cole was using me as a target while throwing rocks to see how close he could come to me without hitting me, but he eventually came too close, pegging me square in the eye. The Big M proceeded to punch him out. Around the same time, when Hank Kunzik, a kid twice my size, took me by one arm and leg and began turning like a whirling dervish, finally releasing me, the centrifugal force launched me like a rocket out into the middle of the road. I got scraped up pretty good when I landed on the asphalt. Once more, it was Michael to the rescue. I didn't see either fight, but I will never forget what Dave Woodson, who lived across the street from us and was a year older than Michael, said to me: "You should have seen what your brother did to Kunzik. Poor Hank had blood all over his t-shirt when Michael was done with him." And then Dave concluded, "I wouldn't mess with Michael anymore. You should feel proud to have a brother like that." And hearing Dave's words, I *was* filled with pride — but at the moment, it wasn't pride I was feeling, but anger and frustration.

Noticing that I was lost in thought, Jeff said, "Hello? You with me, buddy? You alright? You're not yourself tonight."

"Yeah...I'm here. I'm myself. Sorry. My mind just wandered a little."

I tried to hold up my end of the conversation, saying how great I thought my favorite Knick, Clyde Frazier, was and how I felt the Knicks would be a force to contend with next season. But I think Jeff noticed that my heart wasn't really in it. We turned on to Pershing Drive and now just had about a hundred yards to go.

When we got to Duchess, I asked Michael if I could talk to him in the office for a few minutes. This couldn't wait until we got home where there was no privacy anyway. They had just finished the big rush from the dance, so he told Tomaso, who was also on, to keep an eye on the window.

I was hyperventilating as we walked into the office, but I forged ahead. "Did you threaten Daryl Novak tonight?" I asked.

"You bet I fucking did," he responded strongly.

"How did you know I hung out with him?"

"Easy," he said. "The night I went to Brewster, we got back to Ansonia at about 1:00 in the morning and stopped for a bite at the State Diner. Craig Betts was in there having a late night snack, and he said, while he was waiting on a customer, he thought he saw you drive out of the lot in Novak's car. A few days later, I drove by the playground and saw Jeff shooting some hoops by himself. I asked him what you two ended up doing on Saturday night. He told me you had cancelled because you had too much homework. What the fuck is going on?"

"Nothing is going on. Daryl is just a friend," I said defensively.

"What kind of friend? The kid is a hot fucking mess, and you need friends like him like you need a hole in the head! What the fuck would you want to be friends with that loser for?"

I felt a tidal wave of emotion wash over me, swallowing me up. "He's not a loser," I shouted angrily. "He's...not...a...loser! I'm just trying to help him! That's all, okay? Okay? Is that fucking okay with you? Did you ever try to help somebody?"

"You can't help someone like him," Michael reasoned. "He's way, *way* beyond your help."

"Don't say that to me!" I could feel tears filling the corners of my eyes.

"You need to calm down," he ordered firmly. "You're out of control. You really are. I don't get why you even know him."

"I know him because...I know him...because...because his sister Susanna was my friend! Okay? She was my friend!"

"C'mon. Give me a break. How could a Seymour girl have been your friend? Just how?" he asked skeptically.

"Because I met her at the Derby Community Center and I danced with her, okay? I danced with her twice. Even a slow dance. I even think I was in love with her, if that's okay with you! Ask Jeff. He knows. Go fucking ask him!"

The angrier I got, the calmer Michael seemed, which infuriated me even more. More gently now, he said, "Gabe, you're being a little naive and a little irrational even. Dancing with a girl doesn't mean you know her. And how could you have been in love with her?"

His words stung me more than his threatening Daryl had. "Don't say that to me! Do *not* say that to me! Ever! Not ever! Do you hear me? And don't try to control what I do or who I hang out with! Just leave me alone, will ya? Just leave me the fuck alone!"

I pushed through and ran out of the office, smashing into Kevin Binkowski in the process. On foot, I made a beeline for the parking lot exit. I walked past dozens of kids who were hanging out and talking by their cars and headed out to the shoulder of Pershing Drive toward Route 8. Jeff, who was talking to Tomaso in the vestibule, saw me, rushed through the door, and yelled, "Gabe, where are you going? Gabe?"

"Leave me alone!" I yelled at the top of my lungs, not breaking stride and not looking back. "Just, everybody, leave me the fuck alone!"

22

Michael and Jeff didn't pursue me. Seeing how upset I was, they appeared to feel it was best to give me space. Michael wouldn't be finished working for at least another half hour anyway. When I got to the Bradlees Plaza, I stuck my thumb out, kind of hoping that Daryl would pass by. Instead, a middle aged black guy in a beat up Cadillac soon pulled over and picked me up. I was grateful, actually, because I was worried that Michael and Jeff would come by. The driver could see me wiping away tears.

"You alright, young brother?" he asked, his voice like scratchy sandpaper.

"Uhm," I sighed. I was too drained to be anything but truthful. "Not too good actually. I just had a bad argument with my big brother."

"Well, don't let nothin' get in between you and your big brother now, my man. See, I call you 'young brother' because we all brothers to each other — but our *real* brothers — well now, tha's a whole different story. True brotherhood! That right there's the most important kind. Here's my recommendation — you make up right away, now, you hear me?"

Fighting back further tears, I gulped and nodded that I did.

He said he was heading for Bridgeport, so I asked him to drop me off at the top of Exit 14.

The truth is that I didn't listen to the man's advice. Call me defensive, but I didn't like that Michael had called Daryl a "hot fucking mess," and I liked it even less that he threatened Daryl. We didn't speak to each other for at least a week after our talk in the office. Rarely did we even make eye contact. He might have been the Big M, but at the moment, I was having some of my own pretty big negative feelings about him. It's rough living in such close quarters and not speaking, but we somehow managed. I know it seemed to Michael that I went over the deep end, but I took what happened to Susanna and what I feared might happen to Daryl seriously. In a way, I understood where Michael was coming from. Our mom and dad had always told us to steer away from what they called "problem people." I remember when Michael was sixteen, he was dating a girl whose parents were divorced. Dad really got on his case, pointing out that a girl who was from a divorced home was more likely to consider divorce as an option when she had problems in her marriage. As if Michael and this chick were going to end up married. Thinking back on those kinds of teachings from our parents, it got me thinking, once again, that our family had its own problems.

Anyway, I didn't take the advice of the Cadillac man. I didn't make up with Michael. Sometimes, the most important things are left unsaid. That's how it is for me, anyway. But my mother always told me that "time heals all wounds," and I figured that's how it would be for me and Michael.

I didn't get together with Daryl that week either, but I saw him when I worked on Wednesday night. When he came in for coffees, things got majorly uncomfortable because Michael was on the window. They didn't speak at all, and oddly the Big M didn't hand me the list but just went to the coffee machine and made the coffees himself. After he rang Daryl out, he walked to the back of the store, leaving me alone at the counter with Daryl. I mouthed, "I talked to him." Daryl mouthed back, "How did it go?" I gave him a thumbs down and whispered, "Not good. But I'll see you soon." With a look of satisfaction, Daryl nodded and went on his way.

The following Friday we had our third track meet against Amity High School of Woodbridge, a rich town next to Ansonia. In the first two meets of the season, I had won the two mile run with times of 11:03 and 10:56. Those aren't amazing times, but they were good enough to cross the finish line first after eight long laps against Ansonia and against East Haven. At Amity, I was up against Ronald Adams, a senior, who was considered one of the best distance runners in the state. Maybe the very best. To say I was nervous would be an understatement. When the gun sounded, I stayed with Adams for the first three laps, but his pace was too much for me. He was a tall, strong kid, like Daryl, who took longer strides than I did. I seemed to be taking two strides for every one Adams took. There's a point in a distance race where the loser lets the winner go. Once I made that decision, the distance between Adams and me grew and grew over the course of the next five laps, and in the end, he beat me by more than a third of a lap. My first loss of the season. But I was stunned when I heard that my second place time was a new Shelton High School record. My eyes almost popped out of my head when Coach Duggan told me my time was 10:31. The previous record, held by William B. Cross (I had studied his name on the record plaque in the trophy case outside of our gymnasium) of the class of 1957, had been 10:48, so I had beaten it by almost twenty seconds. Adams finished in 9:57, and I was shocked when he didn't look too happy with his time. I would have been thrilled to break the ten minute barrier. I still would be. It was a time that had probably been unheard of in William B. Cross's era. Then again, Adams would probably have lapped William B. Cross.

My teammates shook my hand and slapped me on the back, enthusiastically congratulating me, and I tried to catch my breath after the long race. What got me, though, was I wasn't sure if I was supposed to feel good about the record since I had *lost* the race. Sports, I had learned, was a world where losing, of course, was frowned upon — like, after every away basketball game we lost freshman year and this year, we had to maintain silence on the bus on the way home as if we were in mourning for our dead grandmother or something. Even if we played our very best and lost by one point, still: remain silent...feel bad about yourself. With a different bounce of the basketball, maybe we would have won. That didn't matter. The message was clear. Losing is unacceptable. And now I had gone and broken a long-standing school record but had not won the actual race. What do you do with that one?

I guess track, being more of an individual sport than a team sport, was different because losing didn't seem to diminish the glory of the accomplishment much. Not only had my teammates enthusiastically congratulated me, but on the following Monday in school, I was patted on the back by just about every upperclassman who was a major athlete. Breaking the cross country record brought me some notoriety, but the track record turned out to be a bigger deal. I had gone from practically being a big nobody to a somebody just like that. By lunch time on Monday, Coach Duggan had taken William B. Cross's name off the track record plaque and replaced it with Gabriel DeMarco, there for the entire student body to see. Sorry William B. Cross, but nothing lasts forever. And while it lasted for me, I was going to enjoy the glory. People respected a person who accomplished something like breaking a school record. Even the guys at work made a big deal about it. When I went to work on Saturday night, everyone commented, ribbing me a little, calling me "the lonely distance runner" and asking "What makes Gabriel run?" About the second comment, I wondered myself: What is it, exactly, that makes me run? Or better yet, what am I running to — or away from? Distance running is a very solitary endeavor and takes a special kind of drive because there are no fans and there is usually very little glory. Why I had that drive was anybody's guess.

In the meantime, my feet were still on the ground enough to know that breaking a track record didn't fit in the same category as making a game saving play in football. There were sports like track and cross country and there were sports like football and basketball. Let's just say I wasn't holding my breath expecting girls to swarm around me at the next dance. But, in life, you take what you can get, so I wasn't complaining either.

All of the accolades didn't change the fact that, at the end of the night, I had to clean the parking lot like always, track star or not. Like I said, in life, you get what you get. About fifteen minutes before closing, I was sweeping up the last remnants of trash when I heard a familiar sound. Daryl chugged into the lot and pulled into a spot right next to where I was sweeping.

He jumped out of the car. "My man — Record-breaking Gabriel DeMarco," he said. "Way ta go, Dushess! I read it in the *Sentinel*."

It was true, my name had appeared in the headline of the *Sentinel's* sports page on Saturday morning: "DeMarco Sets New Record in Loss to Amity," and in the text of the article, the copy read "Record-breaking Gabriel DeMarco, who broke Shelton's Cross Country record in October, set a new school record in the two mile run with a time of 10:31, breaking the previous record set by William B. Cross in 1957." Luckily the reporter didn't state Ronald Adams' time, but it was there to see in the list of results at the end of the article if anyone chose to read further.

"Thanks, Daryl," I said humbly. I could tell he was a little drunk.

"You're the man! The Roger Bannister of the Valley! The Valley's own Jim Ryun!" I must have turned the brightest shade of red, hearing myself compared to the most famous Olympic milers ever, even though I was more of a two-miler than a miler. The longer the distance, the better I was, I guess.

"Get out — you must have noticed that I lost the race," I said, sheepishly.

"Who the fuck cares, Dushess? You ran your race faster than anyone in Shelton has been able to run it in more than a decade, which is pretty fuckin' amazing. Your time is probably better than any time that's been run in Derby, Ansonia, and Seymour too. Ever think a that, pal? We'll have to find out. If I'm right...and I think I am, that would make you the greatest distance runner in the history of the whole Valley. And think of this...think how much better you're going to be by the time you're a senior. Man, you'll set a record that no one will ever break!" His words filled me up and changed my perspective. Daryl had this crazy knack for making me feel good about myself.

Maybe he was right. Maybe I needed to let go of comparing myself to Ronald Adams, who was two years older than I was anyway, and just appreciate what my time meant at my school and in the Valley.

"Le's go break into the school buildings and find out if anyone ever ran the race faster than you, Dushess."

"Let's not," I cautioned. "I don't need to do anything else with you that I could get arrested for."

"I'm jus' kiddin', Dushess. Okay, we'll find out some other way. How about this then? How about you and I play one-on-one tomorrow. Le's see if ya got any better in basketball since you became a record-breaking track star. Besides, there's somethin' I wanna show you."

I had no plans for Sunday. "What time?" I asked.

"How about, like, 11:00 a.m.? I'll pick you up at the bottom of Exit 14 under Route 8 like usual. How's that sound?"

"Sounds good."

"You got it," he said, and jumped in his car and pulled out.

"And don't get into any trouble," I called after him, but considering that rattling muffler, I don't think he heard me.

The next morning, Daryl was on time as scheduled. We headed straight to the courts at Nolan Field. I don't know why he chose to play in Ansonia instead of in his hometown. Maybe it was because he didn't want to run into his old friends. In our second game ever of one-on-one, Daryl seemed lethargic after what was probably a late night of drinking and smoking grass. He still beat me with ease, but this time by only eight instead of twelve points. Of course, an eight point loss is still a beating. When Jeff and I played, it usually ended up in a deuce game, and never more than a three or four point difference between us.

As we were finishing the game, two guys from Duchess were heading on foot to the courts — Lance Jefferson and Buster Brookes.

"Yo, what's shakin', Gabriel," Buster said, greeting me.

"Hey Buster...Lance," I replied.

"You boys down for a game of two-on-two?" Lance asked, holding a worn out basketball in his slender fingers.

Buster and Lance were both about 5'10" but sported very different physiques. Buster was seriously muscle bound. I had seen him play in the summer leagues, and his strong body made him a great rebounder, and, despite those signature thick glasses of Buster's, his eyesight didn't seem to be much of a handicap. Though I never heard that he played any high school sports in Ansonia, Buster would have made a heck of a football player. Lance was an athletic player who was long and lean. Even with Daryl, I didn't think we could beat them. Buster and Lance were better than I was. I certainly wasn't going to be able to rebound with either of them. And I was learning that white kids don't usually beat black kids in basketball.

I looked at Daryl, and he nodded, giving the signal that he was in.

"Winners' outs? That's how we do," Buster said.

"Always," I said.

"You take it first," Daryl offered with a playful smile. "But don't miss because once we get the ball, you might not see it again."

"Whoa," Lance shrieked, and Buster broke up in gritty laughter, both guys apparently appreciating Daryl's trash talk.

That's pretty big talk, I thought. But Daryl wasn't too far off. Buster and Lance scored the first three baskets, but after missing the fourth, Daryl and I took over. My game plan was to feed the ball to Daryl and not shoot myself unless I had an open shot. Though Daryl hadn't seemed to work hard in his game against me, he was suddenly rejuvenated. I got to see the competitor that was Daryl Novak in all his glory. He couldn't miss from the outside, and on the inside, neither Buster nor Lance could handle his head fakes and moves around the basket. On one play, Daryl would double pump and then knock it down while they were coming down from their jump, and on another play, he would take the pass from me, dribble into the bucket and drop in a beautiful hook shot. Before we knew it, we were ahead 10-3. Or should I say, it was Buster and Lance, 3 - Daryl, 10? That was okay, though, our game plan was working. Daryl continued to show no mercy, and when he hit the winning hoop, the final score was 21-7. Of our point total, I had only scored three points, but I shot one hundred percent, having taken only three shots on pretty feeds from Daryl.

Buster broke into a throaty laugh. "Whew-hoo!" His voice then whistled out, "You smoked us! This boy the real deal, Gabriel," and he cracked up again. The less boisterous Lance just shook his head and shrugged, trying to comprehend what had just happened to him. What I understood, though, is we had just shared the court with a truly great athlete — a guy who should have been both an All State football player as well as an All State basketball player, if the game of life had only taken a slightly different bounce.

Lifting the front of his t-shirt to wipe his sweaty head, Daryl called out a muffled, "Nice game, guys. You're good players."

"Thanks, man," Buster replied. He nodded at Daryl and added, "You're like some kind of Jerry West." Then Buster and Lance told us they had to be on their way. "If you boys have any Christianity in your hearts, you'll keep the results of this game a secret, especially at Duchess," Buster chortled as they walked away.

"We'll try our best to keep it a secret, Buster," I teased.

"Thank you. You're a good Christian, my man. I guess Big Al is right about you," Buster called back, leaving us with one more of his big belly laughs.

Daryl and I went and sat at a nearby picnic table. "Nice game, Duchess," he said, wiping the sweat off his face with the bottom of his t-shirt.

"Thanks," I smiled, "but it was all you."

"Not true. You made all my scoring possible. You're an excellent passer, and you're going to be a good point guard for Shelton, that's for sure. You'll probably set some assist records to go with your track records."

"I don't know about that one," I replied doubtfully.

"Listen, Duchess, I don't think you get it about sports, so let me clue you in. People say I was a great football player because I scored a lot of touchdowns, but without Ben Andrews, I was fuckin' nobody. He put the ball where I could catch it. Without Andrews, I was a big, fat nothin', and without you a few minutes ago, those two guys might have beaten us. Got it?"

He had done it again...built me up...made me feel good about myself. His compliment left me speechless. I'm not sure if I had ever known a top athlete as humble and as selfless as Daryl. The guys I knew, or knew of, like the Derby players, seemed so full of themselves, and here was Daryl, willing to give all the credit to others. To me. It was really something.

"Remember how I told you I wanted to show you something?" he asked, changing the subject.

"Yes," I said, curious to know what it was.

He trotted over to the passenger door of the Bug, reached into the glove compartment and returned to the picnic table, handing me what appeared to be a folded up page from a magazine or a book. I slowly unfolded the glossy page, and he pointed to the side he wanted me to see. There before me was a photo of a man on fire. Immersed in flames, he seemed to be sitting calmly in the middle of a roadway, a gas can and a car close behind him. A group of Asian men in robes stood a small distance away on the other side of the car. The men looked concerned, but no one seemed to be helping him as he sat serenely in the sea of flames. Under the photo was the following caption:

In June 1963, most Americans couldn't find Vietnam on a map. But there was no forgetting that war-torn Southeast Asian nation after

Associated Press photographer Malcolm Browne captured the image of Thich Quang Duc immolating himself on a Saigon street. Browne had been given a heads-up that something was going to happen to protest the treatment of Buddhists by the regime of President Ngo Dinh Diem. Once there he watched as two monks doused the seated elderly man with gasoline. "I realized at that moment exactly what was happening, and began to take pictures a few seconds apart," he wrote soon after. His Pulitzer Prize-winning photo of the seemingly serene monk sitting lotus style as he is enveloped in flames became the first iconic image to emerge from a quagmire that would soon pull in America. Quang Duc's act of martyrdom became a sign of the volatility of his nation, and President Kennedy later commented, "No news picture in history has generated so much emotion around the world as that one."

After studying the photo and doing my best to digest the blurb, I looked up at Daryl, not quite sure what to say.

"Incredible, right?" he said. "I just wanted you to see this because I didn't know about this when it happened. I mean, I was only about thirteen, and you couldn't have known because you would have been around ten or eleven. Did you ever read about this?"

"No...but…but wait. Where did you get this...and what's the... the point?"

"I came across it in a book in the Seymour Library, and the point is...the point is, first of all, he's protesting the same war that all the hippies are protesting here now. But maybe it's like my dad says. The hippies have no right to protest. Vietnam isn't their country. And besides, the guys in the Army are fighting for our freedom, aren't they? The hippies just carry signs, which seems stupid, but this guy obviously had such strong feelings that he torched himself. He isn't carrying a fuckin' sign. Don't you see? He *sacrificed* himself...maybe because he didn't like his government or whatever. Maybe I'm not making sense, but the point is he had such strong feelings. And just look at him, man — just sitting there so calmly...like...like...like it's no big deal...like he's chillin' out in a park on a Sunday afternoon or something. Talk about guts! That's real courage. Unreal!"

"You tore this out of a *book*?" I asked, incredulously. "You know, you're not supposed to..."

"Yeah, yeah, yeah," he interrupted. "Maybe you haven't noticed, Duchess, but I don't always follow rules."

I was confused. For about a split second, it seemed like Daryl wanted to protest the war, but he didn't like the hippies. Now I was almost sure he was going to join the Army, but not for exactly the same reasons Jeff joined up.

The best thing I could think of to say was: "Well, the caption says he's a Buddhist monk, and those guys are, like, into meditation and stuff like that. I think they have special powers. I just read an article in a magazine about how the Beatles are learning to meditate in India with some swami guy. I think he's cast some kind of spell on the Beatles. It's like that. These guys have crazy mystical powers."

"Vietnam sounds like an interesting place, though, right?" Daryl asked, his eyes squinting in deep thought.

"I guess," I said. "But I don't think I get it. From what I've seen and heard, the Vietnam War is horrendous, and I don't think it's worth the risk of getting killed over. I don't think anything is worth getting killed over."

"I'm not so sure about that, Duchess." Daryl picked up the article off the table and stared at it and seemed to drift into some kind of weird trance-like state.

How could he not be so sure about it? I wondered. To say I was baffled would be the understatement of the year. After I came back to reality, I looked at him sitting there staring at the article, and I broke the trance. "Hello? Are you going to stare at that weird picture all day?"

He looked up at me with what I think was a happy grin and began to carefully fold it back up. "No, Gab-ri-el," he replied mockingly, "I am not. Let's take off."

Here I was again, running after him. When I slammed my door shut, I said, "You've really got me worried, Daryl. You better not be thinking about what I think you're thinking about! You better not enlist like you were saying you might a few weeks ago!"

"Why? Don't you think I'd look good in a uniform? Personally, I think I'd look like a movie star," he chuckled.

"I don't think you're funny."

"Oh, that's too bad. Cuz I think I'm fuckin' hilarious."

"I'm just worried about you because you can act a little crazy sometimes."

"You're a good kid, Duchess...a good Christian like that dude Buster said. But don't sweat it. I've got things under control. I might be a lot of things, but I'm not crazy. You don't hafta worry about that."

As we drove away, he turned on the tape player and started singing along with one of my favorite tunes, Simon and Garfunkel's "Scarborough Fair." Daryl's off-pitch singing didn't improve the song, but it was good to see him so happy. Maybe I didn't need to worry. Somehow, though, his good mood didn't put my mind completely at ease. After all, I had witnessed him running on a railroad track toward a speeding locomotive.

Since it was broad daylight, I had him drop me off at the bottom of Exit 14, so I wouldn't be seen getting out of his car by any of my family members, especially by Michael, who had already caused enough trouble. It sounded more and more like Daryl was going to end up joining the military and getting himself killed in Vietnam. I didn't like that Jeff had joined, but at least Jeff wasn't planning to die. I thought to myself, *Can Daryl possibly be planning to go out as a hero...to sacrifice himself, like the guys in the World War II movies — the heroes that Will said don't even exist in Vietnam? What kind of craziness could possibly be going through Daryl's mind to come up with such a lame-*

brained plan? As I walked up the hill toward my house, I couldn't help but think that the school year was coming to an end and that I had to figure out a way to convince Daryl not to enlist.

23

It seemed ironic that Jeff's birthday fell on Memorial Day that May. He and I didn't exchange birthday gifts because, as guys, that wasn't too cool. As we had been doing for a few years, we hung out and watched the annual Shelton-Derby Parade downtown. It's just your typical Memorial Day parade, probably the same as zillions of towns across the country. The two towns take turns hosting it. The parade alternates from year to year by beginning in one town and ending in the other. The high school band of the hosting town leads the parade. Thankfully, this year Shelton hosted because the Shelton band was absurdly better than the sorry Derby band. Otherwise, the parade features other high school bands from towns that don't have a parade that day, Boy Scout and Girl Scout troops, a few good drum and bugle corps, and some pathetic looking floats. Let's just say that it isn't the Rose Bowl Parade. Still, the parade has its local appeal.

Like never before, I noticed the picnic-like atmosphere with hundreds of people lining the streets, sitting in their lawn chairs, small coolers by their sides, and vendors hawking small American flags, plastic toy guns, and junk like that. Jeff and I walked to Mosci's, asked Lou to make us a couple of hotdogs, and then we claimed a piece of concrete real estate outside the store. Then we sat on the curb because we obviously weren't carrying around lawn chairs.

Some things struck me that I actually hadn't ever thought about before. The first was a formation of jet planes that, moments before the parade began, soared low over our heads. The shrill roar of their supersonic engines pierced the tranquil morning, and, as all eyes looked up to the sky, you could hear a collective "wow" from the crowd. In a flash, the jets were out of sight, but it was the closest most of us will ever get to a military jet plane, and I have to admit that it is exciting. In the past, I had been caught up in the excitement like everyone else, but this year, I felt a surge of anxiety. This year, I felt like an observer looking at the whole scene from, like, the outside. I realized that these were war machines that killed people in Vietnam, and it made me worry that Jeff would end up there, even though he said he probably wouldn't. And now I was pretty sure that Daryl was going to join the military too. Even worse, unlike Jeff, it seemed Daryl *wanted* to go to Vietnam.

Once underway, everyone anticipated one of the parade's highlights, the appearance of the Connecticut Hurricane Drum and Bugle Corps. When the "Hurcs" approached, it brought back a few memories. Jeff had grown up as a big fan of drum and bugle corps and had introduced me to it a few years ago. We'd sit in his bedroom at his grandmother's house, listening to records he had purchased at competitions, and Jeff would describe, in great detail, the uniform styles, the dynamic drum majors, and the intricate marching and maneuvering. As Jeff described each aspect, he always emphasized that the "Hurcs" were the best. He'd say, "The Hawthorne Caballeros wear flat brimmed, Spanish style black hats like Zorro with big white plumes, white shirts with puffy sleeves, red sashes around their waists, and black pants with pencil thin red stripes that flare out at the bottom. So cool." But then he'd add, "But the Hurcs have the *best* uniforms. Their army officer style hats, black shirts and black pants, with a silver lightning bolt sash across their chests are really simple but make them look really bad ass." It was Jeff's goal to someday be a member of the Hurricanes, which I didn't know how he would pull off since he didn't play a bugle or a drum, but maybe they taught a guy how to play. I supposed he could carry a flag and be in the color guard, but I don't think that was his plan. A year ago, the summer before the school year had begun, he and I hitchhiked to Bridgeport's Kennedy Stadium, named for our recently assassinated president, and I enjoyed the competition almost as much as Jeff did. It was majorly impressive.

As the parade reached its mid-point, the crowd came to life as the Hurricanes passed by, playing their theme song, "The Magnificent Seven." Jeff, in a robot-like motion, practically shoved his half eaten hotdog into my chest, stood up, and began clapping enthusiastically for the corps. At that moment, I had a revelation. There was definitely a military regimentation to drum corps — the uniforms, the marching, the precision — and Jeff being drawn to the military life began to make sense.

Finally, something I had paid hardly any attention to in the past were the veterans of World War II, marching in their blue blazers and VFW caps — and, also, the active soldiers in uniform who passed by in olive drab jeeps, trucks, or sitting on some of those pathetic looking floats. I wondered if Jeff would be one of those guys in the parade someday. What I really wondered was whether he would march to commemorate those veterans who had fought for our country or if he would be the veteran who others marched to commemorate. That last thought was rough to think about.

The parade came to its conclusion with the Derby High School Band, all nine of them, playing off key and marching out of step in their red blazers and Derby hats, followed by a lone Derby police car, its light flashing right behind them. I don't know why the cop didn't arrest the members of the band, because playing so badly should be against the law.

As we walked back up the Coram Avenue hill toward our neighborhood after the parade, Jeff sprung something sort of newish on me about his enlistment, because he had been pretty quiet about the details since stunning me with the news weeks before.

"Yeah, so I leave on Saturday."

"Leave where?" I asked, puzzled.

"Home. I leave home — for basic training — this Saturday. Saturday is June 1st, and that's when my new life starts. I'm headed for Parris Island, South Carolina. That's where it's happenin'. That's where they're going to transform me into a Marine."

"This Saturday? Like, in five days, Saturday?"

"Yup, that's right."

"When did you find this out?" I asked.

"I don't know. Maybe three or four weeks ago when I met with Sergeant Higgins at the recruitment office."

"Oh, wow," I said, feeling a gnawing in the pit of my stomach. "And you're just telling me this *now*? How could you have known this for practically a month and not told me?"

"Hey...hey! Relax, cowboy! I wasn't trying to hide anything from you. I mentioned it, more or less, a few weeks back, remember? I just don't like to make a big fuckin' deal out of shit."

"Yeah, I remember, but you didn't give a date. You mean you're not even finishing the school year out at Emmett?"

"No point, partner. I'll be getting a G.E.D. diploma eventually anyway. You just have to pass a test. The sarge says they'll prepare me for the test while I'm serving. So finishing the year out don't matter much if you catch my drift."

"I don't really know what to say." Clamming up, I pursed my lips and shook my head, futilely trying to block out what he was telling me.

"Then don't say anything, brother. But how about this? How about you and me, we go to River Restaurant on Friday night and we celebrate with a couple pizzas."

Jeff and I didn't see each other for the rest of the week. We hadn't been seeing much of each other on weekdays in recent months anyway. Since he had transferred to Emmett O'Brien and was mostly at home in Derby with his mother, and I worked a few nights a week, it was harder to hang out. What I couldn't understand was how he could leave Emmett. He had played basketball for the second half of the season, after transferring from Shelton, and he was averaging twelve points a game for their varsity team as only a sophomore. There was pretty much no doubt he would emerge as an important player not only on their basketball team but also on their baseball team which was really his sport. Why would he give all of that up?

But he *would* be giving it up. Saturday he would leave for Parris Island. It sounded like a vacation place, but I was certain it wasn't. What a way to begin the month of June for him...and for me.

On Friday afternoon, I got home from track practice, had dinner, and thought I'd take a quick nap before Jeff and I met up to head to River, but the phone rang, rousing me from sleep. It was Jeff for me.

"Hey, listen, pal. I'm not blowing you off or anything, but I gotta make it later."

"Why's that?" I asked.

"I'm getting together with Julie to say goodbye. I'm going to hitchhike up to her house and spend an hour or so with her, so how about we meet downtown at Mosci's at about 9:00? I think they usually close at 9:30."

"At the dance you said Julie wasn't that friendly toward you," I said.

"Yeah, well that was before I told her about the Marines. She just wants to say goodbye. I mean...I hope that's not all she wants. So I'll meet up with you at 9:00, okay?"

My mom and dad had gone out for groceries and then to visit my Aunt Sofia and Uncle Vinnie, and Michael, as usual, was out with his buddies, so I hung out at home and watched some TV before heading downtown at 8:45. Mosci's was completely quiet, so I just stopped at the counter and asked Lou for a Coke. Heading to the back of the store, I grabbed a copy of *Tiger Beat* off the magazine rack because a picture of the Monkees on the cover caught my eye. I sat down at a booth and began to thumb through it, wondering if Susanna had liked the Monkees. *Which one would she have liked the most?* I wondered. Most girls liked Mickey Dolenz or Davy Jones the best. I guessed probably Davy Jones because he was what most girls called "super cute." Although Susanna seemed a little quirky so maybe she would have liked Peter Tork or Michael Nesmith. The Monkees were riding a wave of popularity because, unlike most rock groups, they had their own television show, which was a comedy rather than a variety show. I even watched it, but that's not something I broadcast to the guys at school or at Duchess because being the stars of a situation comedy didn't seem like the grooviest thing to be doing for rock stars. You couldn't picture Jefferson Airplane or, like, the Stones, starring in a television comedy. But it was fun anyway. I was pretty sure Susanna would have liked watching the Monkees just like me.

I looked at my watch. It was 9:05, and no Jeff. I was a little annoyed, but I couldn't get too huffy about it because I had blown him off to hang out with Daryl weeks ago. At 9:17, he finally burst through the door.

"Ready, partner?" he asked, slightly out of breath.

"Yup, let's head over."

As we headed toward the bridge, he said, "Let's do a stair race for old time's sake."

Instead of over the bridge, we headed under, down alongside the adjacent sidewalk and made our way toward the factory buildings beneath the bridge. Jeff and I split up and headed to our respective staircases on either side of the bridge. Once in position, he called out, "Ready! Set! Go!" And upwards we climbed at full speed in the darkness. As usual, he hit the top a few seconds before me.

"Nice try," he said, razzing me. "Wait'll I get back from boot camp. When I'm really in shape, I'll give you a worse whooping."

"We'll see," I replied. "So how did it go with Julie?" I couldn't believe I even asked.

"Better than I expected," he said, seeming very pleased with himself.

"You mean?"

"Yup, I mean..." he said.

"But I thought she had a boyfriend."

"Yeah, she does, but she didn't seem to care about him tonight. She told him she couldn't get together with him because she had too much homework."

"Wow!"

"You know what I'm finding out, partner. I think she likes the idea of me going into the Marines, which isn't a bad thing if you know what I mean. She thinks it's sexy or romantic to be apart from each other... to be with a guy who's a soldier, something like that. She likes the idea. I'm pretty sure I'll be seeing her when I come home on leave, boyfriend or no boyfriend if you follow."

"I follow," I assured him.

River Restaurant is right over the bridge. Instead of turning right on Main Street at the Bridge Smoke Shop, you turn left, and then it's just a few doors down. Jeff and I didn't stop in the Smoke Shop like we usually did when walking to Derby. It was too late, so it was closed.

River has two doors because the restaurant is on one side and the bar is on the other. Jeff had told me a year before that Adamo, Grasso and company sometimes get served in the bar. And Shelton football players too, because to a lot of adult men in the Valley, high school football players are like gods. For all I know, Daryl, Ben Andrews, their fellow Seymour players, and even maybe other Valley players have been served there. Lots of adult men, especially Italian guys, like my dad, grew up in Derby and then moved to one of the other Valley towns. Some of those guys hang out at certain bars, and River is a popular spot. I have a hunch some of those guys might have bought the beer Frankie Adamo and his clan got drunk on the night Frankie hit poor Susanna.

The aroma of Italian food cooking as you head down a long hallway is like no other anywhere. First you see the wood-fired pizza ovens and the cooks in their t-shirts and aprons, sweating as they slide the round pies in and out of the ovens with long wooden trays that look like gigantic paddles. Standing nearby at the register is old Nonna Affinito. She isn't my nonna, but that's how I think of her. River is a family business, which the old Italian lady runs with her two sons and her daughter. Usually all four of them are working. Nonna Affinito doesn't seem to do anything except take the checks from the waitresses and give them the change for the customers. She guards the old, brass register like a soldier, stern and unsmiling. It looks like she doesn't trust anyone else to handle the money. She reminds me of my Nonna DeMarco with her stern face, her wavy hair pulled tightly against her head in little silver ripples, her gold wire rimmed glasses, and her black nonna shoes with clunky heels. The difference is my nonna just takes care of her household and vegetable garden, rather than owning a business like Nonna Affinito. In that way, I think of her as Nonna Affinito, just as I think of little Mrs. Vollaro at our local neighborhood grocery market as Nonna Vollaro because she reminds me of my mother's mother, short and soft and gentle. But all of the nonnas wear the same hairstyle, glasses, and shoes. Let's just say that thinking of Mrs. Affinito and Mrs. Vollaro as my nonnas is my own private secret. Sometimes that's how it is to be Italian — you start to feel like you're all part of one big family.

Nonna Affinito's adult sons are hairy men with olive complexions who look like they would break you in half if you made any trouble. I mean, let's just say you'd know they're Italian without even thinking about it. I've been coming to River since I was a little kid with my parents, and it's still a family favorite. As a child, I remember feeling it was weird when I had to use the bathroom because it's located in the bar. It made me uncomfortable to head towards the men's room, smelling the distinct odor of beer and seeing a row of men sitting at the big wooden bar, talking and arguing in a cloud of smoke, often using swear words. Now that I am growing up, I find myself wondering if maybe Jeff and I will be two of those guys someday. Not that I really want to be, actually, but I can't help wondering.

We sat down and ordered a small pizza each and a pitcher of birch beer. As we waited for our order, I said, "I'm not working tomorrow if you want me to see you off on the bus or whatever."

"Thanks, pal, but first of all, we're going by train. Besides that, Sergeant Higgins told me no sentimental goodbyes. I have to be in New Haven at 6:00 a.m., and I don't think you want to get up that early on a Saturday. The sarge said that our parents should drop us off at the recruiting center, say a quick goodbye, and be on their way. I guess they give us a physical, swear us in, and then take us over to the New Haven train station. What did he say it was called...uhm...oh yeah, Union Station. And then we head to South Carolina."

"Wow. It's hard to believe. I guess basic training is gonna be hard, right?"

"Fuckin' A. The sarge says it will be harder than anything I've ever done, but he told me that he knows I'm up to it and that he feels I'll find that it's worth it. He said that the Marine Corps fundamental values are honor, courage, and commitment."

"Oh, wow," I said.

"He said the drill instructors are there to help me overcome any and all challenges. He said that I'll be a man when it's over. He said the Marines don't take just anybody."

"Wow," I said. I felt like an idiot repeating "wow" to everything he said like it was the only word in my vocabulary. *It's going to be awkward having my best friend be a man when I'm still just a kid,* I thought. I wondered if it was true that the Marines didn't take just anybody.

Finally I came up with a few other words. "How long is basic training?"

"Usually three months," Jeff replied, "but with Nam and everything, they are now doing an accelerated program, so it's only two months. He told me not to worry though. Sarge told me if I'm called on to defend my country, I'll be plenty ready."

"But you said you won't have to go to war, right?"

"Yeah...probably not. But if I am called, of course, I *have* to serve."

"Right...right...right." There I went again, talking like an idiot in repeated monosyllables. Then I mustered up a semi-coherent question. "I guess they'll be shaving your head like in the movies, right?"

"Absolutely. But I'm so fuckin' good looking, I'll even look handsome with no hair, right?"

"Right...right...right." Ouch. Back to monosyllables again.

There was no more talk of the Marines or of boot camp while eating our pizzas or heading back to Shelton. We talked about the Yankees, especially how much longer Mantle would play, and about girls — or mainly Jeff talked and I listened. Jeff knew more about the Yankees than I did, and he now knew a heck of a lot more than I did about girls and sex. I didn't talk about Susanna because, like, what would I say? As if Susanna had even been my girlfriend, even though I continued to think of her that way. I knew that wasn't completely normal, but I think that knowing your thinking isn't normal kind of makes you normal, if that makes any sense.

As we headed over the bridge, we ran down the metal stairs on the right side to a little night spot on the Shelton side of the river called the Twin Door which was about fifty yards from the factory buildings. We had heard that they had strippers there, and the door had three small windowpanes, which we always peeked in when we passed by later at night. We never saw any strippers, though. We didn't see any this time either. Someday I'll probably see a naked woman in real life, but for now I'll have to be content with pictures in magazines.

When we got to my street corner, the place where we always parted company, it was time to say goodbye. Jeff said, "Okay, partner...I guess this is it until next time."

"Yeah," I said. "Until next time."

"That's only in two months, though. The next time you see me, I'll be a man in a uniform."

"Can't wait," I said, but I knew I was lying. I wished that I would never see him in uniform. Jeff and I didn't hug or anything like that because it's not cool for guys to hug. I watched him walk up Prospect Avenue in the darkness, and I just wanted everything to go back to being normal, to the way it was, hanging out at dances, getting steamrolled at the Boys Club by Johnny Ping Pong and his thick rubber paddle, playing one-on-one against each other, and racing up the bridge stairs. I felt like nothing was normal anymore since Susanna had been killed.

A good example of how abnormal things were was that four days after Jeff left for boot camp, on June 5th, Senator Bobby Kennedy was assassinated after a political rally in California. My family was, once again, completely stunned, and I'll bet anyone who had any feelings at all was just as shocked. Unbelievably, with the great Los Angeles Rams lineman Rosey Grier right by Bobby's side, some lunatic walked right over to him and shot the popular senator at close range at the Ambassador Hotel in Los Angeles. Even though the shooter had been immediately apprehended, at first the news identified him as "John Doe" because they hadn't found out his real name yet, but later it was reported that his name was Sirhan Sirhan. Who names their kid something like that? Like, what if my name was Gabriel Gabriel? It just sounds dumb to me. The news reports said he had been born in Jerusalem. All I knew about Jerusalem was basically that Jesus lived there. The news also said Sirhan Sirhan was a Christian. Why would a Christian who was born in the same city where Jesus grew up kill Bobby Kennedy?

Twenty-six hours after the shooting, on June 6th, we learned that Bobby Kennedy didn't make it. Although he had made a gallant attempt to cling to his life, he wasn't able to.

My bewildered mom asked repeatedly, "How much more tragedy can the poor Kennedy family endure?" She had a good point with two sons killed by assassins, and also an older brother, Joseph Kennedy Jr., who had been killed in World War II. Between the assassinations of Malcolm X, Dr. King, and now both Kennedys, not to mention all kinds of other civil unrest related to the war and civil rights, I felt the world had really turned upside down. It seemed like the country was beyond hope.

The real sad thing was Bobby Kennedy appeared to be a leader prepared to give America new hope. He had reached out not only to white Americans but to black Americans too. Our history teacher had told us that on the night that Dr. King was killed, Bobby Kennedy had an appearance planned in a black neighborhood in Indianapolis. Despite the police force's refusal to provide protection because the mayor of Indianapolis felt the neighborhood was too dangerous, Bobby appeared anyway. Standing on a flatbed truck, the heroic senator said: "Martin Luther King dedicated his life to love and justice for his fellow human beings, and he died because of that effort. In this difficult day, in this difficult time for the United States, it is perhaps well to ask what kind of a nation we are and what direction we want to move in. For those of you who are black and are tempted to be filled with hatred and distrust at the injustice of such an act, against all white people, I can only say that I feel in my own heart the same kind of feeling. I had a member of my family killed, but he was killed by a white man. But we have to make an effort in the United States, we have to make an effort to understand, to go beyond these rather difficult times."

And now, eight weeks later, Bobby was a victim of the same fate as Dr. King. Even younger kids like me admired Bobby and liked his youthful energy and charisma...and now some nut had killed him. And the thing is, it seemed like no one understood exactly why any of these leaders were killed. Even now, only months later, I am totally confused.

The night after Kennedy was shot, something else that was far from normal happened. Someone other than Daryl came in for the coffees for the crew at Charlton Press. I think Will had come to like Daryl. Puzzled, Will asked the new guy, "Where's my main man, Daryl?"

The guy said, "They told me he got fired. I don't know him, but I guess he didn't show up for work this week, so they got rid of him yesterday."

That isn't good, I thought. *The job is one of the few good things Daryl has going on. Why would he just stop showing up for work?*

The new guy had the same order Daryl always had, and we filled it just like usual, but I kind of resented him. I didn't want anyone taking Daryl's place. I worried when I would see Daryl again, but I didn't have to wait long. He showed up in the parking lot the next time I worked, on Friday night. I saw his car through the window. Luckily, the Big M wasn't working, but it was going to be tricky with Craig Betts. Business was slow, so I told Craig I was going to take out some garbage.

I walked over to Daryl's car, and I saw that his eyes were closed. It was a warm night, so his windows were open. I rapped lightly on the roof of the Bug.

Daryl opened his eyes with a start. "Okay...o-kay, I'm goin', Alfred, I'm goin'."

His eyes began to focus as I said, "No, it's just me Daryl. Are you alright?"

"Oh, yeah...alright...Ahm alright. 's good ta see ya, Dushess."

He was blasted — drunker and higher than I'd ever seen him. Through the window I could see four or five of those big Ballentine bottles on the floor behind his seat. Alarmed, I made my way around to the passenger door and got in.

"Daryl! You shouldn't be driving in this condition. You're wasted," I said.

"Aw...Dushess! You're always tryin' ta help me, ain't ya?"

"What's going on, Daryl? Some kid told me you got fired from Charlton Press. What happened?"

"Yeah...fired. What happened is...is there's jus'...jus' no fuckin' point."

"No point to what?" I asked.

"To fuckin' anything. No fuckin' point to anything," he mumbled as if talking in his sleep.

"Don't say that, Daryl," I said, trying to stay calm.

"Some...some fucker killed Bobby Kennedy, Dushess. Did ya...did ya hear about that? Tha' really...pisses me the fuck off!"

"Yes, Daryl, I heard. Everyone has heard. We're all upset about it. The whole country is upset."

"But can ya answer a question for me, Dushess? Jus' one simple fuckin' question. Cuz...even though...it's a...a real simple question, I don't get it."

"I'll try, Daryl...I'll...I'll do my best." My heart was banging against my chest.

"Okay, Dushess...so tell me this. Why do people hafta die? Ya know what I mean? No...wait. I mean, why do...why do...people who ain't s'posta fuckin' die hafta...die?"

"Oh wow, Daryl. That's not really a simple question. I don't know the answer to that one. I don't...I mean, I don't think anyone knows the answer to that question."

"Yeah, I knew you wouldn't...wouldn't know, Dushess. Tha's okay. Yer still a good kid. Don' worry about it."

His eyelids were heavy and almost closing.

"I'm worried about you. Uhm...you just wait here a minute, Daryl. I'll be right back. Don't move."

I ran back into the store, wondering how I was going to approach this with Craig Betts. Looking at my watch, I saw that it was only 9:53 p.m. I decided to just try to be honest. First I walked over to the coffee machine and poured a large black coffee.

When I got to the counter, Craig said, with no small amount of sarcasm, "Took you a long time to take out a can of garbage, huh? And who's that coffee for?"

"The coffee is for a friend. I'm real sorry, Craig, but listen. I'm going to need to cut out early. A friend of mine is in a bad way out there, and I need to make sure he gets home safely, okay?"

"No, it's *not* okay," Craig replied sharply. "It's that Novak kid, right? Do you think nobody sees you talking to that waste?"

I could feel my throat constrict as the anger rose from deep in my gut, but I had to stay calm. "Yeah, Craig. Except he's not a waste, and he's in trouble so I *have* to help him whether it's okay with you or not."

"I'll have to report this to Howie," Craig said with controlled annoyance. "It could mean your job."

"Yeah, man...well, it'll mean whatever it means." With blood rushing to my head, I added, "Do what you need to do, but he's a good friend, and...and I'm gonna help him."

"And, you're going to have to pay for that coffee, you know?"

"Yeah, I know," I said.

Reaching into my pocket, I slapped a dollar next to the cash register, not waiting for change. On my way out the door, I grabbed a hamburger, tossed my white apron on the sink, and threw my hat in the garbage can. I didn't know if I'd ever be wearing it again.

When I got back into Daryl's Bug, I said, "Okay, Daryl. You're going home."

Once again, appearing to be in a state of sleep, he opened his eyes. "Whataya mean?"

"What I mean is I need to make sure you get home safely. I want you to start the car and drive home...slowly. I'm going to sit here and make sure you stay awake and get there in one piece. But first you're going to drink this black coffee down and eat this burger."

"I don' want that shit, Dushess. I ain't hungry," he complained.

I grabbed his arm firmly and shook him. "It doesn't matter whether you're hungry or not, you hear me, Daryl? You need to sober up a little because I don't know how to drive a car, never mind a stick shift. So start fucking eating and drinking!"

"Dushess, I thought you didn't...didn't swear."

"Only when I'm mad," I replied, honestly.

"Hey, listen, Dushess. You...you can't...you can't...can't save me, ya know. You mighta saved my fuckin' life once, but yer not gonna be able to keep doin' that."

"Maybe not, Daryl...but here's the thing, so pay attention. I'm going to try...and I can keep you safe tonight."

"Okay...okay, Dushess. You win this time."

I practically forced the coffee and burger down his reluctant throat. Then I ordered, "Now start the car, Daryl." We drove out of the parking lot and on to Pershing Drive slowly.

"Keep it slow just like that," I said.

He headed toward Nolan Field. I kept one hand gently on his right bicep and shook him when he looked drowsy. A few times when the car began to swerve a little because of his unsteadiness, I reached over with my right hand and steadied the wheel.

As we passed by Nolan Field, Daryl said, "Hey, Dushess, let's stop and play a little hoop. I'll show ya how it's done again."

"Not tonight, Daryl. You showed me enough. We're just going to get you home tonight."

A quarter mile past Nolan Field, with a little assistance from me, Daryl turned left on Great Hill Road, and we were headed toward his Seymour neighborhood. All the while, I was warning him to go slow and to stay on his side of the white double lines.

"Are we almost at your house?" I asked.

"Yup...yup...this is my street we're on now, Dushess."

He pulled up in front of a small ranch style house with shrubbery on both sides of the front door.

"Now what?" Daryl asked.

"Now I'm going to walk you to the door," I told him.

I walked around to his side of the car, opened his door, and helped him to his feet. Unsteady, Daryl needed plenty of assistance. I grabbed his arm and swung it around my shoulders, guiding him along the flagstone walkway toward his front door. I had to think fast. It would be awkward to talk to his parents. What would I say? "You don't know me, but here's your drunk son"?

When we got to the door, I sat him on the front step, rang the doorbell, trotted across the front of his house, and hid behind the shrubbery.

"Hey!" he shouted. "Hey! Dushess! Where'd ya go?"

He probably woke up everyone in the neighborhood.

Suddenly, a light flicked on over the front door, and I heard the door open. From my vantage point, I could just about see Daryl's dad come out onto the stoop.

"What now, Daryl?" I heard his dad say. "What are you doing now?"

"Hey! Hey, Dushess! Dushess! Can ya hear me?" I heard Daryl yell again. "Come meet my dad. We'll tell 'em how yer always saving my fuckin' life."

"*Quiet, Daryl.*" I had never heard someone speak so quietly but angrily at the same time. Bewildered, his dad looked around. "Who are you talking to? There's no one here, Daryl, but us."

"Right...right. There's no one here but us," Daryl mimicked. "Hear that Dushess? There's no one here but me and my dad!"

A light came on at the house across the street from the Novaks'. *Probably some nosy neighbor,* I thought.

When I saw his dad lift him to a standing position and help him inside, I felt it was safe to be on my way. To be completely sure, I waited for both the Novaks' outdoor light as well as their neighbor's to go out before I jogged across the next door neighbor's yard and out onto the road. I had run many miles during the day, but not at night. With almost no traffic late at night, it looked like I would have to run down Great Hill Road to Route 8 where I could thumb a ride the rest of the way home. It was only about a couple miles, mostly downhill. I could probably do it in ten minutes or less. As I ran on the left side of the road, toward what little oncoming traffic there was, I was grateful that I had gotten Daryl to his house in one piece, but

I also contemplated how I was going to explain this one at home if I got fired. There'd be nothing else to do but tell the truth. As I listened to my heavy breathing, the only sound in the night besides my feet hitting the pavement, I found my mind wandering to thoughts of Susanna. I imagined getting my license and going to visit her in that little ranch house in the well groomed neighborhood. I pictured Daryl and her parents out of the house, and I saw myself making out with her in the basement. I wondered if the kissing would lead to other things like it had done with Jeff and Julie. I knew I wouldn't go there, though, unless we were really in love, and maybe not even then. As I reached civilization and the main drag that connected Seymour and Ansonia, though, my thoughts returned to reality. It was time to get my head out of the clouds and find my way home.

Reaching the entrance to Exit 19, I walked along the wet grass next to the ramp to the closest streetlamp and stuck out my thumb. It seemed ironic since hitchhiking was how I had met Daryl in the first place, and now I was hitchhiking after trying to help him. He had suggested that he couldn't be helped, though, which weighed heavily on my mind.

It wasn't easy getting a ride from this location so late at night. It seemed like only one car passed by every ten minutes. Finally, a station wagon pulled over. I glanced at my watch. It was 11:13, which was perfect. I'd walk in the house at just about the time I would have if I had finished the night at Duchess.

I ran to the station wagon and hopped in. "Thanks for stopping," I said.

"No problem," said a bald guy about my dad's age. "Where to?"

"I live in Shelton, off of Exit 14," I replied.

"I'm headed home to Derby, but you're only one more exit. I'll take you there and then swing back through downtown Shelton and over the bridge."

"That's so nice of you," I said. "Thanks so much."

"Where are you coming from at this hour?"

"Oh...I was visiting a close friend of mine in Seymour. He needed some help with his geometry homework."

"You must be a good student," he offered.

"Yes, I am," I blushed. "Mostly all As." *At least that's the truth,* I thought.

"Well that was nice of you to help a friend," he said.

"Yeah, thanks. Well, it's nice to have a friend like him, so I'm happy to help the kid out."

That was true, too. I did like having Daryl as a friend, even if his behavior was sometimes crazy. We remained quiet for the rest of the ten minute ride home. When he drove to the light at the bottom of Exit 14, he said, "Now where?"

"This is it," I lied. "I live right across the street in that big apartment house." I didn't want him to take me directly to my house. "Thanks again," I said.

"You bet. Good luck to your friend with his geometry course." And he drove down Howe Avenue toward the bridge. Watching him drive off, I stood on the steps of an apartment building I didn't live in and wondered where the driver was coming from, but more importantly, I wondered where I was going.

24

I didn't usually work two nights in a row, but it was how the schedule worked out that week. Michael and I were on Friday night with Tommy Trouble and Bink. I wasn't really in the mood to work again. Mainly, though, I was wondering if Craig Betts had told Howie how I cut out early the night before. Sure enough, when Michael and I walked in the door at 6:00, Howie asked me to come into his office to talk to him.

"Craig told me about last night, Gabe. About you leaving before the end of the night. Not good. Essentially, you left the other guys to do your clean up duties."

"I know, Howie," I replied, "but did he tell you why I left?"

"He said you gave him some rigamarole about helping a friend."

"It wasn't rigamarole. Daryl Novak and I have become friends, and he was out in the parking lot, completely wasted."

"Yeah, Craig told me about how he's seen you hanging out with the Novak kid."

"Well, it's a long story, but it's true. Daryl and I even recently beat Buster and Lance in basketball over at the Nolan Field courts."

"Yeah," Howie said, almost smiling. "I think Alfred told me something about that too. Anyway, I think I'll let this slide since I expect that it was a one time thing...and because Michael is your brother, but it may not happen again, okay?"

"It won't," I assured him.

"Oh...and one more thing, Gabe. I'd be careful if I were you. Take some advice from someone with more experience than you. It sounds like Novak has some problems, and I don't doubt that you have only good intentions, but you're young, and you're impressionable and naive. I would hate to see you get hurt. I hope you understand what I mean."

"I think I do, but don't worry, Howie. Daryl wouldn't purposely hurt me, so I think I'll be okay."

Derby police officer Vincent Mancini finishes his coffee outside of Dunkin' Donuts on Pershing Drive in Ansonia, very near Division Street which separates Ansonia and Derby. Mancini is short and round. His portly belly practically touching the bottom of the steering wheel, Mancini pulls out of his parking space and begins to make his routine late night rounds. It is just after 11:00 on a typical Friday night, and he heads for downtown Derby, turning on to Pershing Drive and then right on Division Street. At the top of the hill, instead of turning on Atwater near the San Marini home, he continues straight on Division toward Griffin Hospital and heads for Over the Hill Tavern on Hawkins Street first. Over the Hill, which Mancini frequents when not on duty, is his favorite Derby watering hole. It sits in the middle of a residential neighborhood rather than the downtown area. Mancini has an eye out for any drunks that may be walking home on foot. All is quiet in the Hawkins Street neighborhood. He turns on Seymour Avenue, which runs almost parallel to Atwater and eventually merges into Elizabeth Street before coming to the small downtown area. Officer Mancini drives slowly around the blocks, passing by the Marchigian Club, the Dew Drop Inn, and River Restaurant...the usual places. Mancini knows the owners of all of the bars as well as the guys who hang out at each one. He has no intention of doing anything other than making sure everyone gets home to their wives and children safely. It is even quieter than usual. Outside of River Restaurant, he spots two friends talking by their cars under a streetlight. Mancini pulls up and rolls down his window.

"What's up tonight, Charlie? Mike?"

"Not a whole hell of a lot," says the taller of the two men. "Just stalling before going home to the wives."

"What's a matter?" Mancini asks. "Not getting any action?"

"Oh, about the same as you," the shorter man offers, and all three men break into laughter.

"How about them Yankees? They lost another one this afternoon," Mancini says.

"Yeah, the glory days are long fuckin' gone," the taller man replies. "It's time to get rid of Houk. We miss Casey Stengel."

"Naw, he's too fuckin' old," Mancini says.

"The Mick oughta be retiring soon, right?" the shorter man asks.

"Yeah," says Mancini. "He's given everything he's got. His good days are over...although he did knock one out of the park today."

"Yeah, every once in a while the Mick shows a flash of his former greatness," the tall one says. "What's happenin' with you tonight? Another exciting night in Derby?"

"You know it," Mancini says. "Well, I better get back to work. You boys stay out of trouble."

It turned out to be a quiet night mostly. Why wouldn't it be? It wasn't like Betts or Fischer were on the crew. And the four of us got along really well. That is, except for the fact that Bink was such an innocent type of kid that he almost invited practical jokes to be played on him. So, the highlight of the night was when Tommy Trouble engineered a good one on poor Bink. Michael was in the office starting to count the cash, and Tomaso had me get on a hose that was next to the orange drink machine right near the front window. He himself grabbed a hose at the shake machine, which was across from the grill. These are high powered hoses meant for filling up a multi-gallon drink container and cleaning out a similar sized stainless steel basin on the shake machine.

Tomaso gave a yell, "Hey, Bink, could you come up here? There's a bunch of customers and we need you."

It was late in the night, and there wasn't a single customer to be found. Tomaso ducked low behind the shake machine, and I did the same at the front counter. When Bink arrived from the back sink, wiping off a giant bun tray, he said, puzzled, "Tomaso? Where are you? I don't see any customers."

At that point, Tommy Trouble yelled, "Now!" and, from two different directions, we both open-fired on Bink. The poor kid, instantly soaked, lost his balance on the suddenly wet floor, and fell on his butt, the tray crashing down with an ear-shattering clatter to the ground next to him. It was maybe the funniest thing I have ever seen in my life.

Other than that, it was the dullest Friday night I had worked in a long time. Basketball season was over, and it appeared there were no dances anywhere in the Valley, so not many kids were hanging out. All through the night, I hoped Daryl would come through because I wanted to know how he was after my adventure making sure he got home safely the night before, but he was missing in action.

On the way home, Michael asked me why Howie talked to me alone in his office. I was surprised that he waited until we were on our way home, but I guess he didn't want to get into a thing around the other guys. At this stage, the only thing I could do was tell the truth, so I explained the whole deal to him, about Daryl's extreme level of intoxication, the ride to Daryl's house, and then my distance run down Great Hill Road to Route 8 so late at night.

I was surprised that he didn't give me a lecture, but he just shook his head in a way that told me he wasn't happy with my story. But what else could I say?

Mancini swings up the hill towards Roosevelt Drive and for the high school parking lot and Osbornedale Park, which is directly across the street from the school, where he will check that there are no high school kids necking in their cars. Like the drunks, if Mancini finds anyone, he will just shag them along, making sure everyone gets home safely for the night.

Then he picks up Route 8 South and gets off Exit 15 heading to Route 34 North. It's a little bit of a drive out to St. Peter's Cemetery, which is almost in Orange on the very outskirts of East Derby. It's another hot spot for amorous teens. Officer Mancini almost always finds a car or two there — young lovers hidden away in darkness. Arriving at the cemetery, he drives along the circuitous driveways that wind about the cemetery, at first not discovering any cars. Suddenly, he hears music playing in the distance. Following the sound of the music, Mancini sees a car with its lights on. Beyond the car, he spots billows of smoke rising into the night air. *What's going on? Something on fire?* Mancini wonders. As he gets closer, he sees the car with its headlights on is a Volkswagen Bug. He recognizes Simon and Garfunkel's hit "Mrs. Robinson" emitting from inside the car. He can see that the passenger side door is open; the interior light is shining, illuminating the shabby interior of the car.

The VW is blocking his view of an apparent fire of some sort. "Fuck," Mancini says aloud. "I thought things were too quiet."

Mancini calls the station and reports what he has encountered so far to the officer on duty at the station, Sergeant McGill. "I'm going to send back-up right now," McGill says. Mancini shines his spotlight on the area where the car is parked and cautiously gets out. He takes out his handgun with his right hand and shines a flashlight with his left. Slowly, he approaches the car. "Who's over there?" he calls out. "Come out with your hands raised!"

When he gets to the car, Mancini looks over the hood to see what is burning. In stunned amazement, he discovers what appears to be a human body, lying still, in what Mancini perceives as a protective fetal position. *What the fuck?* Mancini thinks, *Is this a person or a... what is it?*

"Anyone here?" he calls out louder, but the only sound is the car radio blaring. He circles around the back of the VW and approaches the smoldering body cautiously. As he gets closer, he senses the smell must be burning flesh, and he can see that the badly charred body is a real person, probably a male. Officer Mancini sprints to his squad car where he gets a fire blanket from the trunk, and he races back to the body, covering it with the heavy fabric. Another squad car approaches the scene, and Officer Smolitsky gets out to assist. An ambulance siren, also headed to the cemetery, echoes in the distance. The two officers first lift the blanket off the body, which is blackened beyond recognition. They feel certain that the person is dead. They then check out the car where they find six empty quart-sized beer bottles on the floor behind the front seat, a half smoked joint, and an open bag of marijuana on the passenger seat. On the grass alongside the passenger door is a red, metal can, partially filled with gasoline. The headlights of the car are pointing directly at a gravestone, which reads, "Susanna Marie Novak – Born July 12, 1953 – Died October 21, 1967 – Earth has one angel less, and Heaven one angel more."

"It's that little girl who got killed on Division Street last fall," Smolitsky says to Mancini.

"Yeah, wow! Frankie Adamo drove the car. He didn't mean for it to happen. I'm good friends with his old man," Mancini replies.

"Oh Jesus," Smolitsky replies. "You don't think this body can be Frankie Adamo, do you?"

"God Almighty, I sure fuckin' hope not," Mancini says, taking the palm of his fat right hand and wiping the wet stain of sweat from his forehead.

The ambulance speeds to the grave site, and the EMTs quickly move the body to the vehicle and head for Griffin Hospital, its siren blaring in the night, growing softer and softer in the distance, as it speeds along Route 34.

25

I was awakened out of a deep sleep on Sunday morning by Michael. I felt him gently shake me. "Leave me alone," I moaned, resisting wakefulness. I was exhausted after a long day of hiking with Bink. He had recently gotten his license, and since neither of us was on the work schedule, I let him talk me into going to West Rock in New Haven and hiking up the mountain. He's a good kid, but it wasn't the most exciting day I've ever spent, and it really wiped me out.

Michael shook me a little harder, and half-whispered over and over again, "Gabe...wake up...wake up."

I opened my reluctant eyes and squinted until he came into focus. Sitting on his bed, which in our small room was only a foot or so away from mine, Michael hovered over me.

"What? Leave me alone," I groaned, yawning groggily.

"I have to tell you something," he said. His concerned eyes held my gaze as he offered a section of the newspaper. I pushed my body to a seated position, squinted, and slowly reached for the paper.

"What is it?"

"I'm afraid it's really bad news," he replied soberly.

The header at the top of the paper indicated it was the *New Haven Register*. Right, the *Evening Sentinel* doesn't have a Sunday edition. Also in the header, I saw a bold letter B, page 4, and the word, Obituaries.

"What are you showing me this for?" I complained.

He pointed to an article halfway down the page. My eyes focused, and I began to read:

Seymour Athlete Found Dead in Derby

Derby (Special) — A body found burning in a cemetery after midnight on Saturday has been ruled a suicide and identified as an 18 year old Seymour boy who became despondent after his sister was killed in an auto accident seven months ago.

Police said Saturday that Daryl Novak, of 73 Abbot Road in Seymour, doused himself with gasoline and put a match to his clothing.

The body was found still burning at 12:20 a.m. by a Derby police officer patrolling St. Peter's Cemetery.

Police said a car, registered to the youth's father, was found about ten yards from the body. The engine was idling, the headlights and radio were on, and both the driver and passenger-side doors were open. An empty gas can was found on the grass near the passenger door.

Novak's parents said he had left home four hours earlier, saying he would be gone only a few minutes.

Novak, an outstanding three sport athlete at Seymour High School, was positively identified by a dental chart comparison at Griffin Hospital in Derby.

He dropped activity in football, basketball, and baseball after his sister, Susanna, 14, was struck and killed by a car last October.

During his junior year, Novak was named to the All State and All Housatonic League teams in football as well as the All Housatonic League team in basketball by the New Haven Register.

Dazed, I looked into my brother's solemn eyes and said, "This... this can't...it can't be!"

With tightened lips, he looked down at the floor.

"No way," I continued. "No possible way! Just. . .no...no!"

I could see that Michael was at a loss for words. Dragging myself from my bed, I grabbed my blue jeans and pulled them on, and I slipped my bare feet into my black Converse high-tops.

"Where are you going?" he asked.

"I...I don't know. I just have to...I have to...to think," I replied.

Moving to the door, Michael tried to block my exit. "Listen, it's not good for you to go anywhere right now. You're obviously upset, so I think you better just..."

"No!" I screamed, like a trapped animal, and I pushed him hard, knocking him off balance, in a replay of the night I confronted him about threatening Daryl. In a flash, I was out the door, picking up my basketball at the bottom of the outside stairway. My parents must have still been sleeping — dead to the world — because they didn't seem to hear me scream or see me take off. As far as I knew, neither Mom nor Dad knew anything about Daryl.

I trotted to the corner and headed left on Prospect, dribbling the ball forcefully as I went. Burning tears suddenly began streaming down my cheeks. I stopped at the big Maple by Fowler School. It had always been the best place for thinking.

I thought to myself, *I should have seen it coming. I mean, I did see it coming, but I didn't realize that...that he would do it. That he would end his life that way.* Wiping away the tears with my hands, I rubbed my wet palms on my jeans. About twenty-five yards away, I saw Michael heading for the tree. Of course, he would know where I was going. The Big M would know better than anyone.

When he got to the tree, he grabbed a seat on another root. We sat in silence for a good while, as we had done on another occasion years before. The last time we sat together like this, we were contemplating our own imperfect family. This time, we were contemplating someone else's imperfect family.

Finally, he said, "Listen, I know I came on really strong with Novak about hanging out with you. I'm sorry...but it's just that...it's...

it's only because I was worried about you. I was worried something bad like this could happen. What if something had happened to you?"

I felt the tears release again. "No, I know. I know. He was a good kid, though. I was just trying to help him."

"I know you were," Michael said.

"I should have...should have known he was going to…to…"

"To what?" he asked.

"To...to kill himself...this way."

"How would you know that the guy would light himself on fire?"

"Because he showed me a photo of a monk in Vietnam who protested the war by torching himself like this. Like, he was totally fascinated by the picture of the monk. Fascinated at how calmly the monk was sitting in the middle of the road, with lots of people watching. Almost, like...like Daryl imagined himself sitting the same way, while...while he was burning. Except at the time, I guess I didn't understand that's what he was thinking."

"Yeah, I've seen that photo."

"Daryl said a *lot* of things, though. I thought he was going to enlist in the Army and go get himself killed. You know — like sacrifice himself...on purpose." The thought of how wrong I was about Daryl enlisting caused me to start crying harder. "I figured I had time to talk him out of it, you know what I mean? Because...because as far as I knew, he hadn't taken any steps yet to enlist. I guess I was stupid. It was right in front of my nose. Fuck...just so...so stupid."

"You're not stupid. We can't know what another person is going to do. Look at us. You and I are brothers, but we don't always know what the other is thinking or what he is going to do. I mean, I'm just gonna tell you that there's shit about me that you don't even know... that I don't want anyone to know. There's, like, a private part of me... well, of everyone...that no one else knows anything about. You just can't totally know another person. In a way, we're totally alone on this fuckin' planet. Here's the thing. Anyone with eyes could see that Daryl was really, uhm, I don't know — screwed up in the head. I'm sorry, but that's the best way I can say it."

Now the tears were coming down in buckets. "But, no, he wasn't! It's so easy for you and others to say that because you didn't know him like I did. He was a really great kid and in lots of ways completely normal, just like me and just like you. He was just drowning in guilt because of Susanna. Don't you see? She was walking that night because he dropped the ball. He was supposed to give her a ride, but he screwed up because he was drunk."

After a pause, Michael sighed. "Yeah, I see what you mean. I guess he had good reason to be depressed. If you got killed, I'd be messed up too, especially if I thought it was my fault. But you need to know that there are some things, and there are some...well, some people — that we can't fix. You're not Superman, ya know. Some things and some people...in fact, most things and most people are beyond our control. It's because of that private part of ourselves, that *alone* part of us that I was just talking about."

"Yeah," I said. "Big Alfred said something like that to me a few weeks ago. The night Dr. King got killed."

"Yeah, Alfred knows which end is up. I wish it was different, but it's not. Life can really suck sometimes, but we have to push through. People die. Remember, a few years ago, when Arty Miklos, who lived right there got killed in an accident?" Michael pointed to a house diagonally across from the big tree. "He was driving a VW, just like Novak's. I remember going to the wake and thinking, how can this be? This poor kid got crushed in that car. Arty was one of us. He was only a 16 year old kid."

"Daryl was one of us too, wasn't he?"

"Yes, I guess you're right. I mean, my point is, when you know someone really well and when someone is around the same age as us, it makes them one of us. And it makes it harder to wrap your brain around death. And you got to know Daryl well. Hey, look, there are no answers. We just have to push through when people die."

"But you know how I said he dropped the ball that night? He also felt guilty for literally dropping the ball that morning. Daryl told me that Susanna would still be alive if he had caught that pass at the end of the Derby game. He got all philosophical on me. Something like...like...every single thing that we do...or, let's see...everything that happens to us causes the next thing to happen. He said if he had caught the pass, everything would have been different."

"Gabe, nobody could have caught that pass," he said with a shrug. "Fred Biletnikoff, who's probably got the best hands in the NFL, would have coughed it up. Adamo's timing was perfect. Probably the best defensive play I've ever seen in high school football. And there's no way to know if catching it would have changed anything. Think how many touchdown passes Novak caught. The fact of the matter is, any of us would give our right arm to have had his athletic skills and the high school career that he was having. But tormenting yourself about what might have been is...well, it's just a fucking exercise in futility. I get that he was depressed about his sister, but what he did is the opposite of pushing through, and, I don't know, I don't know what to even think about it."

"Yeah...I don't know what to think either." I looked down and saw that I was peeling little pieces of bark off the root of the tree.

He picked up the basketball and, heading up the grassy bank to the back of the building where the playground was, Michael said, "Come on." Following him reminded me of the many times I had followed Daryl when he led the way. But I guess Daryl was usually leading me down the wrong path, even if it was the path he needed to take. Following the Big M was a lot safer.

He made his way to the sandlot that we called a basketball court, and he took a shot. I slowly walked down the bank onto the cracked asphalt, and he threw me a bounce pass. I shrugged and lofted the ball toward the basket. It hung up on the rim, rolled around a few times, and dropped through the chain net. Lucky shot. We didn't play a game or anything, though. We just shot around. Usually when you shoot around, the person who rebounds the ball only passes it back to the shooter if the ball goes in. It's like a sign of respect — like, "Good shot, take another." You keep making it, you keep getting the ball back to keep your streak going. Today, though, every time the Big M rebounded the ball, he passed it to me whether I had made the shot or not, giving me another turn. Soon enough, I was doing the same for him. Just two brothers on a basketball court, spending time together... shooting around...taking turns...pushing through.

26

I knew in my gut I'd never forget Susanna or Daryl. They had both made an indelible impression on me. On my heart. Susanna because she was so beautiful...and because she was so unique. Even more than those things, Susanna touched my heart with the simple act of resting her head on my shoulder during a slow dance one October night, sort of like she was saying, "I see something in you, Gabriel, that I could really like — maybe even love." In retrospect, at least, that's how I interpret it. That modest display of affection came at a time when I wasn't feeling too great about myself in relationship to girls. It was the sweetest thing that has ever happened to me. And Daryl? Well, I never met anyone with his athletic skills who was more humble. And the way he built up my confidence in myself...I don't even know what to say about that. All I knew was I was sorry I'd never be able to thank him.

A few days after Daryl's death, I received an envelope in the mail. The front of the letter had my name scribbled on it, and it had the words "Maltby Street" with no number and no return address. The postman must have known we were the only DeMarcos on Maltby. As I hastily ripped the seal, a lump formed in my throat when I saw a piece of lined paper all folded up, but not very neatly. With my hands trembling, I unwrapped it and found a wallet sized photo of Susanna. My heart almost stopped beating. A note was scrawled on the lined paper.

Dear Gabriel,

Here is Susie's picture. Something to help you remember her. I wanted you to have it because I think Susie would have liked you. Actually, I know she would have, Duchess, because you're a real good kid. Sorry for what I had to do. I know you tried to save me, but don't feel bad. It couldn't be done. Keep reading books, Duchess. And don't ever stop breaking records.

Your friend,

Daryl

I wondered if he mailed it on his way to the cemetery the night he ended his life. The photo was Susanna's school picture from the beginning of freshman year, the one that was in the newspaper the morning after the accident, but in color. She didn't look quite as mod or fashionable in the photo as she had at the dance. Just pretty and, I don't know how to put it — her face had a warm expression with a kind smile and a genuine look in her eyes that projected a pure spirit and an honest heart.

The school year finally ended, and I enrolled in Driver's Education at Derby High School because Shelton didn't offer a summer program. Every morning for three weeks, I walked or hitchhiked, depending on my mood, to Derby High where the class ran between 8:00 and noon. The guy who taught the class, Mr. Jensen, was such a dweeb. One day, I fell asleep in class and he startled me when he slapped his hand hard against my desk. "Nobody sleeps in my class, *ever*," he said sternly, which kind of surprised me a little, because he was the most boring teacher in the history of Western Civilization. The class erupted in laughter, but it didn't faze me much since I didn't know any of them. On my walk home each day, I passed by the Derby football field, and I replayed the reel in my mind of the night Daryl and I scaled the fence and hung out there. I remembered Daryl running his pass route over and over again, trying to wrap his brain around the most important touchdown he didn't score. It made me sad.

A highlight of the summer occurred on July 31st, when I joined Jeff's mother and grandmother for a three day trip to South Carolina to see Jeff's graduation from basic training. While I hadn't gotten to see him off when he left, I wasn't about to miss his graduation. We left by car that Wednesday morning from Shelton at 8:00 and arrived at our motel in South Carolina at 9:30 p.m. What a long drive. It was the longest trip I have ever been on, and with two adult women to boot. Go figure. Mrs. Pelletier drove and Mrs. Bailey provided sandwiches and snacks for us. My dad had given me money to give to Jeff's mom for the motel and for gas. I told him I would pay for it myself, but he insisted. On the long drive I mostly read. I had finished *Slaughterhouse Five*, and I was now on to a book that a lot of kids were reading — *Siddhartha* by a German author, Hermann Hesse. The book, actually, was written in the 1920s, but a lot of hippies latched onto it, or so I heard. I myself was reading it for my own personal reasons — because it's sort of about the Buddha, and it was a Buddhist monk who had, more or less, planted the crazy idea in Daryl's troubled mind to light himself on fire. I hoped the book would give me some kind of insight. So far, it hadn't. I mean, I was more than halfway through, and it didn't look like anyone was planning to set a match to himself in this story.

Early Thursday morning, we checked in at what was called the Douglas Visitors' Center on the base after making a quick stop for donuts and coffee. Mrs. Pelletier said we had to get there real early because of the schedule of events. The whole deal was called "Family Day." A Marine directed us to a sidewalk on the post where we would see Jeff for the first time since he left Connecticut. The recruits were taking part in what was called a "motivational run." *He's finally a distance runner like me,* I thought. Soon enough a whole mess of guys in lines came running toward us. People began ringing cowbells, and the crowd cheered enthusiastically because, as family members, they were rooting for their Marine. I'm not going to lie — I got caught up in the excitement, so I was kind of hooting and hollering too. The guys in front wore gold t-shirts and green shorts. They weren't kids, so I assumed they were the drill sergeants or officers or something like that. There were some guys in the front carrying gold flags, but they went by so fast, I was only able to read the one closest to me. It had two words, "Semper Fi," but I didn't know what that meant. The recruits themselves ran in step, five or six across, with their shaved heads and green t-shirts and shorts. One guy in each group carried a red flag with a four digit number in gold letters. As each group ran by, they were flanked by their drill sergeants, who were calling out different cadences to which the Marines responded. The clatter of the cowbells and the cheering of the crowd made it hard to hear, but I heard the guys repeating things like "Left foot, right foot, left, right, left, right," and "Marine Corps! Marine Corps!" in what, oddly, were powerful chants.

I was scanning the lines, afraid that I would miss Jeff. But when a group came running toward us with the number 2005 on their flag, Mrs. Pelletier began shouting: "Look! Oh my God! Look! 2005! This is Jeffrey's platoon!" Sure enough, we spotted my pal in the middle of his group. "Jeffrey! Hey, Jeffrey," Mrs. Pelletier yelled, but Jeff didn't look. My guess is that they had been ordered not to look around like they were dumb little Cub Scouts. Jeff sure looked weird with a shaved head.

After the run, we spent some time in a small Marine museum before we attended a meeting called "Liberty Training" where the battalion commander explained to us what the rules were while we met with Jeff. At 10:00, Liberty began, which meant Jeff got to hang out with us for a few hours before he had to be back in his barracks. When we met up with him, he was wearing a green shirt and pants, a matching hat with a front brim, a khaki belt, and black lace-up boots. He must have been hot in that getup because it was a sweltering summer day.

Was I ever glad to see Jeff after two quiet months without him. He looked good in his uniform. "What do they call this uniform? Fatigues, right?" I asked, trying to act like I knew something about it.

"Utilities," he said, correcting me. "The Army calls them fatigues;

we call them utilities." I thought the Army and the Marines were pretty much the same thing, but his emphasis of *we* suggested otherwise.

"Oh, okay. Well, cool hat. It helps hide your shaved head," I teased.

"It's not a hat. We call it a cover," he said, correcting me again with a smile. But there was a seriousness in his explanation that took me a little by surprise. The Marines apparently had their own name for pretty much everything.

The four of us found our way to a picnic table where a boxed lunch of Kentucky chicken was provided. Mrs. Pelletier and Mrs. Bailey gushed with pride, making a big fuss over Jeff. They're really nice ladies.

Mrs. Pelletier gushed as she said, "You look so handsome, Jeffrey." It was true. He did, even though I wasn't about to say it out loud. After we ate, Jeff and I had a chance to take a walk across the post, giving us a little time to ourselves.

"So," I began, "I saw some Latin or some language on the flags. 'Semper Fi' — what's that mean?"

"It's our motto," he began to explain. I assumed by "our," he meant the Marines, not his and mine. "Remember, before I left, I told you about the core values — honor, courage, and commitment. 'Semper Fi' means 'always faithful' to those values and to the corps. It's more than a couple of words. It's a way of life."

"Oh," I said, realizing that I had reverted back to responding to his Marine Corps talk in the same monosyllables I had used before he left.

Jeff must have spent a half hour telling me crazy stories of all the things he had to accomplish and endure during basic training, like having to go from one end of a long swimming pool in full combat gear with his helmet and the whole getup, not to mention a forty pound backpack and a rifle. "I mean, they won't let you drown," he said, "but almost." It was obviously grueling, but he sure was in amazing shape.

He suddenly switched gears. "Hey, man, I was real sorry to hear about your buddy dying. My gramma sent me the article because she wondered if I knew him. That must have been pretty awful." It occurred to me that it was big of Jeff to call someone other than himself my buddy.

"Yeah, it was. Thanks. It happened only a few days after you left." *In a way I had lost two friends in just a few short days,* I thought.

"He had some big problems, huh?"

"Well, it's complicated. He felt responsible for his sister's death because he was supposed to give her a ride home from the dance the night Adamo hit her. It's a long story, but it was all about guilt, not like mental illness or anything like that. You or I would have felt the same way."

"Well...I never had a sister or a brother. I guess you're about as close as I'll ever come. Anyway...I didn't really understand your friendship with Novak, but for what it's worth, you still got me, man. We're still brothers."

I didn't know quite what to say. Jeff is sometimes honest in a way that can kind of set you back on your heels. It was humbling to hear him say he thought of me as his brother. "Thanks. It was a weird coincidence that Daryl and I became friends. I wasn't trying to replace you or anything like that. He picked me up hitchhiking from Duchess, and, well, the rest is history. I guess it was a way for me to hold on to my memory of Susanna. And, well...I don't know...I thought...I thought I could save him. Something like that."

"Yeah, I get it. He must have needed the kind of help that some regular kid like you couldn't give him, though. It's a shame, he was one of the best athletes ever to come out of the Valley."

"Tell me about it," I said. "He steam-rolled me a couple of times in one-on-one. Completely obliterated me. It was kind of like trying to beat Johnny Ping Pong at his own game, but even worse. You know what, though? He was so much more than a gifted athlete. Sometimes people make too much of a big deal about sports. Daryl said it himself. It's like they don't even see the real person. I got to know Daryl — the real Daryl — and he was such a good kid. I really liked him, and I'm never gonna forget him."

The next morning we were seated on a set of bleachers to see the formal graduation. The platoons marched in and stood in four groupings of neat lines. From up in the bleachers it was hard to pick Jeff out because they all looked the same, slim and fit in their uniforms. All of the graduates were now wearing green dress pants with stripes, khaki shirts that looked like they just came back from the dry cleaners, the shiniest black shoes I've ever seen, and cloth caps...I mean *covers.* They looked sharp. They also wore what looked like a ribbon and a medal. Jeff later told me that the ribbon was called the National Defense Ribbon, and the medal was for their level of expertise with a rifle. Jeff said that his medal was the highest level, "Expert," as opposed to either of the next levels, "Sharpshooter" and "Marksman." I wasn't surprised. He had a great eye with a basketball, why not with a rifle? I hoped he would never have to demonstrate his new skill.

Like any graduation, there were a few speakers. One of them, Major General Peatross, a man with a presence that commanded your attention the minute he took the podium, said some things that really hit me hard. "The young man that you sent us is proud — and has every right to be. Certainly you can be proud of him. Recruit Training is a most challenging and strenuous undertaking. It is deliberately designed to be so. Success comes only to those with character and determination. For some, the demands were too great and they dropped out along the way. But your Marine was equal to the challenge. Under the guidance of his Drill Instructors, he has rightfully earned the title of United States Marine. As we look at these young men, I think we have good cause for renewed faith in American youth. These men will live up to the high standards and honored traditions that have been the hallmark of Marines for almost 200 years."

When Major General Peatross said "your Marine," I think he was talking to Mrs. Pelletier and Mrs. Bailey — the parents and the grandparents. But I kind of felt like Jeff was *my* Marine too. I knew Major General Peatross was talking about my best friend...a kid I had known practically my entire life. While I had issues with the war in Vietnam and mixed feelings about Jeff being in the military, it was impossible not to be proud of him. Others dropped out along the way, but Jeff had the character and determination to make it to the finish line. My Marine had been equal to the challenge. It didn't surprise me.

Before I knew it, a lonely summer without Jeff or Daryl had come to an end, and Labor Day was right around the corner. Cool September breezes began to give us relief from what had been a hot, thick August.

On the first day of school this year, our U.S. History teacher informed us we were starting the year with a student teacher, Mr. Cirillo, a cool looking college kid from Derby, who has long, frizzy hair and wears little round glasses like John Lennon. He looks like a hippie in a jacket and tie. He told us to call him "Mr. C" and said instead of starting the year with the same old boring stuff about the early settlers and colonies, he was going to do an overview of the Civil Rights Movement and the assassination of Martin Luther King, Jr. because it is so current. He told us that what is happening right now in America will eventually be in high school textbooks. It makes sense. In class, we have been talking about the importance of Dr. King's life and looking closely at many of the deep things he said, especially in his final speech when Dr. King pretty much predicted his own death:

"I don't know what will happen now; we've got some difficult days ahead. But it really doesn't matter to me now, because I've been to the mountain top. And I don't mind. Like anybody, I would like to live a long life – longevity has its place. But I'm not concerned about that now. I just want to do God's will. And he's allowed me to go up to the mountain. And I've looked over, and I've seen the promised land. I may not get there with you. But I want you to know tonight, that we, as a people, will get to the promised land. And so I'm happy tonight;

I'm not worried about anything; I'm not fearing any man. Mine eyes have seen the glory of the coming of the Lord."

That really blew me away. But one thing he said really grabbed me: *"No one really knows why they are alive until they know what they'd die for."* Wow! As far as I could tell, Dr. King knew what he had to die for. Maybe Bobby Kennedy knew too. I'm not sure. I wonder if Jeff is willing to die for his country...to die in a small Asian country that you can barely find on a map...to die in a war that I can't, for love or money, understand. I guessed Daryl thought he knew what he had to die for. I wish it had been different, though. Guilt seems like a lousy thing to die for. And Susanna? There was no possible way Susanna knew what she was willing to die for. I'm sure death was the furthest thing from her mind. As for me, at only sixteen in 1968, I also don't have a clue what I'm willing to die for. Not the slightest. I don't feel that strongly about anything. According to Dr. King, I guess that means I don't know why I'm alive. I'm just trying to figure out who I am and what my place is on this planet. That's all I can handle right now.

A current event that we spent a lot of time talking about with Mr. C occurred at the Olympics in Mexico City on October 16th. The Big M and I had watched two American Olympians, Tommie Smith and John Carlos, gold and bronze medalists in the 200 meter dash, lift their fists high into the air on the victory stand during the National Anthem. Each of them wore one black glove on their raised fist, and they weren't wearing shoes, but only black socks. Mr. C explained that black gloves signified black power and liberation and not wearing shoes represented poverty. It was the most controversial thing I have ever seen an athlete do, even bigger than Muhammad Ali's refusal to enter the military. Taking it a step further, Carlos wore black beads, which he said was: "for those individuals that were lynched or killed that no one said a prayer for, that were hung tarred. It was for those thrown off the side of the boats in the middle passage." Both athletes had to forfeit their medals and were sent home from Mexico City. In the aftermath of Dr. King's assassination and coinciding with ongoing protests and riots, I was more confused than ever, but Mr. C is helping us understand how the country needs to change its attitude about race, and how guys like Smith, Carlos, and Muhammad Ali, despite their amazing athleticism, transcend sports by standing up for what is right no matter what. I mean, I'm just paraphrasing what Mr. C said because I could never have figured all that out on my own. But it's really been making me think about what's important in life. It hit me that no matter what my father might say, these black athletes, who have risked everything, are true heroes.

On the Saturday after Smith and Carlos did their thing, the Big M and I did our thing. We attended the Derby-Seymour game, still waiting for Derby to get beat. It was mid-season, and Derby still hadn't lost a game. This year Seymour had the home field advantage, which seemed good for me and Michael because we didn't have to pretend we were rooting for Derby since we watched the game from the Seymour stands. I felt an even greater stake in the results because of Daryl. I wanted the Yellow Jackets to win it for him. Michael and I watched the game in pained silence because, unfortunately, there was nothing to cheer about. The final outcome was the same as last season, a victory for Derby, but this time the Red Raiders crushed the Yellow Jackets, 41-7. Seymour didn't score at all until Derby took out its first team late in the third quarter. Gone were the stars from a year ago — Adamo, Grasso, Belchak, Andrews, and, of course, my friend Daryl. The loss of their seniors hurt Seymour but seemed to have no effect at all on Derby. They just picked up where they had left off last year, now with two terrific sophomores at quarterback and at running back. I guess the common denominator was that Derby still had the great Sal Costanzo as coach. Big Sal apparently didn't have rebuilding years.

After the game, I asked Michael if he would mind taking me to St. Peter's Cemetery. "The game got me thinking about Daryl," I explained. "And I think I'm ready to visit his grave." I hadn't attended

Daryl's funeral as I had Susanna's. I couldn't. Going to Susanna's had been one thing, but Daryl and I had become so close. The thought of going to his funeral was just too much for me to deal with. But now I was ready to pay a visit.

"Okay," he responded with a concerned sigh. "I'll wait for you."

"No," I said. "Don't take this the wrong way. I just need some time, and I don't want to keep you waiting...or feel pressured to leave. I can always hitch a ride home."

He reluctantly dropped me off, and I waited at the edge of the grass until the Corvair was out of sight. Then I walked between the tombstones, looking for the Novak graves. I was surprised I remembered because it had been pitch black out on that emotional night when Daryl and I visited the cemetery. Upon reaching Susanna's grave, I saw that Daryl's was right next to hers. Carved into his tombstone were the words:

Daryl Walter Novak
Born March 21, 1950 – Died June 8, 1968
Beloved son and brother

Reaching into my back pocket, I took out my wallet. Besides my license and money, I carried only a few other things — folded copies of Daryl's and Susanna's obituaries, my handwritten copy of Emily Dickinson's poem, Daryl's note to me, Susanna's photo, and the broken lens of her glasses. I pulled out her school picture and gazed at it. I wished I had a good picture of Daryl as well.

I sat in the October grass, gazing at the photo and at the two graves. I wasn't really planning on it, but I found myself talking out loud, breaking the stillness of the afternoon.

"Hey Daryl...hi Susie. I hope you don't mind me calling you Susie, even though we didn't really know each other that good. If we had gotten to know each other, I like to think I would have called you what those closest to you did...what Daryl called you. I should have introduced myself to you, you know? Because, like, maybe if I had, it might have changed your fate, somehow...just like you said, Daryl. Some little thing, like introducing myself, could...uhm...have maybe changed things up. Cuz I would have really liked to get to know you, Susie. Our dance together was...I don't know...I don't know what to say about it. It was just the best thing that ever happened to me. And I'm sorry, Daryl, that I wasn't more help to you. But I really tried my best. I guess you know that, though, huh?"

My cheeks were wet with salty tears, which I could even taste now because tears were even running out of my nose, which probably sounds gross.

"I guess you guys know that they haven't even had a trial for Frankie Adamo yet. I don't understand why it's taking so long. But I guess you probably forgive him anyway, don't you, Daryl? And Susie, you too, probably, right? I guess I probably need to forgive him because...well, I've been pretty mad at him, if you know what I mean."

Of course, they didn't answer me. They didn't even send me a sign. Just silence. I just sat there for a good long while, listening to the birds chirping and the sounds of cars streaming by out on Route 34. I closed my eyes, feeling lonely and incredibly tired. I wanted to lay my head in the grass and just go to sleep, but I knew that wouldn't be the smartest thing to do.

"I don't know what else to say...because...because I never talked to people who died before. So, yeah...like, this is my first time doing that. I guess you guys don't have anything to say. I guess you can't, right? But I just...I just cared about both of you...*a lot*. I never knew you could care that much."

I drifted back into my own quiet place. Daryl had once asked me why people had to die — or, more specifically, why people who weren't supposed to die had to die. I sat contemplating that question. Why did people like President Kennedy...and Dr. King...and Bobby Kennedy have to die? And beautiful Susanna, with her whimsical mod look and those amazingly big eyes — why did she have to die? And, of course, Daryl himself. Why did a good kid like Daryl have to die? I didn't know what the answer was when he asked, and I have even less of an idea what the answer is now. Maybe when it comes to death, there are no answers. I guess it's like what Emily Dickinson wrote — that Death stops for us when he chooses to, and we don't get a say in the matter.

"Because I could not stop for Death –
He kindly stopped for me…"

I'm sure Susanna and Daryl wouldn't have wanted to stop for Death. I just hope Death has been kind to them. They are together now.

Sitting there for a good long time, I took Susanna's broken rose colored lens in my hand, held it in front of my face with my thumb and index finger, closed my left eye, and just gazed around the cemetery, looking through it with my right eye. I guess it was a way of trying to see the world through her eyes. Sadly, it didn't work. *What would it have been like to really find out how she saw the world?* I wondered. Giving up, I just lay back, rested in the grass, and looked up at the bright sky for awhile.

After about an hour, I felt it was time to go or I really would have fallen asleep. Even though I have my license now, I only get to drive when the Big M isn't using the Corvair because it's not like my dad lets me drive his car, so I still find myself hitchhiking sometimes. I walked to the gates of the cemetery, took a deep breath, and crossed to the opposite side of Route 34, leading back to Shelton. As cars zoomed by me, I remembered the night when a drunk Daryl picked me up. It was a ride that changed my life forever.

After about ten minutes, a light blue station wagon pulled over onto the shoulder. I ran, jumped in, and chirped my usual "thank you" to the driver, who was an elderly man. He reminded me a lot of the old guy I had talked to in the park before Susanna's funeral.

"Where you off to, young man?" he asked.

"Just the first exit in Shelton," I said.

"I can help you with that."

After a few moments, he said, "And may I ask, where might you be coming *from*?" Adults always seemed to ask that question for some reason.

"I was just at St. Peter's Cemetery," I replied, "paying my respects to some friends."

"You mean relatives?"

"No, just good friends," I said.

"Seems like you're awfully young to have deceased friends." This guy seemed particularly nosy, but I didn't care.

Feeling a driving compulsion to open up, I said, "Yes, a brother and a sister who died young. Maybe you read in the newspaper about the deaths of two Seymour kids, Susanna and Daryl Novak."

"Oh my, yes...yes I did, young man. The great athlete and his younger sister. So tragic. Tsk, tsk, tsk." Old people are always tsking. "You're saying they were friends of yours?"

A Bible passage from an October day a year ago popped into my head: *To everything there is a season.*

The season of lies and deceits had come to an end, and the season of truth had arrived. "Well," I said. "I didn't exactly know Susanna. I wish I knew her, but I didn't really. I met her at a dance last fall, the night of her accident, and we danced a couple of times together. I was actually surprised that she said yes when I asked her to dance...and then even twice as surprised when she said yes a second time. She was the most beautiful girl I've ever seen. There was her outer beauty, if you know what I mean, but there was also, like, an inner beauty that you can see in a person without quite knowing them. It was just kind of something I saw in her eyes. But her brother, well, that was different. We became super close. I met Daryl a few weeks after Susanna was killed in the car accident. This might sound strange, but he picked me up hitchhiking, just like you, and we somehow became close friends. It was just fate. Daryl totally believed in fate. He had that same rare look in his eyes that Susanna had."

It felt good to finally tell someone the whole truth, even if he was a stranger. I suddenly felt free.

"They say he had a severe problem with mental illness," the man said.

"Oh, yeah. Well, I don't agree with the people who say that. Mostly, he was just a real normal kid, no different from me. Just very upset about his sister. Daryl wasn't only a great athlete, but he was a super good guy too, kind and humble. I'll bet you would have liked him if you knew him. I tried to help him deal with his emotions as best I could, but something interesting ended up happening. While I was trying to help him, he turned the tables on me. He helped me. He kind of...uhm...it's hard to explain...helped me just kind of believe in myself. Because, well...because, like, that's the kind of kid he was — the kind of kid who builds other people up instead of putting them down or bragging about himself."

"Well, it's nice to hear about him from someone who really knew him. And you sound like you have adjusted well to what was a very sad situation. And it also seems to me, young man, like you're the kind of person who sees the best in others."

"I'm trying my best, but if that's true, I owe it to Daryl."

Like so many of my rides, this one ended at the bottom of Exit 14. As I walked from the bottom of Howe Avenue up the steep incline of Maltby Street hill, I gave some thought to what the man had said — that I had adjusted well to a sad situation. I wasn't so sure about that one. I didn't know if I'd ever adjust to what happened. That I was the kind of person who saw the best in others? Well, let's just say I hoped that was true.

What I felt, more than anything, though, was very alone. Maybe aloneness is something we can never escape in this life. And maybe it's not a bad thing. I thought of my relationship with the important people in my life. Michael is now a college junior, majoring in math, and I know that soon he will be starting a career as a teacher. He was born to teach, but as he moves into adulthood, I feel like I'll be left behind for a while. After Michael, Jeff is next in importance to me. Who knows where fate will take him or how often we'll see each other in the next few years? He is currently at Infantry Training at a place called Camp Lejeune in North Carolina, learning how to fight the enemy. Thinking about that, I can't help but wonder who the enemy actually is, though. For Daryl, I guess the enemy was his own guilt, but now there is no more enemy for him to fight. He is finally at peace. He told me from the start that I wasn't going to be able to help him. Big Alfred and Michael and even Jeff said so as well. But like I told the old guy who had just dropped me off, it was Daryl who had helped *me*. After giving it a lot of thought, it struck me that Daryl not only taught me to believe in myself, but by opening up to me in such an emotional way, he taught me something else even more valuable — maybe the only enemy we need to worry about is the enemy in our own minds.

Arriving home, I stood on the sidewalk in front of our big, white house, remembering the various occasions when Daryl had dropped me off after adventures that I never expect to repeat again. I noticed the Corvair in the driveway but not my Dad's new Dodge Polara. *Dad and Mom must be out shopping or somewhere,* I thought to myself. I climbed the side stairs up to our second story apartment. When I walked into the kitchen, I could hear the sound of the TV in the living room. It sounded like Michael was watching an old movie musical. Deciding to leave him alone, I headed into our bedroom, thinking I might take a little nap. There on my bed, though, I found a photocopy of a newspaper article. The headline said, "Novak Leads Seymour to Win Over Derby" with a subtitle that read, "Seymour Star Scores 28 Points." The newspaper copy recounting the big Seymour win was wrapped around a headshot of Daryl with his basketball jersey on. He wore the number 88 proudly on his chest, the same number he had worn in football. I looked at the date: January 14, 1967, Daryl's junior year. I sat on my bed and read the article. I could just picture Daryl giving Derby fits...dropping in 28 points from all over the court. I studied the photo. It was from a happier time. With clear, bright eyes staring at the camera, Daryl wore a carefree smile in the picture that I remembered from some of the better times with him — sliding on an icy pond together in a crazy game of knock the other guy off his feet... Daryl laughing at me when I told him I had quit our football team after only one half of a double session practice...Daryl building me up as the best distance runner in the history of the Valley after my record breaking run against Amity...and even crazier moments like laughing over how I threw his big beer bottle over the Route 8 guardrails at the spot check. Few though they were, these were happy memories that I would cherish.

I walked into the living room where Michael was lying on the floor watching an old Shirley Temple film. It may sound kooky that a twenty year old guy likes Shirley Temple films, but it's one of Michael's many quirks.

"Can I ask you a question? Do you know where this came from?" I asked, holding the article.

"Yeah...after I dropped you off at the cemetery, I stopped at the Plumb and found it in their *Evening Sentinel* archives. That lady with the bald head was about to close up, but I told her it was an emergency, so she gave me fifteen minutes. It actually took me thirty, and was that old bat ever annoyed. I thought it'd be a great way for you to remember Daryl."

"Wow," I said. "I don't really know what to say. That was nice of you. I guess I'll say...well...just thank you."

"It's a reminder that nobody wins all the time. It was a night when Novak stuck it to Derby. I don't know if you checked the box score, but Adamo only scored three points in that game. I only wish we were there."

"Yeah, me too."

It had been quite a ride, starting in the fall of 1967 with a dance, a death, and a funeral. 1968 brought with it a cool student teacher who opened my eyes to racial inequalities in our country, two historical assassinations, my best friend leaving to join the Marines, and the death of an incredible new friend. I had learned valuable lessons about winning and losing. I had learned lessons about people placing too much importance on the value of sports. I had learned that most people judge others without knowing who they really are, and I also learned that most people never *show* others who they really are. Daryl Novak didn't fit into either of these last two categories. He didn't judge others, and he bared his soul to me. I was honored to have been a person he could open up to in the worst of times. And I was grateful.

I went back to our bedroom, grabbed a couple of thumbtacks, and hung the newspaper article over my bed. My mother, who makes our beds every day after we leave for school, has never mentioned it. She somehow knows. Mothers are like that. Michael and I have never talked about it again either. He and I don't need to. We both understand.

Acknowledgments

Writing *Exit 14* has been a true labor of love. First and foremost, I want to thank my family. As had been the case in our life in the theater, bringing this novel to fruition has been a family affair. To my daughter Mia, thank you for working side by side with me and painstakingly editing my manuscript in all of its incarnations. Your meticulous attention to detail and your insightful recommendations have been invaluable. To my wife Francesca, whom I call *Franki* — like everything, we have been partners on this journey. Your input as someone who loves to read and as someone who knows what it means to bring a great story to life, proved to be effective over and over again in the rewriting process. To my daughter Gina, our family entrepreneur, thank you for your marketing recommendations and for your expert assistance in finding a voice-over artist to do what I hope will be an eventual audiobook edition. And, to my grandson Michael, thank you for being my model for the hitchhiker on the cover, for your interest in this project, and for your interest in everything we do as a family. To all four of you: rather than my book, I consider this *our* book. Tengo famiglia!

Next, I'd like to thank one my favorite people on the planet earth, Michael Pereira, for his friendship, guidance, and inspiration. Michael is a limitless person, and his calling is to inspire others to be limitless, including me. Specifically, thank you, Michael, for your help with the design of my website, for your advice about social media, and for your unconditional love and support.

I want to extend a special word of thanks to my three beta readers, Amy D'Amico, Howard Gura, and Megan O'Callaghan — true friends of the Scarpa family. In each case, parts of *Exit 14* were shaped by your invaluable input.

As the saying goes, “It takes a village to raise a child,” the same is true for a book. I am eternally grateful to a community of local writers for their inspiration and advice — several old friends: Sal Coppola, Pax Riddle, Ric Meyers, Amanda Marrone, and Cristina D’Almeida, as well as welcome new friends: Mike Wood, Tarn Granucci, Jill DeChello, Dr. Stephen Hoag, Ian Brooks, Woody Wilkinson, and Andy Merkin. It’s a pleasure to be part of a community of wonderful people who love to write.

Last, but certainly not least, my eternal love and gratitude to my brother Edmund (05/01/1948 – 01/29/2020), to whom I have dedicated this first venture into the world of writing. It was our youth that inspired this story, and my profound loss when he left us that motivated me to sit down and write it.

For more information about books by Gary Scarpa,
visit **www.garyscarpa.com**